No King No Country

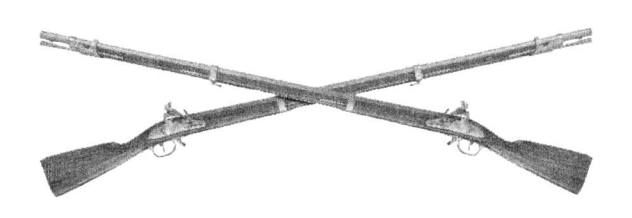

The Inness Legacy
Book 1

Wayne Grant

No King, No Country, Copyright © 2020 by Wayne Grant. All rights reserved.

Printed by Kindle Direct Publishing. No part of this book may be used or reproduced in any manner without written permission, except in the case of brief quotations embodied in critical articles and reviews.

FIRST EDITION

ISBN: 9798686675704

No King, No Country is a work of fiction. While some of the characters in this story are actual historical figures, their actions are largely the product of the author's imagination.

***Cover Art by More Visual Ltd.**

In Honor Of

C.S. Forester, master of historical fiction

Contents

Prologue 1
Part 1: England 3
Dragoon 5
The Purge 17
Flight 35
Liverpool 48
The Smuggler's Trade 59
Part 2: The Crossing 79
Setting Sail 80
Captain Keogh's Table 87
The Bay of Biscay 101
Caledonia MacDonell 113
Tenerife 119
Seven Hundred Leagues West 134
Privateer 151
Pump or Die 169
Aground 176

The Donker Nacht 192

Spoils of War 213

Part 3: A Savage Land 223

Welcome to America 224

No One Owns Juba 236

Jamestown Gaol 249

Mary's Land 265

Potowmac 276

Shenandoah 290

Trouble in Eden 305

Bloodhound 321

Seneca Dawn 328

Return to Eden 343

Historical Notes 353

Useful Terms 360

Books by Wayne Grant 365

About The Author 367

Virginia and Maryland Colonies, 1649

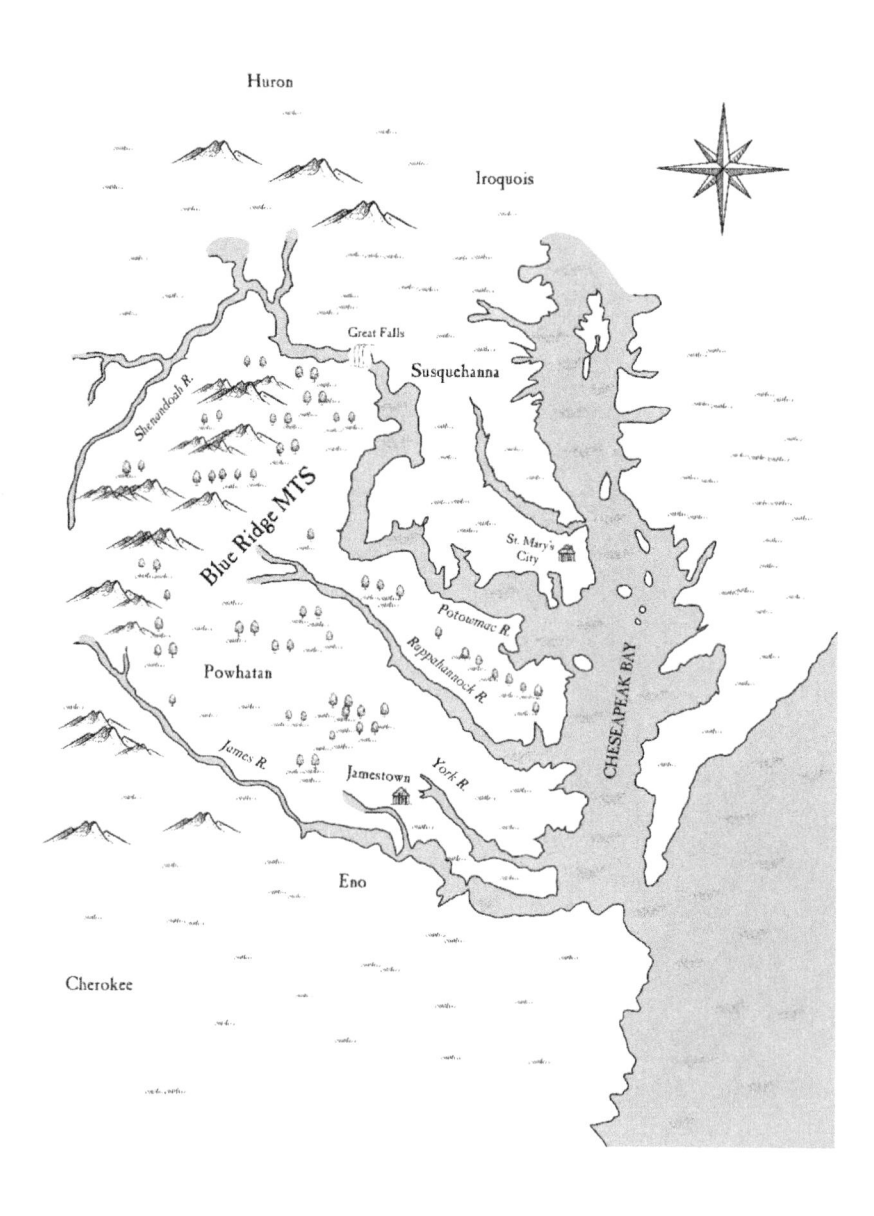

No King, No Country

Prologue

In the Year of Our Lord 1642, England descended into bloody civil war. The causes that prompted Parliament and the King to take up arms against each other had been long in the making, with money, power and religion all playing a role.

After three years of inconclusive bloodshed, Parliament turned in desperation to the brilliant cavalry officer, Oliver Cromwell, to reorganize its forces. Cromwell cast out the high-born officers of the army who had claimed positions based on birth, but lacked military skill and replaced them with capable soldiers drawn from all classes of men.

This New Model Army led by Sir Thomas Fairfax with Cromwell as second-in-command, faced its first test near the small village of Naseby in the countryside of Northamptonshire where it met the forces of King Charles in the summer of 1645. The defeat of Royalist forces at the Battle of Naseby did not end the civil war, but it marked the beginning of the end.

For the forces of Parliament, victory in the civil war had unintended consequences. In the course of the long struggle, a new egalitarian idea took root within the ranks of the New Model Army, the idea that all men, not just the barons and landowners, should have a voice in their governance. It was an idea that would roil the nation and the world down through the ages.

Wayne Grant

Part 1: England

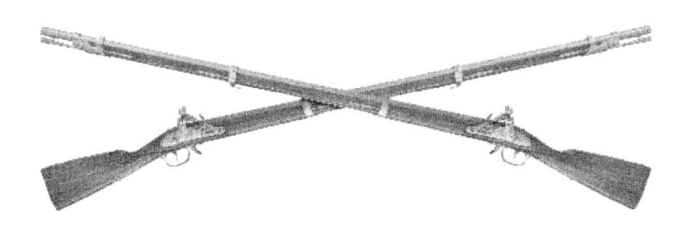

Wayne Grant

No King, No Country

Dragoon

June 14, 1645—Naseby, Northamptonshire

Sergeant William Inness stared into the thick fog clinging to the bottom land, but could see nothing through the grey mist. Out of sight on the high ground to his left and right, he heard shouted commands, the snorting of horses and the rattle of steel. These were sounds he'd come to know well.

They were the sounds of armies preparing for battle.

That morning, his regiment of dragoons had been roused while stars still hung bright in the sky and ordered to mount up. As men rolled from their blankets, their commander walked among them, full of his usual good spirits before a fight.

"Black Tom wants us on the left flank today, lads!" Colonel John Okey loudly announced as men gathered their gear and moved toward the picket line of horses.

Black Tom was Sir Thomas Fairfax, commander-in-chief of the Parliamentarian army. Three days before, Fairfax had broken off the siege of Oxford, leading his army on a forced march north toward Leicester, where the Royalist forces of King Charles had suddenly appeared. Scouts for both armies had clashed in the night and now there was to be a fight in this pleasant little valley where the day before farmers had shooed away birds from the ripening barley.

It was a fight that would test a new way of building an army. After three years of war with inconclusive results, Parliament had ordered the army reorganized and retrained under the watchful eye of Oliver Cromwell, commander of their best division of cavalry. For the New Model Army, as it was called, great lords and landed gentry with little experience or aptitude for war had been purged from the leadership and new formations created. Discipline had been tightened and drill made more rigorous. In the foggy valley north of Naseby, this New Model Army would face its first trial by fire.

Okey's Regiment of Dragoons was a special unit created by Cromwell who'd copied the idea from the Swedes. Mounted like cavalry but armed like infantry, the dragoons would ride to battle, but were trained to dismount and fight on foot. They were not armed with the heavy matchlock muskets with their glowing fuses used by the infantry, but with new short-barreled carbines that were easy to handle from horseback and equipped with flintlocks to ignite the powder in the pan. Okey had driven his men hard to adapt to the new weapons and new tactics.

Now would be the test.

While the troopers saddled their mounts, the Colonel called his officers and sergeants together for a short council of war. When they'd assembled, he pointed in the darkness toward the northwest.

"You all saw the hedgerow off that way before nightfall. Fairfax wants us there and concealed before first light. He and Cromwell expect Prince Rupert will command the Royalist horse on their right and we know that bastard is not one to dither! He's likely to open the action by charging Ireton's cavalry on our left. When he does—and have no doubt, he *will* charge—we're to give him a rude surprise for breakfast!"

There was a low growl of approval at that from the assembled men. Prince Rupert of the Rhine, nephew to King

No King, No Country

Charles and the ablest commander in the Royalist army, had learned his trade in the bloody sectarian wars that still raged in the heart of Europe. Upon arriving in England, he'd brutally applied those lessons in his uncle's cause. He'd burnt Birmingham to the ground, sacked Leicester and executed prisoners, practices common on the continent, but not in England. The German Prince was universally hated by the men who fought for Parliament.

Will Inness had seen Rupert at the battle of Marston Moor and the Prince had cut a dazzling figure. Flamboyant, even by the standards of Royalist Cavaliers, the man rode a snow white charger and carried a pet white poodle into battle with him. But while the Prince dressed like a dandy, Will could vouch for the man's courage. When Rupert saw Cromwell's cavalry turning his army's right flank, he'd led his reserves in a brave but doomed attempt to stem the rout. The Prince lost that battle, but survived the day—though the poodle did not. Now the Parliamentarians were facing him once more in this little valley north of Naseby.

Once mounted, Okey's dragoons had ridden in a wide arc to the northwest then back east to take up positions behind the thick hedge that cut across the valley separating the two armies. At the right moment, the regiment's six hundred men concealed there would fire their carbines into the flank of Rupert's charge shattering the Royalist cavalry. That was the plan, but Will Inness had learned that in war, no plan survived its first encounter with the enemy intact. He doubted this one would either, but one could hope.

Since dawn, he'd been lying on his belly peering through the branches of the hedge and seeing little but a grey haze. As the shrouded sun rose above the horizon and the morning warmed, the little patch of meadow to his front began to come alive with the usual activity of a June morning in the Midlands. Will saw a pale green grasshopper climb to the top of a long stalk of grass, survey his prospects then buzz off to the east to be lost from sight in the fog. A moment later, a toad clambered out from the depths of a muddy hoof print, having missed his chance at a meal. He wondered if any of these local residents sensed the hell that was about to descend on their green valley. He watched as the toad, denied his breakfast, hopped back toward the shelter of the hedgerow.

Perhaps he knows what's coming, Will thought.

Turning to his left and right, he could see that the men of his squad were well hidden, not an easy thing with these damned red jackets issued to the army. Will Inness had grown up hunting in the forests and fields of Cheshire and couldn't understand what sense it made for a man to announce his presence with such brilliant plumage—not when other men were looking to kill him. But he was just a sergeant who had no say in the matter and with this fog, perhaps the crimson lying amidst the green hedge might not be noticed. He felt a tug on his boot and turned to see August Dawes crawling up behind him.

"Thick as porridge," Dawes swore as he came to rest beside Will. August Dawes was a small man, hardly more than nine stone. Lean and wiry with a sharp chin and shock of close-cropped black hair, Dawes was a rarity among men from the Weaver River valley. That region of north Cheshire had been settled by descendants of the Danes who had once conquered half of England with fire and sword. Tall and big-boned, Will Inness could have passed for a Viking, save for his close-cropped brown hair. The two men had grown up on adjoining farmsteads and had been fast friends since they could walk.

For his jet black hair and deep-set dark eyes, some boys around their home of Danesford had called Dawes, "the Spaniard," but none made that mistake more than once. August Dawes was slow to anger, but he was quick as a snake with his fists when provoked. August and Will had enlisted in the Parliamentarian army together. Now, after three years of civil war, they were both sergeants and closer than ever.

"How long ye reckon?" Dawes asked, peering at the wall of grey.

"It'll lift soon," Will said as he looked up at the pale sun burning away the mist. "As soon as it does, they'll be coming. Have your men check the powder in their pans, Gus. This fog is damp."

Dawes grunted. Like his friend, he commanded his own squad of dragoons. Another man might have taken offense at advice from an equal, but August Dawes did not. He was a year younger than Will Inness and had looked up to his friend since they were boys. In his eyes, there was no better soldier on either side in this bloody war and if Will said check powder, then he'd not argue the point. He started to crawl backwards.

"Luck to you, Gus," Will said over his shoulder as his friend moved away.

"And to you, Will. I'll see ye on the other side!"

***

By late morning the sun and a freshening breeze had swept away the last of the fog to reveal a stirring sight. On the northern ridge, Will could see the Royalist forces arrayed in a thick line. Solid blocks of pikemen with their nasty, eighteen-foot, iron-tipped spears were interspersed with ranks of musketeers. A host of proud banners flew behind the line, the largest being that of Charles, the Stuart King.

On the right flank of the Royalist host, rank upon rank of cavalry stood waiting for the order to advance. They were a magnificent sight—all men of quality aboard expensive mounts. Dressed in every color of the rainbow and sporting long curled wigs, they called themselves Cavaliers.

Some were clad in near full suits of armor as though they were medieval knights. Others wore only gleaming breastplates and flamboyant, wide-brimmed hats. At their front, the blue and white banner of Prince Rupert snapped in the morning breeze, though the Prince himself had not yet appeared. Gaudy they might be, but Will Inness knew they were well trained and deadly in a fight.

Looking to his right, the young sergeant saw elements of his own army strung out along the crest of the high ground opposite the Royalists. Colonel Okey had declared that they would outnumber the King's men for this battle, but the Parliamentary line looked oddly thin in the morning light. Will was not privy to the strategy of Lord Fairfax, but Black Tom was a clever tactician and he guessed that the general had concealed most of his strength out of sight on the reverse slope of the ridge.

"He *wants* Rupert to attack," he murmured to himself.

No sooner had he muttered the words than a sharp blast of trumpets sounded from somewhere behind the enemy line. Ranks of heavy cavalry parted and Prince Rupert made a dramatic entrance onto the field, riding his magnificent white stallion. He reined in and swung around in the saddle to address his men. Drawing his sword, he pointed to the thin line of Parliamentarians on the far ridge and shouted something Will could not hear. Whatever the message, the Prince's words drew a lusty cheer from the massed cavalry.

The man nearest Will rolled toward him.

"Cuts a fig're, don't he, Sergeant?" Corporal Baker opined, impressed with the display.

"That he does, Baker. That he does. Now see if you can kill him when he gets close!"

Baker gave Will a wink and rolled back to the place he'd staked out in the hedge.

Will looked back to his front and saw the Prince turn his mount's head to the south and put the spurs to the big horse. The animal pinned its ears back and rumbled down the slope, gaining speed with each stride. Rupert stood up in his stirrups and waved his sword overhead like some wild Cossack from the steppes. Behind him, a thousand horsemen in the first line set their mounts into motion, slowly gaining momentum as they came on.

Will Inness slid his thumb over the carbine's cock and levered it half way back. He glanced down to check his powder. Beneath him the ground began to shake as though an earthquake had come to Northamptonshire. Men in the first wave of Royalist cavalry were whipping their mounts into a gallop to close up around their commander as the Prince reached the flat ground of the valley floor. On the slope behind them, the second wave now lumbered into motion.

Here and there individual dragoons took potshots at the galloping Prince, not waiting to pour volley fire into the close-packed ranks behind him. Will didn't even look down the line at his own squad. He knew his men would not want to face him after the battle if they fired before he gave the order. None did as the Prince rode past, untouched.

Will took a quick look to the south and saw a mass of horsemen, all clad in the thick buff coats of the Parliamentary cavalry, come streaming over the ridge, the blue and yellow banner of Colonel Ireton's regiment in the lead. The first line of Royalist horsemen were now no more than a hundred yards from where he and his squad lay in wait.

"Make ready!" he shouted down the line.

Men cranked their carbines back to full cock as the thunder of hooves swelled. Will heard the first volleys ring out far to his left as the Royalist charge came even with the far end of the dragoon line. The sound of the guns swept down the hedgerow toward him, growing into a roar. He watched as scores of men and horses fell, but the charge of the Royalists surged on, unchecked by such trifling losses. Then the wall of men and horseflesh was right in front of him. He cranked his own carbine to full cock and sighted down the barrel.

"Fire!" he screamed.

There was little need to aim carefully. He simply pointed and squeezed the trigger. The flint snapped forward, striking the frizzen and sending a hot spark into the pan. There was a quick flash as the powder there ignited sending a jet of flame through the touchhole to the powder charge inside the barrel. Will felt the reassuring kick of the carbine's butt against his shoulder. Down the line his squad unleashed a storm of lead into the tight-packed Royalist cavalry.

A cloud of acrid grey smoke engulfed everything for a moment, then the morning breeze blew it away to reveal many horsemen down on the valley floor, but the enemy charge surging on unchecked. By now, the men and horses in the second wave were nearing his position. Grabbing one of the dozen wooden apostles slung across his chest, he poured its carefully measured charge of gunpowder down the barrel of his carbine. Laying a patch of cloth across the muzzle, he rammed a ball home.

Looking up he saw the Parliamentary cavalry slam into the first wave of Royalists with a sound like a thousand blacksmiths hammering steel. Pistols were discharged at point blank range and swords drawn as the two sides went at each other in a melee of blood and steel. The combatants were so thoroughly intertwined that Okey's dragoons could find no shots that didn't endanger their own men.

For the moment Will Inness and his squad could only lay there and watch the bloody spectacle unfold. From where he sat, it looked like the two sides were so evenly matched that they would simply maul each other in the middle of the valley until no one was left in the saddle.

But slowly the tide began to turn in favor of the Royalists.

Here and there, Cavalier horsemen fought their way completely through the Parliamentarian line and were turning to attack its rear. Then, with the suddenness of a collapsing dam, Ireton's regiment broke. First, in twos and threes, then in droves, buff-coated horsemen turned and fled back up the slope in a general rout.

No King, No Country

"Prepare to mount!" Will heard his captain shout behind him. He took a last look at the valley to his front, covered now with the dead and dying on both sides. Riderless horses galloped in every direction, their eyes wide and white with terror. Here and there downed riders staggered to their feet, some gravely wounded and others dazed from being unhorsed. A few of the Parliamentarians recognized the hedgerow as a refuge and stumbled toward whatever safety might be found there, while others wandered aimlessly among the fallen.

A dozen or more Cavalier horsemen had not joined their comrades pursuing Colonel Ireton's routed regiment and were falling on these unfortunates like vultures, shooting the wounded and looting the dead. Some men tried to surrender and were shot down or cut down with sabers where they stood. Seeing the slaughter, those who could now fled in panic toward the hedgerow.

Will saw one of his own cavalrymen struggling in vain to drag himself from beneath his downed horse. The man was only twenty-five yards away and looked to have a leg solidly pinned beneath the dead animal. His struggles had not gone unnoticed among the Royalists shooting the wounded. Three of the gaudy Cavaliers were now picking their way across the field of dead and dying men and horses toward the downed man.

The trapped rider saw them come and drew a long cavalry pistol. Will watched as he took careful aim and fired. The pinned rider was either an excellent marksman or it was a very lucky shot, for one of the riders pitched backwards off his mount, dead before he hit the ground. The other two, enraged at this affront, spurred their horses toward the now helpless man.

"Damn it all," Will swore, scrambling to his feet. Behind him the dragoons were mounting and preparing to move. He knew he should join them, but instead forced his way through the thick hedge into the open, sprinting toward the downed rider who was trying desperately to draw his sword. Behind him he could hear August shouting his name and cursing.

One of the enemy riders saw Will break out of the hedgerow and reined in, taking careful aim with his pistol and firing at the red-coated dragoon. Will saw the pistol come up and lurched to his left as the ball ripped through the fabric of his coat sleeve slicing a burning furrow in the flesh of his arm. But it struck no bone and he kept running, reaching the downed rider ahead of the approaching Cavaliers.

There was no time to try to free the man as the riders were almost on top of them. As he raised his carbine to his shoulder, the lead rider saw the danger and jerked his reins, veering off to the right. Will took aim at the second rider and squeezed off a round, but the rider kept coming. Will cursed the carbine. It was fine if you pressed the muzzle against a man's chest, but beyond that could be wildly inaccurate.

"Take this!" he heard the man on the ground shout.

He looked down to see the pinned rider had pulled a second pistol loose from his belt and was handing it to him butt-first. He grasped it just as the first rider stood in his stirrups and raised his saber over his head. Will stepped over the dead horse, shoved the barrel under the man's breastplate and pulled the trigger. There was a muffled report and the Cavalier stiffened then toppled backwards off the horse.

The last rider now bore down on the two Parliamentarians secure in the knowledge that neither man could reload their weapon before he reached them. He leaned out over his saddle and drew back his saber. For want of any other weapon, Will took his empty carbine by its barrel and parried the slashing attack, knocking the saber from the rider's numb hand.

Shocked, the Cavalier whirled his horse around, drawing his own pistol as he turned. It was a fine display of horsemanship, but too slow. As horse and rider whirled around, Will leapt forward and grasped the man's sword belt, dragging him from the saddle. The Cavalier hit the ground hard, but managed to scramble to his feet in time to take the butt of Will's carbine to his head. He collapsed like a marionette whose strings had been cut.

Beyond the downed Cavalier, Will saw more riders had taken note of the brief fight and were now turning their horses in his direction. The enemy rider on the ground revived enough to grasp a sword laying close at hand and to stagger to his feet. With no time for niceties, Will drew a short dirk from his belt and drove the blade into the man's neck, just above his steel breastplate. The sword dropped from the man's lifeless hand.

Slinging his carbine over his shoulder, Will turned back to the pinned rider, grasping the strap running over the man's shoulder and heaving backwards, dragging him free at last. The injured man tried to stand but the freed leg would bear no weight. Will draped the rider's arm around his neck and began to half-drag him back toward the hedgerow.

By now, a half dozen Royalist horsemen had abandoned their looting of the dead, and were riding to investigate. They were closing fast when a score of red-coated dragoons emerged from the hedgerow, August Dawes at their head.

"Present!" Dawes commanded and the men shouldered their carbines. The riders, looking down the line of black muzzles, swung their mounts about to retreat.

"Fire!" August commanded and twenty lead balls followed the fleeing riders. Four of the six fell from their saddles as the rest rode out of range. August ran to help Will drag the rescued rider back through the hedges.

"You're a damned fool, Inness," Dawes groused as they dragged the wounded man through the hedgerow and out of harm's way. Will was too breathless to reply and what would he say if he had the breath?

It had been foolish.

He'd have busted a corporal for doing what he'd just done, but there had been something about the downed rider's refusal to die without a fight that had compelled him to take a foolish risk. As they neared the picket line of horses, one of his men found a riderless mount and they hoisted the injured man up into the saddle.

"Obliged," he croaked.

"Can you get to the rear, sir?" Will asked, noting the man's captain insignia for the first time.

"Aye, lad. I can manage. You'd best join your mates. Cromwell should be launching his attack on the enemy left about now. I expect our boys have led Rupert on a wild chase all the way back to Naseby where they cannot be of any help to the Royalist infantry when Cromwell strikes them. It's about to get interesting."

"Aye, sir," Will said as he mounted his own horse.

"What's your name, sergeant?" the captain asked.

"Inness, sir, William Inness."

The captain nodded.

"I'm Jack Percival. You've made yourself a friend this day, Sergeant Inness."

No King, No Country

The Purge

April, four years later—London

Night was falling fast as Captain William Inness made his way beneath the arch of Aldersgate and into the old city of London. He nodded at Parliamentarian guards keeping watch there. The sergeant of the guard gave him a perfunctory salute as he passed by, taking little note of a solitary captain of cavalry.

When last he'd passed through this gate two days ago, there'd been half the number of guards, so it seemed Parliament and the generals of the New Model Army were expecting trouble—and little wonder. All of London had been on edge for months since the execution of the King in January and now there was serious unrest within the army itself.

Colonel Whalley's famed Ironside regiment of horse had been brought in from Oxford a month ago and billeted just outside the old city walls of the capital as insurance against trouble from the fickle London mobs, but the regiment had trouble of its own. Will had joined Whalley's command a year ago on Colonel Okey's recommendation. The move had meant a promotion to captain and command of a company, but the new posting had not been without challenges.

The men of his new company were good soldiers, but had received no pay for six months and many had families on the verge of starvation back home. Stationed so near the capital, his lads had seen firsthand how the great men of Parliament lived like princes in their London townhouses. In just a few short weeks, the mood of Whalley's men toward their masters at Westminster had matched that of the London mobs.

Fairfax and Cromwell were not blind to the growing unrest. They'd allowed petitions to be submitted to Parliament for back pay, but these pleas had been met with an inflammatory rebuke that questioned the Army's loyalty. Then came the orders dispatching the Ironsides regiment to Ireland.

It was the last straw.

Outraged, a company from Whalley's regiment guarding London's Bishopsgate stood to arms and refused to go to Ireland. What had Ireland to do with the fight for English rights they'd demanded to know. Their commander, Captain Somerset, pleaded with them to stand down, to no avail. The response from army leaders had been swift and brutal. Cromwell, who had once commanded the regiment, ordered two of the mutinous ringleaders hung and the rest of the company cashiered out of the army with no pay. That had been ten days ago, but the harsh suppression did little to quiet the growing unrest in the ranks.

The day Somerset's two mutineers had gone to the gallows, talk of mutiny had swept through his own company like a gorse fire. He'd been as angry as his men at being ordered off to fight in Ireland and at the harsh treatment of Somerset's men, but he was an officer and had a duty to keep good order. He'd assembled his men in an open field north of Smithfield and addressed them.

"Men of the Ironside regiment," he began, his voice carrying to the last man in the ranks. "You've fought together in every battle from Marston Moor to Naseby and beyond. Some of you have taken wounds and all have seen friends die for our cause. Now you have been insulted and mistreated by the very assembly for which you've made these sacrifices!"

This brought a ripple of angry agreement from the men. Will let the murmurs die down before continuing.

"These grand men of Parliament…you've seen how they live, while your wives and children go hungry at home."

"Down with Parliament!" a man shouted in the back. Will ignored him.

"You are free Englishmen. Your grievances are just and you must be heard!"

Now there was a roar from the gathered cavalrymen and a few men drew their swords. Will felt himself being carried away by the passion of the men—his men—and by the sure knowledge they were in the right. His hand slid down to the hilt of his sword. He was on the verge of drawing the blade and leading them to the halls of Westminster to demand justice when he saw Alfred Treadway, his senior sergeant, eying him uneasily.

When he'd taken this post with Whalley's regiment, Sergeant Treadway and August Dawes had come with him. Treadway had been his senior sergeant for over two years and was as steady a soldier as they come. The sergeant had not drawn his sword, nor was he joining the uproar around him. He was waiting to see what his captain would do.

Then, in the sea of angry faces, Will saw the face of Caleb Jones. Jones was new to the company and looked to be no more than sixteen. He was a brave lad and a superior horseman, but was often homesick and wrote long letters home to his mother in Lancashire. Here was a boy who'd never shaved, nor loved a girl, nor seen much of England except to ride through it on the way to a battle. Now, with mutiny in the air, Caleb Jones looked frightened.

Will drew back his hand from the hilt of his sword as though it was a hot poker. Treadway was a veteran and knew what mutiny would mean and Jones was just a scared boy. Their blood would be on his hands if he acted unwisely in this moment. He calmed his breathing and let the cheering and the shouts die down. Once the crowd grew quiet, he spoke again.

"Your grievances are just,...but to refuse to obey orders.... to contemplate mutiny.... These are grave choices, ones I fear will bring no redress of our grievances, but will tarnish the reputation of us all. Men now speak of the Ironside regiment with awe. You broke the Royalist horse at Marston Moor and Naseby!" he reminded them. "Englishmen will not forget that. You, no less than King Harry's band of brothers, will have a place of honor in the hearts of your countrymen from now until your dying day. Unless we mutiny."

Men had grown quiet as he spoke, but scattered shouts of defiance still erupted in the ranks. Will stood silently until the defiant cries turned to angry grumbling, then spoke again.

"If we mutiny, the glory of Naseby and Marston Moor will be forgotten. We will be branded as traitors to the cause we've fought and bled for and make no mistake. We *will* be punished. You saw what happened to Captain Somerset's company. It will go worse with us. But if you stay true to the colors—our colors—I swear on my honor that I and Colonel Whalley will plead for you. We will make Fairfax and Cromwell listen and they will make Parliament do right by the Army."

The crowd went silent as he ended his speech. Will held his breath waiting to see if he'd moved them, waiting to see if they'd stand down. Then Alfred Treadway stepped out of the ranks and turned to face the company.

"All right, lads," he barked. "That's it then. Back to yer barracks. There'll be an extra rum ration at supper."

Habit is a powerful thing among soldiers. Habit keeps them awake on the night watch and makes them water their horses before they take a drink. Habit make them stand and fight in the face of deadly peril when any sane man would turn and run. It's sergeants who drill these habits into farm boys and clerks and cobblers and it's sergeants the ranks turn to in uncertain times.

Alfred Treadway was a man born to be a sergeant. He delivered his order with utter certainty and habit won the day. There was grumbling, always a soldier's right, but no one challenged the order. In twos and threes they broke ranks and headed for their barracks, content to wait for at least a while to see if their Captain could somehow gain justice for them.

Will had let out a sigh of relief and gone straight to Colonel Whalley, telling him that his hold over the men of his company hung by a thread. Whalley who was cousin to Cromwell agreed to personally press their case with his illustrious kinsman and he had. Cromwell had listened and expressed sympathy, but had agreed to nothing.

Much had changed since, at seventeen, he and Gus Dawes had answered Parliament's call for men. Back then everything had seemed clear to him. The King had trampled on the ancient rights of Parliament and hence on the rights of all Englishmen. Those rights had been worth fighting for, but now, six years later, he had to wonder if *his* cause and that of Parliament had ever been the same.

They'd done away with the divine right of kings when they chopped off Charles Stuart's head, but other promises, promises to the men who'd done the fighting and dying, seemed to have been forgotten. It now looked as though the rights of Englishmen that Fairfax and Cromwell touted were reserved for only high-born Englishmen.

His thoughts returned to the present as he reached the lane where sat the Bull and Mouth Inn. Only a block from Aldersgate, the inn was a popular lodging for senior Parliamentarian officers when duty brought them to London. A captain's purse could not afford a room at the Bull and

Mouth, even when pay was forthcoming, so he had taken lodging at the Cock and Hen a few blocks outside the city walls. There he shared a room with newly-promoted Lieutenant August Dawes. The place was old and not that clean, but it was cheap and quiet. That suited the two young officers from Cheshire. Neither cared much for the rhythms of city life.

Will had been off duty for less than an hour and alone in his room when a boy rapped on the door to inform him that a Major Jack Percival urgently requested his presence at the Bull and Mouth. It had been four years since he'd dragged then-Captain Percival from beneath his dead horse at Naseby and in the intervening years, the war had taken the two men to different corners of England.

But Percival had gone to some lengths to maintain a connection with the young sergeant who'd saved his life. He'd even made a point of being present when his young friend was promoted to captain. Will hadn't seen Percival in over a year, so the summons was a surprise, but the major was not one to idly request an urgent meeting. And Will had news to share with his friend as well. He'd decided this very day to resign his commission and go home to Cheshire. Six years of war had been more than enough for him and August felt the same. They intended to submit their resignations to Colonel Whalley in the morning.

He wondered how Jack Percival would react to that news!

As the boy took his leave, Will had hauled his boots back on and set off toward Aldersgate and the Bull and Mouth. Now as he turned off Aldersgate Road he saw that the street in front of the inn was jammed with horses and carriages, all queued up and waiting for their owners to emerge. Senior officers of Cromwell's New Model Army were never short of invitations to dine with the wealthy merchants of London and men were emerging from the front door of the Bull and Mouth in twos and threes searching for their conveyances as the hour for supper approached.

No King, No Country

Will plunged into the throng near the entrance and managed to shoulder his way inside. The air in the inn's massive parlor was redolent with the smell of ale and tobacco smoke. The messenger boy had told him where to find Percival's room on the third floor and he headed for the wide staircase, taking the steps two at a time. Arriving on the third floor landing he found his way down a narrow hall to Percival's room and rapped twice on the door, eager to see his friend but anxious as to what prompted the urgency of this meeting.

For a moment there was no response, then the door was flung open. Jack Percival offered no greeting, but poked his head out into the hall, glancing in both directions before motioning Will inside. He closed the door and latched it, then turned to extend a hand, though his usual jovial smile was nowhere to be seen. His reception put Will on his guard.

"What's this about, sir?" he asked.

Percival released his handshake and stepped back. Reaching into a pocket of his vest, he drew out a scrap of paper. He carefully unfolded the wrinkled note and handed it to the young officer. Will took it and held it up to a flickering candle to better see what it contained. It was a hastily scrawled list of names, eleven in all. Some of the names Inness knew and others he did not.

His own name was third on the list.

"What does this mean?" he asked quietly.

Percival sighed.

"You're to be arrested, William—this very night."

Inness looked blankly at the major.

"Arrested? On what damned charge?"

"Mutiny, I'm told. Men of your regiment have refused to follow the colors to Ireland."

"*I* have not refused, nor have the men of my company!" Will said, his voice rising. "We took no part in this mutiny, though none of us joined Parliament's cause to go kill Catholics in Ireland."

Percival furrowed his brow.

"I'm relieved to hear that, Will. Never took you for a mutineer, but these orders were issued by Cromwell himself. Why would he…"

Percival stopped, a look of dawning comprehension on his face.

"You spoke at Putney," Percival said.

Will looked puzzled. What had come to be known as the Putney debates had taken place six months ago. Fairfax and Cromwell, aware of growing unrest in the army had felt compelled to meet with representatives of the soldiers at the village of Putney a little ways out from London in the Surrey countryside. Regiments had elected representatives and Will was chosen by Colonel Whalley's men to carry their complaints to Fairfax and Cromwell.

"Yes, I was at Putney. The men picked me to speak for them, but what has this to do with mutiny?"

"I didn't recognize all the names on the list," Percival said snatching the paper back from Will and examining it more closely, "but you and three others I know spoke at Putney. What were your demands there?"

"The complaints I presented came from the men, not from me, though I hardly disagreed with them. My regiment hadn't been paid in six months! So I asked for back pay. I'm to be hung for that?"

"Was there anything else you spoke to?"

"My men favored Colonel Lilburne's position on votes for landless men, Jack. I did lend my voice in support of that. I'm no Leveller politician, but most who fought and bled for Parliament are landless men. Why should they not have some voice in how the land is governed? The good book says all men are equal in the sight of the Lord!"

Percival held up a hand.

"I'm not here to censure you or to disagree with the just demands of your men, but you must understand this, Will. The leaders of Parliament find these ideas dangerous. They

No King, No Country

did not wrest power from the King to simply give it over to landless men. Cromwell and Fairfax may think kings have no divine right to rule, but they believe the lower classes have no rights at all in the matter. And now that Parliament has nothing more to fear from Royalists, they're turning their attention to troublemakers in their own ranks. They mean to crush the Levellers and suppress any further mutinies in the Army. Lilburne they've thrown into the Tower. Him they won't hang—too popular here in London—but they're looking to make examples of some lesser folk it seems—folk like you, Captain Inness. I'm told they'll begin making arrests early this evening."

"So am I to be hung for nothing more than what I think?"

Percival shrugged.

"Ideas have weight, Will. Had Charles not believed in the divine right of kings, he might still sit on the throne today. You and the others on this list harbor an idea that frightens Cromwell and Fairfax and the leaders of Parliament. Men have been put to death for much less."

Percival wadded up the scrap of paper and threw it into the crackling fireplace. It flared for an instant then turned to black ash.

"I'm not one to run," Will said grimly.

"Then you'll die," Percival said, his voice now harsh. "Don't be a fool, Will. They'll not give you a fair trial. You have to run. I've lost a lot of friends in this war. I'd rather not lose another."

For a long moment, Will stood there silently. The Major let him stew. They'd both seen terrible things in six years of civil war, evil things done on both sides in the name of God and justice. Hanging innocent men would not be all that extraordinary and both men knew it.

"So where would I go, Major?" Will asked bitterly. "Where in England can I hide? You know Cromwell. If he is intent on finding me, I'll be found."

Percival nodded glumly.

"You'll not be safe in England. You're a good soldier, Will—one of the best I've seen. Get yourself to Germany or the Low Countries. Both sides there pay well for experienced men such as you."

Will frowned.

"I'm no mercenary, sir."

"Then Scotland, perhaps."

"The Scots turned King Charles over to Cromwell when he sought shelter with them," Will said with a shake of his head. "Do you think they'd not do the same to me?"

Percival stood.

"Where else then?" he asked. "Surely not god-forsaken Ireland."

"No, not Ireland. America, I think."

"America! Why there's nothing there but stiff-necked Puritans and Royalist refugees!"

Will shrugged.

"They say the crown colonies are but tiny outposts in a vast unexplored land, vast enough for a man to find a place of his own, a place away from all this…this intrigue and politics."

"Outside the colonies there's nothing but wilderness!" the major said. "And its full of savages—fierce warriors they are and cruel."

Will Inness nodded and gave the major a small smile.

"Not unlike the English."

Somewhere down below the sounds of a commotion reached Percival's room on the third floor. The major looked worried.

"None of the men on that list lodge here, Will. I'd guess someone saw you enter. I think it best you be gone now."

Will started for the door, but Major Percival grasped his arm. Outside, boots could be heard on the staircase.

"The roof," he said and crossed the room in three quick strides to unlatch the lone window. The young captain didn't hesitate. As he climbed through the window he looked back at Percival.

"Thank you for the warning, Major. I think we're even now," he said as he disappeared into the darkness.

"God go with you, William," Percival murmured as someone began pounding on his door.

***

The slate roof of the Bull and Mouth was mossy and slick, but not too steep. Thankfully, Percival's room was in the rear of the inn. Otherwise the crowd out front might have taken note of a lone man picking his way toward the corner of the inn's roof. Behind him, Will heard men loudly questioning Major Percival who was lying convincingly.

When he reached the edge of the roof, Will looked down upon the top of an attached gallery. Two stories tall, the gallery was used to accommodate those guests who could not afford the inn's more sumptuous salons available in the main building. Will eased over the edge of the main building's roof, hung on the gutter for a moment, then dropped the twelve feet to the lower roof.

He landed softly with knees bent, but this roof was pitched more steeply and his feet flew out from beneath him, sending him sliding down toward the two story drop a few feet away. Desperately he dug in his heels and the palms of his hands, but could not arrest his slide. As his feet slid off the edge of the roof, he was saved by a rickety gutter that caught his boot heels and left him panting twenty feet above the back alley behind the Bull and Mouth.

Recovering himself, he managed to get to all fours and edge his way along the lip of the gallery roof until he reached a thick lead downspout. He muttered a quick prayer of thanks and shinnied down the pipe, alighting in the alley. His arrival startled two curs fighting over a bone. The dogs snarled at him but turned their attention quickly back to the dry bone. At the corner of the gallery the alley met a narrow lane that ran from the rear of the Bull and Mouth to the road in front of the inn. Breathing hard, Will considered which way to turn next.

Passing in front of the inn in sight of the crowd of officers there was a risk, but he had to get back to the Cock and Hen and it was in that direction. He took a moment to straighten his clothes, though there was nothing to be done for the stains on his rear where he'd slid down the roof of the gallery. He let the pounding of his heart slow, then walked up the lane and casually moved through the milling crowd of men, horses and carriages gathered in front of the Bull and Mouth.

Across the crowded street, another dark alley beckoned. With the roundup of the men on the Major's list underway, using Aldersgate was out of the question. He'd needed to find another way to get north of the city wall and the dark, narrow passage ahead ran in the right direction. He slid between a team of horses and the rear of a carriage and had almost reached the far side of the road when he heard a shout behind him.

"You there! Stop!"

He didn't turn to see who had raised the alarm or if it was meant for him. He bolted into the alley and ran. In his wake he heard a hue and cry and, though the space between buildings here was narrow and pitch black, he did not slacken his speed until a mass of stone rose up ahead of him, entirely blocking his path. It was London's ancient wall!

The city had long since outgrown its fortifications and the wall had fallen into disrepair. In many places, it had been incorporated into the walls of new buildings and in others it was left to fall to pieces. To his relief, Will saw there were stone steps at the end of the alley that led up to the old wall walk. The ancient stairs were broken in places, but passable and he took them two at a time. Over his shoulder he saw that men had entered the alley carrying torches. Peering over the battlements, he could make out an expanse of open ground and the dark ruins of St. Bartholomew's Church looming beyond, but in the shadow of the wall below him there was nothing but a black void.

He guessed it was a fifteen foot drop from the top of the wall, dangerous in the pitch dark, but he had no choice as his pursuers were nearly to the stone steps. He hoisted himself up and over the battlements and hung there for a moment.

The he jumped into the blackness below.

***

August Dawes stood concealed in the shadows of St. Bartholomew's watching the street in front of the Cock and Hen. Four Parliamentarian infantrymen armed with muskets stood in front of the inn scanning Aldersgate Road.

Dawes had met these gentlemen a half hour earlier when they'd burst into his room and demanded to know where Captain William Inness was. He'd told them to bugger off, but they'd produced an arrest warrant signed by Oliver Cromwell himself and that shut him up. Still, they'd been most unpleasant until he'd convinced them that he didn't know where his lodging mate had gone.

"Bloody infantry," he muttered as he watched the men across the way from his hidden position next to the church.

As soon as the soldiers left his room, he'd gathered up his kit and Will's things and slipped out the back of the inn, taking a hidden route through stinking alleys to reach this spot. From here he could see up and down Aldersgate Road, for he'd told the soldiers the truth. He didn't know where Will had gone or when he might return, but he was determined to intercept his friend before he blundered into this welcoming committee.

He didn't know what trouble Will had stumbled into and the bloody posse waiting at the Cock and Hen wouldn't say. They'd only shown him the order signed by General Cromwell and that worried August. Oliver Cromwell did not have men arrested for spitting on the street.

***

Will saw Dawes before August saw him. His landing beneath London's old wall had been surprisingly soft and he'd quickly seen why. He'd leapt into Saint Bartholomew's ancient and ill-kept graveyard. Luckily he'd landed among thick tufts of grass growing untended between headstones and crypts that were moss-covered and neglected. He picked his way through the old graves to the rear of St. Bartholomew's and climbed over a rusting fence, alighting on a side street. At the end of the street, he saw August huddled against the wall of the church watching the front of the Cock and Hen.

"Gus, it's me," he whispered as he drew near. Dawes whirled around, startled, but relieved to recognize Will.

"Oh bloody hell, Will, you gave me a start!" he blurted.

"What are you doing here?" Will asked.

"Watchin' for you. Thought you'd be coming up Aldersgate Road and didn't want you to run into that lot," he said, pointing across the street at the red-coated guards waiting near the inn's doorway. "What's this about, Will? They say they have orders from Cromwell for your arrest."

Will nodded.

"I've just come from Jack Percival. He warned me that I'm one of eleven to be arrested for plotting mutiny."

"Mutiny?" August asked, incredulous. "You? You were all that kept our company from joining the damned mutineers after they hung Captain Somerset's lads! Surely such a charge won't stand up at a court martial."

Will shook his head.

"The major says it will, Gus. Parliament has decided to suppress the Levellers and their sympathizers once and for all. They've thrown Colonel Lilburne in the Tower and are arresting others. I'm on that list."

"You're no Leveller, Will!"

"Aye, but I spoke for the men at Putney. I asked for back pay for the troops."

No King, No Country

"Which we're owed six times over!" August said heatedly.

"I also supported Colonel Lilburne's demand for votes for all men, not just the land owners. Percival believes that's what got my name on the list."

"And why shouldn't men who've fought and bled for Parliament have a say in who is chosen to represent them?" August shot back.

Will shrugged.

"This is not the night to debate that, August. The Major says Lilburne is too popular here in London to execute, but those of us on the list are not so lucky. They intend to hang us as a lesson to others."

"Damned if they will!" said August, his voice rising again. "We'll talk to the men. They love you, Will. They'll shoot the first man who tries to lay hands on you!"

"I'll not drag the lads into this, Gus."

"What then? Walk to the gibbet like a sheep?"

"The Major says I must run."

Dawes said nothing for a long time, then he spoke urgently.

"If Jack Percival says run, you must listen to him. I've brought your things," he said, motioning to a bag at his feet and a carbine leaning against the church wall. Will saw that August had his own carbine slung over his shoulder.

"Obliged, Gus, but why'd you bring your own weapon?"

"Thought I might have to shoot someone 'fore the night's done," August said matter of factly.

Will almost laughed at that, but could tell his friend was in deadly earnest.

"This isn't your trouble, Gus."

"The hell it isn't. You always made my trouble your trouble, Will. Ever since we were boys. Do you think I'd not do the same?"

"But this isn't some fist fight with lads from the next village. It's big trouble—deadly trouble. I'm asking you to stay out of it."

"Ask all you like. It will do ye no good," the young lieutenant said with finality. "I'd already made up my mind to leave the army and that was before they decided to start hanging innocent men. Promises were made to those who fought and promises have been broken. More mutinies are coming and I just might join the next one. I think it better to be a deserter than a mutineer."

"Gus,..."

"Shut up, Will. We come in together. We go out the same way. So where shall we run?"

Will wanted to argue more, but he knew Gus Dawes. His friend was as genial a man as he'd ever known, but stubborn as an ass once his mind was set.

"Cheshire first. You should see your folks and I need to speak with Robert."

August stood silent in the shadows of the church for a moment. He wasn't surprised that his friend would look to Cheshire for refuge. It was home to them both and a long way from London. But for Will to seek out his older brother surprised him.

Will and Robert Inness had been close growing up and August had tagged along behind the two on many adventures. Rob, tall and handsome, was a serious and cautious young man, willing to take a risk, but only after careful calculation. Will had been the bolder of the two, forever coming up with clever and sometimes dangerous plans for their amusement.

Between the brothers, there had been a natural balance, but that balance was threatened when their father fell ill with some wasting disease that the local surgeon had no power over. He'd died when Will was fifteen and his mother soon after from a fever that struck the Weaver valley in the winter. As first born, Robert had inherited all the Inness properties including the Cheshire lands and the shipping business based in Chester and Liverpool. He'd been only nineteen at the time and his new responsibilities had put an end to youthful adventuring.

Will had not envied his older brother's new wealth and position. He'd confided to August his relief that it was Rob, not he, who'd taken on the burden of managing the family's affairs. For a time, the two brothers had worked together, Will working the land around Danesford and Robert tending to the family's growing shipping enterprise, but events far from Cheshire had intervened. King and Parliament had fallen out and all across England, counties, villages and families had had to take sides. It had turned neighbor against neighbor and kin against kin. Sadly it had been so with the Inness brothers.

Like most folks in Cheshire, Robert had given his support to the Royalist cause, but Will had seen things differently. He'd found merit in Parliament's grievances with the King and, in time, the disagreement had frayed the close ties between the two Inness boys. Their parting had been bitter, Robert refusing to see Will or August before the two friends left to join the rebel army. As far as Dawes knew, the two had not reconciled in the six years since. But blood was thicker than water. Perhaps Robert would help them, but how?

"What can Rob do?" he asked. "Hide us in his cellar?"

Will shook his head.

"He's a shipper. He can find us a ship."

"A ship? A ship sailing where?"

"To America, Gus."

"America! I hadn't thought we'd have to leave England, Will."

Will looked at his friend in the dim light.

"Still time to change your mind. I'd not think ill of you. But I'm done with England. In America, kings and parliaments are an ocean away and that suits me. But it might not suit you."

August rubbed his chin and looked back across the street at the armed men looking to arrest his friend.

"America will suit just fine," he said, handing Will his carbine.

No King, No Country

Flight

The two men rode through the night, following Watling Street to the northwest and passing through Dunstable a little before dawn. As the sun rose behind them, Will turned his mount off the old Roman road and led August onto an overgrown path that cut through a narrow stretch of woods. Beyond the fringe of trees was a secluded meadow with a small stream running through it. The horses plunged their muzzles into the clear water and the men went down on their bellies to do the same. When they'd drank their fill, the men unsaddled the animals and left them to browse the fresh spring grass of the meadow.

August Dawes pressed drops of water from his scruffy black beard as he rummaged through his bag. He pulled out a small loaf of crusty bread, ripping off a piece and handing it to Will. He looked around the clearing curiously.

"We've been here before," he said, surprise in his voice.

"We have," said Will. "Camped here for a night on the march to Edgehill four years ago."

Dawes gave a low whistle.

"I don't know how you do this," he said shaking his head. "It's been four years and a hundred meadows. I'd have never found this place."

Will shrugged. It was an odd skill he had that he never forgot a place once he'd been there.

"This little meadow is about the only good memory I have from that campaign," he said.

August squinted as a shaft of early morning sun burst through the trees.

"Aye, Edgehill was a bloody mess," he said, shaking his head. "We were green as grass back then and so were our generals! We were lucky the war wasn't lost that day!"

Will nodded.

Edgehill *had* been a mess. Early in the war the ragtag army of Parliament was little more than a gathering of armed bands of militia from all over England. Led by the Earl of Essex, the Parliamentarians had been outmaneuvered and nearly routed by the Royalists at that first great battle. For two more years, Essex dithered and failed to press the outnumbered Royalists until Parliament finally had enough. The Earl was replaced by Thomas Fairfax and Oliver Cromwell and the tide of war quickly changed.

"Essex had no fight in him. You can't say that about Black Tom and Cromwell. They know how to win a war."

"Aye," August agreed, "but now they want to hang the lads who did the fightin' for them. I reckon they know war better than they know men."

Will turned to his friend, who looked as weary and dust-covered as him.

"Still time to change your mind," he said. "Ride back to London and tell the Colonel you were drunk at the Ox Tail and missed morning muster. You'll get nothing worse than a reaming from Whalley."

August snorted as he made himself comfortable on the bed of grass.

"Not a chance, Inness," he said, his jaw set. "I've made my choice. To hell with Cromwell and Parliament. It's America I'm bound for where a man can make of himself whatever he chooses."

"Amen to that," said Will.

***

Oliver Cromwell scanned the paper on the small table in front of him and frowned. One name on the list was not accounted for. He looked up at Colonel Edward Whalley who stood nervously at attention before him.

"One of your officers avoided arrested?" Cromwell asked calmly.

"Aye, sir. Captain Inness was not found."

"I believe you objected to his inclusion on the list, didn't you, Colonel?"

"Vigorously, sir. Captain Inness is the best officer I have. It was Inness and his men who broke through the Royalist lines and turned the tide at Maidstone last year. You approved his commendation for valor, General!"

Cromwell shrugged.

"He's not being arrested for cowardice, Edward."

"But he's no mutineer, sir. He kept his company under control during the affair at Bishopsgate."

"Perhaps he didn't lead *that* mutiny, Colonel, but I heard Inness speak at Putney. This captain of yours has dangerous ideas, and he's just the sort of man others will follow. We cannot have that."

Whalley did not reply. Cromwell was his cousin and he respected his kinsman, but the man was dead wrong about William Inness. He'd argued hotly against the captain's arrest when first the charges were levelled, but his objections had been ignored. Cromwell picked up a second sheet from his desk and scanned it.

"I see another of your officers, a Lieutenant Dawes, has gone missing," he said, laying the paper down.

"Aye sir. He did not report at morning muster."

"Does he have a connection to Captain Inness?"

"Aye, he does. They enlisted together in Cheshire six years ago and served together since. They're close."

"Does this lieutenant have a stronger loyalty to his friend than to his regiment and to Parliament, sir? Would he help Inness avoid arrest?"

"If he thought Captain Inness unjustly accused, I'd expect so, sir," Whalley replied evenly.

Cromwell scowled at the colonel.

"Then this Lieutenant Dawes is a deserter!" Cromwell shouted, slamming a fist down on the table. "I'll want him arrested as well."

The General rose and walked over to a small window that looked out from his office in the Guildhall across the rooftops of London. He was a countryman from the market town of Huntingdon and had never cared much for the city. Its citizens were volatile and easily swayed by the passions of the moment. Now some of those passions were beginning to infect his army. He shook his head sadly.

"These ideas of Colonel Lilburne and the other Levellers are like a festering wound, Whalley. We must cauterize the flesh before it consumes the whole body. Inness and Dawes must be captured and brought back to London for trial. They're Cheshiremen and I expect they'll run for home. I'm ordering you to go after them and bring them back. Take the men from their own company and chase them down. If they resist, or if any of your men balk at apprehending their old commander, you may take summary action."

"You mean shoot them?"

"If needs be," said Cromwell. "I want those men brought back. Understood?"

"To be hung?" Whalley said glumly.

"After a fair trial," Cromwell said with a curt nod. "And Colonel, I will be sending Major Binford with you as an…observer."

Whalley frowned but said nothing. Simon Binford was the army's Provost Marshal, entrusted by Fairfax and Cromwell with enforcing discipline in the ranks of their New Model Army. It was a task the Major seemed born to. When mutinies began to spread though the regiments ordered to fight in Ireland, Binford had used a combination of threats and blandishments to ferret out the ringleaders, then ruthlessly rounded them up in the middle of the night. These were given a speedy trial and half were executed. That too was personally managed by the Provost Marshal. He was a man full of zeal for his work and for that he was universally feared and despised by the men of the army.

Cromwell now busied himself sorting through a stack of papers on his desk while Whalley stood silently at attention. Finally he looked up and seemed slightly surprised to see the Colonel still standing there.

"You are dismissed, sir."

Whalley saluted the General and hurried from the Guildhall. He knew these orders were a test of loyalty for him and the men of Inness' old company, a test to be judged by Simon Binford, the most hated man in the army. It was a calculated insult and it rankled, but he was an old soldier and would follow orders—up to a point.

"I'll be damned if I'll shoot my own men," he muttered as he headed for his regimental headquarters.

**

After five days in the saddle, the two weary riders turned off the road halfway between Coventry and Liverpool and rode down into the valley of the Weaver River. A squall had blown through as they broke camp at dawn and now a steady cold rain fell as they walked their tired horses through the village of Danesford. They had not been home for six years and the village looked largely unchanged. It was a small place with no more than a score of houses laid out neatly on either side of the road. Some of the larger dwellings looked prosperous with half-timbered second stories and attached barns.

No one was about in the weather, though Will knew that there would be unseen eyes warily watching two armed men riding through the center of the town. Danesford appeared to have been spared the kind of destruction they'd seen elsewhere, but after six years of bloody civil war, every town in England had learned to be vigilant.

They followed the dirt road out of town and into open country where spring plantings were showing green shoots in the fields. The road ran along the river and a mile beyond the town it climbed a small rise, then swung down to cross the shallow ford on the Weaver. From the crossing, the road ran on for twenty miles to the Northgate of Chester.

Will reined in his horse as they neared the rise above the ford. He felt a lump in his throat as he looked on the ancient stone fort perched there. The place had once guarded this strategic crossing of the Weaver, but had been abandoned and left to decay long ago. Its walls were overgrown with ivy and crumbling in places but the stone ramparts still looked formidable. The fortress had fascinated him as a boy and he'd spent many an hour standing imaginary guard along its battlements, waiting to repel some marauding Welshmen. But to his deep disappointment, no enemies had ever dared approach. Will clucked to his horse and they trotted past the fort, which looked dreary in the steady rain.

They did not take the bend in the road down to the ford, but rode straight onto an old familiar farm track that continued along the ridge above the river. A quarter mile on, they reached the family burial ground where generations of the Inness clan were laid to rest. Will's mother and father were buried there, side-by-side, looking down on the river. The graveyard held two score stone markers, some new but many so ancient and weathered nothing could be read upon them.

He'd often passed by this place as a boy and wondered about the folk who lay there. There was a family legend that one of the old weathered stones marked the grave of the man who'd built the fort by the ford. He'd been a knight who fought with King Richard in France and the Holy Land—or so the legend had it—and this land along the Weaver had been given to him by the Earl of Chester.

Whether such a man ever existed, Will did not know. More than four hundred years had passed since the reign of Richard I and there were no records from that long-ago time.

No King, No Country

But when he was a boy he liked to imagine what it must have been like to fight the Saracens beside the great Lionheart.

Passing the graveyard, the two riders rounded a sharp bend in the road and reined in their horses. Before he was born, Will's grandfather had built a fine house of stone and timber on this spot. The house was still there—what was left of it. The place had been burned out leaving nothing but low stone walls scorched black by fire.

"Good God!" August exclaimed.

Will swung down from his horse and led the animal up to the ruins. The damage was not new, as brambles and vines had already overtaken the charred skeleton of the house. He peered inside and saw nothing but blackened timbers. He'd spent a happy childhood in this house and the sight made his stomach lurch. Then a spasm of fear struck him.

Robert!

His older brother was the only member of the family who still kept residence here at Danesford, though he was often gone to Chester or the new port of Liverpool on business. Will looked past the ruins of the house. The large barn that had stood a hundred paces off was gone, burnt down to its foundations. An accidental fire in one should not have engulfed the other. That both had burned meant these fires had been set. Danesford had not completely escaped the ravages of war after all.

Will climbed back on his horse. Had Robert been here when the place was torched? He tried to dismiss the thought. Surely someone would have gotten word to him if his brother had been injured or killed. But he'd heard no word of Robert or the fire, so he could not be sure. He glanced over at August and saw him looking anxiously up the farm track toward his own farmstead. They both kicked their horses and rode the next mile through the pouring rain at a gallop, fearful of what they might find.

As they came over an old familiar rise, Will eased back on his reins. The Dawes farm house and barn were still standing. August did not slacken his speed until he reached the front of the house and leapt from his saddle. Splashing through puddles in the yard, he scattered a gaggle of geese that honked and hissed at him as he burst through the front door and disappeared inside.

Will followed him in and was relieved to see a shocked Alfred Dawes staring at his son as though a ghost had appeared in his front parlor. Behind Mr. Dawes, and equally shocked, was Mildred Dawes, who shrieked at the sight of the son she'd not seen in years. Without a word, the three came together in a tight embrace.

***

"I'm sorry for the house, William. I truly am. We saw the smoke and come running, but…"

Will nodded.

"How did it happen?"

Alfred Dawes was slow to answer, but finally began without raising his eyes to meet Will's.

"It was the Royalist army, William. They come up from Chester more'n a year ago. Marching to take Liverpool they was. They crossed at the ford. We stayed clear and their men never ranged out this way, but your stead, well, it was right near the ford…"

"Were any of our people hurt?"

"Nay, Robert was off in Liverpool and the rest scattered as soon as the advance guard of the Royalists started across the river. Some came here to our place and we took 'em in. After, we sent word to Robert of the fire, but he's not returned. He was in Liverpool when the Royalists took the city, but we heard he survived the storming of the town."

Will nodded.

"I thank you for that, Mr. Dawes."

"It was stragglers, Will," added Mildred Dawes who now spoke up with brimming eyes. "Most of the army was on past the town when we saw the smoke. When we came to see about it, there were a few of the King's soldiers still about. They were drunk and totin' off some of your folks fine things, but the house and barn was already burnin'. Wasn't nothing we could do."

Will could tell that recounting these events came hard for the Dawes'. They, like his own brother Robert and most of the west country folk, had strong Royalist sympathies. To see men in the King's army plundering so, and in a region that supported His Majesty, must have been a rude shock.

Will laid a hand on Alfred Dawes' shoulder.

"I know you did all you could. When an army passes through, be it for King or Parliament, few places are safe from ruin."

Will's kind words caused Mildred Dawes to burst fully into tears. Sobbing, she threw her arms around her young neighbor's neck and hugged him to her ample bosom.

"I'm just happy to see you alive and well, Will, and come back home to Danesford now the damned war is over. The place hasn't been the same since you and our August run off to join the army. And with Robert always away on business, it's been right lonely out this way."

Will let the woman cry for a moment then gently untangled himself. He gave August a look and stepped back. His friend sighed and put his hands on the woman's shoulders.

"Mother," he began, "we haven't come home to stay. In fact we are only passing by and must not dally. Will and I are going to America."

The woman looked at her son blankly.

"America?" she asked, unsure if she'd heard correctly.

"Aye, Mum, America. We're done with England."

"Isn't that across the ocean?" she asked, starting to blink back tears again. "Why would you go there? It's a wilderness they say."

August Dawes sighed and looked at his father who seemed to have grasped the situation.

"You can't stay in England, son?" he asked.

"Nay, Father. The Royalists have ample reason to hate us, now their cause is lost, and we've now managed to run afoul of the Parliamentarians as well. When both sides in a civil war count you as enemy, it's time to move on."

The old man nodded.

"I won't ask what trouble you're in, lad, and I don't care. I know ye. Hell, I raised ye! God can strike me down if ye've done anything shameful. And the same for you, William," he said, nodding toward Will. "If ye can't tarry then we won't keep ye long and if anyone comes looking, we'll not have seen ye. But for now, ye both look hungry."

He turned to his wife.

"Mother, can you feed the boys?"

Mildred, given something to do, sprang into action and within a quarter of an hour the dinner table was filled with plates of meat and cheeses, loaves of bread, and pots of stew. The two friends ate until stuffed then rose from the table.

Will turned to Alfred Dawes and shook his hand.

"You've been a good neighbor, Mr. Dawes," he said.

Alfred Dawes gripped his hand tightly and pulled him close.

"Watch out for my son," he whispered.

Will just nodded and found his way back out to the yard. He'd let August have his private goodbyes to the parents he might never see again. After a while his friend emerged, his eyes red-rimmed.

Will looked at him hard.

"Still want to go to America, Gus?"

His friend nodded.

"Aye, Will. And I pray it's better than here!"

***

Forty mounted men rumbled through Stoke-on-Trent as a wall of rain swept in from the west. The few people on the street watched them with a combination of curiosity and apprehension, wondering where a company of Roundhead cavalry was off to in such a rush, now the war was over.

No King, No Country

The men of the company were in a foul mood. They'd once been commanded by Captain William Inness, a clever leader and fair, but now they'd been ordered to arrest him. That their old commander was guilty of nothing more than speaking for them at Putney made this mission all the more galling.

Their Commander, Colonel Edward Whalley, rode at the head of the column and the Colonel's mood matched that of the men. Inness had been his most reliable company commander and a popular leader. He'd planned to promote Lieutenant Dawes and give him a command as well. Cromwell's order to hunt down Inness and Dawes was a calculated affront to him and the men of their company, but thus far the lads had kept their discipline and that at least was a relief.

He glanced to his right and saw Major Binford sitting straight as a ramrod in his saddle. Before setting out, the Provost Marshal had questioned him carefully on how he intended to track down the missing officers. Binford had found no fault with Whalley's plan to ride directly to the men's farmsteads in Cheshire and begin the search there—if they did not overtake the two on the road before then.

"If your birds have not flown home," the Major said with a smirk, "I'm certain someone will know where we might look for them. Panicked men rarely make wise decisions I've noticed."

Whalley did not reply. He'd fought beside Inness and Dawes in three major engagements. Neither man was prone to panic. It was likely the pair had headed for Cheshire, but Whalley harbored the unspoken prayer that they had fled in a different direction, far from his grasp and that of Major Binford. Since leaving London the Provost Marshal had hardly spoken to him. That suited Edward Whalley. Binford's personality was no better than his reputation and the Colonel had no interest in socializing with this catchpole.

As they thundered out of Stoke, the rain hit with a vengeance, the downpour driven by the wind. Whalley slowed the march and lowered his chin against the sting of the wind-driven drops. After four days in the saddle, he could feel every joint of his body protesting.

Not so young anymore, he thought, as he led his men into the teeth of the storm.

***

The rain died away as Will and August rode north for Liverpool. They camped on the last bit of high ground before the land dropped away to the swampy valley of the River Mersey. The next morning they were up at first light and reached the bridge over the river at Warrington. The wet April had the river swollen with spring runoff. Logs and other flotsam bobbed in the torrent, slamming into the piers beneath the bridge and causing the whole structure to shake. It didn't seem to bother two dirty-faced boys who stood on the upstream side of the bridge throwing sticks in and dashing across the span to watch for their prizes to be spit out the other side.

Will and August looked at the scene and smiled. They had played the same game more than once as boys. The two lads looked up and saw the riders with buff coats coming and stood aside, watching warily as Will and August clattered over the wooden structure. They brightened as Will touched the brim of his hat in a quick salute, prompting the boys to wave back cheerily.

"Takes more than a civil war to keep boys from finding some amusement," August said.

"And thank God for that," Will agreed as they rode into Warrington—or what remained of it.

"Oh lord," he said, reining in his horse.

The village of Warrington had once been a small but thriving place, profiting by its location at this furthest downstream bridge over the Mersey. It lay only fifteen miles north of Danesford and both men knew it well. Now it was

No King, No Country

a hollowed out hulk of a town. All about were signs of an army's occupation. A large makeshift corral, suitable for a regiment's compliment of horses, stood not far from the bridge, its posts and railings stripped from nearby houses and barns.

The pen was empty now and neglected, its gate askew and some of its rails fallen to the ground, evidence that whatever unit had taken quarters here was long gone. As they rode up the lane through the town, they could see that the houses had been sacked by the occupying troops. Neither man spoke as they rode out of Warrington, having seen not a living soul beyond the two boys on the bridge.

"The Royalists took Liverpool a year ago." Will said finally, leaving his growing worry unspoken.

"They'd have no cause to molest Robert, Will. He supported the King," August said half-heartedly. He knew as did his friend that when a town fell after a siege, the occupying army rarely made distinctions between friend and foe within its walls. Will said nothing, but touched his horse's flanks with his heels to pick up the pace.

August threw a glance back over the bridge. The two boys had resumed their game and there was no one else in sight, but that gave little comfort. Oliver Cromwell was not a man to be thwarted and somewhere behind them, men would be coming. He turned back and urged his horse into a trot to catch up with his friend.

Will turned as August rode up beside him.

"See anything back there?" he asked.

"Not yet," August said.

Liverpool

As they rode into town from the high ground to the east, they could see right down to the river and the view made Will's heart sink. A half dozen small fishing boats bobbed at anchor there, but not a single tall-masted merchant ship. Before the war, the Mersey would have had dozens of ships, large and small, waiting to take on or offload cargo. Most would be bound for Ireland, but some would set sail on the long voyage to America feeding the growing trade between the mother country and the new English colonies there. With no such ships in sight, Will wondered if fleeing here had been a wise course. He would know soon enough if he could find Robert.

On closer observation, Liverpool showed many signs of the fierce fighting that had swept over the port city during its capture by the Royalists and recapture by the forces of Parliament. The old castle still stood, but its walls were pock-marked with cannon shot from both sieges. Here and there a vacant lot stood filled with rubble and choked with spring weeds, evidence of the destruction that had befallen Liverpool.

The town was now controlled by the Parliamentarian army and the few troops on the street paid no heed to two buff-coated cavalrymen as they rode past. Mr. Dawes had told them that Robert Inness had gone into partnership with another local merchant near the beginning of the war and now kept offices on Water Street, with a small customs house down by the riverside. The two riders passed by the old town hall and onto Water Street walking their horses slowly toward the river and peering at each store front as they passed by. At last, they saw a sign hanging above a door.

Inness & James
Shippers & Customs

Will reined in and swung off his horse. A bell rang above the frame as he pushed the door open and stepped inside, with August at his heels. A plump man with a shiny bald pate was sitting behind a desk toward the rear of the room. The man's head jerked up at the sound of the bell and Will saw just a flicker of fear in his eyes. It was hardly surprising that a merchant whose town had been sacked twice in four years would show fear at the sight of two strange soldiers, but Will was impressed at how quickly the man masked it with a show of calm confidence.

"What can I do for you gentlemen?" he asked rising from his perch behind the desk.

"We wish to see Robert Inness," Will said flatly.

The pudgy man spread his hands.

"I'm afraid Mr. Inness is not available this morning. I'm Asa James, his partner. I'm sure I can help you with any sort of business you have in mind. Are you seeking passage to Ireland? We have a coaster departing on the next tide."

Will shook his head.

"I thank you, sir, but our business is with Mr. Inness. Do you know where he might be found?"

Asa James cleared his throat. Now he looked nervous.

"I wouldn't know, sir. He didn't say. He sent a boy around to let me know he would not be in the offices this morning. Perhaps I could give him a message when he does arrive."

Will stepped forward and glared at Mr. James.

"I'm William Inness, his brother."

James' eyes widened.

"Oh, beg pardon, sir. I meant no offense—none at all. But visits from the military these days…well, one can't be too careful."

Will nodded.

"I understand, Mr. James, but now if you will tell me where to find Robert."

James nodded agreeably and snatched up a wide-brimmed hat from a peg on the wall to cover his slick scalp.

"I'll take you myself, sir, if you'll follow me."

He led the two men back out to the street, turning to lock the door behind him.

"This way," he said, starting down toward the river.

Only a block west of the shipping office they reached a road that ran along the river bank. On the far side were wooden buildings lining the waterfront, some large and new, some small, shabby and old.

"This is our customs house," James said as they passed one of the newer structures. He did not stop there, but continued on past several more customs houses until he reached a series of small shanties that sat on piers out over the water. The merchant gave a quick look around, then led them onto a narrow catwalk that ran along the side of one of these structures.

"I believe we will find him here, this time of day," James said, puffing a little as he made his way along the catwalk to a small door. James gave the door two vigorous raps with his knuckles, then three more in quick succession.

Will glanced at August who shrugged his shoulders.

Some faint reply came from inside and James eased the door open a crack. Will brushed past the man and stepped into the room. Robert Inness looked up from a desk expecting to see his partner, but saw a big man in the buff coat of the Parliamentary cavalry instead. Startled, he grasped a pistol lying on the desk. In one fluid motion he

No King, No Country

raised the weapon, cocked it and levelled its muzzle at Will's chest.

"You would shoot me, brother?" Will asked, raising his hands to show they were empty.

Robert stared at the figure standing before him, then blinked and set the pistol down on the desk. He rose a little unsteadily to his feet, staring at the brother he hadn't seen in six years.

"William?"

Will nodded and returned his brother's stare, not moving. Robert was as he'd remembered him, tall and lean with the strong jaw and fine features that young women had always been drawn to. The face had aged a little with the passage of years, but was handsome still, framed as it was by long brown hair that fell to his shoulders. But there was one shocking change in the man. Robert was missing his left arm to the elbow, judging by the pinned up shirt there. Will did not let his eyes dwell on his brother's injury.

"Aye, Rob. It's me."

Robert crossed the floor in three quick strides and wrapped his good arm around his brother's neck, pulling him close.

"Ah, God, but it's good to see you, Will," he murmured. "I was sore afraid you might be dead, but as a known Royalist, I had no way to reach you. This war…There's been so much death."

Will returned his brother's embrace and the two stood there clinging to each other for a long moment before Robert stepped back. For the first time, he noticed August Dawes standing just outside the door.

"Ahh, the reunion is complete," he said with a smile. "Come here, young Gus!"

August stepped forward eagerly and pumped Robert's proffered hand vigorously, paying no heed to the man's missing limb.

"It's grand to see you, Rob," he blurted.

"And you, Gus, It's been too long since the three of us were together."

Robert cut a quick glance at his partner who still stood at the doorway. Asa James did not need to be prompted that it was best for outsiders to absent themselves when family affairs were to be discussed. He discreetly withdrew from the shanty and returned to his office on Water Street.

***

"You're a customs agent?" Will asked.

Robert shrugged.

"Of a sort. Half the shipping agents in Liverpool have commissions from the King or from Parliament, or both, to collect the fees on imports. It's not a great deal of money, but it's steady."

"You said, 'of a sort,' I believe," Will noted. "Care to explain?"

Robert gave Will a sly smile.

"These have been hard years, Will. First, Parliament's troops took over the garrison here and those of us loyal to the King did what we could to keep our heads down and to keep customs revenue out of the hands of the King's enemies."

"And how was that done?" Will asked, genuinely curious.

"We took up smuggling—an old and honorable activity in these parts," Robert said, still smiling. "We funneled most of the profits into the King's coffers, but I confess we kept a bit for ourselves."

"It must have been a relief for you when Prince Rupert took the city."

Robert frowned.

"Aye, or so I'd hoped after four years of occupation by your lads, but…"

"You were injured—in the siege?" Will said, nodding toward his brother's missing limb.

Robert shook his head.

No King, No Country

"No, not in the siege nor in the fight inside the town. It would have been easier to stomach had that been the case. I, and a good lot of the townsfolk, came out into the streets to cheer when the King's banner rose above the castle's battlements and for a few hours there was joy, at least amongst Liverpool's Royalists. Then the trouble began."

Will sighed. He knew what must come next.

"They sacked the town," he said.

Robert nodded.

"The bastards went mad for two days. Houses were plundered and some burnt, women were dishonored, all by a drunken horde we thought were our liberators. They didn't give one shit if you were a Roundhead or the King's most loyal supporter. I got this when I stood between a neighbor's daughter and three drunken Cavaliers," he said, holding up the stump of his arm. "Was it like this everywhere, Will? Or just here in Liverpool?"

"It didn't start that way, Rob, but it became that in the end. Liverpool is far from the first or last town to be plundered in this war. I wish I could say such outrages were only the work of your Royalists, but that would be a lie. My regiment kept good discipline after our victories—Colonel Whalley saw to that—but not all regimental officers were as honorable. I expect it was the same with the King's army."

Robert sat in silence for a while, then looked up.

"The King is dead and Parliament has triumphed. Is that not the end of it?"

Will sighed.

"No. There's ferment in London and trouble within the ranks of Parliament's army. Many of the men feel they've shed their blood only to exchange the King's rule for rule by the great land-owners."

"And they do not want that?"

"Most do not. I do not."

"So what is it you *do* want, Will?"

"You know why I enlisted with Parliament in the beginning, Rob. We argued about it long enough. You thought we were best ruled by a wise king accountable to God. I thought we'd be better ruled by wise men accountable to the people. In the end, neither of us got what we hoped for. The men who fought and bled for Parliament are coming to believe that their leaders are as feckless as your King. They want a voice."

Robert gave Will a wry smile.

"Are you one of those…those followers of this Lilburne fellow we've been hearing about? Is it votes for all?"

Will did not return the smile.

"And why not? Why should only a handful of men have a voice in our rule. You may vote for Parliament, Rob, because you own the Inness lands. I may not. Am I a lesser man?"

Robert shook his head.

"No, you are not. In fact, you are the better man. You at least went to war for what you believed. I…I just tried to stay out of the way and you can see what that brought me. But now I must wonder, why you are here, Will? Have you come home now the war is over? The folks in Danesford would rejoice if it's true."

Will shook his head and stood up.

"No, not back to Danesford. We stopped there a day ago."

Robert's face looked pained.

"Word reached me after the Royalist army moved on that they had burned our place. I couldn't bear to go back to see it. Is it truly gone?"

Will nodded.

"Aye, Rob, burnt down. Mrs. Dawes says it was stragglers that did it."

"Father's books…" Rob said mournfully.

"All gone."

No King, No Country

Robert reached out and grasped Will's hand, his eyes brightening.

"You could rebuild! You know the land, Will. It's not too late to put in a crop and I have money for seed corn, horses and plows—whatever you need."

Will drew his hand away.

"I cannot, Rob. There is a warrant for my arrest signed by Cromwell himself I'm told."

"For what crime?" Robert asked indignantly.

"Mutiny, and they intend to hang me if I'm caught."

"Good Lord, Will. You spoke of trouble in your army, but mutiny?"

"He did nothing more than stand up for his men!" August put in. "He's no mutineer."

Will nodded.

"I led no mutiny, but Cromwell and Parliament fear I might, so I am to hang. Men will come looking for me in Danesford and no doubt here as well. They'll be no more than a day behind us. Gus and I need to leave England, Rob. Can you help us?"

***

The storm had long past when Colonel Whalley led his company of horse off the old Roman road and down into the valley of the River Weaver. When they reached the village of Danesford, they stopped to make inquiries, but none in the town admitted to seeing two riders come through the day before. They did tell the Colonel where he would find the Inness place, but that he'd find no one there to speak to.

So the troop rode on out of the town and did not pause at the crumbling fort by the ford or the burnt country manor, halting only when they reached the farmstead of Alfred Dawes. The old man came out to greet them, his wife hovering in the doorway.

"Mr. Dawes?" Whalley inquired as the man approached.

"I'm Alfred Dawes. What can I do for you?"

Whalley cleared his throat.

"I'm Colonel Edward Whalley. We were looking for your son, Mr. Dawes. It seems August has gone missing along with his friend William Inness. Have you seen the lads?"

"Missing?" Dawes asked, rubbing his chin. "What do ye mean?"

"He missed morning muster five days ago, sir. We thought he might have come home for a visit."

Dawes looked skeptically at the forty men sitting their horses behind Whalley, an unlikely concerned search party.

"I'm sorry to hear that, Colonel, and appreciate yer worry over my boy, but I've not seen either lad for six years or so. Not since they run off to join up. Got a letter from August last year, but nothing since. He seemed well at the time."

He turned and spoke to his wife.

"Mother, the Colonel says August's gone missing."

Mrs. Dawes hand went to her mouth.

"I begged my boy not to join up with those Parliament folks!" she wailed, on the verge of tears. "Now he's gone missin'. He shoulda never left Cheshire!"

Whalley waved his hands.

"I didn't mean to distress you, Mrs. Dawes. I'm sure he's alright. We just need to find him."

Major Binford brushed past Colonel Whalley.

"We'll need to search your property," he said abruptly, paying no heed to the distraught Mrs. Dawes.

Mr. Dawes cocked his head.

"What's the point?" he asked. "We'd a surely seen the boy if he was around here."

"Don't play me for the fool, sir!" snarled Binford, turning and summoning the company's senior sergeant.

"Twenty men to search the house and barn," he ordered. "Another twenty to search the land from here down to the river."

Sergeant Treadway glanced over at Colonel Whalley who turned to Binford.

"May I remind you that you are here as an observer, Major."

"I..."

Whalley raised a hand for silence.

"As an observer, Major," he repeated. "Those were Cromwell's exact words. Do you dispute that I command here?"

For a moment the two stood a few feet apart, glaring at each other. Then Binford shrugged.

"As you wish, Colonel. I'll observe carefully and report in detail as to how you and your men carry out the General's orders. You can be sure I will note any lack of diligence I witness."

With that, Major Binford turned and marched back to his horse. Colonel Whalley motioned to Treadway.

"Search the place," he said quietly. "If anything must be disturbed, it will be put back in place gently. Understood?"

"Completely," the sergeant said. "And if we find them, sir?"

Colonel Whalley grimaced.

"I fear we must do our duty, Sergeant Treadway. It is duty and discipline that distinguishes us from an armed mob."

The sergeant saluted and began barking orders to the men. For two hours they searched the property while Mr. and Mrs. Dawes offered drinks of cool well water. Finding nothing, Colonel Whalley ordered the men back on their horses. Alfred Dawes came out of his cottage to see them off.

"You'll send word if you find my boy, Colonel?"

Whalley nodded solemnly, but did not reply. If word was to be sent to the Dawes' it would likely be that their only son was dead or imprisoned for desertion. He led his troop back up the road to Danesford. Alfred Dawes spat on the ground when they were out of sight.

In the village more townsfolk were questioned at Major Binford's insistence. Now money was offered for information and, in due course, someone spoke up. Two riders *had* been seen passing through the town and headed north the day before—and one thing more.

Inness had a brother in Liverpool.

No King, No Country

The Smuggler's Trade

Apprised of his brother's urgent need, Robert Inness turned his considerable experience and energy to the task of getting William and August Dawes out of England. Leaving the two in his small office, he went first to his banker, then shuttled up and down the riverfront of Liverpool speaking to men he trusted and avoiding those he did not. Information was gathered, bargains struck and plans made. He returned at sundown to the office where the two fugitives had remained hidden.

"There is a ship bound for the Virginia colony that was to have sailed from Southampton four days ago," he announced. "She's to make port here in Liverpool to take on cargo for delivery to Jamestown. She's called the *Fair Wind* and if she's not had foul weather, she'll anchor in the Mersey by tomorrow afternoon. The ship is owned by a man who owes me a favor. I can get you aboard, but all passenger berths have been sold, so you'll be quartered on the tween deck with the crew, though you'll mess with the passengers. It's the best I could do on short notice."

"That should do fine, Rob," Will said. "We've slept in much worse these past few years. You have our thanks."

"And your destination—I would have preferred a ship bound for Massachusetts Bay or perhaps the new Connecticut River colony where the Governors have sworn allegiance to Parliament. Virginia is rife with Royalist emigrants and sympathizers. I should know, I've helped many a one flee England in the last year."

Will shrugged.

"Virginia or Connecticut—it matters not. I've managed to make enemies of Royalists and Roundheads alike and have no plans to tarry long in any settlement. It's a new land. I'll find my own place."

Robert rubbed his chin.

"It's a wild place, Will."

"I'll take my chances, Rob."

Robert nodded. He'd heard this tone of stubborn defiance from his brother many times before and knew it was no use to argue.

"You'll need supplies to survive outside the settlements and some are hard to come by in the colonies. I'll see what I can arrange."

***

The sun had fallen below the horizon when Robert exited the small office to make the rounds of a different set of acquaintances. Before he left he rummaged through a cabinet at the back of the small room and pulled out two woolen blankets.

"I've much to attend to," he said, tossing each a blanket. "Try to get some sleep. It's best you stay here. Only a few of my trusted associates know that this shack is mine, whereas everyone in town knows my house. If someone comes looking, they'll likely look there first. I'll send someone around if there's trouble."

After he'd gone, August wrapped himself in his blanket and curled up on the floor.

"What sort of supplies will he be wanting for us?" he asked as he stifled a yawn.

"A few I can guess," said Will. "Lead, powder, an axe or two, iron pots for starters. Robert has no doubt provisioned others crossing to the colonies and will have learned what's needed."

"I've never been to sea," August put in drowsily.

No King, No Country

Will lay down beside his friend. He was no old salt, but he'd spent many winter months as a boy plying the waters between Chester and Liverpool and the ports along the Irish coast. It had been his father's wish that he and Rob understand the sea and the vessels that were the basis of their shipping business. Having spent three seasons each year working the land around Danesford, he'd always welcomed these winter voyages. The work had been hard and at times dangerous, but for an adventurous boy of ten, the deck of a ship and the men who sailed her offered an exciting look at a wider world.

"I'll not let you fall overboard, Gus" he said.

The only reply he got was a soft snore.

***

When Colonel Whalley's troop of cavalry clattered over the Mersey bridge at first light there were no boys playing there, nor was a soul to be seen in the ravaged village of Warrington as they passed through. At midmorning they crested the high ground east of Liverpool, descended to the Towsend Bridge and rode into the center of town, only drawing up when they reached the main gate of the castle that loomed over the town and the riverfront.

The Colonel ordered a halt, instructed his men to see to their horses, and rode across the drawbridge, through the massive gatehouse and into the outer ward of the castle, Major Binford by his side. The approach of a troop of cavalry had not gone unnoticed by the watch and an officer was waiting in the castle ward to greet them.

"Major Chester Atherton, Garrison Commander," he said by way of introduction.

"Colonel Whalley and Major Binford," Whalley replied, noticing just a hint of apprehension in Atherton's expression at the mention of Binford's name. "We have orders for the arrest of Captain William Inness and Lieutenant August Dawes. We have reason to believe they are here in Liverpool seeking aid from Captain Inness' brother, a local merchant in the shipping trade. Our orders are from General Cromwell."

Cromwell's name had the desired effect.

"Of course, of course. You will want to speak with Mr. Robert Inness," the Garrison Commander eagerly volunteered. "Tall man, dark hair—a Royalist sympathizer, but of the quiet sort."

"There must be more than one tall, dark-haired Royalist in this town," Major Binford said acidly. "How would we know this man if we saw him on the street?"

"Oh, you'll have no trouble," Major Atherton replied. "The man lost half his left arm when the town fell to Prince Rupert. And he is often found in his offices on Water Street. I'll have one of my lad's show you the way."

Whalley nodded.

"Obliged. And Major, we'll expect any spare men in your garrison to assist in locating and apprehending these two criminals."

"Whatever you need, Colonel!" Major Atherton declared, saluting smartly and barking an order to his adjutant.

***

There was no knock on the door to announce the arrival of visitors at *Inness & James Shippers & Customs*. Only the tinkle of the bell over the doorjamb. Asa James' head came up to see a burly colonel of cavalry approaching his desk with a razor-thin major in his wake.

"Can I help you gentlemen?" he inquired politely.

"We are here to see Robert Inness on official business," the colonel stated politely.

"Official, you say?"

"Yes, yes. We are here on orders from General Cromwell himself!" the skinny major threw in.

"Cromwell! Now that does sound official," James agreed heartily. "Is it about the customs payments? We keep very careful books you know."

No King, No Country

Reaching behind him, the bald merchant grasped a hefty ledger and plopped it on his desk.

"It's all here—every farthing," he insisted, opening the ledger as though opening his robe for all to see, a little hurt that any doubt might have been cast on the firm's accounting.

"No, no, no!" the major said, slamming the book shut and almost pinching one of Asa James' pudgy fingers. "We don't give a damn about your customs collections, sirrah! We are searching for deserters and traitors, one of whom is brother to your Mr. Inness. Has your partner had any visitors in the last day?"

Asa drew back in alarm.

"Deserters you say! Robert's brother? Oh my."

"Have you seen two young men with Robert recently?" Colonel Whalley asked quietly.

"Well, aye, sir. Robert met with two young Presbyterian ministers and the Bishop late yesterday to arrange for passage to Ulster, but they seemed strangers to him—the ministers, not the Bishop of course."

Binford, his face turning crimson, reached for the long cavalry pistol at his side, but Colonel Whalley laid a restraining hand on the major's own and turned back to Asa.

"Mr. James, where would Robert Inness be now? We should speak to him directly."

James scratched his bald head and furrowed his brow.

"It's hard to say, sir. He left an hour ago for George Thomas' pier. The one at the far end of the riverfront. Some business about delayed cargo. You might find him there or encounter him on the way back. He has a townhouse on James Street, but is rarely there during the day."

"Thank you, Mr. James," the Colonel said politely. "We'll leave you to your business." With that, he opened the door, ignored the tinkling bell and waved Major Binford outside.

"What a fool!" Binford snapped as they emerged onto the street.

"More liar than fool," Whalley said, "and loyal to his partner. I'll send men to Thomas' pier and to this house on James Street, but I'll wager we'll find nothing in either place. We'll need someone less attached to this Mr. Inness to help us. You have silver left?"

Binford nodded.

"Let's hope it takes less than thirty pieces to buy Judas," Whalley said as he made his way back toward Liverpool Castle.

***

The boy sent by Asa James found Robert Inness just exiting the establishment of a Mr. Albert Rose, Liverpool's most prominent ironmonger. He breathlessly related Mr. James' recent encounter with the two cavalry officers at their Water Street office. Robert gave the boy his thanks and a message, then flipped him a coin and continued on his rounds.

***

"I can sort this for you, Colonel," said Major Atherton with confidence. "Half the merchants in this town sided with us during the war and half with the King. Inness was a Royalist, so I suggest we seek information as to his whereabouts from the Parliamentarian sympathizers. It so happens I have an accurate list of these men and would be happy to assist you."

"That would be most appreciated, Major," said Colonel Whalley. "I'm sure General Cromwell and Black Tom will be pleased to hear that Liverpool is in such capable hands. So where do we start?"

The Garrison Commander returned to his desk and shuffled through some papers in a drawer before drawing forth his prize, a list of reliable Parliamentarian supporters in the town.

No King, No Country

"Ah, here it is! And the first name on the list is....Mr. Albert Rose."

***

Will heard two sharp raps on the door followed by three others in quick succession, the signal of a friend come to call. He arose a little groggy and was startled to see sunlight streaming in from the lone window in Robert's office. It seemed he'd slept through the night and well into the morning. Curled up in the corner, August still snored contentedly. Crossing to the door, Will opened it a crack and peered out. There was a boy waiting patiently on the catwalk.

"Mr. Robert says t' tell ye a troop of Roundheads rode into town this morn and are askin' questions. Mr. Robert says ye should keep yer heads down."

The boy did not wait for reply, but turned and set off at a run, other duties to perform. August sat up in the corner.

"What's afoot, Will?" he asked.

Will closed the door and threw home the bolt.

"Hounds on our scent, Gus."

***

With the names of Liverpool's known Parliamentarian sympathizers apportioned out, mixed squads from Whalley's cavalry and the garrison descended on merchants and tradesmen from one end of the city to the other with silver in hand. Major Binford took the first name on the list and led his squad to the establishment of *A. Jones, Ironmonger*.

A clerk led the Major through a large shop displaying a great variety of domestic and agricultural tools available for purchase. In the rear a door led out to a large covered shed where a half dozen smiths were hard at work, some heating metal in blazing forges, some hammering glowing rods of steel into shape or plunging them into cauldrons of water sending plumes of steam up toward the roof of the shed.

Mr. Rose, a short man with the shoulders of one twice his size, stood amidst them all observing their work. He saw the clerk and the visitors and, wiping a sheen of sweat from his brow, left his post to see to them. With conversation impossible amidst the pounding of steel, he beckoned them to follow him into the shop.

"What can I do for you gentlemen?" Rose asked once they'd assembled inside.

"We wish to question Mr. Robert Inness," Major Binford began, "on an official matter. Do you know his whereabouts?"

Albert Rose stuffed the sweaty cloth in a rear pocket and scratched his head.

"Inness? Haven't seen the man lately, but hope you find the Royalist bastard! Now I must be..."

Binford cut him short.

"We can pay for your help, Mr. Rose, in silver," he said, laying a small leather sack on the desk that jingled as it came to rest.

Rose picked up the little sack and felt its heft before setting it back down with a shrug.

"I'd love to take your money, gentlemen, but as I said, I haven't seen the man and I have a rather important order to fill." With that, Rose turned his back on his visitors and returned to his post amongst the smiths.

Binford clinched his fists as he watched the man's back disappear through the door, but held his tongue. Snatching up the purse from Rose's desk, he stomped out of the ironmonger's shop. Having no luck with Albert Rose, Binford moved on to the next name on his list, a Mr. Jacob Murray, Liverpool's most prominent cooper and a staunch Parliamentarian. But his results there were no better. Murray hardly knew the shipper, he'd declared.

As the afternoon progressed, drapers, cordwainers, slaters, butchers and shippers all across the port town proved unable to pinpoint the current location of Mr. R. Inness. Two merchants happily took the Major's bribe and claimed to have seen Robert Inness at opposite ends of the town around noon, but searches turned up nothing. Binford sent men to retrieve his silver, but the recipients could not be located.

In port cities the world over, politics weigh little against the interests of business. Whether Royalist or Parliamentarian, the tradesmen of Liverpool were businessmen first.

And Robert Inness was one of their own.

***

Robert Inness returned to the shed at midafternoon, his rounds complete.

"Your ship has been sighted coming upriver," he said to the two fugitives. "She's a fully-rigged merchantman bound for Virginia. The ship's owner says she'll only drop anchor long enough to take on fresh water and provisions and a few items of cargo, then sail on the ebb tide. The town is crawling with Roundheads looking for me, so they can find you, but with luck the *Fair Wind* will be in and out before they notice. A tender will swing by this pier as soon as the ship reaches its anchorage."

Will nodded.

"We're obliged, Rob."

Robert threw his good arm around his brother's neck.

"It breaks my heart to see you leave England, Will," he said, his voice cracking. "These are foul times for our country."

"Aye, Rob. The war's over, but what will follow it? I don't think it'll be peace."

Rob released his grip on his brother and drew out a small pouch from his coat.

"It's not a fortune, but it will help get you by until you find your way."

Will felt tears well in his eyes. It had been a long time since he'd cried, but he cried now as he pulled Robert close and hugged him. He whispered in his brother's ear.

"If ever you are in need, Rob, send for me. I will come."

***

The *Fair Wind* dropped anchor an hour before sunset and was soon joined by a few small tenders sent out from docks along the waterfront, some delivering cargo and supplies for the long over-ocean voyage and others offloading goods sent from Portsmouth. One among the tenders also delivered two fugitives who slipped aboard and were ordered below and out of sight.

The *Fair Wind*'s crew and the men aboard the tenders moved with long-practiced efficiency and hardly an hour had passed before the boats began to return to shore, their work done. But those in Liverpool's shipping trade were not the only ones to take note of the arrival of the *Fair Wind*. Word had spread through the town that a Roundhead Major was offering silver to locate two deserters and while the merchants and shippers might turn up their noses at that, not every denizen of Liverpool's waterfront felt obliged to keep silent.

A frustrated Major Simon Binford was leading his squad down James Street when a man hailed him furtively from an alleyway. He told Binford he didn't know where Robert Inness was, but had a notion where these deserters might be. Binford was about to dismiss the man as just another of Liverpool's liars until the fellow demanded silver, the first person in the town to do so. Still skeptical, he counted out a handful of coins, which the man took eagerly. He then stepped into the street and pointed at the ship swinging at anchor in the Mersey. For Binford, the sight of the vessel provided a jolt of clarity to what had become a murky business. Why had he not thought of this?

Robert Inness was a shipper!

What better way to spirit his brother out of Parliament's reach than to ship him out of England? He turned to the sergeant leading his escort and pointed to the river a block ahead.

No King, No Country

"Find me a boat, sergeant. We'll have a look at this ship in the river."

***

Abraham Keogh, Captain of the *Fair Wind*, stood on the quarterdeck watching as his men hauled a large wooden box up from a tender, swung it over the rail and lowered it through the hatch into the ship's hold, setting it down as gently as a feather. Keogh was a small, compact man dressed all in black save for the white collar above his coat and he stood with feet apart as men do who've spent years keeping watch on a pitching deck. The Captain noted with satisfaction how well his crew handled the onboarding of the cargo. Most had sailed with him for three years or more and all knew their jobs well.

As he watched the men go about their duties, something on the river caught his eye. It was a skiff jammed with soldiers sliding away from the bank and pulling toward his ship. As he saw the men straining at the oars, he uttered a brief curse under his breath.

"Forgive me, Lord," he murmured, embarrassed at his own vulgarity.

He'd been a sailor since he was nine years old, working his way up from ship's boy to ship's master and had heard every blasphemous oath invented by the mind of man—had used most of them himself! But late in life he'd met and wed a good, God-fearing woman who did not approve of such language. So he'd affirmed, before Nellie and Almighty God, to curb his tongue, and for the most part, he'd kept that oath, but…there were times when nothing less than a sincere curse would do.

This was one of those times.

He had hoped he could get into and out of Liverpool with no trouble, but here was trouble rowing right towards him. Like all ship's masters in all ages, Keogh exercised complete authority aboard his own vessel, but even a sea captain's power had its limits. Under sail he was supreme, but ships eventually had to make port where the authority of landsmen came into play.

Had this been a skiff filled with brigands and pirates in the harbor of Tortuga, he'd have ordered his first mate to send a shot across their bow from one of the *Fair Wind*'s eight 12-pounders and if that did not dissuade them, he'd have turned the skiff into kindling with his swivel gun mounted on the fo'c'sle. But this was Liverpool and the men rowing toward him were no brigands. He would have to exercise his authority delicately.

For he had something to hide.

Only an hour before, he'd taken two men aboard bearing a message from the owner of the *Fair Wind*. The note directed him to provide Captain Inness and Lieutenant Dawes passage to Virginia as "special passengers." Given the number of Royalists he'd secreted out of Liverpool and the southern ports during the civil war, Captain Keogh knew what the owner meant by "special passengers."

These men were fugitives.

Having no berths in the few passenger cabins aboard, he'd ordered the two quartered with the crew in the tween deck and they'd not complained—a welcome change from many of the more refined Royalists he'd smuggled out of England these past years. He'd noted their buff coats, sure signs that they'd been Roundhead cavalry, and wondered why, with Parliament victorious, these two had to flee England. Time would tell, as few secrets withstood a long sea voyage. He could wait to satisfy his curiosity. Of more immediate concern was the skiff full of soldiers bearing down on him.

"Mr. Berrycloth," he called, and his first mate hurried to his side. Where Keogh was a small man both in height and girth, John Berrycloth was neither. It was a wonder a man of his bulk had found his calling within the exceedingly cramped quarters of an ocean-going merchant ship. But Berrycloth, for all his size, was nimble and could slip through a passageway or scramble up the ratlines like a ship's boy when needed.

"Aye, sir," the mate said when he reached the captain's perch on the quarterdeck.

"You'll note we have visitors," the captain said pointing to the approaching skiff. "I expect they'll be looking for our newest guests. It will be awkward if they're found."

"Aye, Cap'n," Berrycloth replied and disappeared. He found the two men where he'd sent them—out of sight below on the tween deck.

"Soldiers coming aboard, lads," he warned. "Best shed those clothes."

Will and August looked at each other.

"We've no other," Will admitted.

Berrycloth nodded.

"Stand fast, then."

The big man hurried down the crowded passageway that ran the length of the tween deck and flung open a trunk jammed between barrels stacked three high. He rummaged through the chest and hurried back with a bundle in his arms. Sizing the two men up, he tossed them loose shirts and looser pants with drawstrings to preserve modesty.

"Get 'em on quick now and act busy. They'll search I expect."

Will and August quickly shucked off their uniforms and the high leather boots favored by cavalrymen, stuffing these along with their weapons under the thin mattresses they'd been assigned as bedding. The clothes hung on them shapelessly, but fit after a sort if they tied up the drawstring of their trousers. Newly outfitted, they stood for Berrycloth's inspection. He grunted.

"Ye'll do. But stay below. Down here, they might not notice yer not burnt as brown as a seaman." With that the mate disappeared up the ladder to the main deck.

***

On the quarterdeck, Captain Keogh watched as the skiff clumsily came along side. He stepped to the railing and looked down on a scene that might have been humorous in other circumstances. A thin man, obviously an officer, was standing in the center of the boat screaming at the man handling the tiller who was screaming at the oarsmen.

After much bouncing against the hull of the *Fair Wind*, a line was finally secured from the skiff to the ship and the thin man began scrambling up the jack ladder, followed by two of his soldiers. The officer pulled himself over the rail and onto the deck as Mr. Berrycloth emerged from below. The mate went to greet the visitor, offering a proper salute as Binford, breathing hard, straightened his jacket.

"Welcome aboard, sir," the big man boomed. "if you'll follow me, I'll take ye to the Captain."

Without looking to see if his charge was following, Berrycloth scampered up the ladder to the quarterdeck. Binford hurried to keep up. When finally he arrived before Captain Keogh, the Major took a long moment before speaking, still breathing hard from his climb up two ladders. At last he managed an introduction.

"Major Simon Binford, Provost Marshal of the Army," he announced.

Captain Keogh looked him up and down.

"The Parliamentarian Army, is it? I've been at sea a great deal these past years, Major. It's been hard to keep up with the course of events on land. The Parliamentarian faction won the war then?"

Binford sputtered, unsure if this little ship's captain was ignorant or insolent.

"Won? Of course we won!" he said. "We executed the King in January, or hadn't you heard."

"Ah, yes. I think there was talk of that in Southampton," Keogh observed, "but they say the King has a son who'll be back on the throne in no time. Wasn't sure if that had happened."

"It hasn't and it won't!" Binford sputtered. "Now you have my name, but…"

"Oh, forgive my manners, Major. Aboard ship everyone knows who the Captain is and I do sometimes forget that visitors might not!" Keogh said cheerily. "I am Abraham Keogh, master of the *Fair Wind*. How may I be of service to you and your men?"

"Captain, we have reason to believe that two fugitives wanted for mutiny and desertion are on this ship."

Captain Keogh's eyes grew wide.

"Mutineers, you say? Nothing lower in my book, Major! I brook no mutiny aboard the *Fair Wind*, I assure you, But why would you suppose army mutineers would be aboard my vessel? We've taken on no one here or in Southampton who could possibly be involved in such an affair."

Binford arched an eyebrow.

"Perhaps these men slipped aboard without you noticing, Captain Keogh, so I must insist on searching the ship and examining all aboard myself."

This drew a pained expression from the Captain.

"But, Major, we are ready to hoist anchor and catch the ebb tide! Miss it and we lose a half day's sailing, which we can ill afford as we're bound for Virginia."

"Your desire for haste cannot preempt the requirements of the law, Captain. In the name of Parliament, I order you to turn out your crew and all passengers!"

Keogh sighed. The owner of his vessel had requested he slip two young men out of the country quietly—as a favor to a friend. He'd agreed readily enough as it would not be the first time he'd smuggled wanted men out of England. But his instructions did not extend to provoking a confrontation with the Provost Marshal of the New Model Army. He would not risk damage to his patron over two fugitives.

"Very well, Major, but I doubt anyone could have come aboard this ship without my knowledge."

He turned to the first mate.

"Mr. Berrycloth, please assemble the crew and ask our passengers to join us on the main deck."

"Aye, sir."

***

Twenty-eight men and a ship's boy stood in two lines along the larboard rail of the *Fair Wind*. Twenty-six of the men were crew. Two were not. Will and August had considered concealing themselves somewhere on the ship, but the small vessel was jammed with cargo that filled every nook and cranny, leaving no suitable hiding places. So they'd joined the crew, finding spots on the back row some distance from each other. The seamen of the *Fair Wind* showed no reaction to having two strangers suddenly join their ranks. In a less organized fashion, five passengers were gathered in a group near the bulkhead of the sterncastle. From the quarterdeck, Captain Keogh looked down impassively on the scene.

As Will lined up on deck, he'd been chilled to see Simon Binford leading the search party. He'd seen Binford once before and the occasion had left a mark. His company had been ordered to witness the hanging of the two mutineers from Captain Somerset's company and Major Binford had conducted the gruesome proceedings. There was no mistaking the sharp features and cold countenance of the Army's Provost Marshal.

Thankfully, Will and August had been but two obscure faces in the crowd that day, so Binford would have no cause to recognize either. Still, it was a shock to think that the Army had sent their most senior enforcer all the way to the west of England in search of them and nerve-wracking to stand there as the Provost Marshal scanned the faces of the crew and passengers.

The major gave a clipped order to the two local garrison soldiers who'd followed him onto the deck of the ship. The two slung their matchlocks over their shoulders and disappeared down the stairs to the tween deck and the hold, no doubt to begin their search of the ship. The major then turned and called down to the skiff below. Three more men appeared in due course and were ordered to stand ready should there be any resistance once the deserters were found.

Binford began with the passengers. The sun was low on the horizon as he passed among the well-dressed group by the sterncastle. There were two young women and three men. One of the women wore silk and looked highborn. Next to her stood a second woman, who by her plain dress looked to be her servant.

Two of the men in the party were as richly dressed as the young woman, sporting expensive cloaks, kid gloves and the long curled wigs favored by the gentry. The exception was a squat man who wore plain, sturdy garments that marked him as a tradesman. As Binford looked them up and down, the tradesman looked bored, but the two gentlemen looked nervous—and with good reason. They'd hardly be mistaken for deserting Roundheads, but the times did not favor those sporting the customary dress of Cavaliers, especially with a senior Parliamentarian officer glaring at them.

"Off to Virginia, gentlemen?" the major asked acidly.

Neither answered.

"When you get there, inform the rest of the Royalist traitors who've washed up on those shores that the writ of Parliament will be along soon enough!"

This brought a swift response from the well-dressed young woman.

"Who are you to bully us, sir?" she snapped, her eyes flashing.

"I am Major Simon Binford, Madam," Binford snapped back, "Provost Marshal of the army, sent here by General Cromwell to serve arrest warrants on a mutineer and a deserter. And as for bullying, you Royalists have had your day. Your lording it over Englishmen ended when your precious king's head toppled into the basket!"

Anne Bingham did not quail at the Major's harsh words.

"The people of England will wish us back soon enough after they've had a belly full of your precious Parliament!" she hissed. "Then you'll not be so bold with your words!"

The color rose in Major Binford's face, but before he could reply a voice came down from the quarterdeck.

"If you have no warrant for any of my passengers, Major, you will leave them be!" Captain Keogh snapped, his voice full of authority, all deference gone. "I have a tide to catch, so inspect my crew and be done, sir."

Binford turned his glare on the Captain, but held his tongue and turned to the crew standing in two loose ranks. He scanned their faces searching for some clue that the men he sought were among their number, but the sailors all looked more put out than nervous. Then he brightened and hurried back to the rail, calling down once more to the skiff.

A few moments later, a new man pulled himself over the railing. Will felt his stomach knot. It was Sergeant Treadway, the senior sergeant from his old company, a man who knew him well and one he'd never known to shirk his duty. He stole a glance at August, who'd gone pale at the sight of Alfred Treadway.

"You were with Inness' company were you not, Sergeant?" Binford asked as Treadway cleared the rail and joined him on the main deck.

"Aye, sir," Treadway replied readily.

"Then point him out, if you please," Binford ordered, gesturing toward the two lines of seamen.

Treadway snapped a salute and turned to the assembled crew. He walked briskly down the front rank taking a long look at each man in turn, then turned to Binford and shook his head. The major motioned for him to continue. Treadway turned and walked down the rear rank. Will stared straight ahead as the sergeant drew even with him. Treadway who'd spent most of every day with Captain Inness over the past two years stared blankly at him with no hint of recognition and passed on. He did the same as he moved past Lieutenant Dawes. At the end of the line, he marched back to Major Binford and saluted.

"Not in this lot, Major, sir," he said with a hint of disappointment in his voice. Binford scowled, but nodded.

"Very well, Sergeant. See that the search of the vessel is thorough. I want every berth, including the Captain's, inspected as well as all decks below. They may be hiding somewhere amidst the cargo."

"Aye, sir," Treadway growled.

As the sergeant stepped through the hatch and into the cramped passageway of the sterncastle to begin his search, he let out a sigh of relief and shook his head.

"Duty be damned," he muttered to himself.

***

The anchor was hauled up before the skiff full of soldiers reached the riverbank and the *Fair Wind* began to drift down the Mersey carried by the current and the ebbing tide. On Captain Keogh's orders, riggers scrambled up the ratlines to set the sails, which billowed like grey clouds in the twilight. On a ramshackle pier at the river's edge, Robert Inness watched the ship gather headway.

An hour before he'd felt his heart sink as a skiff bearing a squad of soldiers swept out to midstream and boarded the *Fair Wind*. He'd used all of his connections along the Liverpool waterfront and a substantial sum of money to get his brother and August Dawes on that ship and now he feared that all might be for naught. For an agonizing hour he'd watched until, finally, the soldiers had clambered back down into their boat, empty-handed.

As the skiff headed for shore, he'd watched the ship weigh anchor with a mixture of relief and melancholy. Politics and war had once driven a wedge between him and his brother, but Will's unexpected arrival in Liverpool had managed to close that breach. Now politics was forcing them apart again, with an ocean to divide them. As the *Fair*

Wind picked up speed in the offshore wind, Robert raised his good arm and waved at her stern.

"God go with you, little brother," he whispered and turned away.

No King, No Country

Part 2: The Crossing

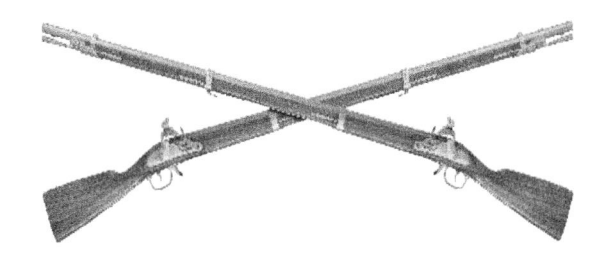

Setting Sail

The ship was barely underway when Mr. Berrycloth summoned the objects of the Provost Marshal's search to the quarterdeck where Abraham Keogh stood waiting. As the crew fell into their long-practiced routines, Captain Keogh looked over the new arrivals carefully, a stern expression on his face.

"Captain Inness and Lieutenant Dawes, is it?" he asked at last.

"Aye, sir," both men answered at once.

Keogh clasped his hands behind his back and thrust out his chin.

"I'm not a man to judge another on the word of a stranger, no matter his rank," he began. "This Provost Marshal says you're deserters and mutineers. What say you?"

"I'd say he's half right," Will replied. "I've been charged with both crimes and Mr. Dawes with desertion only. As to that offense, we must both plead guilty. As to the other, that charge is a damned lie. I've taken no part in any mutiny."

"So I'm to believe that such a serious charge has been made out of whole cloth?" Keogh shot back.

August answered before Will could.

"Captain, a month ago a company in our regiment stood to arms and refused orders to deploy to Ireland to put down the Catholics. There was strong sentiment in our own company to do the same, but Captain Inness kept the men in good order, sir. None joined the mutineers."

"So were you in favor of going to fight the Irish, Captain Inness?" Keogh asked mildly.

"No...no I was not, sir," Will answered truthfully. "Lieutenant Dawes and I joined Parliament's army because the King was trampling on the rights of Englishmen. We didn't join up to fight the Irish. Let them settle their own affairs."

"If that was your sentiment, why did you oppose the mutineers?"

"It was my duty...as I saw it," he answered at last.

"To obey your superiors," Captain Keogh added.

"Aye that, but more than that. I did not want to see my men die in a fight they could not win. I once sat across the table from General Cromwell at Putney and took the measure of the man. I'd no doubt Oliver Cromwell would crush any uprising within the ranks. I didn't want to have that blood on my hands."

"So you stood against the will of your men and your own sentiment and still you were charged with mutiny?"

August jumped back in.

"The big men, Cromwell and Fairfax, they fear they'll lose control of the men in the ranks and well they might. The men of our regiment looked up to Will. He'd stood with them in demanding their back pay and that marked him as threat. A senior officer warned him that a warrant had been issued for his arrest."

Keogh was still looking at Will as August spoke.

"So you chose to desert."

Will nodded.

"Aye, it was that or swing for a crime I didn't commit."

The captain turned back to August.

"And you Lieutenant Dawes? How do you fit in this drama?"

"Captain Inness is my friend, sir, and I was there the day he stopped the mutiny at Smithfield. He kept faith with the Army. Then the Army broke faith with him—and me as well!"

Captain Keogh rubbed his chin.

"This sergeant who was ordered to pick you out of the crew, he was from your regiment?"

"Sergeant Treadway was senior sergeant of my own company," Will replied.

"He did not give you up."

"No, he did not."

Keogh let his gaze move from the two men standing before him to the search party disembarking on the river bank. He nodded.

"Very well, gentlemen. Welcome aboard the *Fair Wind*. You'll take dinner with the crew tonight, but will join me and the other passengers for dinner on the morrow." He paused and looked them over still dressed in their common sailor's garb. "Dinner will be an hour past sunset and you will want to dress."

With that, Captain Keogh turned to his helmsman and gave him a small course correction to keep to the center of the river channel, a clear signal that their interview was at an end. Mister Berrycloth led the two men back down to the main deck.

"You two 'ave made a good impression on the Captain," he said as they crossed the deck toward the ladder that led to the tween deck. "I'm wondering if your words were clever or just lucky."

"How do you mean?" asked Will.

"You said the Irish should settle their own affairs," Berrycloth replied.

"So?"

"What do you know of the Captain?"

"Nothing," said Will.

Berrycloth shook his head and laughed.

No King, No Country

"Then it's lucky you are. Captain Keogh is Irish don't you know."

***

As Abraham Keogh watched the two men go below, he allowed himself a small smile. Contrary to what he'd told Major Binford, he was well acquainted with the latest political news from London and beyond. He took no sides in the civil war the English had embarked on, save to hope that by fighting amongst themselves, the English would leave Ireland to its own devices.

As for his two new passengers, he'd withhold judgment. He'd been impressed by the young captain's answers to his questions, but at the first sign that Inness and Dawes were stirring up trouble with his crew, he would happily slap them in irons for the remainder of the voyage.

He hoped that wouldn't be necessary, for having two more experienced fighting men aboard the *Fair Wind* might prove useful. The course he'd plotted for Virginia would take them through some dangerous waters where piracy was a growing menace. If it came to a fight, these new passengers would be welcome. And adding these two to the captain's table should make for lively dinner conversation. Two Roundheads breaking bread with four Royalists and one German.

Lively conversation indeed!

***

As the *Fair Wind* gathered speed, the passengers retreated to their berths while the crew went about their duties. A dozen topmen scampered aloft to trim the sails while two men hurried forward to take soundings as the ship moved down the narrow channel of the Mersey toward the Irish Sea. Eight men of the first watch took their supper rations from the cook who'd begun frying up fatback in his galley in the fo'c'sle. Will and August joined them and wolfed down their food, surprised at their own hunger.

Two miles beyond the headlands at the mouth of the River Mersey, the *Fair Wind* heeled to larboard as the Captain called down a compass heading of due west. With a freshening breeze filling her sails and the bottom falling away beneath her keel, the ship dove into the light swells, white spray flying out from her bow.

As the two men finished their meal, Will beckoned August over to the larboard rail and pointed to the shore.

"This might be our last look at Cheshire, Gus. Come morning we'll be off the coast of Wales."

Overhead a spray of stars began to speckle the evening sky. To the south the low coast of the Wirral could be seen sliding by. Not very far beyond the eastern horizon lay Danesford, their home.

"Do you think we'll ever see it again?" August asked.

Will shook his head.

"God only knows, Gus. Never thought I'd leave. Now I must doubt I'll ever come back."

"I'd like to come home someday…a rich man. I've heard there are fortunes to be made in the Americas."

Will laughed.

"Aye, if you're a Spanish grandee with a silver mine! But we English? We managed to plant our flag in the only part of the New World with no silver or gold."

"That's why our English lads turn to piracy," August said with a gleam in his eye. "If there's no riches in the north, we can do as Drake did and take it from the Dons in the south!"

Will shook his head.

"Piracy means killing, Gus, and I've killed enough men for one lifetime. I did it for a cause I believed in, but I'll not do it for riches. Whatever I make of myself, it will be through my own sweat, not by stealing another man's treasure—even if he be a Spaniard."

August threw an arm over Will's shoulder.

"Then here's to sweat," he said solemnly.

No King, No Country

Ahead the broad estuary of the River Dee now appeared. A smattering of small boats that fished these waters could be seen heading back to whatever small landings they called home in the lingering twilight. Behind them, the ship's bell rang eight times marking the beginning of the first watch. Will slapped August on the shoulder.

"Let's see what provisions Rob managed to scrape together for us."

***

They borrowed a pry bar from the ship's carpenter and Mr. Berrycloth told them where in the hold their crate was stored. The two men had to squeeze between hogsheads of water and stacks of other cargo to find the crate. Scratched in the wood on its top was the name "INNESS."

August went to work with the pry bar and the top of the crate came loose with a screech as nails were wrenched from the wood. Lifting off the top they looked in on a treasure trove. August reached in first and pulled out two long-handled axes. Nestled together in one corner of the box were a paring spade and a turning spade. Stacked up along one side of the crate were iron pots, skillets and a host of cooking and eating tools. Will saw something on the bottom of the box and fished out two plow blades. Beneath them were two scythes and a pair of skinning knives.

"Clothes!" August shouted as he drew forth a wrapped bundle of shirts and pants.

"Powder!" Will practically whooped as he popped the bung on a small barrel and used a finger to scoop out a pinch of grainy black gunpowder. Next to the barrel were lead ingots that could be melted down and formed into shot.

"Rob was busy while we hid away," August said as he surveyed the bounty.

"Aye, he got us things we'd have a hard time coming by in Virginia. Rob gave me money, but these things…" He stopped, overwhelmed by the parting gift his older brother had given them.

Slowly the two sorted through the remainder of the trove. As they neared the end of their inventory, August fished out a small wooden box. There were elaborate carvings on the lid and Will recognized it instantly. It had sat in a place of honor on the mantel above the fireplace in his father's small library at Danesford for all the years of his childhood. He took the box with trembling hands and flipped the latch. Holding his breath, he opened it.

Mounted in the box was an ancient dagger, its blade well-honed and its grip wrapped in worn leather. Imbedded in the hilt was a single red stone his father said was a ruby of great worth. This blade had been passed down from father to son in the Inness family for as far back as any could recall. Will's grandfather told him that the dagger had once been the property of the man who'd built the ruined fort at Danesford, but that was little more than a family legend. No one living knew for certain how it had come into the possession of the Inness clan.

"It's yer father's blade!" August said, with a touch of awe.

Will nodded silently, then gently lifted the weapon from its case. He'd seen it many times, but had never been allowed to hold it as a boy. Now the worn leather handle settled naturally into the palm of his hand, the blade perfectly balanced. By tradition, the dagger passed to the eldest Inness son on the death of the father. Will felt his throat tighten as he thought of Rob placing it in the crate for him to carry with him. He touched the blade's edge with his thumb and felt its razor sharpness. This might be a family heirloom, but it remained a lethal weapon. He took up the leather sheath folded within the wooden box and slipped the blade into it, then tucked it into his boot.

The dagger had been an heirloom long enough.

No King, No Country

Captain Keogh's Table

Will rose with the morning watch and, leaving August snoring contentedly on his mattress, followed the eight men of the watch up to the main deck. Overhead the stars still burned brightly, though the first faint signs of dawn could be seen over the stern of the *Fair Wind*. Off the larboard bow, the dark mass of Anglesey was just visible.

Relieved of duty, the men of the middle watch did not linger, but filed below to sleep. Will looked up at the sterncastle and saw the huge frame of John Berrycloth on the quarterdeck. The big man stood casually observing the new watch take up their duties, but gave no orders. None were apparently needed—the mark of a veteran crew.

As the new helmsman entered the steering room and took control of the long whipstaff, Berrycloth stirred himself to call down a small course correction. Satisfied with the new heading, the first mate leaned back on the railing and lit a pipe. Will climbed the ladder to the quarterdeck to join him.

"Mr. Berrycloth, my compliments to your crew," Will said. "The men look able."

Berrycloth nodded slowly.

"They are that, Mr. Inness. But most landsmen wouldn't know the difference. Have you been to sea?"

"Aye, winters as a boy. My family has a small shipping business, mostly between Liverpool and the Irish ports. When the harvest season was done in Cheshire, my father would dispatch my brother and I as ship's boys and later as crew during the winter months. Said it was the best way to learn the business."

"A cold and stormy time to be sailing in the Irish Sea," Berrycloth commented.

"It was," Will agreed. "I recall mornings when every line was sheathed in ice an inch thick. We'd use knotted ropes to break it up on the reefed sails and sheet 'em home. That first winter I thought I'd never be warm again."

Berrycloth blew out a long column of smoke that was snatched away by the wind, then fetched a nail from his pocket to stir the embers in the pipe bowl.

"Well then, you'll appreciate that we're not taking the northern route on this voyage. There are still bitter cold days off Greenland and Newfoundland in May and even June and the seas at those latitudes have icebergs as big as Westminster Hall, but for this crossing, we're taking the southern route, south to the Canary Islands to replenish our consumables then follow the currents across to Barbados. We have cargo for there and will take on sugar to be sold in Jamestown. From Barbados it's up the coast to Virginia, assuming we don't catch a blow and end up God only knows."

Will nodded.

"I've heard tales of terrible storms down there in the southern seas, great cyclones that no ship can sail through."

Berrycloth nodded.

"I've heard the same, though I've not lived through one myself. The Spanish call such a storm a huracán. They say there are waves thirty feet high and wind that'll strip canvas from the yards and suck men right up into the sky." Berrycloth shrugged as he puffed on his pipe. "Maybe they're just tales. Sailors love to scare folk with stories of monsters in the deep and such, but I do know of at least one sound ship that was lost during the storm season somewhere between the Canaries and Barbados."

No King, No Country

Will tried to picture thirty foot waves as he looked across the deck of the *Fair Wind*. Such a wave would swallow a ship this size.

"When is the storm season?" he asked.

Berrycloth took another drag on his pipe, the glow of the burning tobacco in the bowl illuminating his features in the dark. He blew out the smoke, then spoke.

"Soon," he said with a grin.

Will wanted to learn more, but Berrycloth turned to stare intently at the coastline to the south, then called down to the sailor manning the whipstaff.

"Come to west by north!"

Will heard a muffled "aye" come back from the steerage room and felt the slight heel of the ship as the rudder turned her bow to starboard. Not wanting to distract Berrycloth's navigation, he turned to head back to the main deck, but the first mate called him back.

"So tell me, Captain Inness, what did you do in the war?"

It was an unexpected question, but Will felt obliged to reply given Berrycloth's willingness to answer his own inquiries about the *Fair Wind's* course for the Americas.

"Dragoons at the start, then cavalry for the past year. Fought at Edgehill, Marston Moor, Naseby and a lot of places whose names I can't remember."

"Dragoons, they ride to the battle and fight on foot?"

"Aye, mostly."

Berrycloth nodded.

"Good. I saw you brought weapons aboard."

"Aye, Mr. Dawes and I have our carbines and pistols."

"Ever handle cannon?"

"Not as a gunner, but dragoons oft times were placed to guard our artillery. I could do the drill in my sleep."

That produced a smile on Berrycloth's face.

"You come in as a captain?"

Will shook his head.

"Hardly. They made August and I sergeants because we owned our own horses."

Berrycloth took another long drag on his pipe.

"Good then. As ye earned yer rank and didn't have it handed to ye, you might know what yer about in a fight."

"You expect a fight, Mr. Berrycloth?"

"No, but I'd be a fool to not be ready for one. We'll be sailing through some dangerous seas once we reach the Indies. If it comes to it, you and your friend may be called upon."

"If the ship is in danger, Mr. Berrycloth, you'll not need to call us."

Berrycloth nodded at that then turned away looking back toward the shore that was emerging from the darkness with the approach of dawn. Sensing their conversation was done, Will made his way back down to the main deck and found a spot where he would not be in the way of the morning watch going about their duties. He sat for a long time, watching the slow brightening of the sky astern.

There'd been precious little time in the past week for quiet contemplation. He'd gone from officer to fugitive and from Englishman to a man without a country in what seemed the blink of an eye. He wondered about the other ten men on Jack Percival's list. Had they been taken? Had they been led to the gallows? What would have been his fate if he'd not run? The questions plagued him, but as the *Fair Wind* left England in its wake, he felt a strange new sense of freedom. He was alive and at liberty and in the new world of America, anything might be possible for a free man.

Behind him he heard the ship's bell ring seven times. At eight bells the forenoon watch would relieve the men of the morning watch. In the fo'c'sle he could hear the cook preparing breakfast for both watches. He got up and made his way down to the tween deck where he found that August had just risen.

No King, No Country

"Not the comfiest bed in the world," he said, stretching and yawning, "but a damned sight better than hard cold ground. Where have you been?"

"Up with the first mate for a bit, then watching the sunrise."

"What did Mr. Berrycloth have to say?"

"A good deal, starting with the course they've set for Virginia. We're south to the Canary Islands then west across the southern ocean."

He took a moment to pass on to August the rest of what he'd learned from Berrycloth about their route to the Americas and the first mate's interest in their fighting abilities.

"He said he may need our help should the *Fair Wind* be threatened."

"Pirates?" August asked, fully awake now.

"Aye, or the Spanish. They have no love for English ships in those southern waters."

August was about to reply when the ship's bell sounded eight times and the smell of boiling oats reached his nose. He pulled on his boots.

"Let's eat," he said and joined the men of the forenoon watch as they shuffled sleepily up to breakfast.

***

Will lingered after he'd had his breakfast to watch the Welsh coast slide by to the south. Ahead, he recognized the rocky outline of The Skerries approaching off the larboard bow. Like the Tuskar Rock that lay near the east coast of Ireland, the shoals around these low islands had sent many a ship to the bottom.

On the quarterdeck, Keogh eyed the approaching hazard warily, but satisfied he was well clear, kept his course steady. Once The Skerries were far astern, he gave the order to change the *Fair Wind's* heading to south by west. With but few minor corrections, the ship would stay on that heading for a fortnight.

Through the long afternoon the ship plowed through the Irish Sea. Far to the east, a dark line on the horizon marked the great mountains of Wales. During the first dog watch, Will and August retreated to their humble lodging on the tween deck and sorted through the bundle of clothes Robert had sent for them, picking out the most suitable for dinner with the Captain. The evening breeze on the open sea was chill and finding no cloaks amongst their new clothes, they donned their buff coats. brushing the dirt of the road off as best they could.

Will sniffed at his coat and wrinkled his nose.

"It stinks."

August sniffed at his own coat and shrugged.

"It's smelled worse, I reckon, but the Cavaliers amongst the passengers will no doubt disapprove of the fragrance."

"I'm sure it's what they expect from two Roundhead cavalrymen, so why disappoint?" Will said with a grin.

***

The cook and the captain's steward had taken down the movable walls of the chart room to magically convert one end of the Captain's quarters into a serviceable though cramped dining room. The passengers who'd boarded in Portsmouth had already staked out their places when Will and August ducked through the door from the passageway and entered. There was an empty chair at the head of the table set aside for the Captain and the steward waved the two newcomers toward two empty stools at the far end.

As they gingerly picked their way past the other diners to take their places, Captain Keogh emerged through the narrow door to his sleeping berth and took his spot. He looked up as Will and August settled onto their stools.

"Perhaps introductions would be appropriate as we have two new passengers aboard," he said. "Our new arrivals are Captain William Inness and Lieutenant August Dawes, originally from Cheshire and late of the Parliamentarian cavalry. They are bound for the New World to seek their fortune."

The Captain then turned toward a handsome and impeccably-dressed young woman on his right.

"May I present Lady Anne Bingham, of Northumberland. Lady Anne is bound for Jamestown where she is to be wed to Sir Thomas Lunsford, Captain General of the Virginia Militia."

Will and August sprang hastily to their feet, as was only proper upon being introduced to a lady, but neither took account of the low ceiling and both banged their heads on the oak beams there. This produced a cackle of laughter from the young woman sitting between Lady Anne and the Captain.

"Callie!" Lady Anne scolded as the girl's hand flew to her mouth in embarrassment, her face flushing red.

Undaunted by the interruption, Captain Keogh continued, nodding toward the girl trying mightily to quell her laughter.

"The lady who finds you gentlemen so amusing is Miss Caledonia MacDonell, Lady Anne's companion."

Will nodded toward the girl who'd finally composed herself. The MacDonell girl was dressed very plainly, but in her way, was more striking than her mistress. She was half a head taller than Lady Anne with long auburn hair framing a face whose pale skin was made more interesting by a sprinkle of freckles across the bridge of her nose. The girl kept a straight face by biting her lip as she met Will's eyes, giving him a quick nod before casting her eyes back down.

"MacDonell might be Irish or Scottish, but Caledonia suggests Scotland," he said. "Do you hail from there, Miss MacDonell?"

"Born there, sir," she replied, lifting her head and fixing him with dark green eyes. "Came to Northumbria three years ago."

As the lady offered no further details, Captain Keogh turned to introduce the man seated on his far right. Will and

August sank back on their stools, resisting the urge to check their scalps for lumps or bleeding.

"This gentleman," Keogh said, "is Sir James Bingham, Lady Anne's distinguished brother who has purchased land for a tobacco plantation along the James River."

Bingham, a tall man with a carefully groomed black beard and a flowing wig of curled brown hair, looked at the two men at the end of the table with bored indifference, but returned their small nods of greeting. Keogh then turned to his left.

"This young gentlemen is Lieutenant Henry Grey from Yorkshire, formerly of His Majesty's cavalry—Langdale's regiment of horse I believe. I'm sure you will have much to talk about in our time together."

Lieutenant Grey looked barely old enough to hold the rank of an officer. He had pale blue eyes set in a roundish face that sported a sparse patch of hair at the chin, a poor attempt at a beard. Unlike Sir James, Lieutenant Grey favored the men at the foot of the table with a broad grin.

"Roundhead cavalry!" he exclaimed excitedly. "I'd guessed as much from your dress. I was late to the war—only joined Langdale's horse in forty-eight. By that time all the big battles were done. I must wonder what they were like--Edgehill, Marston Moor, Naseby. I'd be most obliged to hear your accounts of those great struggles, gentlemen."

Will returned the young Cavalier's smile.

"If you wish, Lieutenant, though for my part, I've no desire to dwell on the war."

Grey's smile faltered a bit, but he nodded.

"I understand, Captain. The memories must still be fresh."

"You saw no action, Lieutenant?" August asked.

"Well, yes, some. When the King raised his standard after his escape, Baron Langdale raised a new regiment of Royalist horse in Yorkshire. I was finally old enough to join up. We took Berwick with little bloodshed and would have secured the north for the King if your General Cromwell hadn't come up through Cheshire. He caught us at Preston Moor in Lancashire. Were you and Captain Inness with him that day at Preston?"

August shook his head.

"Our company was left behind in Oxfordshire to keep watch on what remained of the Royalist force there. We missed the final battle of the war—and thankful for it."

Grey gave a rueful smile.

"Aye, Preston Moor was the end of things for Langdale, our King and for my career as an officer of cavalry. Over before properly begun, I'd call it."

"You should count yourself lucky, Lieutenant," Will said. "Many a man's career ended less happily than yours at those battles you speak of. They lie beneath the ground."

Grey nodded gravely.

"Well, perhaps one day, when we are old soldiers and the past takes on a rosy glow—as I'm told it does—we'll share a pint and tell lies about our exploits back in the mother country. But for now, I hope that recent adversaries might become, if not friends, then peaceful acquaintances!"

"I'll drink to that," Will said and raised his wine glass in a salute to the Cavalier officer.

Lieutenant Grey raised his own glass to return the salute.

"To peaceful acquaintances!"

None of the other passengers joined in the toast. Behind Grey, both Binghams frowned and Lady Anne appeared ready to say something more, but Captain Keogh was not to be diverted as he turned to introduce the last passenger.

"Gentlemen, the guest to your right is Herr Mathys Beck, who hails from Freiburg in the Black Forest of Germany. Herr Beck is a metalworker and gunsmith by trade. I've personally examined a pistol of his manufacture and can vouch for the quality of his workmanship."

Mathys Beck was a man built like a tree stump, with the arms and shoulders of a blacksmith and a bullet-like head covered in close-cropped grey hair. He had a livid raised scar that encircled his thick neck before disappearing down the front of his shirt. The gunsmith's appearance was enough to frighten small children and give pause to fully-grown men who might have reason to quarrel with him. Upon introduction, the German simply turned to the two men next to him and gave a quick bob of his head.

"My English...not so good," he said and turned his gaze back to his plate.

"It's much better than my German, Herr Beck," said Will.

Beck shrugged.

"When Hapsburgs take Frieberg, they bring English soldiers with them. Their guns break, they come to me. I learn a little of their speech, mostly swear words, like...."

He stopped in mid-sentence, his cheeks reddening. He turned to the two ladies at the table, shame-faced. "My apologies to you," he said gravely.

Will stepped in to ease the awkward silence that fell over the table.

"Perhaps I could prevail on you to look at my carbine, Herr Beck. I fear the frizzen spring has seen better days."

Beck looked at him, but not with gratitude. He scowled, as though Will's request was somehow an insult.

"Carbine," he muttered the word with a sad shake of his head. "This is your weapon?"

Will nodded, not knowing what had provoked the German's ire.

"You are lucky to be alive," Beck declared with utter conviction. "Forget frizzen spring, Captain. Just use carbine as a club. It's all it's good for!"

The gunsmith was about to speak further when the steward arrived carrying a large tray that he set down with a flourish before the Captain. Behind him, the cook came with a large cauldron, wisps of steam rising from within. Captain Keogh saw his opportunity to cut off the indignant German and took it.

No King, No Country

"Ox tongue soup, cured ham, roast carp, boiled cabbage and fresh oysters," he announced proudly with a nod to his steward, who beamed.

"Well done, Mr. Goodacre," he continued, "especially the oysters!"

He turned back to the guests around the table. "I urge you all to savor this feast, ladies and gentlemen, for hereafter we'll dine on beef, salt pork and smoked fish for the most part."

The aroma of the soup and the sight of the heaped up tray of food caused Will to forget about the truculent German sitting next to him. He reddened a little as his stomach growled audibly. The sound must've carried as he noticed Miss MacDonell look his way and bite her lip once more. But he and August had not eaten since before dawn and they soon turned all their attention to the banquet on the Captain's table. Will had just stabbed an oyster with his fork when Lady Anne spoke up.

"Should we still address you as Captain, Mr. Inness, considering you've clearly left your army and not it seems on honorable terms?"

Will set his fork down as a nervous silence fell over the diners and all turned to see how he would answer the young woman's insult. He smiled at Lady Anne.

"Mister will do nicely," he said, "as I no longer hold a commission as an officer in the Parliamentarian Army. As for my honor and the circumstances of my departure from the service, you have no basis to judge, miss."

Will picked up his fork and stabbed another oyster, popping it into his mouth and chewing happily. For her part, Lady Anne appeared to find this reply unsatisfying.

"Having been rousted out of our quarters to be gawked at and threatened by one of your damned Roundhead officers yesterday gives me more than enough grounds to judge, *Mister* Inness. He named you a deserter and a mutineer!"

"And he named you traitors, miss." Will answered mildly.

Before Lady Anne could respond, Lieutenant Grey broke in.

"Lady Anne, it seems to me that most who take this long voyage have their reasons for leaving the mother country for the New World. I know I have mine! Shall we all lay bare our situations for judgement here at the Captain's table? Or shall we leave behind our sins in England and make a new start in America?"

Lady Anne's face flushed, but her brother laid a hand on the girl's arm to silence her.

"Forgive my sister, gentlemen. She's not herself. Travel by sea does not agree with her. She meant no offense."

Will looked at Lady Anne and the look he got back gave the lie to her brother's assurance. The girl had every intention of giving offense. But he had no interest in an argument with the opinionated Miss Bingham—not when there was still a plate of good food before him.

"No offense taken, sir," he said to James Bingham, then turned to Lady Anne.

"I'm sorry my troubles followed me aboard and troubled you, my lady."

For a moment, there was a slight softening of the girl's expression, but that was quickly erased. She eyed him coldly.

"You'd best hope they don't follow you to Virginia, sir. They do not tolerate such there."

"Virginia is a vast land, my lady, and I intend to go where my troubles will not follow. If they do, they will find me ready to meet them."

Captain Keogh cleared his throat loudly.

"Ladies and gentlemen. You will be in close quarters for the next month or so, with plenty of time to further your acquaintance. But at the moment, our dinner grows cold, so pass the oysters," he said politely.

No King, No Country

***

Taking their lead from the Captain, the passengers passed the rest of the meal more in silence than conversation. In due course, the oysters were reduced to empty shells, the ham to a lonely soup bone and the carp to a picked-clean skeleton. Finishing off the final oyster with a satisfying belch, Captain Keogh, excused himself to return to the quarterdeck and the passengers housed in the sterncastle retired to their berths.

Will and August made their way back out to the main deck to find it fully dark. Overhead the grey sails of the *Fair Wind* were stretched taut in a following wind. Above the masthead, the sprinkling of stars Will had seen at twilight now presented a grand display, like a fortune in glittering jewels spilled across black velvet. For six years he'd only seen the stars through the smoky haze of hundreds of campfires as the army campaigned from one end of England to the other. He'd forgotten what the night sky looked like from the deck of a ship at sea.

He let his gaze drop closer to the horizon and over the starboard rail found a familiar cluster of stars. From long practice his eyes followed a straight line from the two leading stars of the Plough to find the pole star. From its position he could tell the ship continued on its southwesterly course that would take them down the Irish Sea and out into the open ocean.

He turned to look off to the east and could see a dark line where the west coast of Anglesey met the sea. To his surprise he saw a small light flare on that dark shore. To be seen so far out to sea, the flame had to be considerable. He wondered if it was some spring celebration that called for a bonfire. More likely it was a homestead being burnt in one of the eternal feuds the Welsh seemed to delight in. Nowhere it seemed did peace hold sway for long. Certainly not in England or Ireland or Wales whose histories had always

been written in fire and blood. Would America be more peaceable? Would the new world be different than the old?
  He doubted it.

No King, No Country

The Bay of Biscay

For a day and a half, they sailed southwest through the Irish Sea. Three days out from Liverpool, the passengers who came on deck got a final glimpse of England as the rocky tip of Cornwall slid by to larboard. On a glorious clear day and under full sail the *Fair Wind* left the shallow Irish Sea behind and sailed into the Bay of Biscay.

Here the bottom fell away sharply and the swells doubled in size. The increased motion of the ship was hardly noticed by the crew, but for some aboard who'd never been to sea, the change was distressing. Hardly an hour had passed since the last view of Cornwall when Caledonia MacDonell appeared on deck carrying a bucket at arm's length. She checked the wind and went to the starboard rail to empty the bucket's foul contents over the side. Will watched the girl gamely handle her chore and smiled.

"Eat the ship's crackers, Miss MacDonell. They'll settle your stomach," he said.

The girl looked at him and hesitated.

"I'm not to speak to you, Captain Inness," she said at last and turned away.

"Seems you just did, Miss MacDonell."

The girl turned back around.

"Well, it's impolite to not answer when spoken to," she said, frowning, "but henceforth, we are not to converse."

"And why is that?"

The girl pressed her lips together, determined not to answer, but the habits of courtesy finally overcame her resolve.

"My mistress believes you to be a traitor to your King and to your rebel Parliament as well. She has forbidden me to speak with you."

Will laughed.

"A double traitor! I suppose if I'm caught they'll chop off my head twice."

Will saw a brief flash of amusement in Callie MacDonell's eyes at that, but the girl quickly stifled it. To avoid any further violations of her orders, she turned once more and made for the sterncastle. As she stepped through the door she looked over her shoulder.

"It's not *my* stomach that's the issue, Captain Inness, but I'll fetch some crackers for my mistress."

With that, she disappeared inside. Will stood staring at the sterncastle door for a moment, oddly pleased that she had called him Captain and not Mister as her mistress had insisted on doing.

"A comely lass."

Will swung around to see August grinning at him. He felt his face redden a little.

"I was just passing the time," he said.

"I could see that. And a pleasant time it appeared to be!"

Will sighed. August Dawes knew him all too well.

"Very well. I confess. She's a lovely girl. It's been a long time, Gus."

August put a hand on his friend's shoulder. When they were boys, there was hardly a girl within ten miles of Danesford that Will Inness had not tried to woo, if he could get there before his brother Robert. But there'd been precious little opportunity for courtship these past six years. The few young ladies they'd encountered on campaign were often frightened refugees from one side or the other or camp followers and those had not appealed to either man. So, yes, it had been a very long time.

"Sadly it appeared Miss MacDonell was impervious to your charms," August said

Will smiled at the younger man.

"That's where you're wrong, my friend. It's clear she's taken with me."

"Oh, I hadn't noticed that. Was that the part where she said you two 'weren't to converse'?"

"Just a delaying tactic, Gus, a fighting retreat. One day I'll teach you to know the signs."

August laughed at that.

"Little good it'll do me, Inness. I'd as soon face a regiment of Cavaliers as talk to a girl."

Will threw an arm around August's shoulder. His friend's shyness with females was an old story and an affliction that six years of war had provided little opportunity to cure.

"Never fear, Gus. When we land in Virginia, those colonial girls will melt at the sight of you."

August hooted at that.

"And what of you and the Scottish lass?" he asked. "I hear a ship's captain can marry ye."

Will gave his friend a shove and laughed.

"No danger of that! If I take a wife it'll not be until we've set down roots in America."

August arched an eyebrow.

"Then perhaps you'd best steer clear of Miss Caledonia MacDonell," he said.

***

For five days the *Fair Wind* rode the swells of Biscay Bay with blue sky overhead and a favorable wind off her starboard quarter. For Will the smell of the sea, the creak of the rigging and the ship's bells that marked the watches brought back memories of his years sailing the Irish Sea. For a boy who'd grown up on a modest farmstead in Cheshire, even one with an ancient fort on the land, the chance to go to sea had seemed a grand adventure and three days of puking over the rail on his first crossing of the Irish Sea had done little to dampen his enthusiasm for shipboard life.

The work itself was often drudgery of the first order. Carrying out the captain's chamber pot, holystoning the deck on your hands and knees until both bled and mucking out shit from the hold when horses or cattle were transported all fell within the duties of the ship's boy. On his first voyage the crew had eyed him warily, waiting to see if the son of a Chester shipper would find the work of a ship's boy beneath him, but Will had taken on each task with a cheerful energy and no complaints. Soon he was all but adopted by the veteran sailors. From them he'd learned much about ships, the sea and the wider world.

But the death of his father had put an end to his life at sea. Robert had taken charge of the Inness shipping business and Will had worked the family land in the Weaver valley for two years until he'd answered the call of Parliament. Now, as the *Fair Wind* plunged through the swells, the old rhythms of shipboard life came back.

With little else to occupy his time, he found himself lending a hand here and there. He was not the size of John Berrycloth, but he was bigger than most of the crewmen and more than pulled his weight. Men gave him skeptical looks, unsure why a paying passenger was exerting himself, but none challenged him. As he hauled away on the lines, he joined in the shanties the men sang as they worked, some he knew and others he learned. The man who led the singing was a gnarled Yorkshireman named William Barley, a seaman as brown and weathered as old leather but with a high tenor voice as clear as a chime.

Bill Barley would sing out a line and the crew would take up the next, all the while bending their backs to haul on the heavy lines.

No King, No Country

When I was a little lad and so me mother told me,
Way haul away, we'll haul away Joe.
If I didn't kiss the girls me lips would grow all moldy.
Way haul away, we'll haul away Joe.

Way haul away, we're bound for better weather.
Away haul away, we'll haul away Joe.
Way haul away, we'll haul away together.
Away haul away, we'll haul away Joe.

St. Patty was a gentleman. He came from decent people.
Way haul away, we'll haul away Joe.
He built a church in Dublin town and on it put a steeple.
Way haul away, we'll haul away Joe.

August, bored with watching the show, soon joined in. From boyhood days aboard ship, Will had a good understanding of the rigging of a sailing vessel and readily fell to when a line needed to be snubbed down or the capstan turned. For August it was all new, but he followed Will's lead as best he could and was soon hauling away at the sheets and braces with the rest. As the days passed and the men of the *Fair Wind* saw that this wasn't a passing fancy for these two passengers, they slowly came around.

The *Fair Wind* crew was a veteran lot, skilled in their trade and rough as a holystone. Hardly a man among them went by his Christian name. All had been rechristened by their crewmates. There was Knocker Chance and Coops Arnley, Nobby Postlethwaite and Daisy Meadows to name a few.

Will advised August that it was best not to inquire about a sailor's nickname as some were touchy on the subject. The wiry little Cheshireman heeded that advice, worked hard and spoke little. What he lacked in experience he made up for in cheerful enthusiasm and impressive endurance. By the third day he was leading shanties of his own invention, in a voice that verged on baritone. The crew, used by now to these volunteers, gamely learned the new chants and sang along lustily.

From their station on the quarterdeck, Captain Keogh and John Berrycloth watched the two sweating at the thousand and one chores that occupy a sailor.

"What do ye make of those two?" Keogh asked Berrycloth.

"Haven't decided yet," Berrycloth replied.

***

It was Captain Keogh's custom to take dinner with his passengers on the first night at sea and on each Sunday thereafter. In between times the steward served passengers in their berths. Their food was of a higher quality than that reserved for the crew, but Will and August preferred to take their rations with the men. What the crew's meals lacked in quality and variety the cook made up for in quantity. Manning a square-rigged ship was hard work and Keogh had ensured that his men had enough food to sustain them.

A pound and a half of beef or salt pork, a pint of peas, a pound of ship's biscuit and a gallon of beer was a usual ration for a day's work aboard the *Fair Wind* with salted or dried fish thrown in for variety. Later in the voyage the butter would grow rancid and the biscuits weevily, but none of it inedible for a sailor.

While Will and August slept and ate with the crew, the other passengers took pains to stay out of the way. Only once in the crossing of the bay did Lady Anne make an appearance on deck. On that occasion, the sight of the rolling swells drained what little color was left in her face and she hurried back to her berth in the sterncastle, a hand clutched over her mouth.

The lady's brother, Sir James, kept to a regular schedule, coming up on deck to smoke a pipe each day at midmorning and midafternoon. These were solitary outings as he engaged with no one and retreated to the sterncastle once he'd satisfied his tobacco craving.

No King, No Country

Callie MacDonell appeared fairly regularly to empty the contents of her mistress's rebellious stomach over the side, but made a point of avoiding Will on those occasions. One day, she'd spent half the morning on deck, bent over a wooden tub washing out what seemed like half of Lady Anne's traveling clothes. Once thoroughly scrubbed she'd laid the clothes out to dry.

Will had used the opportunity to stroll about inspecting the lady's garments hoping to get a rise out of the girl, but she'd acted as though he wasn't there. Later that day, as he lounged on a huge coil of rope and leaned against the bulkhead of the sterncastle he could hear through the wall Lady Anne giving Callie a tongue-lashing for displaying her undergarments so publicly. The servant girl did not shrink from the scolding, but fired back that there was no discreet place to do the drying and that the sailors of the *Fair Wind* would not likely be shocked at the sight of lady's drawers. That put a smile on Will's face for the rest of the afternoon.

Mathys Beck, the oldest of the passengers, also came on deck twice a day, but not to smoke. The German would appear before breakfast and after the evening meal to tramp vigorously up and down the main deck, pumping his arms and breathing deeply of the sea air. This he would do for a half hour as marked by the ship's bell, taking pains to avoid interfering with the crew's duties.

"He'll not go soft on this voyage," August observed one morning as he watched Beck marching briskly up and down.

Will nodded. Before the gunsmith began this morning routine, Will had only seen him at their first dinner at the Captain's table and hadn't judged how powerfully built the man was. He might be balding and grey of hair, but his years working metal showed in his heavily-muscled arms and shoulders.

"Aye, nothing soft about Herr Beck," he said.

The most frequent visitor among the passengers was Lieutenant Grey who came on deck for long stretches to linger at the railing watching the sea foam around the ship's hull. After a day or so, he'd hit upon a new amusement to pass the time— tossing crusts of bread from the deck to see gulls swoop and fight over the morsels. On their fourth day out from Liverpool he interrupted his game to hail Will who was between chores on the main deck.

"Captain Inness!" he called, "Come join me."

Will made his way across the deck to where the Lieutenant stood at the rail.

"Why don't we dispense with ranks, Lieutenant, now we've both left our former employ. Call me Will."

"Splendid, Will! Then you must call me Harry. All my friends do."

"Harry it is, then."

"I see you've become a member of the crew," Grey said, idly tossing his last piece of bread into the air and watching two gulls almost collide trying to capture the prize. The crust fell into the blue green water and was swept away. "I'm sure the Binghams would disapprove of such mingling with the lower classes, but I applaud your industry."

Will smiled at that.

"You're welcome to join us, Harry. It helps the time pass."

Grey laughed.

"Oh, I'll stick to my game with the gulls, Will. I fear I'd get tangled up in all these lines like a fly in a spider's web. More trouble than I'd be worth, I expect."

"You could learn."

Grey shrugged.

"I'm curious, Will. What was your station before joining up with the Roundheads. Were you a sailor?"

"From time to time. My family was in the shipping business. I worked our land in the planting and harvesting seasons and took ship in the winters."

"So you're not of the common stock then. I suspected you had good breeding."

No King, No Country

Will gripped the rail and turned to look at Grey.

"Breeding is for cattle, not men, Harry. I learned long ago that what separates a commoner from a gentlemen is not blood. It's money."

For a moment Grey bristled, but then he shook his head and gave Will a rueful smile.

"I dare say you may have something there. A gentlemen's blood looks much the same as a foot soldier's when they're both lying dead on the battlefield."

"Perhaps in the Virginia colony, distinctions of class will be less than in England," Will said. "In a wilderness, a man's worth should be judged by what he can do, not the condition of his birth."

Lieutenant Grey wrinkled his brow.

"I wouldn't count on that, Will."

***

On the fifth day out of Liverpool, the lookout Keogh sent up to the topsail yard sighted the coast of Spain. It was a rocky headland at the very shoulder of the Iberian peninsula and at its tip was the ruins of a great tower.

"The Tower of Hercules," Mr. Berrycloth announced. "Built by the Romans they say."

"Looks long neglected," Will said.

"Aye, the Dons all say they'll rebuild it one day, and with all the silver they've found in Mexico they just might afford the repairs, but I doubt it."

"Why is that?"

"Privateers."

"Like Sir Francis Drake?"

"Of a sort. Sir Francis had letters of marque from Queen Elizabeth, but King Charles didn't want trouble from Spain and curtailed the practice. Some say it was because of his Spanish wife. Others claimed he was a secret Catholic, but whatever the reason he would not sanction English privateers."

"So who are these privateers if not English?"

"Oh, they're English right enough! Having no slip of paper from a King would hardly stop bold English seafarers from going after the Spanish treasure ships. They, and a few Dutch corsairs operate out of Tortuga and the Bahamas."

"And the Spanish tolerate this?"

"Not in the least. They've cleaned out Tortuga at least twice that I know of, but then they leave and the privateers return. It's why the Spaniards spend half their loot on ships and men to protect the other half."

"Leaving nothing to repair their tower."

Berrycloth nodded.

"And it's why they're touchy about English vessels in their waters."

"That's the trouble you spoke of my first day aboard?"

"Aye, an English pirate will take our ship if we're unlucky enough to cross paths, but might not kill us out of hand."

"And the Spanish?"

"Oh, the Don's will blow us to splinters and let the sharks take the rest."

***

Colonel Edward Whalley and Major Simon Binford stood at attention in the tent that served as Oliver Cromwell's field headquarters, their uniforms covered in dust from the road. They'd ridden hard from Liverpool to London, then on to Romford where Cromwell had gathered three regiments of the Army for drill. The General was not pleased with their report.

"You tracked them to Liverpool, but failed to apprehend them?"

"Aye, sir," Binford replied. "They were seen in Cheshire and locals reported Inness had a brother in the shipping business there. We have some reason to believe he and Dawes may have taken ship."

"The brother told you this?"

Binford frowned.

No King, No Country

"We could not locate the brother, sir."

"You could not locate a shipper in Liverpool?" Cromwell asked, incredulous. "When I was there last, every one of the blackguards had a sign over their door!"

"Aye, sir," Whalley put in, "and we found Robert Inness' shop straight away. We questioned his partner."

"We questioned them all," Binford added.

"Except for this Robert Inness," Cromwell said.

"Aye, except for him," said Binford. "In the end, none of the information we gained from the shippers proved useful. We ran patrols throughout the town. We located the brother's apartments and searched them from top to bottom and found nothing of note. We boarded and searched the one ship in the harbor. It was bound for the Virginia colony."

"But no brother and no deserters."

"No sir."

Cromwell came around the small field table in the middle of the tent and glared at the two officers.

"Do we not have a garrison at Liverpool?" he demanded.

"Yes, sir," Binford replied.

"Do we not, therefore, control the town?"

Binford hesitated and Whalley, for the second time, spoke up.

"We control the town, General, but not, apparently, the shippers of Liverpool."

Cromwell shook his head.

"Out," he ordered, and the two officers wasted no time in complying.

Cromwell returned to his desk and began to sort through the stack of papers there. He had decided to commute the sentences of four of the men on the list with wives and children—as a show of mercy. The other six would hang as a show of resolve that mutiny would not be tolerated. The execution and commutation orders were at the top of the stack and he signed them one by one. When he'd set down his quill, he got up and walked to the entrance of his field tent and pulled back the flap. The day's drill done, his men were settling into camp for the evening. As he watched campfires being kindled he returned to the nettlesome issue of Captain William Inness.

The failure to capture Inness troubled him. The Captain was well known and liked in the army and news of his escape had spread quickly. Just that morning word reached him that soldiers were offering toasts to Inness' escape in taverns all over London. That wouldn't do!

He would dispatch agents to Liverpool to continue the search for the illusive Captain Inness, though one thing in Binford's report rang true. If Inness and his friend had gone to Liverpool they'd most likely have been looking for a ship to get them out of England. It would make sense for these men to seek refuge in Ireland or one of the English colonies in America. Parliament's control over those possessions was weak at present and they might find sanctuary, but he would be remedying that in due course.

He and Fairfax had already discussed sending a fleet to America in the spring to root out any Royalist strongholds there. He'd be sure that arrest warrants for Inness and Dawes would go with them along with clear orders to track down and capture the fugitives.

If the two had fled beyond England's reach, to the continent or to one of the rival Dutch or French colonies in America, so be it. Inness was a man with dangerous ideas. Votes for landless men?

Let him infect the Dutch or French with such madness!

No King, No Country

Caledonia MacDonell

The *Fair Wind* followed the coast of Spain and then Portugal southward under fair skies and favorable winds until they neared Cabo de Roca, the rocky headland north of the Tagus River estuary. Here storm clouds began to build out to sea and the swells grew. Captain Keogh altered course toward the storm, choosing to weather the approaching squall as far from a lee shore as possible.

As the dark clouds gathered along the western horizon like a line of black-clad infantry, Will scrambled up the rigging with the forenoon watch to reef the main topsail. High above the pitching deck, he looked back toward shore and saw white spray exploding skyward against the high cliffs and jagged rocks there. Overhead, the sun still shone down from a clear blue sky, but in the distance the tops of the advancing thunderheads pulsed with heat lightning.

With the sails reefed, he followed the watch back down to the main deck and took up station on the starboard railing to watch the storm come in. As the wind kicked up, spindrift began to fly from the tops of the approaching whitecaps. Will leaned into the wind and a line from Shakespeare came to him.

"The storm is up and all is on the hazard," he said quietly. His words were soft but carried on the wind. Behind him a softer voice replied.

"Now let the wind blow, waves swell, and ships sink!"

He turned in time to see Callie MacDonell join him at the rail. The girl gripped the smooth wood and looked off to the west, the wind whipping her long red hair into tangles behind her.

Lovely, he thought.

"I thought you were forbidden to talk to me," he said.

"I am," she agreed, but did not move away.

"You know Shakespeare's plays, Miss MacDonell?"

"Some," she said. "I like Macbeth."

"Of course, the Scottish play."

She laughed.

"When shall we three meet again, in thunder, lightning, or in rain?" she said quoting from the first act.

"When the hurly burly's done, when the battle's lost and won." he answered with a grin.

She turned to look at him.

"I'd not expect a soldier to be a student of Will Shakespeare, Captain Inness."

Will shook his head.

"I'm hardly that, Miss MacDonell. My father was a lover of books. His library had near thirty volumes—Bacon, Chaucer and Milton among them. And two works by Shakespeare, Julius Caesar being one and Macbeth the other. My brother and I read them all, more than once. But what of you? It seems as likely a soldier would quote Shakespeare as a lady's companion."

"It would seem that our expectations are often unreliable, Captain. You had a life before you became a soldier and I was not always a servant. My father was an educated man, a cousin to Aeneas MacDonell, our clan chief."

"Tell me then. How did you come to be here, in service to the Binghams?"

Callie wrinkled her brow as though considering whether to answer.

"You've heard of Montrose?" she asked finally.

No King, No Country

"Who hasn't," Will said. James Graham, the Marquis of Montrose was a feared name among Parliamentarian forces. As head of Clan Graham, he'd raised an army of Highlanders to support the Royalist cause in Scotland. For two years the daring Marquis swept to victory after victory over the Scots Covenanters who'd allied themselves with the English Parliament. By the end of 1644, he'd secured Scotland for the Crown as far south as Glasgow.

"He was the terror of the north for years, until General Leslie beat him at Philiphaugh. Last I heard, he was still at large."

"You're well informed, Captain. Montrose raised the clans, including my own Clan MacDonell. My father and brother marched out of Glengarry to join him. They never returned. I'm told they fell at Philiphaugh. After that battle the surviving men of Clan MacDonell scattered into the mountains and the Covenanters fell upon Glengarry like wolves. Houses were burnt and crops despoiled. Had I not fled, I'd no doubt have been raped and killed. Many were."

She paused as a clap of thunder rumbled out of the advancing squall line.

"It was a bitter time for the clans that rose for the King and many went hungry in the Highlands that winter. Having no family left, I made my way south. My father had an old comrade in Northumbria. He'd served with Sir Charles Bingham in the Low Countries and I sought him out. Sir Charles was a kind man and welcomed me into his home. He treated me like kin. But his children never did. When he passed, Sir James offered me a choice—serve Lady Anne or be turned out and be left to my own devices. With no money and no connections, I really had little choice in the matter. Then, with Royalists out of favor in England, the Binghams chose to cast their lot in Virginia, where it's said adherents of the King are welcome. So here I am on the *Fair Wind*."

Another rumble of thunder swept across the sea as the first drops of rain struck them, flung almost horizontal by the wind.

"So we are both fugitives of a kind," Will said gently.

Callie MacDonell nodded.

"So it would seem. And now that I've told you my tale of woe, what of yours? Are you a deserter and mutineer as that Roundhead officer claimed?"

"I confess to desertion, as my other choice was hanging for some mutiny they feared I might someday lead."

"They would hang you in advance?"

"So they intended. There is unrest in the Parliamentarian army these days. I had presented my men's rightful grievances to Cromwell and Fairfax in the spring and that apparently marked me as a troublemaker. When mutinies began to break out a month ago, I kept my men loyal to the colors. That did me no good. I was warned by a senior officer that I was to be arrested and that I would receive no fair trial. So I ran."

When he'd finished, Callie stared at him for a long moment, her green eyes boring into his. The wind kicked up and she pulled her shawl tighter around her shoulders.

"Life is unfair, isn't it?" she said finally, turning back to stare at the darkening horizon.

As the wind continued to grow she spread her arms and her shawl fluttered out behind her like the wings of a bird.

"I always loved storms as a child," she said as a jagged bolt of lightning leapt across the sky. "In the Highlands the thunder would echo down the valleys and frighten my mother, but I loved the sound for some reason. Of course my enjoyment was enhanced by the sure knowledge that no matter how the wind blew or the rain swirled, I'd be safe and dry inside. I expect a storm at sea is another matter."

"Aye, miss, it is. And as you say, best observed from shelter."

No King, No Country

With that he led her to the fo'c'sle and drew her into the cook's galley. The cook was snoring in his berth, undisturbed by the approaching tempest. Across the main deck, the rain now began to fall in sheets, blown by a howling wind as the squall struck. Callie watched it from the refuge of the galley, her eyes shining.

"You've seen it, Captain, a storm at sea?"

"Aye, miss. Not one of the great storms of the southern oceans, but even the Irish Sea can make a man wish he'd never left dry land. As a ship's boy I sailed aboard a two-masted ship bound from Chester to Cork. A winter storm caught us at night in St. George's channel."

"A storm at night sounds terrible. Were you frightened?"

"Scared out of my wits. We were short of crew and the captain had to send me up the rat lines along with the rest to reef the sails. I was twelve years old. I'll tell you, hanging onto the main yard with a pitching deck below and the wind howling like a banshee, is no place to be in the dead of night. From up there I saw waves crashing on a jagged shoreline dead ahead. It was the Tuskar Rock."

The girl was no longer watching the storm outside, but was staring at him, her eyes wide.

"And what is that?"

"Oh, it's a treacherous spot, miss. It's only a quarter mile across and so low it's hard to see, even in daylight. The Tuskar Rock has torn the bottom out of ships in the Irish Sea since the days of the Vikings and from where I clung to the main yard I could see the waves dashing against the black rocks as the wind drove us toward them."

"What happened!" she demanded, breathless.

Will shook his head sadly.

"Tuskar Rock ripped out our bottom and we all drowned, miss."

The girl's mouth popped open, then clamped shut. She glared at him. Then Callie MacDonell laughed. It was the sweetest sound he'd heard in a long time.

"Captain Inness! I'd not expected you to be a man who'd cozen a lady!"

Will smiled at her.

"Someone once said that expectations are oft times unreliable."

That brought another laugh from the girl.

"You have me there, Captain."

"Perhaps if you hadn't spurned all attempts at conversation, you'd have come to know me better by now."

"Perhaps you didn't try hard enough," she said tartly as she stepped out of the galley.

With startling abruptness, the squall had passed over the *Fair Wind* and blown off toward the coast of Portugal. Will watched the girl make her way across the rain slick main deck.

Perhaps I didn't, he thought as she disappeared into the sterncastle.

No King, No Country

Tenerife

"Land Ho!"

The cry came down from the topgallant yard where Keogh had sent a man at first light to watch for a landfall to the west. Will and August had been lending a hand with the forenoon watch since breakfast, but now lay down their mops and made their way forward to the bowsprit. At first they saw nothing, then a dark smudge appeared peeking over the curve of the earth. Slowly the smudge took on the shape of a mountaintop, then other peaks appeared flanking the first in a ragged line against the blue morning sky.

August had feared they might miss the islands entirely in the vastness of the southern Atlantic, but Will had watched Keogh use his navigation tools for a fortnight and found no fault with the Captain's instruments or his skill in using them. To avoid missing his landfall, Keogh had cleverly followed a compass heading that brought the ship within sight of the Moroccan coastline well north of the islands. They'd followed the coastline south until Keogh's quadrant showed they were nearing the twenty-ninth parallel where the Canaries lay. There, he'd ordered a sharp turn to the west. On this course, the *Fair Wind* could hardly miss the islands.

As the ship plowed on through the shallow swells a second island appeared just south of the first and the Captain headed his ship toward the narrow channel between the two.

As the land slid by on either side, whirlwinds of red dust swirled up from flat, treeless plains that girded the island's peaks. Will could see no signs of human habitation and it was little wonder as the islands looked nearly barren from shoreline to mountaintops.

"Volcanoes," a voice said.

Will and August turned to see that Mathys Beck, the German gunsmith, had joined them at the bowsprit.

"They grow from the bottom of the sea, little by little," he said.

Will had heard of volcanoes, but had never seen one. They were said to spew melted rock into the air. Looking at these two desolate islands he could imagine that they'd been vomited up from some hellish underworld.

"Herr Berrycloth says a day and a half more to Santa Cruz de Tenerife," Beck added, then turned to make his way back toward the main deck.

"Mr. Beck, we've not had many opportunities to speak. I'd be interested in what plans you have for Virginia."

Beck turned, but did not answer right away as though assessing whether these two near strangers could be trusted with his plans.

"Not Virginia," he said finally. "I go north to the Maryland colony. More like me are der."

"Germans?" August asked.

"Catholics," said Beck. "I think we are not so welcome in your Protestant Virginia."

Will had little reason to doubt Beck's claim. Catholics were barely tolerated and often oppressed in England.

"Do you have people there, sir?"

"People? No, Captain. I have no people."

This last he said with a trace of bitterness before turning away and climbing back up on the fo'c'sle.

"Something is troubling that man," August observed as Beck disappeared from view.

"Aye, Gus, and it's not just our carbines."

No King, No Country

***

Once the *Fair Wind* had cleared the channel between the two rocky islands, Captain Keogh called down a course correction to west by south and the ship held to that course through the rest of the day and into the night. It was nearing noon on the following day when the lookout again sighted land. That announcement turned out all of the passengers to view their landfall, including Lady Anne who looked pale but somewhat recovered from her chronic sea sickness.

Dead ahead, there was a line of white where waves dashed against a breakwater enclosing an anchorage. Inside the protected harbor two dozen masts could be seen and beyond those a cluster of buildings climbed up a long slope toward a steep ridge to the west. On a rocky promontory off to starboard, a massive fort stood guard over the town and the harbor.

As the passengers crowded onto the fo'c'sle to get a better look, Captain Keogh called out a course correction to the steerage room and the *Fair Wind* came a few degrees to larboard, heading for the harbor entrance. Will was impressed. After sailing nearly two thousand nautical miles southward, much of the time out of sight of land, the Captain had guided the *Fair Wind* to Santa Cruz harbor like a pigeon coming home to a familiar roost.

Approaching the channel that cut through one end of the breakwater, Keogh ordered the topmen to furl the topgallant and the deckhands to luff the mizzen. The *Fair Wind* obediently lost headway, gliding gently through the opening and into the protected cove.

"Make ready the anchor," Keogh commanded and deckhands leapt to attach the heavy anchor cable to the stopper. From his perch on the quarterdeck, the Captain judged the distance to the ships already in the anchorage, then gave the order.

"Let go the anchor."

The heavy iron anchor hit the water with an audible splash plunging to the bottom of the harbor as the coils of cable played out across the main deck and through the hawser hole.

Will watched the operation with keen interest. He'd known captains on the Irish run who'd delighted in charging into a crowded harbor with all sails set, intent on impressing the locals with his seamanship and putting a scare into men aboard the ships already in the anchorage. He'd seen them wait until the last possible moment to drop anchor and lurch to a jarring halt mere yards from a disastrous collision.

While locals ashore were often amused by such antics, rival crews were not. Will learned that first hand after his captain had engineered a near miss in Cork harbor. He'd boarded the ship's pinnace to go ashore with the crew. As they approached the dock, they saw a gang of aggrieved sailors waiting for them. The crewmen ordered Will to stay in the small boat while they dealt with the mob. That had seemed cowardly to him. After all, he'd been in fights before--what farm boy hadn't? So he'd followed them onto the dock and plunged into the fray, fists flailing.

He was eleven years old.

He quickly learned that scuffles with neighbor boys had ill-prepared him for the violent mayhem of a sailor's brawl. Noses were broken, teeth knocked out, and ribs cracked as the crews went at each other. Will managed to land one solid punch to the gut of a beefy man who only seemed annoyed by the blow. With blinding quickness, a meaty fist connected with his ear and stars exploded before his eyes, followed quickly by blackness.

He woke up on the pinnace alone, save for the man who had given up his liberty to row him back to the ship. In the end, he'd suffered nothing worse than a split lip, a bloody ear and an eye swollen shut for his efforts and the ship's cook had cleaned those up nicely. To the crew his wounds were like a Roman general's laurel wreath and they never again looked upon young Will Inness as the privileged son of a shipper. In fact, the most skilled fighters among the crew took it upon themselves to teach the boy all the tricks they'd learned in brawls and knife fights from Toulon to Dublin. It was an education that had saved his life more than once on the battlefield.

As the anchor chain played out, Captain Keogh stood on the quarterdeck calmly issuing orders to furl the sails and showed no interest in putting on a show for the port of Tenerife. The ship drifted slowly forward until its anchor snagged, bringing it to a stop as gently as a sparrow alighting on a thistle. They were half a cable's length from the nearest vessel.

Once the ship had come to rest, the crew set about securing her sails and lines while the first mate supervised the launching of the pinnace that would ferry needed supplies from the quay to the ship. The night before, Captain Keogh had informed the passengers that they would be at liberty to take the ship's boat to shore and attend to whatever interest they might have there, but to take care. Any port had its dangers for the unawares, and Santa Cruz was no exception. He reminded them that it was a Spanish port and while Spain and England were currently at peace, there was no love lost between the kingdoms. Spanish authorities should be avoided where possible. Now, as they gathered on deck he issued his final advice.

"Stay together, stay near the waterfront and be back onboard when we weigh anchor at sunset. Anyone still ashore will be left behind. That is all."

All the passengers had chosen to spend this day in port on solid ground and jammed into the small boat wherever they could find room between the empty water barrels. Lady Anne made a point of sitting as far away from Will as she could, which suited him nicely as it meant that Callie MacDonell had to sit opposite him in the small boat. He smiled brightly at the girl as she settled herself among the hogsheads. Callie met his eyes for a moment, then looked away. Had he seen a hint of a smile there? She, at least, hadn't frowned. Will counted that as a victory.

When they reached the quay, there were two bored looking Spanish officials waiting to greet them. Mr. Berrycloth bounded off the pinnace and the two men took a step back, a little cowed by the man's sheer bulk. But like petty officials everywhere, these were men used to having their way and they recovered quickly. The smaller of the two Spaniards, who was dressed in what appeared to be a uniform with a yellow sash across his chest, began to pepper Berrycloth with questions.

Will understood none of it, but to his surprise, the first mate did, slowly answering each inquiry in the Spaniard's own tongue. Whether it was his answers or the small leather pouch he passed slyly to the man with the yellow sash, the port officials at length agreed that the *Fair Wind* and her passengers had legitimate business in His Catholic Majesty's port of Santa Cruz de Tenerife. They handed him a slip of paper and departed to check on other arrivals at the quay. Berrycloth stuffed the paper in a pocket and waived the passengers ashore. Will was the last off and as he alighted on the quay, the first mate addressed the group, repeating the Captain's caution.

"When the sun drops below there," he said, pointing to the sharp ridgeline to the west of the town, "be back here. I won't come to gather ye up if any of you ladies and gents are dawdling about the town."

Having said his piece, Berrycloth turned to his work detail, ordering them to begin hoisting the empty water barrels out of the pinnace.

"Impertinent man," Lady Anne sniffed in a false whisper loud enough for all to hear.

Berrycloth paid her no mind as he supervised the unloading of the barrels. Will looked around at the quay, which was bustling with sailors and locals going about their business. Warehouses and taverns crowded along the waterfront with neat residences trailing away up the gentle slope behind them. Beyond the houses one could see some stunted trees, low scrub brush and barren rock, but little else—another barren island belched up by the fires within the earth.

Not in England any more, he thought.

Among the passengers gathered on the quay, Sir James Bingham seemed to be the only one in a hurry to be off. He took Lady Anne by the elbow and led her briskly away toward the center of the port town, with Callie MacDonell hurrying to catch up. Lieutenant Grey watched them go, but did not follow. He stood with his hands on his hips, swaying slowly from side to side.

"Sea legs," Will said with a grin. "It will take a bit for the solid ground to feel steady under your feet, Lieutenant."

Harry Grey found the sensation amusing as he surveyed the inns and grog shops along the waterfront.

"Well, if I'm to weave about like a drunkard, I might as well make the most of it!" he announced. "I've heard the Spanish have decent wine. Who's with me?"

"Thank you, Herr Lieutenant," Mathys Beck said, "but I must decline." The quiet German said nothing more, but set off across the quay in the opposite direction from the Binghams.

Having no pressing business to attend to, Will and August followed Grey toward a tavern that sported a painted sign of a buxom woman with a basket of grapes under her arm. It was a little past noon and the place was not crowded. They found a table near the door and had hardly settled into their seats when a burly woman sauntered over. Given her substantial bustline, Will guessed that she had once been the model for the sign painter—perhaps twenty years ago.

"Señores?" she asked, feeling no need to be more specific.

Grey didn't hesitate.

"Tres vinos, señorita," he said holding up three fingers.

"You speak Spanish?" Will asked.

"A little," Grey said. "My father brought a Spanish boy back from the wars in the Low Countries. He managed our stables and taught me a bit, though most of the words I can't use in polite company!"

"Well, we've none of that here," said August with a smile.

Grey laughed at that as the serving woman returned with a large pitcher and three goblets.

Grey seized the pitcher, filled the cups and raised his in a toast.

"To the New World and a new start!"

"To the New World," Will and August echoed him.

They took deep draughts from their cups as Grey tilted his head back and drained his. He set it down and refilled it.

"Your father was a soldier?" Will asked.

Grey nodded

"For most his life and all of mine."

"He must have been pleased that you followed in his footsteps."

Grey shrugged, then upended his refilled goblet and drank it down.

"Not bad wine, this," he said as he wiped a hand across his lips and poured another cup full.

"Sir John Grey is a great man, a soldier of renown on the continent I'm told. He was rarely home when I was a boy and I think that suited my mother. She was a delicate woman and he was anything but that. My father's visits always made her anxious, but for me, it was like the return of a knight from the Crusades."

Grey stopped to gulp down most of his cup of wine before continuing.

"He rarely stayed more than a few days," he said, his voice turning bitter and his words starting to slur. "Just enough time to chastise the household staff, complain to Mother about our finances and ignore me."

No King, No Country

August shot Will a glance. It appeared that Lieutenant Grey was not a man accustomed to strong drink and it was loosening the young officer's tongue. As soldiers, it was not the first time they'd seen strong spirits induce personal confessions. In such cases it was best to sit back and listen quietly.

"He…was a hard man," Grey said. "Didn't like me much. Thought Mother coddled me. He was not a man much given to praise. He'd say 'Weakens a man's backbone.'"

This last was said in a blustery, officious voice, that would have been humorous if the words weren't so sad. Will saw the young officer's eyes welling up with tears. Grey turned his head and wiped his eyes before draining his cup once more. He picked up the pitcher to pour another, but found it empty. Holding it up to the light, he looked at it quizzically.

"Must have a hole in it," he pronounced loudly and called for another pitcher.

"Surely your father appreciated your service in the war…" Will began.

"Hardly," Grey said mournfully, "and with good reason. Why do you suppose I'm on this boat bound for America?"

Will said nothing for a moment. Men oft times betrayed confidences when drunk that they later regretted and he did not want to encourage Grey to say more about the affairs of his family.

"As you said at the Captain's table," he said gently, "perhaps its best if we leave behind our troubles in England and look to a new start in America."

Grey looked up at him, his eyes red-rimmed.

"Can you ever leave cowardice behind, Captain?"

***

Harry Grey had panicked at Preston.

His first action after joining the Royalist cause had been at Berwick-upon-Tweed a fortnight before the battle at Preston Moor. It had been an almost bloodless affair. The small garrison of Parliamentarian troops had fired a few volleys in their general direction as a matter of pride before laying down their arms and surrendering. That day, the sound of lead balls whizzing by overhead had added a bit of zest to the proceedings but had hardly been a baptism by fire. Still, it gave the young Lieutenant the sense that he was prepared for sterner tests.

Such a test had come two weeks later at dawn on the barren moor above the town of Preston. The sudden appearance of Cromwell with six thousand hardened veterans joining the outnumbered Parliamentarian force at Preston Moor had sent the Royalist forces reeling back toward the town and the bridges over the River Ribble to the south.

The Duke of Hamilton, in overall command of the Royalist force, ordered Langdale's horse into the town itself in a desperate bid to stop Cromwell's advance long enough for his army to escape over the bridges that spanned the river south of town. Lieutenant Grey had ridden forward with the rest, prepared to do his duty, but at the edge of town he'd looked up at the treeless moor to see Cromwell's vaunted cavalry bearing down on him.

Unlike the loose formations of local militia cavalry he had grown accustomed to in his month with Langdale's horse, these men rode knee to knee in a tightly packed, unbroken line that surged toward him like some huge scythe come to cut down a field of wheat. The breath caught in his throat as he felt the very ground tremble beneath him from the pounding of their hooves. As they came on, a bugle sounded and two thousand men drew sabers, the wicked blades gleaming in the early morning sun. Grey drew his pistol and tried to calm his breathing, but all around him men began to break and flee back through the town.

It was too much.

He fired off a wild shot at the onrushing Roundhead cavalry then whirled his horse around and followed the rest of his regiment streaming through the narrow streets of Preston, desperate to reach the bridges over the Ribble before they were ridden down by Cromwell's killers. When he reached the river he found the bridges jammed with panicked riders. Behind him he could see the enemy cavalry pouring into the town. He tried to force his horse into the river, but it balked. In desperation, he leapt off the animal and plunged into the water.

The Ribble was wide at this point and Grey had to fight to stay afloat, weighed down by his heavy boots and shiny steel breastplate. Somehow he kept his head above water long enough for his feet to touch bottom on the far side. He crawled out of the river exhausted, but there was no time to rest. Cromwell's troopers had reached the opposite bank and were falling savagely on the rear of the retreating Royalists.

Bullets whistled past him and struck the bank sending up little eruptions of mud as Grey climbed up the slippery slope with nothing but an empty pistol still shoved in his belt. He stripped off his breastplate and managed to grab the reins of a riderless horse wandering aimlessly amidst the chaos. He hauled himself into the saddle and didn't stop riding for two days, finally reaching the north of Yorkshire and his home. In a sad bit of irony, Sir John Grey had arrived the day before. The welcome he offered his son was not a warm one. Once the truth of what had happened at Preston was laid on the table, Sir John had exploded.

"You ran in the face of the enemy?"

"The whole army ran, Father!" Grey protested. "What was I to do? Those who didn't run fast enough are all dead."

"That would have been preferable to dishonoring your family name!"

For a day and a night, the house was filled with recriminations. Lady Francis tried to shield her son from the wrath of his father to little avail. On the morning after his return home Sir John called him into his private study.

"I will not have a coward under my roof," he said simply. He held out a small pouch of silver. "Your Mother insists I give you this, but I do so on one condition. You must leave this country and never return. Your mother has a cousin somewhere in the Virginia colony, perhaps you can find some use for yourself there."

All this and more, Harry Grey poured out to his two fellow passengers as they sat in the tavern.

"So you see, gentlemen," he said at last. "That is why I am on this boat to America."

Will shook his head.

"You're on this boat because your father is an ass, Lieutenant. Believe me, we ran more than once when our lines were broken early in the war and lived to fight another day. You did no worse than that."

"We ran like rabbits at Edgehill," August put in.

"But you did fight another day," Grey protested. "I deserted!"

"Then you are in good company with us," August said.

"And now, I think it time we take you back to the ship," Will added, throwing a few coins on the table.

Will and August got on either side of the drunken young man and helped him stumble out of the inn door and across the quay toward where the pinnace was tied up. Further down the waterfront, Will saw the Binghams and Callie MacDonell standing near a pier where a small merchantman was tied up. Sir James Bingham was in an animated conversation with a man there while the two ladies stood off to the side. Glancing back to the west, Will saw that the disk of the sun had begun to dip below the ridgeline above the town. He was turning toward the pinnace when he heard a piercing cry of pure rage and anguish come from the vessel docked at the pier.

He looked up in time to see a black man, wholly naked, leap from the railing of the ship and plunge into the water of the harbor. Other men, white men, appeared at the ship's railing cursing and pointing at the man who had begun to swim toward the opposite side of the harbor. An order was given and the ship's boat was lowered over the side. A half dozen sailors scrambled down the jack ladder and set off after the escaped African.

"Get Grey to the pinnace, Gus," Will said and, releasing his hold on the drunken Lieutenant, he rushed to the edge of the quay to see how the drama played out. It didn't last long. The man swimming for his life didn't make it half way across the harbor before he was overtaken and dragged into the boat by the crewmen sent to fetch him. As he was being hauled out of the water, Will saw that the man had a metal collar around his neck.

"Good God," a voice said behind him. Will turned to see that August had returned in time to see the African dragged into the boat.

"God has naught to do with this," Will said grimly.

Though Will's father had scorned the slave trade, there were English shippers who profited from it. There'd been a prominent English merchant in Chester who'd regularly sent ships to the west coast of Africa to pick up consignments of men, women and children to be sold in the islands of the Caribbean. The man had even kept two Negro boys as footmen for a time, until the local Bishop of Chester threatened to chastise him from the pulpit on Sunday.

Will wondered now what had happened to those boys. Had their silk liveries been stripped off and iron collars bolted around their necks? He watched as the ship's boat reached the pier and saw the escaped man dragged ashore. As he struggled to rise to his feet, two men beat him savagely with wooden truncheons until he fell face down on the pier. Two more men grabbed the slave's wrists and dragged him, unconscious, toward the gangway of the merchantman.

Will had seen a good deal of cruelty in the war, but this sight made his stomach turn. Almost against his will he found himself moving toward the slavers and their captive.

He was brought up short by a hand seizing his arm in an iron grip.

"Not your business, Captain."

He swung around to see Mathys Beck standing there.

"You can't help him, Inness," the German said grimly. "You try, they beat you bloody. And I know these Spanish. They put you in stinking cell here to rot. Maybe Keogh get you out. Maybe not."

Just then John Berrycloth appeared and pointed to the setting sun where only the rim still shone above the mountains.

"It's time gentlemen. Best get yerself to the pinnace."

Will turned back to see that the African man had already been hauled back aboard the slave ship. Whatever his fate was to be, it was out of his hands. Resigned he turned to follow the first mate back to the ship's boat. Then the Binghams arrived, their faces alight with excitement.

"Quite the show, that!" Sir James exclaimed, his eyes shining.

"For a bit I thought the brute might actually make good his escape," Lady Anne put in, breathlessly.

"But they were on him like a pack of hounds!" Sir James added gleefully.

He was about to say more when Will grasped him by the lapels of his coat and jerked him close.

"You miserable shit," he growled, his faces inches from Bingham's. "They almost killed that man!"

James Bingham lurched backwards in a panic and managed to break free from Will's grasp. He was reaching for something in the folds of his coat when Berrycloth stepped between the two men and turned to Bingham.

"I wouldn't advise that," he said quietly, though his tone was more of an order than a request.

Bingham hesitated, his face a mask of fury, but finally brought forth his hand, empty.

No King, No Country

"He laid hands on me!" he screamed, pointing a finger at Will.

"Hardly mussed yer coat," said Berrycloth calmly. Then he turned on Will.

"He may be a miserable shit, Mr. Inness, but we'll have no rough stuff amongst the passengers. Clear?"

Will nodded. It had taken a force of will, but he'd managed to get his own fury under control.

"Clear."

Berrycloth grunted, then pointed once more to the ridgeline behind which the sun had now entirely disappeared.

"Now if you gentlemen and ladies would kindly get yer arses on the pinnace. We've an ebb tide to catch."

No one spoke on the trip back to the *Fair Wind* with John Berrycloth sitting in the bow and glowering at the passengers. Sir James would not meet Will's eyes and Lady Anne stared straight over his shoulder. Next to her, Callie MacDonell met his gaze and gave him the slightest little nod.

Seven Hundred Leagues West

As was his tradition, Captain Keogh invited the passengers to join him for dinner on the first night out of port. On this night the Binghams made excuses and absented themselves, leaving Will, August, Herr Beck and Lieutenant Grey as the only guests at the Captain's table. Beck sat silently as always while Lieutenant Grey, pale but surprisingly sober, was for once as taciturn as the German. When all were seated, Captain Keogh entered and took his spot at the head of the table.

"So, Mr. Inness," he began, "Mr. Berrycloth informs me you had a busy day in port."

Will nodded.

"Lost my temper, Captain. I will try to do better."

"I would appreciate that, sir. It's bad for business if my passengers kill each other."

"I understand, sir."

"And you should also understand that the slave trade is deep-rooted in the Virginia colony. They're convinced they cannot raise tobacco, their only cash crop, without enslaved Africans to provide the labor. They will not take kindly to those who disapprove."

"Have you ever transported Africans to America, Captain?"

Keogh set down his cup of ale, a scowl on his lips.

"The slave trade is an abomination in the eyes of the Lord," he said firmly, "and I take no part in it, but if you are to trade in Virginia, or settle in it, sir, you'd best accustom yourself to the practice."

"The buying and selling of men will be hard to get used to, Captain."

"Women and children as well, Mr. Inness," Keogh added brusquely. "Women…and…children! They breed 'em and sell 'em like cattle."

Just then the steward came in with a huge platter and laid it with a flourish at the center of the table. At its center were three large broiled fish, the likes of which Will had never seen. The things had beaks!

"Parrotfish," the steward announced proudly. "A delicacy in the Canaries."

The fish were surrounded by stacks of small lobsters boiled to a bright red, and tiny limpets still in their shells.

"Let us abolish the slave trade after dinner, gentlemen," the Captain declared. "And since no ladies are in attendance, you may dig in without regard for the niceties!" Keogh punctuated his comment with a satisfying belch and scooped up a heap of the limpets.

Will had little appetite for the bounty on the table. What he'd seen this day had been unsettling and if Keogh was right, such sights would be commonplace in the Virginia colony. He took a small portion of the strange fish and found it tasted much better than it looked. He waited until Keogh had finished his mound of shellfish to speak.

"Captain, what do you know of the lay of the land in Virginia?"

Keogh helped himself to half of one of the parrotfish and didn't answer while he delicately removed the fish's spine. Once that operation was complete he looked up.

"Not much, Mr. Inness. Small settlements have spread up the James River as far as the falls I believe. There was a war with the local Powhatans a few years back, with a good deal of slaughter on both sides, but that seems to have quieted down. Somewhere far off to the west are mountains

I'm told. To be honest, what I know is the shipping trade out of Jamestown. You'd best speak with James Oakley. He spent four years as a waterman on the great bay there and tells stories about venturing up the rivers that run toward the mountains. He'll know far more than I."

With that, Keogh signaled the end of the dinner conversation by stabbing a fat lobster, expertly splitting its shell and popping the fleshy meat of the tail into his mouth.

***

There was a full moon hanging just above the horizon when Will emerged from the narrow passageway in the sterncastle onto the main deck. Tenerife had long since disappeared over the curve of the Earth behind them while off to starboard a dark shape loomed—another rocky island in the chain. Above the black outline of the island, he found the north star and from its position could tell that the *Fair Wind* was sailing southwest. He'd heard Berrycloth say they'd stay on that heading for four days until they reached the westerly current that would speed their progress to the Americas.

August stumbled on deck behind him and, full of parrotfish and limpets, yawned and said his goodnights before shuffling down to the tween deck to sleep. Will didn't follow. The events in Tenerife had left him on edge and he knew sleep would come slowly tonight, if it came at all. He leaned on the rail and looked at the wide strand of silver cast on the dark waters by the moonlight. The sight was so beautiful it made the breath catch in his throat, but did little to ease his mind. He heard soft footsteps behind him and turned to see Callie MacDonell slipping across the deck to join him at the rail.

"I can only be a moment or I'll be missed," she whispered urgently, looking over her shoulder. "You made a dangerous enemy today, Captain. Sir James is a man who holds grudges."

Will shrugged.

"He seems more the sort to threaten than to act, miss."

Callie shook her head.

"Then you have misjudged him, sir. He'll not come at you direct. He's too much the coward for that, but cowards can be dangerous. Do not take him lightly."

"He was reveling in that man's degradation!" Will said in disgust.

"He doesn't see those poor devils as men," Callie said quietly. "What do you think he was doing all afternoon? I watched him strike a deal with a slave trader to have a score of Africans delivered to him in Jamestown. They'd just shaken hands on it when the man leapt from the ship."

Callie paused, searching Will's face.

"You seem a decent man, Captain. James Bingham is not. He is clever and ruthless. I have seen him ruin men for far less than what you did on the quay today."

He'd listened to her words, but found himself distracted by the moonlight reflecting off the girl's lovely face—until her worried expression broke whatever spell the moon was casting. He laid a hand on her shoulder.

"Thank you for the warning, Miss MacDonell. But don't fear for me. More dangerous men than Bingham have set about my ruination and I've survived."

Callie shrugged off his hand and fixed him with a look that was at first hurt, then withering.

"I've noted how well you've survived, Captain. Here you are in the middle of the ocean on the run from charges of mutiny and desertion! You've a gibbet awaiting you back in England and as far as I can see your prospects in Virginia are now nil. Perhaps you give yourself too much credit!"

Will's face reddened. He wanted to give back something clever, but the girl's words had struck too close to home. He'd been dismissive of her warning and boastful in the bargain. Callie did not wait for his response as he stood there flustered. She turned on her heel and stomped across the main deck, disappearing into the sterncastle.

***

Will found his way to his thin mattress atop the cargo on the tween deck and crawled up beside August who was already asleep. All around were the familiar sounds of the crew quarters after dark. Most of the morning watch were snoring in their own spots while a few were gathered around a flickering lantern quietly playing a game of thirty-one. He tried to sleep, but sleep would not come. Again and again, his mind played back the events of the day, but this rehashing did little to bring him rest.

He thought back on the Chester merchant with his African footmen. When he'd seen those two boys riding past on the back of the man's coach it had been nothing more to him than a distasteful novelty. But what he'd seen today went far beyond distaste. He'd witnessed the harsh reality of the slave trade. The black man's cry of despair still echoed in his ears and he could only guess at what horrors would be seen in the hold of that slave ship. He knew his assault on Bingham had been pointless. It could not help the escaped slave and had made him a new enemy and he'd made enough of those lately to suffice. He'd lost his temper and that was always a mistake. But he had to confess.

It had felt good.

Then there was Callie MacDonell. The girl had taken a risk to warn him of danger and he'd made light of it, hoping to impress her. How cocksure she must think him and with good reason! What's more, her description of his current circumstances had been painfully accurate. A noose waited for him back in England and in Virginia he'd managed to make a powerful enemy before ever setting foot there. It had been a bad day and much of it of his own making.

Somewhere on the tween deck a man gave a little yelp, having cast the dice and come up thirty-two. Will rolled over and tried to clear his mind of dark thoughts but long after the game had broken up he still lay awake.

***

No King, No Country

Will waited until Jamie Oakley came off the forenoon watch and sat down to his midday meal to approach him. Like all the crew, he'd gotten to know Oakley a bit on the voyage from Liverpool down to Tenerife and had found him to be a relentlessly cheerful and talkative man.

"Captain Keogh tells me you're well acquainted with the land and the settlements in the Virginia colony, Jamie. As I'm bound there, I've a wish to know what's ahead."

Oakley gave him a grin, displaying two missing teeth in the front.

"'Course, Will," he said, as he stabbed a chunk of salt beef and stuffed it in his mouth. He chewed energetically on the tough slab of meat for a moment then gulped the bite down.

"The Cheseapeak is a bigger bay than any you'll find in England or France and I worked most of it," he said, "fishin' and crabbin' and pickin' oysters. Never saw coastal waters as rich as those. It must be all the rivers drainin' into the bay. Every few leagues, there's another one! I once worked my way as far north on the bay as the new Maryland colony."

He paused to spit a chunk of gristle over the side.

"Full of Papists, but far as I can tell they ain't botherin' no one. The Virginia colony is at the south end of the bay and between the two colonies there's four big rivers comin' in from the west."

He held up four fingers and ticked off the river names.

"Potowmac is the biggest, then there's Rappahannock, York and James. I been up all four to the fall line and such rivers they are! Every one as wide as the Thames or Severn!"

The old sailor's eyes shone as he thought back on these mighty streams that poured into the Cheseapeak.

"The Virginia colony has grown up along the James which is the furthest south. Jamestown's near forty miles upriver from the bay. Not the healthiest spot for a town as it's surrounded by bogs, but that's the spot they chose forty years ago and by time I left, there was a couple thousand souls there. But it's no surprise that folks spread out and found better places. Last I knew there were four settlements on higher ground upriver and they was building forts of some sort above the fall line. Same thing on the Appomattox River and the Chickahominy."

"Chickahominy?"

"It's another stream that feeds into the James a few miles upriver from Jamestown. It's a Powhatan name. Lots of them in Virginia. Names that is. Not so many Powhatans anymore. They rose up against the English right before I left the colony in forty-four. Killed five hundred—men women and children. Wiped out a couple a' those settlements up river I heard. My luck, I was fishing for crabs on the bay when they struck. It was all over time I got back. If them Powhatans had kept at it they might have run the whole lot of English right out of the country, but Indians, they don't think like us. They did their killin' and just went back to their wigwams and smoked their pipes."

Finishing his meal, Oakley set down his bowl and drew out a twist of tobacco, stuffing a strand in his cheek.

"Finest tobac ye'll find anywhere is growed right there in Virginia," he observed as he chewed contentedly on the cured leaf.

"You were saying about the uprising of the Powhatans…"

Oakley spit a stream of brown liquid over the rail and nodded.

"After all that slaughter, Governor Berkley had to show them who was the boss along the James. He turned Lunsford on 'em and the colonists had their vengeance and then some! That's when I decided it was time to go back to sea. Captain Keogh was in port the day I got back from crabbin', so I signed on with him."

"You said he turned Lunsford on the Powhatans."

"Oh, aye. Sir Thomas is the man ye want if it's a massacre yer lookin' for. Killed every one of the Indians he could lay hands on. Women and children weren't spared. Burnt their villages, took their food—and that was after the harvest so's they'd not have nothing to eat over the winter. Lunsford's not to be trifled with during peaceable times either. Keeps everyone in line he does. That's one reason I worked the bay. Thing's was too strict-like there in Jamestown. Not sure who fears the bastard more, the savages or the English."

Will wondered if Lady Anne Bingham was aware of her future husband's reputation or whether it mattered. Surely Sir James Bingham would know what sort of man Lunsford was. And if the Binghams were to be joined by marriage to the Captain General of the colonial militia, Callie's warning the night before was even more worrisome.

"So there are few Indians left in the land?"

"Few Powhatans anymore, but there are strong tribes further west and north, warlike tribes that even the Powhatans fear."

"How far from the sea to the mountains?"

Jamie scratched his chin.

"Don't rightly know, Will. Don't think any white man has been that far."

Then that's far enough, Will thought.

"Could you help me fashion a map?"

Jamie gave him another gap-toothed grin.

"'Course, Will."

***

On the fourth day out from Tenerife they struck the great equatorial current that swept relentlessly west from Africa to the Americas. Captain Keogh altered course to due west and the *Fair Wind* plunged through the swells like a great sea creature. Indeed, on the following day, the lookout spotted a pod of twenty or more whales just to the north. All of the passengers gathered on the starboard rail to witness the spectacle. Even the Binghams put in an appearance, though they kept their distance from Will and August. Will split his attention between the great behemoths and Callie MacDonell, but the girl stared resolutely at the whales and when they finally sounded, she followed the Binghams back into the sterncastle.

As the crowd dispersed, Will saw Mathys Beck still standing at the rail staring at the empty ocean where the great sea creatures had been. Since leaving Tenerife, Will had only seen the beefy gunsmith during the German's daily exercise routine on deck and hadn't wanted to disturb the man. Beck had almost certainly saved him from a beating or worse at the hands of slavers there and he'd never properly thanked him for his intervention. He took a spot by the rail next to the man and started to speak, but Beck spoke first.

"Captain Inness, you are well?" he asked.

"Passable, Herr Beck, passable. I wish to thank you for restraining me in Tenerife. I might still be there now if you had not stopped me."

The German shrugged.

"These slavers, they are brutes, Captain. And I know the Spanish. It would not have ended well."

"Indeed," Will agreed. "And how are you, sir?"

"Gut. I am gut. I have wanted to speak with you, privately."

"Of course, sir."

Beck looked around. No one stood near them on the deck. He leaned in close and spoke in a hushed voice.

"Captain, my berth is next to that of the Binghams," he began. "I am not one to…belauschen…." he searched for the English word.

"Eavesdrop?" Will offered.

"Ya, eavesdrop! I do not do this, but the walls, they are thin and I hear. The man, Sir James, has spoken of you, Captain. It was not pleasant. He means you harm."

Will nodded.

"You are not the first to warn me of this, Herr Beck, and I thank you."

No King, No Country

Beck shrugged.

"Men like Bingham are everywhere, Captain. There were men like him in Germany and there will be others like him in America. Of that there is no doubt."

Will heard no despair in the German's voice, just a flat statement of fact. Having had his say, the gunsmith turned to go, but Will beckoned him to stay.

"Herr Beck, you know why I had to leave England. May I ask why you left Germany?" It was a question he'd wanted to pose since he'd first met the gunsmith.

Beck hesitated, then nodded.

"Freiburg…I could not live there any longer. First the Austrians came. They raped and killed the Protestants. Then the Swedes came. They raped and killed the Catholics. Then came the French. Then the Spanish. They were all the same. Always killing in the name of God. Like wild animals they were. I lost my wife to the Swedes. I'd hoped to live peaceably when the Spanish came. They were Catholics like me, but they took my only child, my son, for forced labor. I never saw the boy again."

"Your wound, Herr Beck," Will said nodding toward the nasty scar that circled the man's neck. "How did you come by it?"

"When they come for my boy," Beck said, "I fight them. But there are too many. They tie a rope around my neck and drag me through the streets until I pass out. I woke up half dead, but I lived. For a long time I search for Johan, for my boy. After a year, I was told he died when a ditch he was digging collapsed on him. My boy," he said, his voice cracking, "my boy was buried alive!"

Will had never heard the sound of a man's heart breaking before, but he heard it now in the mournful voice of Mathys Beck. He stayed silent for a while as he watched the German struggle with this memory. After a bit, Beck looked up, his eyes damp.

"I knew I must leave Freiburg, but there was one thing I would have before I left—justice, for me and for Johan."

"Did you have your justice, Herr Beck?" Will asked gently.

Beck nodded grimly.

"The man who took my son—I put a rifle ball through his brain. That was my justice."

***

For three weeks, the *Fair Wind* kept to a westerly course. Each night when the sky was clear, Captain Keogh would take out his quadrant and sight on the North Star to determine if his ship was staying close to his plotted course of ten degrees north latitude. He made little effort to determine his longitude, having little faith in the instruments available to measure his position east to west.

"We stay on this course and we're bound to sight land by and by," he told Will. "Then we turn north."

Will and August took their turns on watch and often spent the evenings on deck. The tween deck smelled of mildew and sour sweat from twenty-six crewman and the May nights at this latitude were mild. They lay side by side gazing up at the sky ablaze with stars. and sorting out their plans for a new life in America.

"Farming," August proposed. "It's all I know besides soldiering. We must find what food crops grow in the Virginia climate and cash crops as well."

"Aye, I've a mind to find some decent land, well-watered and timbered," Will said. "Jamie Oakley says there are mountains far inland that white men have never reached. I've a hankering to see those mountains."

"I've heard the forests there are filled with game," August said. "You could cut some good staves and fashion longbows for us."

The crafting of this most venerated of English weapons had been passed down for many generations by some folk who dwelt in the valley of the River Weaver. In the days of the Plantagenet kings and their heirs, the men from this region of Cheshire were renowned for their skill with the bow. They had fought with the Black Prince at Crecy and with King Harry at Agincourt, where they'd slaughtered the flower of French chivalry.

In the years since, the bow had fallen out of favor as the musket replaced it for military use. The longbow might be accurate up to two hundred yards and capable of launching twelve shafts a minute, but the cost of maintaining men who could wield the weapon had just been too much. Later English kings chose to stick a musket in a farm boy's hands and have him blast away at two rounds a minute standing twenty-five paces from the enemy.

Despite its fall from grace, the longbow was something of a family tradition in the Inness family. Will had learned to fashion bows from a stave of yew at his father's knee. His brother Rob had not been interested in the craft or the weapon and his young friend August hadn't the patience to spend hours in the Inness barn paring down staves to be fashioned into bows. But he'd happily joined Will as they hunted grouse and red deer and hares in the wood and fields along the Weaver, with both boys becoming, in time, competent with the bow. And when stealth was required, the longbow had one other advantage over a firearm.

It was silent.

"They say the natives in America still use the bow," August observed.

"And the war club and lance and tomahawk," Will added.

August gave a little groan.

"Sounds more deadly than a line of muskets. You've talked about leaving the settlements behind, Will. Can we survive among the savages?"

Will took a while to answer. He knew little of the native inhabitants of this new land beyond the little Jamie Oakley had told him, but he was certain of one thing. Men were men, wherever they were found.

"We'll have to prove we are not enemies."

August frowned.

"That might not be easy. We won't be the first Englishmen they've dealt with. They'll bring with them whatever opinions they've already formed of our kind."

Will did not answer. He knew Gus was right and that was a worry.

***

"Can I help with that?"

Will had hoped for an opportunity to make amends with Callie MacDonell and had seen his chance as the girl struggled to haul a tub of dirty laundry water to the rail.

She sat the tub down and looked at him a little doubtfully, then shrugged.

"If you wish," she said and stepped back.

Will lifted the tub of soapy water and started for the lee side rail.

"You've been avoiding me," he said as he lugged the heavy tub.

He turned to see Callie wrinkle her brow at that and knew he'd made a poor start.

"You flatter yourself, Captain," she said.

"I spoke foolishly when last we met," he offered.

"I noticed," she gave back.

He reached the rail and dumped the laundry water into the ocean. This was not going as he'd hoped. Perhaps contrition had not been the best approach. He resolved to try plain honesty. He turned and handed her the empty tub.

"I boasted…to impress you," he confessed.

This admission brought just the hint of a smile to the girl's face.

"Bravado doesn't impress me, Captain Inness," she said gently, "but honesty does. So does standing for what's right. That day in Tenerife—there was nothing you could do for that poor man, but I saw the look on your face when they

No King, No Country

began to beat him. You were going to challenge those wretched slavers, had Herr Beck not stopped you."

Will found himself off balance by this turn in the conversation.

"It's a foul practice, slaving," was the best he could manage.

"It is that," she said lifting the laundry tub and resting it on her hip. She turned to go and was halfway across the deck when she stopped and looked back.

"Oh, and one more thing. You were foolish to seize Sir James by his lapels, but *that* did impress me."

As she disappeared into the sterncastle Will stood there wondering what had just happened.

***

It was just as the Captain said. On the twenty-third day out of Tenerife, the call came down from the topsail yard that land was in sight dead ahead. Once more, the passengers gathered on deck to get their first look at the New World. There wasn't much to see. A fringe of white beach backed by an impenetrable wall of jungle stretched endlessly to the north and south. There was no sign of human habitation on this wild coast and soon it was left behind as the Captain laid in a new course of north by northwest.

For another six days they followed that heading until the rocky east coast of Barbados came into view. Keogh took the ship around the southern end of the island and into the small port of St. Michael's Town. Unlike Tenerife, the Captain did not offer his passengers liberty to explore the town.

"It's a hell hole," he declared, "and having shown your propensity for mischief in the last port, you shall remain aboard." Sir James Bingham made as though to object, but Keogh turned his back on the knot of passengers before he could speak and began barking orders to the crew. In little more than three hours, they'd taken on a shipment of sugar bound for Jamestown, fresh water, a few baskets of fruit and a steer to be butchered. Before the cook could go to work on the hapless animal, the *Fair Wind* weighed anchor and was bound northward once more.

***

Two days north of St. Michael's Town, Will sat on deck studying the map that Jamie Oakley had painstakingly sketched for him. The old waterman's map began well north of Spanish Florida and showed a number of great bays cut off from the sea by long sandy islands. Will traced a finger north until he reached the broad open mouth of the Cheseapeak.

The map showed a long finger of land forming the eastern shore of the bay and four rivers draining into it along its western shore. Oakley hadn't been sure of the spellings, but had marked the rivers from south to north as James, York, Rappahannock and Potowmac. All the rivers ran off generally to the northwest. The English had chosen the James River, nearest the mouth of the bay, to plant their colony.

"What have you there, Captain?"

Will looked up to see Callie standing over him and scrambled to his feet. He spread open the map and showed it to her.

"This is Jamie Oakley's work."

The girl studied the map for a long time saying nothing.

"What is this?" she asked finally, pointing to a jagged line drawn to the west of the headwaters of the rivers.

"Mountains, Jamie says, but no English have actually seen them that he knows of. The local Indians call them Quirank but he says all the tribes have different names for the rivers and hills. I've a mind to go see those mountains."

The girl nodded

"I gathered you were looking to make your own way from what you said that first night at Captain Keogh's table, and given the friends you've made of the Binghams, I'd think the

Virginia colony might not be hospitable. But so far? Will it not be dangerous?"

"Perhaps. Jamie says the Powhatans call this area the empty land," he said pointing to the middle section of the jagged line on the map. "No tribes dwell in these mountains, though they hunt there and follow paths that run north and south to trade and make war."

"More war," she said sorrowfully.

Will shrugged.

"I know little about these natives of America, but it's said they make war upon each other and value bravery in battle above all else. As for me, I've had a belly-full of war and will seek to avoid it, unless it comes to my doorstep."

Callie nodded and ran a finger slowly along the jagged line.

"I miss my mountains," she said wistfully, "and Jamestown I'm told is low and swampy."

"Not a fit place for a highland lass," Will said.

"It will have to do, for a time at least. I will owe the Binghams six months of service to pay off my debts to them."

For a while the two stayed silent, but at length Callie drew her eyes away from the jagged line in the west and pointed to a mark on a point of land just north of the northernmost river on the map.

"What's this?" she asked.

"St. Mary's City—though Jamie says it's not much of a city. It's the main town of the Maryland colony."

"Mr. Beck says that's where the Catholics have settled?"

"Aye, he told me the same."

"Did you know I was Catholic?" she asked him.

Will nodded.

"I saw you once standing by the rail. You were murmuring something I couldn't hear, then I saw you holding the string of beads that Catholics use in their prayers."

"You have sharp eyes. It's not a thing I often do where others can see."

"It's hard not to notice you when you're on deck," Will said honestly.

She looked at him with mischief in her green eyes.

"Why Captain Inness, are you wooing me?"

"Would you object if I was?"

"I asked you first," she said with a laugh.

"Then, yes, I'm wooing you, Miss MacDonell."

"Does it not bother you that I'm a Papist?" she asked, serious now. "My faith is not much in favor in England these days."

"We are not in England anymore, Callie, and no, it doesn't bother me. Worship how you wish."

"And what of you, William? What flavor of Protestant are you."

Will shrugged.

"The plainest I suppose. Church of England, but there's been little time for church these past six years and to be honest, I haven't missed it. Does that trouble you?"

"We can work on that," she said with a smile. "At least you're not a Puritan!"

No King, No Country

Privateer

They were seven days out of Barbados when the call came down from the lookout.

"Sail t' larboard!"

Will set down the rope he was splicing and looked off to the west. He shielded his eyes from the glare of the setting sun, but could see nothing from his vantage point save a low, scrub-covered island not unlike a dozen others they'd passed since entering the waters of the Bahamas.

He saw Captain Keogh extend his spyglass and slowly traverse the western horizon. At a little south of due west he stopped and held steady for a moment then jerked the glass down and summoned Mr. Berrycloth. Will watched the two briefly confer, then the first mate began to shout orders.

"All hands on deck! Stand by to make sail!" he boomed.

The first dog watch ceased whatever minor duties they were attending to and moved to man the sheets and braces. From the tween deck, men of the off-duty watches poured onto the main deck, hurrying to their assigned stations. August came up with the rest and sought Will out.

"Trouble?" he asked, breathless.

Will nodded.

"Ship to larboard, beyond the island there and a little astern of us. Keogh didn't like the looks of it."

"Mr. Barley to the Quarterdeck!" Berrycloth shouted from the railing just above their heads.

Bill Barley hurried smartly to the bulkhead of the quarterdeck as Berrycloth leaned over the rail.

"Standby the gun crews, Mr. Barley," he said calmly.

Barley turned to the men assembled on the main deck.

"Gun crews, man yer guns!" he bellowed. "Sternchaser crew to the quarterdeck. Powder monkey to the magazine!" Eighteen men and one boy sprang to comply.

From his position on the quarterdeck, Keogh watched his men move to their stations.

"Ready about!" he ordered.

A moment later the cry came back from the main deck.

"Ready to come about!"

As the last of the gun crews disappeared below, Keogh bawled out his next command.

"Come about!" he roared

Below, the helmsman leaned into the whipstaff to shift the rudder. On deck, men began to haul on the braces and sheets. The *Fair Wind* had been running close-hauled on a larboard tack for hours, but now Keogh was putting her on the opposite tack. Close hauled on the starboard tack, she would keep her speed, but put more distance between her and whatever ship was behind the island.

As the *Fair Wind* came about, her sails luffed for a few moments as the bow passed directly through the prevailing wind, but they tautened as her momentum kept her out of irons and put her on the starboard tack. The merchantman's rigging and timbers groaned as she heeled over and turned toward the northeast.

Will couldn't gainsay Keogh's caution. Putting distance between them and an unknown vessel in these waters seemed only prudent. In the West Indies, experienced ship masters assumed bad intentions. Will watched Keogh turn once more to John Berrycloth and the big first mate hurried to the ladder that led to the tween deck.

"Mr. Barley, run out your guns on the starboard side if you please!" he shouted down.

No King, No Country

Will could feel the rumble through the deck as the starboard twelve-pounders were run out, shifting the ship's weight and helping the *Fair Wind* grip the water and run faster on her new tack. Whatever Keogh had seen through his glass, the Captain wanted no part of.

"You two!"

Both men turned to see Bill Barley had come back on deck and was beckoning them.

"Are ye crew these days or passengers?" he asked curtly.

"Crew," they both said at once.

"Good, then I'll want you lads in the tops with yer weapons," he said. "If our friend is hostile, I'm sure the Cap'n would be pleased if you would shoot anyone you see on her deck."

"Aye," both said at once.

Will followed August back below deck to retrieve their carbines. On the tween deck men stood by the guns on the larboard side as the ship's boy staggered down the center aisle with an armful of muskets and cutlasses. As he passed each gun crew the men there picked their weapon of choice. Will absently reached down to assure himself that his ruby-handled dagger was snugly in place in his boot and fervently hoped he wouldn't have need of it in the coming hours.

When they returned to the main deck Will saw the other passengers had emerged from their quarters to see what the alarm was about. None of the crew paid them any attention as the little knot of passengers stood about, gawking at the frantic activity. Finally, Callie MacDonell separated herself from the group and crossed over to where Will and August stood checking their carbines.

"What is this, Captain?" she asked.

"Unknown ship, Callie, tracking north on the other side of that island," Will said nodding toward the low spit of land to the west. "Somewhere ahead there'll be open water. If she turns east toward us, it likely means trouble."

Callie wrinkled her brow.

"Privateer?"

"Don't know rightly, but Keogh is not taking chances."

"Can we outrun them?"

Will shrugged.

"Won't know until she shows herself. The Captain glassed her, but I'm not sure he could see anything but her masts."

"And what if it comes to a fight?"

Will looked her in the eye.

"Gus and I will be aloft," he said, pointing to the tops.

"Taking the high ground," Callie said, eyeing the small platforms thirty feet up. Will grinned.

"A Highland lass would understand that," he said.

She nodded.

"And those of us who aren't combatants?"

"Get yourself to the sterncastle and keep as much oak as you can between you and whatever they send our way."

"And if they sink us?"

Will shook his head.

"They won't do that. They'll be after whatever we have on board and won't want to send any valuables to the bottom. They'll try to board us, but if I know Keogh and Berrycloth, they'll play hell taking the *Fair Wind*."

His words carried far more conviction than he felt, but he saw no profit in frightening the girl. What would happen would happen.

Callie nodded.

"Thank you," she said and started to go, then turned back and laid her hand on his arm.

"God watch over you, William."

Will met her green eyes.

"And you, Callie."

***

She came out of the west, black as a shadow and sleek as a racehorse. She had a lateen sail on a single tall mast and two jibs marking her as a sloop and as soon as she cleared the northern end of the low island, she'd tacked hard to starboard, falling in a league or more behind the *Fair Wind*. There could be little doubt now as to her intentions. She was a privateer and the merchantman was to be her prize.

There'd been few sloops plying the shipping lanes between England and Ireland when Will was a boy, but those he'd seen had been fast—faster than any square-rigger. The fact that the sloop had given chase suggested her captain knew he had the faster boat. The question was, how much faster? For the sun had now dropped below the horizon and twilight was gathering. If the *Fair Wind* could manage to stay ahead of the pursuit for another hour, she might slip away in the darkness.

Will looked astern and could already see that the sloop was gaining on them. With the sails trimmed and the ships eight guns loaded and primed, the *Fair Wind*'s crew stood by waiting for orders and tending to their cutlasses and pistols. If the men on the sloop wanted this ship, they would pay a price in blood for her.

Across the main deck, Will saw that the Binghams had retreated to the relative safety of the sterncastle taking Callie with them, leaving Lieutenant Grey and Mathys Beck gathered at the rail straining to see this mystery ship following in their wake. After a time, Grey broke away and joined Will and August.

"Will they catch us?" he asked nervously.

Will looked back and saw that the sloop was indeed getting closer. Above he saw the evening star hanging above the horizon in the fading light. It would be a close run thing.

"I don't know, Harry. She's fast, but if they don't reach us before full dark, we might give them the slip."

Grey nodded, his face pale.

"I see you've armed yourselves."

"Aye, Mr. Barley has asked us to man the tops and fire on the crew of the sloop if, as seems likely, they prove hostile."

Grey looked up at the platforms swaying high above the deck and shook his head.

"I don't envy you your post," he said, laying a hand on the butt of the pistol jammed in his waistband, "but if it comes to it, I intend to give a good account of myself down here!"

Will nodded.

"I know you will, Harry," he said, then paused. "As you will be here on deck and Gus and I will be in the tops, I would ask a favor of you."

"Of course, Will."

"If they board us, have a care for Miss MacDonell. She's a headstrong girl and may put herself at risk."

That brought a faint smile to Grey's face.

"Of course, Captain. It's only right to be concerned for headstrong girls."

August cleared his throat loudly.

"Pretty ones, too," he muttered.

Will felt his face flush, but knew it would be useless to try to defend his motives. Any denial would only prove the case.

"Thank you, Harry," was the best he could manage.

Grey nodded, then wandered back to the larboard rail to keep watch on the sloop. Will took the opportunity to carefully inspect his carbine. He knew it was unloaded, but checked the pan to be certain there was no powder there. Having checked that all was safe, he cocked the weapon and pulled the trigger. The flint slammed into the frizzen striking a good spark. Satisfied that the gun was ready save only for loading, he wiped a soft cloth over the stock and barrel.

Across the way he noticed Beck kept turning away from the rail and casting glances at him. After a time, the German disappeared into the sterncastle, only to reappear a few minutes later carrying a large bundle in his arms. He crossed the deck to where Will and August sat.

No King, No Country

"Captain, you have been asked to fire on the ship?" he asked, jerking his head toward the stern.

"Yes, if she fires on us, Herr Beck. Mr. Dawes and I will position ourselves up there," he said pointing the tops, "and try to dissuade that sloop from getting too close."

Beck looked up at the small platforms above the mainsail and mizzen sail and hesitated before speaking. Then, as though reaching a decision, he laid his bundle on the deck and kneeling beside it, began untying the leather thongs that secured it. As he undid the bindings, he nodded toward the short carbine laid across Will's legs.

"Carbines, are schlecht, Captain. You could barely hit the ocean with them, but these!"

He threw back the folds of the bundle to reveal three guns. Will had never seen anything like them. They were almost six feet long with stocks of burled maple, intricately carved and polished to a high sheen. There was exquisite scroll work on the lock plates and the barrel itself was octagonal, the metal a dark blue-black.

"Herr Beck!, These are beautiful!" Will exclaimed.

"They are jaeger rifles of my own design, Captain. I felt there would a market for them on the frontier."

"May I?" Will asked.

Beck nodded and Will picked up the weapon. It was heavier than his carbine by a considerable measure, but the balance was perfect and it felt natural in his hands.

"You say it's a rifle? I've heard of such but have never seen one. They say grooves are etched in the barrel." He swung the barrel around and gazed into the muzzle.

"By God, there are!"

Beck nodded.

"Just as fletching makes the arrow to fly true, grooves makes the ball to spin. Spinning ball will fly straight, not flutter like ball from musket or worse—a carbine!"

He reached into his coat pocket and produced a handful of balls and a small wad of cloth patches. He handed one each to Will and August. They each took one of their apostles and poured a measure of powder down the barrel, then slid the rammer from its slot, draped a cloth patch over the muzzle and tamped the ball into the cloth. It took more force to ram the ball home than was the case with a musket or carbine.

"Slow to load," August muttered.

"Ya, Herr Lieutenant, slow, but you will hit what you shoot at—if you aim proper!"

Beck took a moment to explain the open sights of the rifle, a vee shaped piece of iron a third of the way down the barrel and a small stub of brass near the muzzle.

"When stub lines up with bottom of the groove, you shoot!"

The German looked around the deck and saw a discarded biscuit tin by the galley. He carried it across the deck to the starboard rail and set it there. It was twenty-five paces away. Will looked over his shoulder and saw Captain Keogh watching the proceedings with interest.

"Fire away, Captain, but try not to splinter my rail." Keogh said.

Will raised the jaeger rifle. The barrel was a good foot longer than the few matchlock muskets he'd shot and two feet longer than his carbine. He ratcheted the cock back and nestled the butt against his shoulder. Despite its length, the rifle's perfect balance reduced any strain associated with its greater weight. He pointed the muzzle toward the biscuit tin and carefully lined up the front and rear sights. He took a breath, held it and squeezed the trigger.

The cock sprang forward, its flint striking the frizzen and sending a spark into the pan. The rifle barked and grey smoke obscured his vision for a moment. He prided himself in being a good shot with a carbine, but at this distance he would not have expected to strike a target that size more than once in three shots. As the breeze blew away, he saw that the railing was empty.

No King, No Country

"Well done, Captain!" Keogh called from above. "Dead center it looked."

Will shook his head. A weapon like this—what could it do on a battlefield? Pikes would be worthless. Massed muskets would be decimated from afar. He looked at Beck who showed no surprise at the result. The German didn't have to rummage for a new target. The cook brought out an empty bottle and set it on the rail as the crew looked on, curious about this long firearm.

August raised the rifle to his shoulder and squinted down the barrel. The aiming instructions were clear enough and he adjusted the weapon until the stub sat down neatly in the vee. He squeezed off a round. The bottle shattered in a halo of glass shards and the crew raised a spontaneous cheer. August beamed as Will slapped him on the shoulder. He turned to Beck.

"You've built a wonder here, Herr Beck. Will you join us in the tops?"

A look of horror came over the man's face.

"Nein, nein, Captain," he said shaking his head. "Too far up. I cannot stand such a place. You take my rifles up there. I shoot from down here."

Will nodded sympathetically. He'd known boys who quailed at the notion of climbing into the high branches of a tree and men who'd go nowhere near the top of a cliff. His German friend might fear heights, but given the trouble the man had seen, Will doubted he feared much else.

The shooting demonstration complete, the crew of the *Fair Wind* returned to their stations and waited. There was little else to do as the distance between the merchantman and the sloop closed. Overhead, the sky slowly grew darker, but it was late June and the days were long, causing the twilight to linger. The sloop was now less than a half mile astern and gaining steadily.

On deck, the men had grown quiet, with the only sound the hiss of the water rushing past the hull. Then a new sound broke the quiet. A resounding boom echoed across the water and a splash went up fifty yards astern of the *Fair Wind*. The sloop was ranging them.

"Time to get aloft, Gus," Will said.

The two men slung their bandoliers of apostles over their shoulders, stuffed their pockets with lead balls and cloth patches, then crossed the main deck to the shrouds. Will took the mizzen top to place him as close as possible to the stern as Gus clambered up the ratlines to the higher main top. The tops were cramped, but Will hooked an arm through a stay to steady himself against the roll of the ship and braced his left shoulder against the mast. It was an awkward firing position, but stable enough. Below he saw Mathys Beck sprawled on his belly on the starboard side of the quarterdeck, his longer jaeger rifle at the ready. Looking over his shoulder, he saw August had twined his arm around a halyard and braced himself against the mainmast. His friend gave him a wave.

"Luck to you, Will!" he shouted across the distance.

"And to you, Gus!" Will shouted back.

Just then Captain Keogh bawled out an order.

"Mr. Barley, man the stern chaser. You may fire when you judge it time!" he intoned.

"Aye, Captain."

Barley moved to the nine pounder perched as far astern as possible on the quarterdeck. He stared at the sloop as it steadily drew closer. With the experienced eye of a trained gunner he waited until a swell lifted the *Fair Wind*'s stern. then set the smoldering linstock to the touchhole. The ship gave a little shudder as the powder in the chamber ignited and the gun recoiled. Barley leaned out over the stern railing and watched his round fall just off the bow of the sloop.

As he considered his near miss, the gun crew swabbed out the barrel, shoved in another bag of gunpowder and rammed home a new shot. They hauled on the pulleys rolling the nine pounder back into its firing position. Barley stepped forward

No King, No Country

and slid a long quill through the touch hole to prick the powder bag. Then he waited.

The sloop was closer now. He ordered his crew to use two long wooden spars to hoist the rear of the cannon and the old seaman slid a block underneath. He sighted over the top of the gun, and made a small adjustment to the block beneath it. Again he waited for the stern to rise, then touched off a round. All watched as the ball tore a clean hole in one of the sloop's forward jibs.

A moment later the bow chaser on the sloop spit fire and a round ripped through the stern rail three feet from where Barley stood. It sailed through the forest of masts and rigging on the main deck and dropped into the ocean to starboard without hitting another thing. But its damage had already been done. At the stern, Knocker Chance, who'd crewed the stern chaser, lay dead in a pool of blood, the round having cleanly taken off his right arm. Another man staggered away, a jagged splinter the size of a knife blade lodged in his shoulder.

Barley looked about for a replacement as the two remaining crew hauled on the ropes to run out the nine-pounder once more. He yelled at the nearest man who hesitated for a moment then stepped over the dead crewman, picked up the swab and rammed it in the muzzle of the gun.

It was Harry Grey.

The young officer hoisted a powder sack into the muzzle, a surviving member of the gun crew rammed it down and Grey shoved an iron ball into the mouth of the cannon, ramming it home.

"Stand clear, sir," Barley ordered calmly. Grey, realizing he was standing in the path of the gun's recoil, jumped back as Barley pricked the powder bag and sighted down the black barrel.

"Shift 'er t' me, lads!" he bellowed as he raised up. Harry Grey put his shoulder to the rear of the gun and pushed with the rest of the crew.

"Good there!" Barley shouted and, hesitated a beat—long enough for the crew to draw back—then touched off another round. It blasted a ragged hole in the sloop's hull, two feet above the waterline. A ragged cheer went up from the *Fair Wind's* crew at the hit and another when the return round from the sloop did nothing more than put a rip through the fore topsail.

From the mizzen top, Will could see that the hit on the sloop had not slowed the pursuit and as it drew nearer he got a better look at the vessel. It was a daunting sight. There were at least eighteen cannon mounted on the main deck, manned and ready to unleash a broadside if the sloop could draw abreast of the *Fair Wind*. If nine guns tore into her at close range it would rip the hull of the ship into kindling. He guessed that was not the privateer's intent, for gathered between the guns were scores of men, all well-armed. They meant to take the ship, not sink her. If they boarded he knew it would be a bloody affair, but in the end the *Fair Wind* would be taken.

The distance had now closed to two hundred yards and the bow chaser on the sloop barked again. Will felt a shock wave of air as the ball passed within a few feet of him. It hurtled onward clipping ten feet off the main yard. The yard jerked violently, but did not tear free from the main mast. Will's breath caught in his throat as he watched August thrown about like a ragdoll from the impact, saving himself only by clinging to the topsail shrouds. Once he regained his perch he waved at Will as though nothing had happened.

The next round went higher, clipping off the mast head of the foremast.

"They want to demast her," he muttered to himself.

Put a hole in her hull and the whole thing might go to the bottom taking any booty with it. But take down one or more masts and a ship slows or goes dead in the water. Then she can be boarded with ease. It made sense, but for a man

No King, No Country

sitting atop the rearmost mast, the logic of the sloop's tactics was cold comfort.

Below him, Barley fired once more and a new cheer went up from the *Fair Wind's* crew as his round struck one of the sloop's deck-mounted guns, demolishing its carriage and laying low three gunners. But the sloop came on. Will did not know the effective range of this new weapon Herr Beck had given him, but it was time to find out as the sloop crept ever closer.

He raised the rifle to his shoulder and steadied himself, aiming at a man on the sloop's crowded deck then waited for the *Fair Wind* to reach the top of a swell before squeezing off a round. The ball missed his intended target, but the man standing directly behind him lurched backwards and dropped to the deck. Will gave a low whistle. At nearly two hundred yards the bullet had struck within a foot of where he'd aimed! Had it been luck? He shook his head.

He'd never had that kind of luck with a carbine.

Behind him he heard a sharp crack as August discharged his first round. He scanned the sloop's deck and saw a man clutch his arm and spin around. He heard August whoop, excited that he'd hit his mark.

Quickly he set to reloading, his pulse pounding. It was slow and awkward work in the tiny space of the mast top, but he knew with practice it would go quicker. He finished ramming a ball home and poured a pinch of powder in the pan as the sloop's bow chaser sounded again. This shot struck the starboard chains of the mizzen mast, severing the shrouds. Will felt his platform lurch beneath his feet, but the arm he'd wrapped around the stay held him steady. With the starboard shrouds cut, the braces and stays groaned, but they held, keeping the mast almost vertical and its sails functioning.

With a fresh round in the barrel, Will settled himself and aimed once more at the sloop. It had gained another boat's length on the *Fair Wind*, its bowsprit now less than a hundred yards astern. In another ten minutes she'd pull alongside and grappling hooks would be flung across the gap. Once secured, the ship would be boarded. No matter how brave its crew, they could not stand against the scores of men waiting to pour over the rail and seize their prize.

Shooting random targets on the deck of the sloop would not materially change the likely outcome of a boarding, The privateer just had too many men, all experienced fighters no doubt. Now that he knew what this gun could do, he was determined to make every shot count. Once more, he raised the butt of the rifle to his shoulder, picked his target and squeezed the trigger. The man at the sloop's tiller jerked backwards, the tiller falling from his lifeless hands and leaving the rudder free to travel. Like a drunken man, the sloop bore off sharply to starboard, its sails starting to luff. The *Fair Wind* quickly widened the distance between her and her pursuer.

As Will reloaded, he saw a big man scramble to seize the unmanned tiller and put the boat back on its tack. The sloop was starting to respond when Will heard the bark of August's rifle behind him. The new helmsman staggered then toppled over as the sloop once more veered off its close-hauled tack losing steerage and speed.

It was then that Will noticed a tall man in a crimson jacket on the sloop's deck. He was shouting orders and pointing at the tiller, but men shied away from what had become a killing ground. He saw the man in red draw a pistol from his belt and point it at one of his crew. The lucky crewman eased toward the tiller as though it was a hot iron.

Will lowered his rifle and took aim. He had a more valuable target now. Visibility was dropping rapidly in the fading light as he lined up his sights on the flash of crimson near the sloop's helm. The bow chaser on the sloop barked again, but now the round splashed just short of the *Fair Wind's* stern. Will squeezed the trigger and felt the jolt against his shoulder. The man in the red jacket clutched at his arm, but did not go down. He turned and stared at the stern of the *Fair Wind*, his eyes traveling upwards until they reached the mizzen top.

He pointed directly at where Will clung to the tilting mizzen mast and screamed out an order. Will couldn't hear it, but he didn't need to as a dozen muskets rose as one and pointed at him. He lurched backwards, trying to put as much of the mast between him and those raised muzzles as possible. Then a storm of lead balls buzzed through the riggings all around him. Splinters exploded nearby as a few of the musket balls struck the mast and the mizzen top platform. Most flew by harmlessly, poking holes in the mizzen topsail.

The last ball in the volley blasted a smallish splinter from the mizzen mast that lodged in his cheek. He ripped it out and started to reload. Below him, he heard a weapon discharge and saw Mathys Beck roll onto his back and begin reloading. Astern, the sloop again veered off its tack, the German having taken out yet another helmsman.

On the sloop a brave man climbed over the dead bodies and, crouching low, grasped the tiller. He shoved it hard to starboard to try to bring the boat back to its close-hauled tack, but from his crouch he couldn't judge the angle of the wind. The sloop's bow swung around too far, until it was nose-on to the wind. The great triangular sail went slack, then began to flap fitfully as the privateer slowed to a near stop.

"By God, she's in irons!" Berrycloth shouted.

Captain Keogh nodded, a weary smile on his weathered face.

"That she is, Mr. Berrycloth. That she is."

Below him, Will heard the crew raise a relieved cheer, followed instantly by a command from Keogh.

"Silence on deck!" he thundered, and the cheers died away.

From the mizzen top Will watched the sloop recede in the distance until it was lost to sight in the deepening dark. In a quiet voice, but one that carried to every man in the crew, Keogh issued a new command.

"Stand by to come about."

Men laid hands on the braces and waited for the signal.

"Come about!"

The helmsman leaned into the whipstaff and the deck crew hauled on the lines. The nose of the *Fair Wind* passed once more through the wind as she returned to a larboard tack.

Will slumped back against the mast and shook his head. The privateer would not stay in irons for long. They'd get her nose turned about and take up the chase once more, but in the dark her crew wouldn't know that Keogh had already changed course. Where they would be searching, they'd find nothing but empty ocean.

***

The ship's bells were silenced as the *Fair Wind* sailed quietly to the northwest. More islands could be seen off to leeward, their white sand fringes visible even in the dark. Will and August climbed wearily down from their perches in the tops and were met by a beaming Mathys Beck on the main deck. It was the first time Will had seen the German smile.

"Excellent shooting, gentlemen!" he said in stage whisper. "We kill the hand on the tiller—we stop the boat!"

Will threw an arm around the broad shoulders of the stocky German.

"Herr Beck, your rifles! They are…magnificent! They must have an effective range of…."

"Two hundred yards, for a marksman," Beck said finishing his sentence, "and you are that for certain."

"Someday, if I live and prosper, Herr Beck, I will come to Maryland and purchase one of your rifles," Will said as he handed the weapon back to Beck.

Beck handed it back to him.

"You keep for now, Captain. It's a long way yet to Virginia." He turned to August. "You too, Herr Lieutenant."

August nodded his thanks.

Beck made a little bow and made his way back toward the sterncastle as Caledonia MacDonell came out on deck. She frowned when she saw Will in the dim light.

"You're hurt," she said, taking Will's chin in her hand and turning his head to examine the gash left by the splinter in his cheek.

"Get me a lantern and a clean rag," she ordered August, who leapt to comply.

"It was just a splinter," Will said.

"Aye, and a small one it must have been," she agreed looking at his wound in the dim light. "I just helped the cook dig a piece of the stern rail the size of a meat cleaver out of a man's shoulder. It was a jagged mess, but I think he'll live."

August appeared with a lantern and square cloth and Will noticed for the first time the blood on the girl's frock. Callie dipped the cloth in a bucket of sea water and held the lantern over Will's head to have a better look at the gash in his cheek. He winced a little but tried to stay still as she dabbed away the dried blood with the brine. She set down the rag and used her thumb and forefinger to snag a fragment of the mizzen mast still lodged at the edge of the wound.

"There! If it doesn't putrefy, you should be right as rain," she said.

"Obliged, Callie."

"You're welcome, William," she said. "I must get back to help cook. We're sewing up Knocker in his mattress cover. We'll consign him to the deep come morning."

Will nodded. He'd heard the cheerful crewman had lost an arm and died of shock, but he and the *Fair Wind's* crew had had little time to mourn.

"It's a kind thing you're doing, Callie."

The girl just shrugged.

"You did what needed doing in the fight," she said. "I'm doing what needs doing now."

No King, No Country

Pump or Die

Abraham Keogh stood on the quarterdeck keeping a wary eye astern and on the string of islands to leeward, their white sand shorelines just visible in the dim light. It had been nearly an hour since they had broken contact with the privateer, but he knew that jackal of the sea would be out there somewhere, searching. At some point the sloop's captain would realize that the square-rigger had changed its course and would adjust his own. But Keogh was not over worried.

It was a big ocean and a dark night.

As for the islands, he knew the Bahamas angled off to the west as they stretched northward. On an overcast night with no stars to steer by, they pointed like beacons toward the coast of Spanish Florida. They would be his guide.

Their encounter with the privateer had been a close run thing and they'd been fortunate to escape. But Keogh knew their good fortune had not simply been luck. He'd seen musketeers fight from the tops before and they could be deadly at close quarters, but the display put on by his two fugitive Roundheads with Herr Beck's rifles had been a shock. He'd watched at least three men killed or wounded at the helm of the sloop at distances that were hard for him to fathom. Beck, he thought, would get rich selling such weapons in America. He was considering whether he should purchase one of these rifles for himself when he noticed something odd.

As the ship passed over a swell it had seemed to wallow a bit. He'd spent a good many years on the deck of the *Fair Wind* and had never felt it move in this sluggish way. Keogh was not an alarmist, but this strange behavior of his ship put him instantly on edge. He moved to the quarterdeck ladder and summoned Jamie Oakley who was leading the first watch.

"Mr. Oakley, sound the well if you please," he ordered.

"Aye, Cap'n," said Oakley, and hurried over near the main mast where the aperture for the ship's well was located. He picked up the weight attached to a coil of rope and let it fall through the tube until he felt it hit the bottom of the hull with a thud. He quickly drew the line back up, hoping to feel only a few inches of moisture.

In that, he was disappointed.

He hurried back to the quarterdeck. Keogh met him at the top of the ladder.

"Three feet wet, Cap'n," Oakley reported.

Keogh nodded. No wonder the ship was moving so listlessly. All wooden vessels leaked and the *Fair Wind* was no exception, but in a calm sea, there should not have been even a foot of water in the bilge. Somewhere below her waterline, the *Fair Wind's* hull had been breached.

"Call out the crew, Mr. Oakley, and fetch Mr. Berrycloth."

***

Will and August turned out as soon as Oakley sounded the alarm, wondering if the sloop had somehow managed to find them in the pitch dark. When they arrived on deck, it was clear there was a problem of a different sort.

"Middle watch, man the pumps!" Berrycloth ordered. "Morning watch, stand by to relieve."

"Are we sinking?" August whispered.

"Don't know, Gus, but we must be taking on water."

No King, No Country

As the men went below to man the pumps, Will saw Jamie Oakley conferring with Berrycloth. When the old sailor broke away, Will intercepted him.

"What's happening, Jamie?"

"She's holed below the waterline. Barley thinks it was the last ball from the sloop. Thought it missed us, but must 'a struck the stern. We've three feet in the bilges and rising. If we can pump out enough, we might get to the hole and plug it. If not…"

Oakley turned to head below, but Will touched his arm.

"What can we do?"

"If ye want t'be useful, follow me and bring a lantern," Oakley said as he headed to the ladder leading to the tween deck and the hold. Will and August followed him, grabbing a lantern as they went. Below deck the men of the middle watch began the back-breaking work of operating the bilge pump. Four men at a time grasped the long wooden spar of the pump handle and began to lever it up and down, pulling the foul water of the bilge up from beneath the deck and out the scuppers. Oakley led them past the bilge pump toward the stern then down a ladder to the bottom of the ship's hold, where Will was alarmed to see water beginning to seep up through the decking at his feet.

Oakley shook his head.

"She's down at the stern."

"Can you fix it?" August asked, looking nervously at the damp deck. Above them they could hear the men on the pumps begin a chant and, with each stroke of the pump's arm, the sound of water gurgling up through the pipe.

"Depends," Oakley said. "If the hole is small enough, the pump might get ahead of the leak and bring the water in the bilge down enough to get back there and plug her."

Oakley cocked his head, listening to the water being sucked up and looking at the puddles forming on the deck and shook his head.

"But I doubt it."

Inspection complete, Oakley headed back up the ladder with Will and August right behind and was met by the first mate on the tween deck.

"Looks bad," Oakley said. He had August carry the lantern back down the ladder and Berrycloth peered at the rising water in the hold.

"Can't get to her?"

Oakley just shook his head.

"Right then. We'll take a look over the side," the first mate said, then beckoned to Will and August.

"You two with me."

***

Berrycloth led the two men up to the quarterdeck and back to the stern railing, half of which had been blown away by the round that killed Knocker Chance. He'd brought a coil of rope with him and looped it around his waist, tying it off with a bowline knot. August looked at Will and then at Berrycloth.

"Makes no sense to send you, Mr. Berrycloth," he said. "No offense, but you're as big as an ox. Not sure Will and I could hoist ye back up. I should go."

Berrycloth eyed him.

"Can ye swim?" he asked.

August laughed.

"Yes, but this ain't the River Weaver, so let's not find out how well. Make that knot a good one."

The first mate nodded and undid his bowline before looping the rope around August's waist and retying the knot.

"Very well, lad. All's we need to know is how far below the water line and how big the hole. We'll lower ye slow till yer up to yer waist. When yer ready t' go under, give us the signal and we'll play out some slack. You find that hole, then pull yerself back up t' the surface. We'll do the rest."

August nodded. Without a word he climbed over the remaining rail and handed the end of the rope to Berrycloth. The first mate took up the slack, and nodded to the smaller

No King, No Country

man. Will stepped in behind Berrycloth and looped the rope once around the breach of the nine pounder. He'd be damned if they'd lose August Dawes at sea.

Together they began to ease August over the side and into the dark. Berrycloth kept a close eye on him as he walked backwards down the stern of the *Fair Wind* until he reached the sea a good twenty feet below. August hesitated there for a moment, as the ship's wake foamed whitely around his ankles. Then he signaled to Berrycloth to let out more line. The big man played out the rope hand over hand as August slid into the foaming wake until only his head and shoulders were visible. He looked up.

"Slack!" he yelled and took a deep breath.

The men on deck played out the rope around the cannon and over the rail as August slid under the water. Long seconds passed as the men on the quarterdeck peered over the rail, searching the spot where the line disappeared into the dark water. It had been nearly a minute when August's head burst above the surface. He sucked in air then looked up at Berrycloth.

"Another three feet," he ordered, taking a deep breath and sinking once more below the surface as Will and the first mate played out more line. Silently, they began counting the seconds. At sixty, Will looked at Berrycloth.

"Not yet, Captain. Not yet," the first mate said.

They counted another thirty and were bracing to haul August up whether he wanted to or not, when the man burst back to the surface, gasping.

"Up!" he ordered and the two began hauling him back up to the quarterdeck. As he flopped over the rail they helped loosen the rope around his waist.

"The hole…it's big…" he said between huge gulps of air. "Four feet wide by two feet."

Berrycloth shook his head.

"Too big for the pumps to hold."

Together they crossed the quarterdeck to where Keogh stood waiting above the steerage room. When he reached the Captain, Berrycloth shook his head.

"It's a big one, Captain. Looks to 'a missed the rudder by just three feet. Pumps won't do."

"Fothering?" Keogh asked.

Will had heard the term before. It involved dragging a section of canvas sail laced with rope strands over the breach and letting the water pressure force it into the hole.

Berrycloth shook his head again.

"Too big," he said "and might foul the rudder."

Keogh nodded.

"Never works well on the stern in any case. How far below the waterline?"

Berrycloth turned to August who was dripping water at his feet.

"Three feet at the top, five at the bottom, Captain."

"Thank you, Lieutenant Dawes. Mr. Berrycloth, we will find a spot to go aground before we sink. Tides are five feet or so in these waters. We have thirteen feet of draft and may settle another foot through the night as we take on more seawater. Come morning, we find a nice soft patch of sand to run her aground at high tide. At the ebb, the hole should be clear. Then we work like hell to plug it. In the meantime, keep the pumps going."

"Aye, sir," Berrycloth said and headed for the tween deck.

Keogh looked at the two men still standing there.

"We'll need every able-bodied man to work the pumps and sail the ship, gentlemen. Please organize the male passengers to assist."

***

Will, August, Mathys Beck and Harry Grey relieved four men of the middle watch at the pump and levered the heavy handle up and down for fifteen minutes until relieved in their turn. Sir James Bingham had refused to join them. Every fifteen minutes they returned to their labors and as the night wore on, hands blistered and backs protested from the strain, though no man faltered.

During the long night men lost all track of time. No ship's bell sounded to mark the watches as the *Fair Wind* sailed quietly on. Will had lost count of their turns at the pump and during a break went up on deck to get some air. He was surprised to see the grey light of dawn. He walked to the larboard rail and saw that the *Fair Wind* was easing through a narrow channel between a string of small islands. Standing in the portside chains, a crewman was sounding, calling out depths as the lead touched bottom.

"By the mark, five!" he called.

Thirty feet, Will calculated in his head. *Too deep*.

As he started back down to the tween deck, he heard the next sounding.

"And a half, three!" he sang out.

Shallowing fast.

"All hands brace!" Keogh commanded from the quarterdeck and the command was echoed across the deck and to the men on the pumps below.

Will gripped the rail of the ladder between the decks and braced himself.

"And a quarter two!"

There was a rasping sound as the keel began to slide along a sandbar. A moment later he was thrown forward as the *Fair Wind* lurched to a stop, heeling over just a bit to larboard. A strange silence fell over the ship for a moment, broken quickly by Mr. Berrycloth who ordered the forenoon watch into the yards to furl the sails.

The first mate saw Will standing at the ladder.

"Six hours to ebb tide, Mr. Inness," he said. "We must pump till then."

Aground

Foul water poured from the *Fair Wind's* scuppers as the men at the pump kept up their labor through the long morning while the tide slowly receded. Those not working the pump arm lay exhausted on the tween deck from the long night and morning of unrelenting labor.

The gash in the stern of the vessel came into view by late morning, but there was no letup in the pumping. The ship's carpenter had torn up deck planking in the ship's hold to get at the breach, but the braces needed to shore up the hole had to be set in the bilge, which was still waist deep in water. They had two, maybe three hours to drain the bilge and plug the hole before the tide rose once more above the breach in the ship's stern. With luck, the *Fair Wind* would be water tight by then, or at least floatable when the next high tide came near sunset. Captain Keogh was prepared to attach a cable to the pinnace and have the small boat haul her off the sandbar if the tide alone did not refloat her.

Relieved at the pump, Will and August had gone up on deck. They lay back against the fo'c'sle bulkhead awaiting their next turn at the pumps. August held up his hands. They were rubbed bloody.

"You'd think I'd been a bloody clerk all these years," he said wearily.

Will didn't answer. His own hands burned like fire and every muscle in his body ached. A few feet away, Harry Grey was curled up on his side, sound asleep. He looked hardly more than a boy lying there. But these last days had tested the Lieutenant's mettle and had not found him wanting. Grey had stepped in when the crew of the sternchaser had been blown to ribbons by a ball from the sloop's gun. And later, when they'd been called on to pump for their very lives, he'd neither flagged nor complained through the long night. Whatever the lad thought of himself, Will now knew that Harry Grey was a man to be counted on.

Near August, Mathys Beck, who'd taken his turns at the pump handle with the younger men, stood up and marched in place for a few moments pumping his arms. Will looked at him and shook his head. Beck saw the look and threw his arms wide, taking in a deep breath of the morning air.

"Best to keep blood flowing," the German said and continued with his exercises.

Across the way, he saw the other knots of weary men sprawled out across the deck suddenly stir and rise painfully to their feet. He turned to see the cook and Callie MacDonell emerging from the fo'c'sle. In their wake, two men staggered forward, carrying a burden slung between them. It was the mortal remains of Knocker Chance, killed when the privateer's cannon shot took off his arm.

The body was sewn up in a shroud made from the cover of his thin mattress. His two shipmates set Knocker down gently on the deck. Captain Keogh came down from the quarterdeck and stood over the sad remains. He took off his hat and cleared his throat, then spoke in a husky voice.

"Arthur Chance, known to ye all as Knocker, was a good sailor. He was a dependable man, in fair weather and foul. Knocker never shirked his duty. May God keep him."

Finishing his eulogy, Keogh made his way back up to the quarterdeck while the members of the crew not employed on the pump walked gravely by the corpse to pay their last respects to their shipmate. Will watched Callie MacDonell cross herself then lean over and speak to John Berrycloth. The first mate nodded, then addressed the crew.

"We need to lay Knocker to rest, lads, but we can't be droppin' him over the side in but six feet of water. I'll want a detail to row the pinnace over to dry land and bury the poor sod. He can't stay here."

No one challenged Berrycloth's assertion or his plan for seeing off Knocker. It would be hours yet before the ship was repaired, refloated on the rising tide and reached deep water for a proper burial at sea. And though the tropical sun was low in the eastern sky, soon enough it would be blazing overhead. A body would get ripe quickly in the heat. Will climbed to his feet and tried not to groan with the stiffness in his arms and shoulders. August followed him.

"We'll see him buried proper," Will said.

Berrycloth nodded.

"Pick a burial detail, Mr. Inness. I'll order the pinnace lowered over the side."

Will scanned the men on deck. Those not present were attending to duties onboard or working the pumps below.

"I'll take you two," Will said, pointing to Jamie Oakley and Daisy Meadows.

Before he could pick another man, Harry Grey raised a weary hand.

"I'll go. Anything to stay off the damned pump."

"And I," chimed in Mathys Beck. "It will be good to touch ground once more, even if it is but sand."

With August, he had his detail. As men went about lowering the pinnace over the side, Bill Barley appeared with a long-handled shovel.

"It's all we have, Cap'n. Use it t' shovel shit out of the hold when we carry livestock."

Will nodded. It would do for sand. As the detail gathered by the larboard rail, Mathys Beck appeared carrying his jaeger rifle, a bag of powder and a bag of shot.

"Expecting trouble, Herr Beck?" Will asked.

"Always," the German replied without a smile.

Will looked at August, who nodded.

No King, No Country

"I'll fetch ours," he said.

***

The island to starboard of the grounded ship was closer, so the burial detail rowed over and hauled the pinnace up on a small strip of white sand tucked along a shore thick with mangroves. Two large wading birds burst from cover as they hoisted Knocker out of the boat, so startling Daisy Meadows that he almost lost his grip on the shroud.

They picked their way inland for fifty paces through thick brush until they found a small clearing with a patch of shade beneath a stunted tree. Then they set about digging. It was hot work and each man took his turn on the shovel. An hour later they had a suitable grave dug. They gently lowered Knocker in and Daisy said a few words.

"Cap'n Keogh said it good and I've little to add. Knocker was a good shipmate and a friend. He owed me two shilling three pence, but I say let bygones be. I hope old Knocker finds a safe harbor on the other side."

With that they filled in the grave and marked it with a rude cross made of driftwood and lashed together with vines. Their mournful duty done, they were making their way back to the pinnace when all froze at once. Off to the left, above the strip of mangroves that fringed the island, the top of a single tall mast could clearly be seen coming up the same channel the *Fair Wind* had used to find her grounding spot.

"The privateer?" Harry Grey whispered.

"Maybe," Will said. It was a big ocean and hard to believe the privateer had managed to find them once they'd lost contact in the night, but what other single-masted ship was this likely to be?

"What'll we do, Will?" Grey asked. Will turned to see all of the men were looking to him. It was a look he'd seen many times on the battlefields of the war.

"Get the pinnace out of sight," he ordered and that simple command galvanized the burial detail. They raced down to the tiny patch of beach and hauled the small boat up from the water's edge and into the cover of the mangroves. There they waited and watched. Soon enough the black-hulled sloop appeared around the edge of the island, like a wolf that had run its prey to ground..

***

Callie MacDonell came on deck when she heard the lookout shout that a sail was in sight. She heard Mr. Berrycloth order all hands to their stations and all around her, men raced to obey. Climbing up the ladder to the quarterdeck she joined Captain Keogh at the stern railing.

At first all that could be seen was a single tall mast, the rest being hidden by the small island where the burial detail was laying poor Knocker Chance to rest. The grim look on the Captain's face told the girl to expect the worst, but her heart still sank as around a point of the island the black sloop of the privateer sailed into view.

The ship had a shallower draft than the square-rigged *Fair Wind*, but its captain was taking no chances in the narrow channel. He stayed in deeper water a half cable's length away, turning the sloop broadside to the stranded ship and dropping anchor. From this position, he had nine cannon that could turn the *Fair Wind* into a smoking patch of driftwood in minutes if he gave the order.

As though to leave no doubt as to that point, fire spat from a single cannon on the sloop's deck, the round landing thirty yards off the *Fair Wind's* larboard quarter and sending up a geyser of sand and seawater.

Bill Barley and his crew had been standing by their nine pounder at the stern rail when the cannon on the privateer fired. The old gunner blew life into the coal of his linstock fuse and prepared to return fire, but Keogh ordered him to stand down.

"Can't fight a broadside with a sternchaser, Mr. Barley," Keogh said quietly. "Ask Mr. Berrycloth to run up a white flag on the mizzen."

No King, No Country

Barley grumbled but hurried to follow Keogh's order. In due course a patch of white cloth was hoisted to the mizzen masthead. It didn't take long for the privateer to respond. As soon as the white flag was flown, a boat was lowered over the sloop's side and ten men clambered down the jack ladder, two taking up positions at the oars, one manning the tiller, one taking a spot in the bow and the rest finding places forward and aft of the oarsmen. Once all were settled, the tillerman shoved off from the black hull of the privateer and the oarsmen began to pull toward the grounded ship. Keogh turned and beckoned to Berrycloth.

"Lower a ladder, John."

"Aye, Cap'n."

"Miss MacDonell, you should alert your mistress and her brother that we are to be boarded."

Callie nodded.

"What will they do with us, Captain?"

Keogh shook his head.

"I don't know, lass. I don't know."

Callie knew the Captain had much to consider and left him alone with his thoughts. When she reached the main deck she looked off to starboard toward the island where Will Inness and his detail were burying Knocker Chance. She'd seen the ship's boat pulled up on a narrow strip of sand there when she'd first come on deck. Now it was gone. Its disappearance meant that the men on the island had seen the danger and concealed themselves.

If they stayed hidden they might escape whatever fate awaited those still aboard the *Fair Wind*. Perhaps they'd even be able to sail the pinnace to the nearest friendly port and report the loss of their ship. But little good that would do for those who were about to fall into the privateer's hands.

Good for them, she thought, *but no help for us*.

***

"Surrendered?"

Anne Bingham blinked as though she didn't understand the word as Callie gave her the grim news.

"Aye, miss. Captain Keogh had no choice."

Anne Bingham wrang her hands.

"Why have we given up? You must go to the Captain immediately and demand we resist!"

"Miss, we can bring but one gun to bear, while the privateer has nine I'm told. If we fight, we will die."

At that moment, Sir James entered his sister's cramped berth. He looked agitated, but tried to speak calmly.

"Anne, this will be alright. You must stay calm. These freebooters are only interested in money and will no doubt ransom us."

And leave me to my fate, Callie thought.

"They won't... violate us?" Anne asked, her voice breaking.

"No, no, Anne. They may not be gentlemen, but they will not jeopardize a ransom payment by something so vile."

Sir James sat down beside his sister on her narrow bed and threw an arm around her as she began to sob quietly and shudder. Callie eased out of the berth and made her way back to the tiny nook where she slept. She sat on her bed and took a deep breath, fighting the wave of despair that threatened to overwhelm her. What would these privateers do with a young woman no one would ransom? The possibilities were bleak. But whatever her fate, she was certain of one thing.

She would face it like a MacDonell of Glengarry.

***

From the cover of the mangroves the men on the island watched the boat shove off from the black sloop and pull toward the *Fair Wind*. Will studied the deck of the privateer and could see a tall man in a red coat watching the proceedings, a black boot planted on the sloop's starboard rail. This was the man who'd been giving the orders during the fight at sea. He was sure he'd winged this man with a shot from the mizzen top, but the sloop's commander looked none the worse for it as he watched his boat tie up at the *Fair Wind*.

Whoever this privateer was, Will had to give him credit for his seamanship. Finding a ship, even a three-master like the *Fair Wind*, in this multitude of islands was impressive. As he studied the sloop, Mathys Beck crawled up beside him and braced his jaeger rifle on the low branch of a mangrove.

"I can shoot him from here," he whispered to Will.

Will shook his head. He had already thought of that and had dismissed the idea. It was a very long shot, over two hundred yards and whether they hit or missed, they would give away their location. In their current position it was best the privateer didn't know that some of the *Fair Wind's* crew were not aboard their ship. It wasn't much of an advantage, but it was the only one they had at present.

"No, Mathys. We wait."

Waiting was not a thing that came naturally to him. When faced with a problem, he always felt compelled to act, not to wait, but war had done much to temper that in him. Act too hastily and men died.

"For what do we wait, Captain?" Mathys asked.

For that, he had no good answer—yet.

***

The emissary from the privateer climbed over the larboard railing and surveyed the crew gathered on the main deck. He was as tall as John Berrycloth, but unlike the *Fair Wind's* first mate, he was thin as a rail and dressed as though attending a military ball. He straightened his short jacket that was adorned with silver braid, adjusted the green sash around his waist, then stepped aside as a half dozen heavily armed men from the sloop followed him over the rail, fanning out and standing with weapons leveled at the crew. Keogh and Berrycloth stepped forward and the Captain spoke.

"Abraham Keogh, Captain of the English ship *Fair Wind*." He nodded toward his mate. "John Berrycloth, first mate."

The emissary nodded in return.

"I am Pieter Van Wyke, first mate of the *Donker Nacht*," he began in good English but with a distinct accent. "Captain Baltazar de Graff sends his compliments."

"You're Dutch?" Keogh asked.

"I am, as is my captain, though we have a good many English amongst our crew."

"English, Dutch, it's all the same to me."

Van Wyke raised an eyebrow.

"It's said the English corsairs treat their own merchants leniently. Taking their goods, but not their ships or their lives. Would you not expect favorable treatment from your own countrymen?"

"I'm Irish, so I expect nothing from the English."

Van Wyke sniffed at that.

"Ireland, the island full of unruly Catholics."

"Only to foreigners who seek to lord it over us. Now what may I do for you, Mr. Van Wyke?"

The tall Dutchman smiled now, but there was no warmth in it.

"You will place all weapons by the main mast. My men will search your vessel. We will take note of your cargo and if we find weapons, one of your crew will be shot. You will complete repairs on your stern with dispatch and you will bring out your passengers now. They will accompany me back to the *Donker Nacht* to be interviewed by Captain de Graff. That's what you can do for me, Captain!"

***

Callie MacDonell sat quietly as the privateer's pinnace was rowed back to the sloop. She had not been treated roughly by the Dutch officer or his men, though some had made crude remarks when she and Anne Bingham had climbed down the jack ladder to the small boat, revealing more of their stockinged legs than propriety would wish. Even this mild abuse halted as soon as the pinnace tied up to the black hull of the privateer. Waiting at the top of the ladder for the three prisoners was a man of striking appearance.

Captain Baltazar de Graff was a remarkably handsome man with a square jaw, bright blue eyes and golden hair falling in ringlets to his shoulders. He wore a scarlet coat that hung to his knees where the hem met the top of shiny boots of fine black leather. If ever a man looked the part of a dashing pirate, Callie thought, this privateer captain did. Once Sir James and the ladies had assembled on the deck of the sloop, de Graff gave a formal bow.

"Welcome to my ship," he said. "I know you must be anxious as to your fate, but you may put your mind to ease. I will not cut your throat!" This he said with a grin as he drew a finger slowly across his neck.

As his crew burst into laughter, Anne Bingham fainted dead away, saved from collapsing only by the quick reaction of her brother who caught her as she fell and lowered her gently to the deck. The privateer captain looked genuinely concerned. He bent over Anne as her eyes fluttered open and patted her hand.

"My pardon, miss. It was but a jest. You are entirely safe with me. We need only to establish what your ransom shall be, receive the funds and release you on your way. It rarely takes more than three months."

At that news, Anne Bingham fainted again.

"What is wrong with this woman?" de Graff demanded.

"She has a fragile constitution," Sir James said as he gently slapped Anne's face to revive her.

De Graff stood up, put his hands on his hips and shook his head.

"It's going to be a long three months," he said to no one in particular. Then he looked at Callie MacDonell and smiled.

"Or perhaps not."

***

On the island, the burial detail watched the privateer's pinnace carry the *Fair Wind's* passengers, prisoners now, back to the sloop. Will felt a pang of fear and rising anger as he watched Callie MacDonell sitting proud and tall in the small boat as Anne Bingham cowered in her brother's arms. He wanted to launch their own boat and intercept the privateer's vessel, but he knew that would only end in disaster, so he did nothing. He watched as Anne climbed up the ladder and disappeared over the sloop's rail.

He had to think.

***

Jan Verbeek climbed over the rail of the captured square-rigger and looked around. Behind him, a man with a pistol and a cutlass took up station scanning the crew for any sign of trouble, but Verbeek expected none. Before he shoved off from the *Donker Nacht*, Van Wyke had assured him that this prize would be no trouble. And it had been his experience that all the fight went out of these merchant vessels as soon as their white flag went up. Besides, Van Wyke's men had gathered up all the weapons on board, so they'd have nothing to fight with even if inclined to. Verbeek beckoned to a huge man on the main deck who fit the description he'd been given of the *Fair Wind's* first mate.

"Are yer repairs complete?" he asked.

"Our carpenter sent word he's finished his shoring in the bilge and the hull is watertight," Berrycloth said.

Verbeek nodded and looking around the deck he noticed something missing.

"Where's yer ship's boat?" he asked.

"Lost," Berrycloth replied. "Your bow chaser blew it to splinters yesterday. We tossed what was left over the side."

The Dutchman let his eyes rove over the deck of the merchantman as though to verify the first mate's claim.

He'd been ordered to ferry the captured crew of the ship over to the nearest island and leave them there. He'd come in the sloop's small boat, but had hoped to use the *Fair Wind's* pinnace to make the job move more quickly. But there was no boat in sight.

"Pity. This'll take longer then. Line up yer crew, twelve to a bunch. Any man among them with good skills may join us if Cap'n Baltazar approves. The rest will be marooned."

"We'll need water," Berrycloth said.

The man hooted.

"That's none of my concern."

"We'll have a hogshead of water, or we'll not go."

The voice came from behind him and Verbeek whirled around to see a short man dressed all in black standing there with a pistol trained on him. He silently cursed Van Wyke for missing a weapon in his search of the ship. Verbeek's eyes darted to his escort who had his pistol pointed at the man in black, but was vexed to see the big first mate had stepped in close to his man and had a knife pricking his ribs.

This sudden show of resistance was annoying. He wished that that tarted-up dandy Van Wyke could see this! Of course this little rebellion would come to naught. The captain and first mate had but a pistol and a knife, while his captain had nine cannon trained on the *Fair Wind*. An unequal fight to say the least. As he stared down the barrel of Keogh's pistol, his annoyance grew.

"Kill me and Cap'n Baltazar'll blow ye out of the water and leave ye for the sharks!"

"But you'll be dead all the same, won't you?" Keogh said calmly. "You put us on one of these islands with no fresh water and we'll all be dead in three days, so we have nothing to lose."

Verbeek glared at the Captain, but then saw something in the man's eyes.

This fool will pull the trigger, he realized.

"My water?" Keogh asked calmly, keeping his gun trained on Verbeek.

The Dutchman sighed. Baltazar would surely have him and his man flogged for being taken off guard like this, but there was no need for the captain to learn of the incident. His man with the knife in his ribs certainly wouldn't say a word.

No point dying over a barrel of water, he thought.

"Very well, one barrel, but be quick about it," he said.

Keogh nodded and lowered his pistol. Across the deck, Berrycloth slid his blade into his belt. Verbeek nodded to his escort, who un-cocked his pistol and shoved it in his belt.

An unspoken understanding had been reached,

Within minutes a sling was fashioned and a barrel of water lowered into the sloop's boat. Once the water was secured, Keogh ordered ten men into pinnace. Verbeek climbed down and took up his position at the tiller, his guard sitting beside him on the bench nervously watching his passengers. There was a freshening southern breeze and that decided his course. He'd drop the prisoners on the island to the south. It was a bit farther away, but the wind was in his favor. The prisoners could bend their backs rowing against the headwind and he'd sail back to the *Donker Nacht* with the wind at his back.

Captain Baltazar had decided to sell the merchantman and its cargo in Santa Domingo or perhaps in Spanish Florida as the ship was too slow for privateering work. Verbeek had been ordered to shuttle the dozen men of the prize crew from the sloop over to the English ship once he'd dropped his first load of prisoners on the island. He'd be happy to do so. Let them deal with the troublesome captain and mate of the *Fair Wind*!

***

Will saw the sloop's boat return to the *Fair Wind* and in due course, a barrel was hoisted over the side followed by crewmen from the captured ship. The small boat shoved off

No King, No Country

and headed south toward the island on the opposite side of the channel.

Will was both relieved and troubled at the sight. Daisy Meadows had mournfully predicted the crew would all be slaughtered outright, but Jamie Oakley had felt confident they'd simply be put ashore and left to die. It appeared that Jamie had been right and that was a relief, but he'd hoped the crew would be marooned on the island where he and his detail lay hidden. Instead the crew was being taken to the island on the far side of the channel. He would have welcomed the help and advice of Captain Keogh and John Berrycloth, but that was not to be. August watched the small boat pulling away toward the other side of the channel and turned to his friend.

"Looks like we're on our own, Will."

***

It took most of the afternoon to ferry the crew of the *Fair Wind* to the island and replace them with the prize crew from the *Donker Nacht*. None of Keogh's men sought to join the crew of the privateer. Aboard the *Fair Wind*, Pieter Van Wyke surveyed his new command with satisfaction. He'd long thought he should captain his own privateer. After all, a captain's share of booty was twice that of a first mate's and why should Baltazar have a seaside mansion in Tortuga while he had a few rooms in the port town? Perhaps this was his opportunity. Should this merchantman he now commanded somehow lose contact with the *Donker Nacht* in the night, it would be a simple thing to make for a different port, sell her and buy a fast sloop of his own.

Of course, he must be cautious. If Baltazar had any inkling of his ambitions, he'd be hung from the yardarm after hot irons had been applied to places on his body he chose not to think of. But life was risk was it not? As he stood on the quarterdeck of the square-rigger he felt the slightest movement beneath his feet. Sunset and high tide was an hour away, but the *Fair Wind* was beginning to stir.

***

All afternoon Will watched the sloop's pinnace shuttle the crew of the *Fair Wind* to the island south of the channel and bring over men from the privateer to take control of the square-rigger. Meanwhile, the waves that lapped gently on the strip of sand to his front broke further and further up the beach as the tide rose.

"She'll float off in another hour," Daisy Meadows observed sullenly as he watched the tide rise around the ship.

Will didn't answer. He'd been thinking furiously since the sloop dropped anchor on how to rescue this situation, but had not yet seen a way. But one thing was clear to him—whoever controlled the eighteen guns on the privateer would determine how this all ended.

He'd been encouraged as he watched two dozen men transfer from the sloop to the *Fair Wind*. But that still left at least twenty men aboard the sloop, and boarding her seemed impossible. The sloop lay a good two hundred yards off shore. There was no way to cross that distance in their boat without being seen and blown out of the water. Their chances would be better on a dark night, but high tide would come around sunset and the *Fair Wind* might well float free by early evening. Then both vessels were likely to make sail and leave them and the rest of the English crew to their fate, not to mention putting any chance of rescue for the imprisoned passengers out of reach.

Frustrated, he turned away from staring at the two vessels in the channel. At that moment a strong gust of wind swept across the channel from the south rippling the placid water and sending a spray of loose sand to pepper the mangrove leaves around him. Men shielded their eyes and turned away from the blast. It died as suddenly as it had come, but in its wake a low rumble followed.

Will turned back to look at the channel. Beyond the narrow strip of water and the island that bounded it on the south, black thunderclouds had appeared.

No King, No Country

"That's a bad blow comin'," Daisy observed as he stared at the southern horizon.

Jamie Oakley sniffed at the wind and nodded his agreement. He jerked a thumb toward the sloop.

"They'll not make sail in this. Not when they can lay up in a protected anchorage."

Will looked back at the black-hulled sloop, tugging now at its anchor in the growing breeze and for the first time since he'd seen the privateer come up the channel, he had a glimmer of hope.

Wayne Grant

The Donker Nacht

The storm came on fast, boiling out of the south with bolts of lightning leaping across the cloud tops and sheets of rain blown sideways by the wind. Captain Baltazar de Graff had seen it coming and knew they could not weigh anchor and sail for Santa Domingo until this weather passed. He ordered his pinnace hauled up and secured on deck. Even in a protected anchorage a storm like this could roil the water enough to smash a small boat to splinters against the sloop's hull.

As his crew set about securing the lines and equipment on deck he looked up the channel at the square-rigger that was only now starting to lift off the sandbar. Getting the fat merchantman off the bottom and into deeper water in this blow would be tricky. There was a danger the storm could drive the ship into shallower water and beach her for good. He'd sent his first mate over with half of the sloop's crew to man his prize and was anxious to see how they fared, but as the sky darkened and the wind driven rain swept across the channel, he could barely see the *Fair Wind*.

Van Wyke is on his own, he thought.

De Graff scanned the deck and rigging of his own vessel and, satisfied that the *Donker Nacht* was secured against the gale, kept two men topside to keep watch and sent the bulk of the crew below to get out of the weather. Wavetops were already beginning to splash over the side of the sloop and wash across the deck.

He ordered the two men left topside to finish sealing the hatches with canvas and wooden battens. That task was barely completed when the storm redoubled its fury. Waves were now cresting over the gunwales of the sloop and eddying ankle-deep around the mast and the raised frames of the hatches.

De Graff retreated into the sterncastle, leaving one unfortunate man to stand watch on deck and ordering the other to take up station outside Van Wyke's small cabin, where his prisoners were now confined. Down a narrow hall was his own, more spacious cabin. In between was a small nook where his steward Mateo was quartered, ever ready to answer his captain's summons.

He paused at the door of the first mate's cabin and thought he could still hear moaning inside. He shook his head and wondered if anyone would be willing to pay good money for such a childish woman. But her brother had confessed that his sister was betrothed to Sir Thomas Lunsford, the Captain General of Virginia's colonial militia.

Lunsford's name was not unknown to de Graff. Another Dutch privateer had foundered near the mouth of the Cheseapeak Bay two years ago and Lunsford had hanged the few survivors. The Captain General had also acquired large tracts of land along the James River and was said to be the second or third wealthiest man in Virginia. Surely that meant a rich pay day.

But God's breath, the woman was irritating!

If she kept up this caterwauling much longer he'd be tempted to sell her to a brothel in Tortuga. He made his way down the narrow corridor and into his own cabin, beating the rain off his hat and settling down into the high-backed leather chair he'd taken from a Spanish galleon earlier in the spring. He slipped off his soaked red coat and poked gingerly at the bandage around his left arm. He lifted it and sniffed, but smelled no putrefaction.

He was curious about this wound. Someone on that square-rigger had shot him at a distance far beyond the range of a musket. True, a musket ball aimed in the general direction of the sloop might chance to strike him, but he was certain this shot was no accident. He'd seen a man in the mizzen top and another in the main top of the merchantman. They'd both had what looked to be muskets. But no muskets he'd ever seen could have shot dead two of his men at the sloop's tiller at that range. His wound and the two dead tillermen were proof enough that somewhere on that square-rigger was a weapon that could kill at astonishing distances—and he wanted it.

When Van Wyke had returned with a mound of surrendered weapons from the *Fair Wind*, he sorted through them anxiously, but had seen nothing out of the ordinary. He'd casually asked the brother of the weeping wench about this, but the man was unaware of any such weapon aboard the ship.

He sighed and pulled a cord that would summon his steward. As he waited for his man he felt the *Donker Nacht* buck like a wild horse at the end of its anchor chain. It was going to be a rough night, but he was happy to be in this sheltered channel while the storm blew through. If the merchantman survived the night, they'd weigh anchor at first light and sail for Santo Domingo.

His steward, Mateo Rosales, knocked gently on his cabin door and entered. Mateo was the only Spaniard on his crew. In addition to his excellent service as a steward, he was often called in as a translator when demanding the surrender of a Spanish ship or interrogating its passengers and crew.

"Wine, Mateo," he murmured.

Mateo bobbed his head and turned to go, but de Graff had another thought.

No King, No Country

"Bring two glasses and fetch the servant girl in Van Wyke's cabin." Mateo gave him a sly smile and backed out of the cabin.

Servant girls always pay more attention to what's going on around them than their masters do. They have to. Perhaps this girl would know something of this strange weapon he sought. And if she couldn't provide information, perhaps she could be of some other service. She was a strikingly beautiful young woman after all and unlikely to bring much of a ransom. And on the *Donker Nacht,* all had to pay their freight, one way or another.

***

On the island, men took what shelter they could amongst the mangroves as wind and rain lashed at them. As night fell it became difficult to see either the *Fair Wind* or the privateer, but that suited Will. If they couldn't see the ships in the channel, then lookouts on the ships couldn't see them. As the first rain squall hit, he'd gathered his burial detail together and turned to Jamie Oakley.

"You're a waterman, Jamie. Could you get the pinnace down the channel in this?"

Oakley turned and looked through the mangroves at the growing chop in the narrow waterway. He rubbed his chin.

"Might make it," he said, "or might swamp. Why'd ye want to be boatin' down the channel? We can wait out the weather right here."

Will nodded.

"I know, Jamie, but if we wait out the weather, that sloop and the *Fair Wind* will make sail come light and leave us and the rest of the crew here to starve or die of thirst. Your pinnace won't carry twenty-eight men."

"But the pinnace is all we have," said Daisy Meadows, confusion in his voice.

"Not if we take the sloop," Will replied.

"Take the bleedin' sloop?" Daisy asked, incredulous. "We'd as likely swim to Virginia!"

"They've at least two dozen armed men on board!" Oakley objected. "I can maybe sail her over, but we can't fight that many."

Will shook his head.

"We won't have to. She'll be battened down against the storm with most of the crew below decks.. If there's a watch on deck, they're not likely to see a small boat in these rain squalls and they for sure won't hear us in this wind. We slip up beside her under cover of the storm, deal with the watch and block the hatches."

"It could be done," Mathys Beck said thoughtfully, "though in this rain, my rifles will be useless." He held up his sodden bag of powder to drive home the point.

"I've no desire to starve or die of thirst on this damned island," Harry Grey put in.

Will turned to August.

"In for a penny," his friend said.

He turned back to Oakley.

"We need you to pilot the pinnace, Jamie. What say you?"

The old sailor sat silent for a bit as a new burst of wind and rain drenched them. When it passed, he looked up and nodded.

"In for a pound."

***

Callie did not like the way the steward leered at her when he announced that Captain de Graff wished to see her in his cabin, but she knew there was little choice but to comply. She looked at the Binghams, but found no sympathy there. Anne sat there whimpering with a blank look on her face and Sir James refused to look at her. She got up, straightened her dress and followed the little Spaniard down the hallway to the Captain's cabin using her hands to steady herself against the corridor walls as the ship pitched and rolled in the gathering squall. Mateo knocked, then opened the door and stood aside for the girl to enter.

No King, No Country

Captain de Graff rose as she walked into his cabin and gave a small bow.

"Welcome, miss. I fear I did not get your name earlier when you came on board."

"Caledonia MacDonell," she replied evenly.

"Scottish?"

"Aye, Scottish as the thistle," she said and thought of Will Inness who'd asked her the same question.

Baltazar smiled.

"Are you as prickly?"

"Some would say."

De Graff seemed pleased by her answer.

"Please, Miss MacDonell, take a seat."

Callie pulled up a chair opposite the Dutchman and sat.

"Wine?" he asked, pouring himself a cup.

"No thank you, Captain."

"Ah, a wise girl who keeps her head!" Baltazar said with a smile as he set the bottle down. "I have a question, miss. Do you see this wound on my arm?"

Callie nodded.

"Someone on your ship gave it to me and I would like to congratulate that man on his fantastic marksmanship. But sadly, your ship's crew seems to have no knowledge of such a man. I thought you might help me."

Callie furrowed her brow and stared at the bandage on de Graff's arm. She'd heard what Herr Beck's guns could do and had a good notion who'd shot the privateer captain, but wasn't about to tell.

"Pity the man's aim wasn't better," she said.

It took a moment for de Graff to take her meaning, then he roared with laughter.

"Very good, Miss MacDonell. Very good indeed!" he said dabbing a tear from his eye. "You have wit to match your beauty—a rare find in these parts. But you haven't answered my question."

Callie sighed and tilted her head as though trying to recollect a name or face, but then she shrugged.

"I'm sorry, Captain. I was below when all the fighting was taking place. I couldn't possibly know who might have shot you."

Baltazar raised an eyebrow.

"You're lying of course, but that is to be expected," he said, rising from his chair and walking around the small table. He stopped behind Callie's chair and laid his hands on her shoulders.

"So what am I to do with a prickly Scottish thistle?" he asked.

Callie didn't answer, certain that Baltazar already had some notion in mind.

"Perhaps you should switch your allegiances, Miss MacDonell, and abandon those two you serve."

"To what purpose?" Callie asked.

"Why, to serve me, of course."

His offer didn't surprise her. She'd seen the way he'd looked at her when she'd first been brought on board the sloop. She'd gotten those looks from men since she was fourteen years old—and offers too. Since she was entirely at the privateer captain's mercy, the best she could do for the moment was to buy time and hope for a miracle. She shrugged off the man's hands and stood to face him.

"Is this an offer of employment, a marriage proposal, or something more tawdry, Captain?" she asked evenly.

Baltazar's face reddened a little, but the desire in his eyes still burned.

"Perhaps something between the three," he said with a sly smile.

Callie nodded.

"Very well then, I'll consider it. Now if our business here is done, may I leave?"

No King, No Country

Thrown off balance by the girl's directness, de Graff seemed at a loss for words for a moment. Then he nodded toward the door.

"Of course, my dear. But I will expect your presence for dinner and your answer as well."

Callie jerked the door open only to find Mateo listening on the other side. The steward leapt back in confusion as she stomped past him down the corridor and back to her berth with the Binghams. Her two fellow prisoners didn't bother to look up as she returned to captivity.

***

Night had fallen completely when the six men of Knocker Chance's burial detail dragged the pinnace from its hiding place down to the fringe of sand and launched it into the channel, frothing now with whitecaps. At Oakley's command, Daisy Meadows climbed over the gunwales and into the bow, followed by Will and August who took up positions at the forward oars. Mathys Beck and Harry Grey followed and manned the aft oars. Finally, Beck hauled Oakley aboard and he took his place on the stern bench and grasped the tiller. As men fumbled with their oars the churning seas turned the pinnace side on to the waves and the small boat began to swamp.

"Pull away, damn you!" Oakley screamed and the men at the oars managed a ragged pull, granting the pinnace just enough headway to give Oakley steerage. The old waterman turned the small boat's nose into the wind and the oncoming waves as Daisy Meadows frantically bailed the calf-deep water that had flooded into the bottom of the pinnace. As the wind howled, the men at the oars quickly fell into a rhythm and the pinnace, pitching and rolling, crept down the channel toward the sloop, invisible at this distance.

Halfway to their destination, a jagged bolt of lightning leapt across the sky illuminating the channel in a ghostly glare and making the dark shape of the sloop stand out in stark relief. Off the starboard quarter, the men could make out the bulk of the *Fair Wind*, but couldn't tell if the bigger vessel had floated free or not. As darkness fell back over the channel, Will pulled with all his might and prayed no one aboard the sloop had seen them.

***

On the deck of the *Fair Wind*, Pieter Van Wyke shielded his eyes from the driving rain and leaned over the starboard rail. One of his men was clinging to the mizzen chains and sounding the depth there. Van Wyke could tell from the motion of the merchantman that it was off the bottom, but he had to get to deeper water if he didn't want to be high and dry come the next low tide in five hours.

"By the mark three!" his man screamed above the howl of the wind.

Van Wyke turned away from the rail. The sounding told him he had no more than six feet of water between his hull and the bottom. It wasn't enough and the wind was pushing him back toward the lee shore and shallower water. He'd ordered all the sails reefed as the storm bore down on them, now he ordered men back up to the fore and mizzen yards. His only hope was to set enough canvas to give him the headway and steerage he needed to ease the merchantman to windward where the water deepened. But he had to take care. Too much sail and it would be impossible to control the big ship in the narrow channel.

As his men struggled up the ratlines, Van Wyke looked astern toward where he knew the *Donker Nacht* lay safely at anchor. He imagined Baltazar was enjoying his dinner about now.

"Bastard," he said, but his curse was whipped away by the wind. He was about to turn away when a thunderbolt lit up the sky and for an instant turned night into day. He could see the sloop in the distance, bobbing like a cork, but secure in its deep anchorage. But to his surprise he saw the pinnace rowing towards it.

"What the devil?"

No King, No Country

As quickly as the channel had been illuminated, it went dark again and Van Wyke could see nothing astern of the *Fair Wind*. But he'd seen what he'd seen.

What was de Graff up to sending the Donker Nacht's pinnace out in this weather? he wondered.

Had de Graff sent men to bury part of the booty ashore so he could cheat Van Wyke out of his share? The thought galled him, but he had little time to dwell on it. He made his way to the quarterdeck as the mizzen course and the fore course were set. As the canvas filled and tautened, the *Fair Wind* began to gain headway.

"Hard t' larboard!" Van Wyke shouted down to his man on the whipstaff in the steerage room. And the *Fair Wind* eased away from the lee shore.

***

On the storm-lashed deck of the *Donker Nacht,* Andrus Roll wiped the rain from his face and cursed the weather and the bosun who'd set him to stand watch in this tempest. He knew Karl Munch had it in for him over a woman in Tortuga—and for no good reason! Hell, he hadn't known she was the bosun's woman. She'd not acted attached when she'd settled herself on his lap at the Rusty Nail the night before they sailed!

As it always does in Tortuga, word got back to Munch and the bosun had believed the word of his woman over that of his shipmate. It made one wonder how such a fool could have risen to the rank of bosun. Now as he was getting drenched on deck and staring into near utter darkness, he thought of Munch sitting warm and dry below deck, sipping rum and throwing dice with the rest of the crew. It was damned unfair!

He'd found what little shelter he could against the sterncastle bulkhead where a lip of the quarterdeck formed a small overhang. It didn't keep him dry, but at least cut the wind a bit. He was pulling his oilskin cloak up around his neck when a mighty flash of lightning tore across the dark sky. In the sudden brilliance, Roll could clearly see the rigging and deck of the *Donker Nacht* and the surrounding waters. An instant later, the light faded and a new torrent of rain swept over the deck of the sloop. Roll closed his eyes tightly, and could see the stark after image against his lids. And in that image was something odd. He could have sworn he'd seen a small boat near the middle of the channel. He closed his eyes again, but the after-image had faded.

He opened his eyes and stared out into the storm. The bright flash of light had ruined his night vision and he could see nothing there now. But he was sure he'd seen something. It had looked like a boat, but he knew that was really not possible. He could make out the shape of the sloop's own pinnace lashed down on the *Donker Nacht*'s deck and he'd heard Verbeek report that the captured square-rigger had lost its own small boat. Surely no locals would be out in this foul weather.

He stepped from beneath the overhang at the sterncastle and, leaning into the wind, made his way to the rail. He stared hard into the pelting rain and saw nothing but whitecaps.

Imagination, he thought. *It'll play tricks*.

He staggered back to the sterncastle overhang and resumed his position. It was going to be a long watch.

***

The knock on the cabin door made Callie jump, though she'd been expecting it. She got up and looked at Sir James Bingham who didn't meet her eyes. She'd turned to him after her visit to the captain's cabin and had asked him outright if she'd be ransomed along with him and his sister. He'd given her no reassurance.

"We will, of course, communicate with Captain General Lunsford and inform him we have a servant as part of our party," he said half-heartedly, "but he will decide if you're to be included in the negotiations. It may depend on the price this blackguard demands for you."

No King, No Country

"So I'm to be dickered over like a pig at market."

"Well, I wouldn't put it quite like that," Sir James replied, but she noted he did not suggest another way of putting it.

I'm on my own, she thought, but she'd known that since the day she'd fled from Glengarry. She reached for the handle of the door and murmured to herself.

"Face it like a MacDonell!"

She swung open the door and, ignoring Mateo, marched down to de Graff's cabin. She entered without knocking just as a bolt of lightning illuminated the bank of windows along the stern bulkhead of the Captain's cabin casting an eerie luminescence around the room.

"Ah, a dramatic entrance!" de Graff said, handing her a cup as a roll of thunder echoed over the ship.

Callie took the cup of wine, drank it down and slammed the empty vessel on the table.

"I'll not be your wife, or your serving girl or your doxy, Captain. So let's get that out of the way."

De Graff arched an eyebrow.

"A strong opening to negotiations, Miss MacDonell," he said refilling her cup. "Now please take a seat. Mateo will bring our meal shortly. After we've dined, you can hear my counter offer."

***

As they neared the sloop, Jamie Oakley deftly steered the pinnace to the ship's lee side where the waves and wind were dampened a bit by the bulk of the anchored vessel. With ten feet between his bow and the hull of the privateer, he quietly ordered the men on the benches to ship oars. The old sailor then let the boat's momentum ease it up next to the hull of the pinnace like a kestrel touching down on a safe perch in a hurricane.

As they'd planned, August stood up, his legs spread and knees bent. Mathys Beck and Harry Grey grasped his belt on either side to steady him as he leaned his back against the hull of the sloop and laced his fingers together. Will stood next, trying to keep his balance as the pinnace pitched and rolled in the heavy seas. He planted his foot in August's cupped hands and his friend launched him up along the slick hull of the sloop. At the top of his lunge, his hands sought frantically for the small ledge that supported the starboard chains. His wrists scraped over wood and his fingers closed around cold wet iron. Planting his feet against the hull, he hauled himself up and onto the narrow shelf where the shrouds were secured to pulleys.

He turned and reached a hand down to take one of Beck's jaeger rifles, secured it behind the shrouds, then signaled for the next man. August launched Harry Grey upwards, but in the dark, his hands missed the chains. Will managed to grasp one of his flailing wrists before he fell back into the boat. As the lieutenant hung there he tried to plant his feet, but his good shoes found no purchase. Finally, Will reached his free hand down and grasped the collar of Grey's jacket, hauling him up to sit beside him amidst the pulleys and shroud lines. For a moment the younger man sat there gasping for breath.

"Obliged," he whispered finally.

Will didn't answer. He drew the rifle from behind the shrouds and slipped over the larboard rail, dropping into a crouch as Harry reached down to help August. He was relieved to see that the hatches were battened down against the storm as he'd hoped. He started to rise when he heard a loud thud below as a wave drove the pinnace into the side of the sloop. He froze, scanning the deck. Had someone on watch heard that sound? For an agonizing half minute he expected a lookout to sound an alarm, but none came. He knew there had to be a man on watch somewhere, but could see no one through the driving rain.

He was rising from his crouch when he heard the familiar sound of a gun being cocked. Instinctively he jerked to the side as he heard the flint strike the frizzen and saw a spark out of the corner of his eye. But no shot followed. The rain that had made Mathys Beck's rifles worthless as firearms had ruined the powder in the pistol the guard still pointed at him. Andrus Roll's curse was lost in the wind as he moved to draw his sword. He never freed it from its scabbard as Will drove the butt of his rifle into his chin. Roll dropped in a heap just as August climbed over the rail.

For a moment, both men stood still, waiting to see if others might have heard the skirmish on deck, but they could see nothing moving. The storm seemed to be reaching its peak, as a furious gust of wind caused the sloop to buck and roll and sent a foot of sea water sweeping over her deck. The wave surged around the mast and the two hatches that led to the lower deck of the privateer. Canvas, stiffened by wooden battens, kept the surging sea from getting below decks, but what would keep out seawater would not keep a determined crew from breaking out if an alarm was sounded. Those hatches had to be secured if they were to gain control of the privateer.

Will looked up as Harry Grey crawled over the rail and splashed through the wash on deck to join them. Mathys Beck followed close behind. Beck and August each held a jaeger rifle while Grey carried nothing but a belaying pin.

The decision had been made before they launched the pinnace that Daisy and Jamie would deliver them to the sloop then make for the island to the south where their shipmates were marooned. If the four men on deck could not take control of the privateer, the pinnace would be the only chance of survival for the crew of the *Fair Wind*. Keogh had taken the damaged merchantman well off the usual trade route up the eastern side of the island chain and it was unlikely any passing ship would find them before they all perished from thirst and exposure. But the pinnace could make it to Eleuthera, no more than a few days sail to the northwest where a rescue might be organized.

His boarding party now complete, Will pointed at the two hatches.

"That canvas won't hold if the crew tries to come on deck," he shouted over the howling wind. "We have to block them!"

August had already been considering that problem and pointed to the far end of the deck.

"Booty from the *Fair Wind*!" he shouted back.

Stacked near the sloop's bow were crates and hogsheads, not yet lowered into the hold. Will turned to Harry and pointed toward the sterncastle.

"Watch the door!" he ordered.

Grey nodded as August leaned his rifle against the bulkhead and started forward. Will and Mathys followed him across the pitching deck until they reached the stacks of cargo. August grasped a heavy barrel standing upright, tilted it on edge and began rolling it toward the forward hatch. It took all three men to heave the thing over the raised lip of the hatch and settle it on top. As they stepped back, Beck leaned a shoulder into the barrel and it barely moved.

"It will hold!" the German declared and the three set about selecting and rolling a second barrel toward the aft hatch. They had nearly reached it when the sterncastle door popped open and a head peeked out. Harry Grey did not hesitate. He brought the belaying pin down smartly on the man's head. Stunned the man staggered out onto the deck where Harry whacked him again. The guard went to his knees and toppled over, senseless on the deck. Harry turned and gently shut the door to the sterncastle.

August tilted the second barrel and together the three men leveraged it up and onto the aft hatch, trapping the crew below deck. All that remained was gaining control of the sterncastle and, presumably the privateer's captain.

"August, you and Beck stay on deck, Will shouted above the roar of the storm. Watch the hatches. Harry and I will see what's in there!" he said pointing to the door of the sterncastle.

No King, No Country

August and Beck nodded and each moved to stand near one of the blocked hatches. Will looked at Harry.

"Ready?"

Grey nodded, brandishing his belaying pin now as though it was a broadsword. Will took a deep breath and pulled open the sterncastle door. It was dark inside, but he could see a faint glow coming from beneath two doors, one to his left and the other at the end of a narrow hall. That would be the captain's quarters. He stepped inside and rubbed the water from his eyes. Harry Grey crowded in behind him. Will pointed at the door on the left.

"Watch this door," he whispered and moved on down the hall. Halfway to the Captain's door, a man's head suddenly popped out of a small alcove to Will's right. Mateo Rosales was about to ask the guard posted in the hallway to help him carry the plates of food in to the Captain, but he never got the chance to make the request as a fist slammed into his temple and a constellation of stars exploded in his head. Will caught the little man before he hit the floor.

Easing on down the hall, he stopped at the final door and put his ear to it. He could make out muffled voices above the roar of the storm. He gently tried the lever and it moved. Satisfied the door wasn't locked, he took a step back and kicked it in. Light flooded into the dim hall almost blinding him as he burst into the captain's cabin.

Callie MacDonell sat with her back to him at a small table. There was a man sitting opposite her and at the first sound of the door splintering, he reached across the table, grasped Callie by the wrist and yanked her to his side, tumbling the table over. She struggled, but he savagely twisted her arm behind her back and forced her to his front as a shield. The man raised a pistol and pressed it to her head. As she felt the cold muzzle at her temple, she stared at this drenched apparition who'd burst through the door. Her eyes went wide when she recognized Will Inness.

Will did not return her look, but kept his useless rifle pointed at the sloop's captain.

"You're my prisoner, captain," he said. "My men have secured your crew below decks. Put the gun down."

The captain cocked his pistol.

"Put *your* gun down," de Graff retorted, "or I will spill this girl's brains all over my cabin."

Will shrugged.

"She means nothing to me, though as a matter of principle, I'll kill you if you do."

The privateer gave him a cold smile.

"Then we would seem to have a standoff, except for one thing."

"What is that?"

"I have a shield and you don't!"

As he spoke the words, de Graff lowered his pistol from Callie's temple and pointed it at Will's chest, his finger tightening on the trigger. Callie MacDonell had waited for this chance. As the pistol came down, she drove a sharp elbow up and into the man's throat. The gun went off with a deafening roar in the cramped cabin, the shot splintering the teak doorjamb above Will's head.

Gasping for air, de Graff reached for a second pistol on the bunk behind him but his hand never touched the grip. Lunging across the cabin Will drove the maple stock of Mathys Beck's beautiful rifle into the man's the temple. For a moment he stood over the fallen privateer breathing hard, but de Graff wasn't moving. He turned to the girl.

"Callie," was all he said.

She threw her arms around him and sobbed with relief.

***

A little after midnight, the wind began to die as the storm drove northward toward Spanish Florida. With it went the rain squalls and the storm surge that had roiled the waters of the channel. On the *Donker Nacht*, Captain Baltazar de Graff, two of his crewmen and Mateo the steward sat bound

No King, No Country

and sullen in the large cabin under the watchful eye of Callie MacDonell, armed now with two loaded pistols. De Graff's left eye was swollen shut and starting to blacken.

On deck, Will, August, Harry and Mathys undid the lashings that secured the sloop's pinnace and lowered it over the side.

Grey had helmed a small boat before and took the tiller in hand while August took his place on the oarsman's bench. The second rower was Sir James Bingham. He'd refused a request to help until Will had leveled a pistol at him and ordered him into the boat. Properly manned, the pinnace shoved off from the *Donker Nacht* and made for the southern island where the crew of the *Fair Wind* were marooned.

Through the small hours of the night, the sloop's pinnace, joined by the *Fair Wind*'s small boat shuttled Captain Keogh and his men from the island to the sloop and by first light half were safely on board. They armed themselves with the weapons that had been taken from them on the *Fair Wind* and Keogh ordered the nine guns on the larboard side of the sloop to be readied to fire a broadside at the *Fair Wind* should the privateer's crew aboard her prove troublesome.

Below decks, the crewmen of the *Donker Nacht* were just awakening. A man came to the aft hatch and called up through the canvas covering for the morning watch to clear the hatch. Getting no response, the man pushed tentatively at the canvas only to feel the solid wood of the hogshead sitting atop the covering.

This created a stir below. More men shouted for the watch on deck to open the hatches and some tried to force both the aft and forward hatches to no avail. Finally, Mr. Berrycloth addressed the situation by dragging Baltazar de Graff out on deck and putting a gun to his head.

"We'll have 'em up, one by one, unarmed like good lads. If any cause trouble, you'll be the first t' die."

For de Graff, the cold metal against his temple was convincing. He cleared his throat and called down through the aft hatch.

"This is the Captain. They've taken our ship. You are to come on deck, one man at a time. You won't be harmed."

De Graff paused and Berrycloth pressed the barrel of the pistol harder against his head.

"Any man armed will be shot," de Graff added, plaintively.

Berrycloth lowered his gun and signaled to the men he had standing by at the aft hatch. They rolled the heavy barrel off and set to work with pry bars to loosen and remove the wooden battens. Finally the canvas was drawn back and the woebegone crew of the *Donker Nacht* filed on deck one at a time. Each was searched for weapons and herded up to the bow of the sloop.

As de Graff was being ushered back to his confinement in the sterncastle, the privateer suddenly turned and stared at the rifle in Will's hands.

"Was it you in the tops who gave me this?" he asked, raising his bandaged arm..

Will nodded. De Graff pointed at the rifle, then at his puffy eye.

"Why did you use it as a club?" he asked. Then he shook his head. "Ah, of course, the storm—wet powder." Still staring at the rifle in Will's hand he spoke again.

"Name your price!" he begged. "I will buy it from you!"

Will shook his head.

"Not for sale, Captain."

***

Pieter Van Wyke had managed to free the *Fair Wind* from the sandbar and find a deep enough anchorage during the night. An excellent feat of seamanship, if he did say so. But as daylight arrived, he found himself perplexed. Standing on the quarterdeck of the merchantman, he tried to make sense out of what he was seeing off his stern. The *Donker*

No King, No Country

Nacht was where she'd been anchored when the storm struck—nothing odd about that—but he could now see two small boats tied up to the sloop.

The sight brought all of his suspicions from the night before back. Where had an extra boat come from and what was Baltazar de Graff up to? With de Graff he could be sure it was not good. He raised his spyglass to his eye and focused on the deck of the sloop. The sight made his stomach lurch. For standing on the deck of the sloop looking back at him through a his own spyglass was a stocky little man dressed all in black. He whirled around and screamed at his mate.

"All hands on deck! Weigh anchor!"

But events were moving quickly beyond his control. From down the channel came the familiar sound of a twelve pound cannon firing. He lowered his spyglass and watched the ball land thirty yards off his larboard bow. The shot was well placed, landing square in the center of the only deep water the *Fair Wind* might use to try to escape. Van Wyke's shoulders slumped. Behind him he heard the men straining at the capstan to raise the anchor.

"Belay that!" he ordered, then turned to his mate.

"Find a white flag."

***

The captain, first mate and crew of the *Donker Nacht* were marooned on the island south of the channel, though Captain Keogh insisted on leaving the sloop's pinnace and two barrels of water with them.

"They're blackguards, I know, but I'm a Christian man," was his only comment when John Berrycloth questioned the decision.

Captain Baltazar de Graff was last to take the short voyage over to the island. As he stood at the rail of his former ship he gave Callie MacDonell a sweeping bow.

"If you ever find yourself near Tortuga, Miss MacDonell, my proposal still stands."

Callie looked at him coldly.

"Count yourself lucky I didn't say yes, Captain, for I would have made your life miserable."

"Ah yes, ever the thistle," de Graff said with a sigh, then turned to Will.

"And you, Captain Inness. I hope we meet again someday. If we do, you'd best have that wonderful gun of yours close at hand!"

***

As the small boat carrying Captain de Graff launched, Will turned to Callie.

"So what was his proposal?

She shrugged and gave him a coy smile.

"What's it to you, William? You told him I meant nothing to you!"

Will returned her smile.

"True, but I also said I'd kill him if he harmed you."

She laughed.

"Now those are words to turn a girl's head!"

"I hope so," he replied.

No King, No Country

Spoils of War

Captain Keogh left John Berrycloth and half the *Fair Wind*'s crew to man the sloop and together the two ships weighed anchor and sailed for Eleuthera on the afternoon ebb tide. The English had settled the island only two years before, but there was a fine natural harbor there and some prospect for disposing of the *Donker Nacht* for a price. By the afternoon of the second day the long narrow island emerged over the horizon.

There were four ships in the half-moon bay that served as the port's harbor when the black-hulled privateer and the merchantman dropped anchor. Keogh took the pinnace over to the sloop to pick up John Berrycloth and the two were rowed to the small dock that jutted out into the pale blue water of the bay. Two hours later, they were back and the pinnace began ferrying the considerable store of pirated booty from the Donker Nacht's hold over to the *Fair Wind*. As Captain Keogh climbed over the rail he asked Will to join him in his cabin.

"Captain Inness, I didn't want you on my ship," he began, bluntly. "I don't favor mutineers or deserters, or Englishmen for that matter, but I will confess, I've grown to like you, lad. If you ever grow tired of the land, there'll be a place for you on the *Fair Wind* and for Lieutenant Dawes as well."

"Thank you, Captain. You run a good ship and I'd be proud to serve under you, but we are bound for the Virginia frontier, so I will have to decline."

Keogh chuckled.

"I expected as much, but in either case we have some business to conclude."

"Business?"

"Aye, business. And I must apologize. We could have fetched maybe three thousand pounds for that sloop in Bermuda, but that was a bit out of my way. The best I could do here was five hundred pounds sterling."

Will looked at him blankly.

"How is that my business, Captain?"

For a moment, it was Keogh's turn to stare blankly. Then he realized he hadn't made himself clear.

"Captain Inness, you commanded Knocker Chance's burial detail. On your own initiative, you boarded the privateer and seized control of the ship, along with some of your fellow passengers. Therefore, by custom, if not by law, you have a right to a share in the proceeds of her sale."

"Captain, I…"

Keogh held up a hand.

"You used my crew and my small boat in the action. I say the money from the sale should be divided evenly between you and I. If you agree, I'll see to the shares for Meadows and Oakley and you can decide how to split your share with the men who boarded her with you."

With that he handed Will a leather sack heavy with coins. Will felt its heft and shook his head. He'd never seen so much money.

***

As the *Fair Wind* weighed anchor and set sail, Will gathered August, Harry Grey and Mathys Beck together atop the small fo'c'sle and divided up the prize money, each man receiving the princely sum of fifty pounds sterling.

"I'm rich!" Harry Grey exclaimed as he hefted the leather bag full of coins.

No King, No Country

"This is generous, Captain," Mathys Beck said. "With this I can build a metalworking shop—the finest in the colonies."

Will nodded and handed Beck his jaeger rifle.

"With weapons such as these for purchase, you will be the richest man in Maryland I think."

Beck chuckled at that. It was the first time Will had heard the German laugh. Then he handed Will the rifle back.

"It is yours, Captain. You have earned it."

He turned to August and pointed at his gun.

"And you as well, Herr Lieutenant. When men in Virginia see my guns, they will come to Maryland to buy more. So you do me a favor!"

Will and August started to protest, but Beck refused to hear their objections. Will looked down at the gun and ran a hand over the beautifully carved stock.

"I'm honored, Mathys."

August held up his bag of silver and jingled it.

"And what will we do with all this wealth?" he asked with a silly grin on his face.

Will wrapped an arm around his friend's shoulders.

"Well, we start by buying new coats. The ones we have stink to high heaven."

***

As the sun set, Will saw Callie come on deck. He hadn't had much opportunity to speak to her since they'd reboarded the *Fair Wind*, but the girl had been much on his mind. She stepped to the starboard rail and he joined her there as the last bit of the sun eased below the horizon. The western sky was a blaze of reds and golds.

"I never saw skies like this in Scotland," she said as he stood beside her.

"Nor water this color in the Irish Sea," he replied.

For a while they watched the sunset in silence. Finally he turned and handed her a leather bag. She took it, with a quizzical look.

"So what is this?"

"Your share of the prize money from the *Donker Nacht*."

Callie frowned.

"My share? How am I owed a share? I'll not be taking charity, William."

"Oh, this is not charity, Callie. I saw where that pistol barrel was pointed. But for you, Captain de Graff would have put a ball through my heart, then he'd have rallied his crew and the boarding would have failed. That elbow of yours saved us all."

Callie wrinkled her brow, considering his logic.

"So how much is in this bag?" she asked.

"Twenty-five pounds sterling."

Her eyes widened a bit.

"A princely sum," she said quietly. "Enough to pay off my debts to the Binghams."

"And fairly earned," Will said.

Callie nodded.

"Thank you, William."

As the sun disappeared below the western horizon, the sky lit up with a momentary flash of green. Callie gasped at the sight.

"This new world…it's a beautiful place," she said.

"Aye, it is that," Will agreed. "What will you do now, Callie, now you're free and clear of the Binghams? Will you take ship back to Scotland?"

The girl shook her head.

"There's nothing for me back there, even with a bag of silver in my purse. No, I will see what this America has to offer a girl. Why do you ask, William?"

"Well…I…." Will felt sweat break out on his brow. "I thought since you'll be leaving the Binghams you might take up a new position."

"A new position?" she asked turning and staring at him. "As what pray tell?"

"As a wife, Callie. As my wife."

No King, No Country

***

"Married!" August blurted. "Oh Lord, Will, I knew you were sweet on the girl, but married?"

"You disapprove, Gus?"

"Well…no, actually. I've liked Callie from the moment she laughed at us banging our heads at dinner that first night. And then, when she went right to work on the wounded from the privateer's guns, I knew the girl had grit. And she'll need it where we're going."

"True enough—so I have your blessing?"

"Of course, Will. It's just that…"

"What?"

"Well, you'll have a wife now…and…"

"I'll still have need of my best friend," Will said gently.

August's face darkened.

"Well of course you'll need me! Callie's a lovely lass, but not as good a shot as I am I'll wager. What I was saying is that now you have a wife, I'll need to find one of my own."

***

Callie counted out twelve pounds three shillings and set the coins on the small table next to Anne Bingham.

"What's all this?" Anne demanded.

"Settling our accounts, Anne. I am no longer in your employ."

James Bingham leapt to his feet.

"This is preposterous!" he snapped as he towered over her. "Where did you get this money?"

"That is none of your concern," Callie said.

"But who shall wait upon me?" Anne whined.

"We are less than a week away from Jamestown. Surely you can do your own laundry until then."

"Insolent girl!" Sir James snarled and raised his hand as though to strike her.

Callie turned on him.

"Hit me and you will regret it," she hissed.

For a long moment the two stood and glared at each other, but Sir James' hand never moved. Callie turned and stepped out of their berth and was surprised to see Will there. She frowned.

"I'm not to be looked after like a child, William."

Will reddened.

"I feared Sir James might…"

Callie shook her head.

"Strike me? Oh, he wanted to, but I knew he wouldn't. That's not how he does his damage. We must watch our backs once we land in Virginia, but I'll not be hovered over like a child."

Will slipped an arm around her waist and pulled her to him. What had the privateer called her?

Oh yes, a *thistle*.

***

Captain Keogh wasn't surprised in the least when Captain Inness informed him of his wish to marry Miss Caledonia MacDonell. He'd seen enough love struck sailors in his day to know the signs and these two had been showing them since before Tenerife.

There was, of course, the not inconsiderable problem of one being Protestant and one a member of the True Faith. Such a match was frowned on by both churches. Inness struck him as an upright man, but not much for religion, while Miss MacDonell, he knew, was a good Catholic. He'd watched her cross herself before meals and had heard her praying the rosary more than once as he passed by her tiny berth. She'd apparently known Keogh was Catholic as well and had come to see him on this very point.

"What does the church say on this, Captain? There's naught but Catholics amongst the MacDonells of Glengarry and none that I know of ever married outside the church. Are we allowed to marry a Protestant?"

Keogh sighed.

No King, No Country

"Only with the permission of your bishop and most bishops I'm acquainted with are inclined to say no I'm afraid. I pray that will change, my dear. I don't think God wishes to keep his people apart. But it's not just our church. The Church of England also prohibits its congregants from marrying a Catholic."

Callie's shoulders sagged.

"What am I to do, Captain. I love him."

Keogh patted the girl's hand.

"My dear, I'm an Irish Catholic, but few know that I'm married to a Presbyterian from Ulster. We're recognized by neither church, but we read the same Bible and follow the Lord's commandments—as much as possible. We've not let the Pope nor John Calvin come between us. If you love Captain Inness and intend to follow him out to the Virginia frontier, you'll find no priests or preachers there. Nor do the laws of Crown or Parliament reach must beyond the coast. I say, take a Bible with you and keep the commandments. Then you'll be man and wife in the eyes of God, if not your churches."

Keogh's words made Callie straighten up.

"Thank you, Captain. The churches may do as they please, but I hope you are right about God."

"So does my dear wife," he said with a gentle smile.

Callie stood and to his surprise, threw her arms around his neck and hugged him tightly.

"You'll conduct our ceremony?"

"I'd be honored, my dear."

***

Will Inness stood beside the mainmast of the *Fair Wind* and fidgeted. Harry Grey had helped him select a proper suit for his wedding from stacks of plundered clothing confiscated from the *Donker Nacht*. Now, as he waited anxiously for his bride to appear, he tugged at the tight linen collar at his neck and felt beads of sweat beginning to form between his shoulder blades and run down to collect at the base of his spine.

Harry had urged him to try some of the more flamboyant silk coats and billowy satin trousers Captain de Graff had looted, but he'd looked ridiculous in such finery. In the end, he'd found a long buff leather coat trimmed with silver gilt braid at the collar and cuffs that suited him. Unlike his cavalry buff coat, this garment was pliable and soft to the touch, its previous owner no doubt having no need to fend off saber slashes. Linen trousers and knee-high black leather boots completed his wedding suit as he stood there in the tropical sun waiting, with August Dawes by his side.

It was a thankfully short wait. The door to the sterncastle opened and Mathys Beck appeared, dressed in a rather severe black suit. The German gunsmith held the door as Callie MacDonell stepped out into the morning light. She had likewise been given her choice of garments from the bounty of the privateer's loot and had selected a simple gown of soft satin, its color the pale green of spring buds. She had a strand of small pearls at her neck and her auburn hair fell gently upon her shoulders as she took Beck's arm. Together they started across the deck.

Crowded along both rails, the crew of the *Fair Wind* murmured appreciatively as Callie beamed at one and all. When she reached Will, Mathys withdrew his arm and stepped back. She held out both of her hands and Will took them in his, staring into her green eyes.

Captain Keogh stood nervously next to the mainmast and fiddled with a scrap of paper in his hand. As Will and Callie turned toward him, he reached into his black coat, drew forth a pair of spectacles and set them in place on the bridge of his nose. Clearing his throat, he looked out at the crowd gathered on deck. The entire ship's company had turned out save for the helmsman and the Binghams who'd refused to attend.

No King, No Country

Atop the quarterdeck, Daisy Meadows played a sweet tune on a fiddle as the wedding party assembled while Jamie Oakley followed him deftly on a pennywhistle. Keogh nodded toward Bill Barley who then sang the only hymn he knew in his fine tenor voice.

Preliminaries done, Keogh cleared his throat once more and looked down at his paper where he'd carefully written out the key parts of the marriage vows, with a few editorial changes of his own.

"Dearly beloved friends," he began. "We are gathered together here in the sight of God, and in the face of this crew, to join together this man and this woman in holy matrimony, which is an honorable state, instituted of God in Paradise, in the time of man's innocence, signifying unto us the mystical union that is betwixt Christ and his church. If any here know cause why these two should not be bound together in the sight of God, let him speak now."

There was no sound on deck save for the creak of the rigging and the squawk of a curious seagull hovering over the fo'c'sle. Keogh turned toward Will.

"William Inness, wilt thou have Caledonia to thy wedded wife, to live together after God's ordinance in the holy estate of matrimony? Wilt thou love her, comfort her, honor, and keep her, in sickness, and in health? And forsaking all other, keep only to her, so long as you both shall live?"

"I will."

Keogh turned to Callie.

"And wilt thou, Caledonia Macdonell, have William to thy wedded husband, to live together after God's ordinance in the holy estate of matrimony? Wilt thou obey him and serve him, love, honor, and keep him, in sickness and in health? And forsaking all other, keep thee only to him so long as ye both shall live?"

"I will."

"Then I pronounce you man and wife!"

A cheer went up from the crew as Will swept Callie up in his arms and kissed her.

No King, No Country

Part 3: A Savage Land

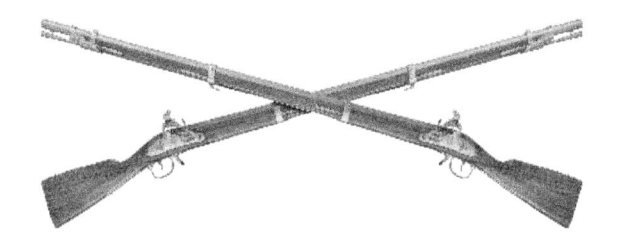

Welcome to America

For two days and three nights the *Fair Wind* sailed to the northwest. John Berrycloth graciously gave up his small cabin for the newlyweds as a wedding gift. At dawn on the third day they struck the great warm current that sweeps up from the south Atlantic, along the coast of America and on to the far north where it meets the icy waters of the Arctic Sea. An hour later, land was sighted off the larboard bow.

When the lookout's call rang out, Will and Callie untangled themselves from their bedclothes and dressed hurriedly, both anxious to get their first glimpse of this huge unknown land. When they reached the deck, they found August, Harry and Mathys already staring off to the west at a low coast that ran out of sight in both directions.

"Four thousand miles," Beck observed. "I've heard it said this coast runs that far from north to south."

Will looked at the white fringe of beach backed by a wall of green and tried to conceive of so much land. How far must it extend westward from this coast? No white man knew. He wondered if even the natives of the land could grasp its size. A man on a good horse could ride the length of England from the north of Scotland to the tip of Cornwall in a fortnight. To ride the length of this land would take three months if there were roads—and there were none.

No King, No Country

"A man could disappear into such vastness," Harry Grey said in an awed voice as the fringe of Spanish Florida slid by.

"You might disappear from English eyes mayhaps," Will observed, "but the land is not empty." He leaned in close to Harry. "I expect there are folk over there on the shore, watching us now."

Harry shot him a look and seemed to shiver just a bit.

"I don't fancy being watched from behind trees and bushes," he declared. "I'll likely plant myself in Jamestown or thereabouts. My mother has a cousin somewhere in the colony. Perhaps he can advise me on where to invest my prize money from the sloop."

"An inn, perhaps," August suggested.

Harry wrinkled his brow.

"Now there's an idea! When I took ship from Portsmouth there were two other merchantmen beside the *Fair Wind* preparing to sail for Virginia with passengers. And with settlements growing upriver, men will be coming to Jamestown for supplies and other business. An inn might turn a profit."

"As long as you don't drink it up."

Harry laughed and shook his head.

"Sworn off Spanish wine, I have, and any other strong spirits. My head pounded for three days after Tenerife!"

Will smiled at this back and forth and pulled Callie closer to him. America might be vast, but that suited him. He'd find a place there, not in any settlement, but out there along that jagged line on Jamie Oakley's map, out beyond the writ of English law. Callie would be by his side as would Gus Dawes.

If that was disappearing, he would take it.

***

An hour after sighting land, the lookout shouted down a new alarm.

"Sail! Off the larboard bow!"

Keogh extended his spyglass and scanned the northern horizon. The approaching ship was laying in closer to shore to avoid the strong northern current that hurried the *Fair Wind* along. Soon it could be seen with the naked eye and it was a grand sight. Will and August were on deck lending a hand with the morning watch and paused to gawk as a majestic Spanish galleon, four-masted and with acres of sail set bore down the coast toward them.

Keogh gave no orders. A Spanish ship of this size in these waters was likely a cargo vessel. If that was so, it would have no interest in a much smaller English craft, as long as the *Fair Wind* made no threatening moves. And if she was a ship of war, Keogh was confident that, with the current pushing his vessel ahead at three to four knots, he could outrun her.

"She'll be out of St. Augustine," John Berrycloth observed as the massive galleon passed by without even hailing the *Fair Wind*. "The Don's control everything from the tip of Florida north for four hundred miles and it's another seven hundred to the English colonies on the Cheseapeak."

"What lies between?" August asked.

"Wilderness," the first mate replied, "and Indians."

***

For five days and nights, the merchantman sailed northeast, well off shore but within sight of land. In the run up the coast, Will, Callie and August talked long into the night, discussing and sometimes arguing over their plans once reaching Jamestown. It was agreed they'd purchase needed supplies in Jamestown and a boat to carry them up the James River to the fall line. At the falls they would sell their boat at the fort or abandon it and travel overland, following the river to its headwaters in the mountains.

Once there, they would seek out a sheltered valley with good water and timber and enough flat land to put in a crop. All agreed with the object of finding suitable land somewhere far to the west. The arguments came over who would seek out that place.

"I'm no weak, lowland, English girl," Callie protested when Will said she'd have to stay behind in Jamestown until he and August found a proper place to settle.

"Callie, I'd not be asking you to make your home in this wilderness if I thought that, but we've only the slightest notion of where we are going or what we may find along the way. We may have to range over a lot of the country, so we must travel light."

"I'd be no trouble," she insisted. "I can carry my share of the supplies."

"I've no doubt of that," Will said gently. "But we don't know if the native people inland will be hostile or not. If they are, then you would be a hinderance."

"I'd be a hinderance?" she asked, eyes flashing.

Will was unmoved by her anger.

"Think, Callie! Can you shoot a gun? Can you shoot a bow? If you can't defend yourself, then August and I must protect you and that will be a hinderance."

Callie frowned at him, but had no ready answer for his blunt logic.

"Let Gus and I find our new home and a safe passage to it," Will said quietly. "Then we'll come fetch you and you can show me what load you can carry."

The girl stewed for a bit, then nodded.

"And you'll teach me how to shoot, once we are there."

"If you wish."

"Very well. I'll wait for your return in Jamestown, but William," she said, fixing him with a hard look, "don't make me the richest widow in Jamestown."

***

Aided by favorable winds and the steady flow of the Gulf Stream, the *Fair Wind* reached the broad mouth of the Cheseapeak Bay on the morning of the sixth day. Taking advantage of the flood tide, Captain Keogh guided the ship into the mouth of the James River and headed upstream.

Now, with land close at hand off both sides, all of the passengers came on deck to watch. Even the Binghams, rarely seen since the fight with the privateer, put in an appearance at the rails. On a spit of land to the north could be seen an abandoned palisade, its walls falling down. Will remembered from Oakley's map that there had once been a small fort on what Jamie labeled as Point Comfort. Its chief purpose had been to watch for possible Spanish warships, but since none had ever appeared, the fort had been abandoned.

In the five hour sail up river, signs of more recent English habitation began to appear. Small fishing boats slid past, their one or two man crews waving cheerily at the square-rigger in the middle of the channel. Here and there, small wattle and daub huts that would be recognizable to any English farmer were set back from the river banks.

As the big ship eased its way around a long bend in the river, a lone paddler in a dugout canoe slid by. This was no English settler. The man was tall and well-muscled, with close-cropped hair. His only clothing was a sort of short skirt about his waist and his naked torso was adorned with red tattoos. August gave the man a wave and the canoeist paused in his stroke, but did not return the gesture. Then the *Fair Wind* was around the bend and the man and canoe were lost to sight.

The ship tacked to larboard to take the next sharp bend in the river, As they came around the turn, a low swampy peninsula appeared off the starboard bow and on the far side of this finger of land, the tops of tall masts could be seen. Jamie Oakley walked up to the rail and looked across the peninsula at his former home where a dozen columns of smoke rose from unseen houses. He spit a brown stream of tobacco juice into the swirling waters of the James River.

No King, No Country

"Jamestown," he muttered, "good fer nothing but pestilence and fine tobac."

***

As the *Fair Wind* rounded the blunt end of the peninsula, the waterfront of the settlement came into view. The ship whose tall masts they'd seen from downriver was tied up on the upstream side of a long pier that extended well out into the swirling current of the river. A second pier looked to be under construction as a pile driver, its weight drawn up by a brace of oxen, was pounding pilings into the mud of the river bottom.

Along the waterfront were a few rough-hewn buildings that no doubt served as shops and warehouses with a score of smaller but tidier dwellings set back from the riverbank on higher ground. A few hundred yards inland a grander, two story house stood with a church next to it.

"Governor's house, I'd wager," Harry said as he pointed to it.

On the quarterdeck above, Captain Keogh issued a stream of orders to his crew as he delicately maneuvered the big ship into position against the river's strong current. To no one's surprise, the merchantman slipped perfectly into its intended spot by the pier, where men ashore caught the mooring lines and made her fast.

Then the stench hit them.

"Good God, what is that?" August said, wrinkling his nose. The breeze from upriver was rife with the odor of human waste and worse. Further down the rail, Anne Bingham clutched a lace handkerchief to her nose and fled from the deck.

"It's a slaver," Bill Barley said in disgust. "They throw the poor sods in the hold, chain 'em up together and that's where they stay for the crossing. Give 'em a little water and enough rotten food to keep 'em alive. A lot die. It's the only way out of the chains, then it's over the side with 'em. At sea you can smell a slaver a mile off."

It appeared that the sad cargo had already been put ashore as there was no activity aboard the slave ship. By contrast, the waterfront itself was bustling. Here and there you could see men, some white but many black, rolling barrels into a warehouse, sawing wood into lumber and carrying on the hundred and one tasks commonly found at any port.

If the waterfront was bustling with activity, the *Fair Wind* was no less so as the crew secured lines and furled sails. Mr. Berrycloth was already ordering the lines and pulleys run to the yardarms to begin hoisting up the merchantman's cargo from the hold. Other crewmen ran a wide gangplank down from the larboard side of the deck to the pier.

Captain Keogh had announced he would tie up at Jamestown for three days before continuing up the bay to St. Mary's Town. He had trade goods and other supplies for the Maryland colony and one remaining passenger to deliver in Mathys Beck. He agreed to keep Will's crate aboard the *Fair Wind* until they could find storage for its contents in Jamestown.

Will, Callie and August gathered at the rail and waited for the gangplank to be secured. The long voyage from England was over. It was time to set foot in a New World.

***

The three did not linger on the pier with the disgusting odor coming from the nearby slave ship. Once on the solid ground of the waterfront, they agreed to split up. Having accepted the need to remain in Jamestown, Callie would seek lodging there while August looked for the supplies they would need for their first trip out to the frontier. Will would stay down by the river and look for a suitable boat to buy. Despite the fact that they were now three thousand miles from England, all three agreed it would not be prudent for Will or August to stay in the English colony any longer than needed.

As Callie and August set out in the direction of the large house and church in the town, Will walked along the riverfront noting the various tradesmen clustered there. He passed a smith pounding away on a glowing rod of iron and a cooper sitting at a bench drawing a two-handled blade over a barrel stave. An ancient hound was curled up at the man's feet, his fur covered with the wood shavings. The dog watched Will pass by without raising its head.

Upstream beyond the waterfront, he could see a well-tended field with long rows of upright plants sporting large fronds on all sides. Will had never seen a tobacco plant, but he guessed this was what the crop looked like and this field looked bountiful. Beyond the tobacco patch was another field with slender green stalks growing twice as high as the tobacco. Another plant he would need to learn about.

Having reached the end of the waterfront and seen no small boats at all, he turned and started back in the other direction. At the pier he saw James and Anne Bingham come down the gangplank, followed by two black men carrying their baggage. There was a fine carriage waiting for them drawn up near the riverbank and the two did not dawdle with the stench still wafting over the pier. As James helped Anne into the carriage he looked past her and saw Will coming toward them. The two locked eyes for a long moment, before Bingham turned away, climbing aboard the carriage and ordering the driver to depart.

Off to meet her bridegroom, Will thought.

He continued down the river bank until he came to a small dock at the far end of Jamestown's waterfront. It hardly amounted to a pier as it projected no more than ten feet out into the river, but there were two boats tied up there, one a rowboat and one a dugout canoe, much like the one they'd passed coming upriver. Both had seen better days.

Will stepped onto the dock and took a closer look. He'd never seen a dugout canoe before and was not impressed. He could not tell if this craft was crudely made or standard for such watercraft. It simply looked clumsy. The rowboat was little better. The oarlocks were thick with rust and one of the gunwales was clearly rotting.

"Interest ye in a boat, fine sir?"

Will turned to see a wiry little man hobbling along the river bank toward him.

"Are these yours to sell?" he asked.

"Maybe, if the price were right," the man said as he sized up Will. "Ye fresh in off the merchantman?"

Will nodded.

"How much for the rowboat?" he asked.

"Lots a folk comin' over from the auld sod these days," the man said, ignoring Will's question. "Mostly Royalists runnin' from the Roundheads. But ye don't look like much of a Cavalier. You a Roundhead?"

Will had been bent over testing the oarlock on the rowboat, but raised up and faced the man.

"You've lots of questions, mister, and none of the answers are any of your concern. What I am is a customer and if you can't sell me a boat, I'll find someone who can."

The little man laughed at that.

"Well I'll know yer story soon enough I suppose. No secrets here, my fine sir. Jamestown is like the tiniest little village in England. Everyone knows everyone's business here. No need t' get yer back up. I'll sell ye the rowboat for six pounds."

"It's a rotting hulk and it has no oars. I'll give you three."

The man swept his arm back toward the bustling waterfront.

"Did ye see another boat along there, fine sir? No? Well then, it'll be six pounds." Will sighed and reached for the pouch of silver he had tucked in his belt. He'd left the bulk of his treasure aboard the *Fair Wind*.

Six pounds poorer, he made his way to one of the warehouses where he had seen what looked to be a carpenter at work. He found a man planing a wooden stave that was taking on the shape of an axe handle. The man looked up.

No King, No Country

"Help ye?"

"Just bought a boat and need two oars."

The man straightened up.

"What'd old Bert take fer it? It's got a rotted gunwale, ye know."

Will nodded.

"Aye, I saw that. Maybe you could fashion a patch."

The man nodded.

"That'll be a pound six shillings fer the patch and the oars. Ready by morning."

"Obliged," Will said and counted out the coins. As the man took the money, his face clouded and Will sensed movement behind him. He turned to find four men coming through the broad door of the warehouse. The big man leading the group had a sword belted to his side. The others all had long wooden truncheons shoved in their belts. He regretted now he'd left his weapons on board the *Fair Wind*.

"William Inness?" a big man in front asked.

Will glanced around the shop. He could see only one exit and no way to get past these men to reach it.

"Who's asking?"

The leader didn't answer Will's question.

"Yer under arrest. Take him, lads."

As a man reached to seize his arm, Will laid him out with a straight right to the jaw. He reached behind him and snatched up the half-finished axe handle and brought it down on the head of a second man. In the corner of his eye he saw the leader drawing his sword. He was turning to meet that threat when his head exploded in stars and his world went black. He crumpled unconscious to the dirt floor of the carpenter's shop.

The leader of the arresting party stood over him for a moment to see if he'd move, then kicked him in the head for good measure. He gave a quick hand signal to the man who'd laid on the blow and the two grabbed their prisoner's arms and drug him upright, draping Will's arms over their shoulders. The man who Will had punched staggered to his feet, but the third guard was out cold on the floor. They left him there as they dragged Will out of the carpenter's shop.

The carpenter waited for them to get clear, then set aside his planer and hurried to the pier. He hadn't recognized the arrested man, which meant he must have just arrived in the colony on the ship now tied up there. He made his way up the gangplank and was greeted by a huge man smoking a clay pipe.

"I believe one of yer passengers was just arrested," he said pointing toward the rutted dirt road that led to the church. "Inness he was called."

John Berrycloth looked up the road and saw four men heading away from the waterfront. Two dragged a man between them and the fourth followed behind, holding his jaw. Berrycloth gave a weary sigh.

"Obliged, sir."

The carpenter nodded.

"Don't like t' see my paying customers abused," he said.

"Neither do I," Berrycloth replied.

***

Callie managed to secure a small room at the poor excuse for an inn on the town square of Jamestown and August purchased twenty pounds of beans and a like amount of bacon to sustain he and Will on the journey west. They had just rendezvoused at the church when they saw a squad of men coming up the muddy road from the waterfront.

Two were dragging a third man up the road toward the center of the settlement, with a fourth following behind. The man being dragged appeared to be unconscious, his feet dangling behind him and his head hanging down, concealing his face. But Callie knew the shape of the man, as did August.

"What the…" he sputtered, starting toward the group. Callie grasped his arm and pulled him up short.

No King, No Country

"No, August," she hissed. "If they've taken William they may be looking for you as well. You must stay out of sight and get yourself to the ship. Captain Keogh must be told what's happened."

August angrily tore his arm away from the girl's grip, but did not move, torn between flying to his friend's aid and the girl's wiser counsel.

"I can't afford to have you both taken," Callie pleaded. "I'll need you if we're to help Will."

A little groan of frustration escaped August's lips as he turned to look at the girl.

"What of you, Callie?"

"I'll go to the Governor. I've no warrant out on me, so I'll be safe enough," she said with more confidence than she felt. "Get yourself to the ship now. We have friends there and will need them. I'll see what I can learn and join you later."

August took a last look at the squad dragging his friend up the road.

"How could they know about us?" he asked angrily.

On that score, Callie had no doubts.

The Binghams.

No One Owns Juba

Will flinched as something cool and damp touched his swollen left eye. His head throbbed painfully and without looking he could tell he was lying on a hard dirt floor. It took an effort of will to force his right eye open and for a moment he saw only a dim shape hovering over him. He blinked and it felt like he'd taken another blow to the head, but his vision cleared a bit. There was man leaning over him with a wet rag and a look of concern. The man was as black as night.

Will stirred and tried to sit up, but the man put a strong hand on his shoulder to restrain him.

"Too quick, too quick," the man murmured. The English was good, but the accent was strange.

"Where am I," Will managed to croak.

"Jamestown gaol, mister."

"Who are you?"

The man sat back and crossed his arms.

"Who are *you*?"

Fair enough, Will thought.

"Inness, William Inness."

"Inness William Inness, a strange name for English man."

Will shook his head and wished he hadn't. After the throbbing eased, he gave a weak smile to his cell mate.

"Inness will do, and you?"

"I am Juba."

No King, No Country

Despite the pounding of his head, Will squinted to get a better look at the man and it was an odd and imposing sight. Juba's head was shaved bald and gleamed, even in the dim light. His dress was strange. He wore a loose shirt made of some sort of soft leather and no trousers, only a cloth that covered his manhood and what looked to be leggings made from the same soft leather as his shirt. His shoes were also leather but looked more like low stockings than proper footwear.

Juba held out a hand and Will took it, managing with help to rise to a sitting position. He turned to the side and vomited on the dirt floor. Juba handed him the cloth and he wiped his mouth.

"Bad hit on the head, Inness. Make you empty stomach. It will pass."

"Are you a surgeon?" Will asked, curious despite his wretched condition.

Juba took a moment to answer, then shook his head.

"I am thought a healer among my people, though my skill is not great. I learn more from them than they from me!"

"And who are your people, Juba?"

The man gave a little chuckle.

"Very good question, Inness. Very good. Sometimes I'm not sure of the answer. For five summers now I live among the Cherokee. Their home is in the high mountains far south of here. They are a strong people with many great warriors, but I am not of their tribe. Before I came to live with the Cherokee, I am in Jamaica. I learn English pretty good there in sugarcane fields."

"You were a slave."

Juba shook his head emphatically.

"Not slave. Never slave. Prisoner! In Jamaica, they look away one little bit. I run. They catch, they whip. They look away again, I run. Always the same. English man in Jamaica, he grow sick of me. Sell me off to man in Virginia, but the ship, she sink, far south from here. I make it to shore.

Most do not. The land there had no English, but I knew they would come by and by. So I must get away."

"I follow rivers toward the setting sun. I hide at day and go at night. Sometimes I see Indians. Many tribes between the sea and the high lands in the west. Then one day I see the rivers drop down through the rocks and the land rise up to the sky. It's a place of deep valleys and hidden ways. There I am safe from the English. There I find the Cherokee or, they find me. They never see Yoruba man before. They decide not to kill me and I repay them with healing and other knowledge."

"You were taken from Africa?"

Juba nodded.

"I was but twelve summers old when my uncle sold me to slavers."

Will wanted to learn more of this strange man, but he felt another wave of nausea overtake him and retched again, heaving until nothing came forth but bile.

"You rest now, Inness. Better in morning."

Will nodded. There was one small, barred window high up the wall of his cell and through it he could see from the angle of the light that it was late afternoon. He wanted to get to his feet. To scream for his jailers. He worried about Callie and Gus, but his head was spinning now. He eased back down and Juba patted his shoulder.

"You rest now, Inness."

***

Callie rapped on the door of the Governor's house and waited. After some time, the big oaken door swung open and a thin black man in a fine livery peered out at her.

"Can I help you, miss?" the man asked politely.

"Yes, please, sir. My name is Caledonia Inness. My husband and I have just arrived on the merchantman tied up down at the river. There's been some kind of mistake as men have taken my husband, Captain Inness, to the gaol and confined him there."

No King, No Country

The man at the door shrugged.

"That would not be the Governor's concern, Mrs. Inness. And he is absent in any case. I suggest you inquire next door at Sir Thomas' house. The Captain General handles all issues of law here in Virginia." He didn't wait for Callie to respond, but closed the door in her face.

She turned and trooped directly to the house next to the Governor's. This dwelling was not quite as grand, but finer by a good measure than any other house in the town. She took a deep breath and knocked on the door. She waited for a long time and was about to knock again when the door swung open.

The man in the entrance was no servant. He was tall and well-dressed after the fashion of a Cavalier. He was of middle age with a few streaks of grey in the light brown hair that fell to his shoulders. More grey showed in the neatly trimmed wedge of beard at his chin. What was most arresting in his appearance were his eyes, which were a dark brown and slightly bulging.

From the moment he'd opened the door, those eyes had been carefully inspecting Callie from head to toe. It was far from the first time she'd been looked at in this way and his gaze made her uncomfortable, but it was too late to turn back now. She stood her ground and addressed him.

"You are Sir Thomas Lunsford?"

"I am. And who might you be?" he asked. "I thought I knew all the beautiful girls in Virginia, but I seem to have overlooked you, miss."

"My name is Caledonia Inness, my lord. It seems men have seized my husband and I would like him returned to me."

This caused Lunsford to arch an eyebrow.

"Inness? Oh yes, the mutineer and deserter. I just received word that we have taken him into custody and are still searching for his companion, a Mr. Dawes, I believe. Would you know his whereabouts?"

"I do not, but please tell me on what basis have you charged my husband with these offenses?"

Lunsford rubbed his chin as though considering her question.

"Why don't you come inside and we can discuss it, Mrs. Inness."

Every instinct told her to turn and walk away, but with Will locked up, her instincts could be damned.

"Very well, my lord," she said and followed him through a small alcove and into a spacious room with a desk and a half dozen chairs clustered by a fireplace. Anne and James Bingham occupied two of the chairs. Sir James rose out of habit when he saw a lady enter, but sat back down when he saw it was their former servant.

"I believe you might know my fiancé and her brother," Lunsford said airily.

Callie ignored the two and turned to Lunsford.

"I believe you need an arrest warrant for detaining a man under English law," she began, but Lunsford quickly raised a hand to cut her off.

"English law is a bit like fresh fruit, Mrs. Inness. It does not travel well across a great ocean. Out here, we must shift for ourselves. But I've been informed that such a warrant exists."

"So you would take the word of these two alone," she said nodding toward the Binghams, "to knock a man senseless and confine him?"

Lunsford seemed amused at her question.

"Well I'm sure you'd agree, it would be rather rude for a prospective bridegroom to doubt the word of his intended," he said, giving a little bow toward Anne who sat stone-faced and said nothing.

"But you are all adherents of the King," Callie pressed. "Why would you punish a Parliamentarian captain for mutiny? Wouldn't you want to encourage such behavior?

You should be hailing him as an example for others to follow!"

Lunsford looked at her, no longer amused.

"That's a novel idea, girl, but haven't you heard? They chopped off the King's head! I'm not fool enough to remain loyal to a corpse. We're a long way from England, Mrs. Inness," Lunsford said, sticking a thick finger in his mouth then holding above his head, "but I can tell even here which way the wind is blowing. Within the year I expect to see a half dozen Parliamentarian warships drop anchor right down there in the river. They will come with a stiff broom to sweep away any whose loyalty they doubt. What better way to show my allegiance than to hold a prisoner they seek?

I understand that the arrest warrant of which we speak was issued by none other than Oliver Cromwell himself who sent his Provost Marshal all the way to Liverpool to catch your Captain Inness. I've heard of Major Binford and know of his reputation. He's not a man dispatched on idle business. It seems your husband, madam, has made powerful enemies in England and I intend to make his enemies my friends!"

Callie's heart sank a little, but she hadn't truly expected help from this quarter. At least now she knew what Lunsford had planned for Will. She turned to go, but stopped and turned back.

"When those Roundhead warships arrive, I hope they hang the lot of you for traitors."

***

Will had started to nod off when the sound of the cell door opening roused him. He sat up, a little too quickly, his head swimming. The feeling passed quickly and he was relieved to find the throbbing had eased a bit. He squinted at the tall thin man standing in the doorway who was casually watching him.

"You are William Inness?" the man asked.

"Who's asking?"

The man at the door gave an exasperated sigh and, stepping out of the doorway signaled to someone behind him. A beefy guard strode across the floor and slapped Will across the face. The slap stung his cheek, but it also caused his vision to blur and the pounding inside his skull to return with full force.

Juba started to rise, but the guard raised a pistol and pointed it at his head.

"Don't you move," he growled and cocked the pistol.

"Now, Captain Inness," the tall man said quietly. "in answer to your impertinent question, I am Sir Thomas Lunsford, Captain General of the Virginia Militia and what passes for the law in this colony. I simply want to confirm that you are Captain William Inness, wanted by the new government in London for mutiny and desertion."

The guard now pointed his pistol at Will.

"He will shoot you, Captain Inness," Lunsford said. "I've told him to do so if you won't obey and I'm sure that would distress your lovely young wife."

Will's head came up at the mention of Callie.

"Oh, yes, Captain. I've just left her. She pleaded for your release, but of course, the law is the law. It's sad that she's to be left to shift for herself. It's hard on women here who have no husbands to look after them."

"If any harm comes to her...," Will said, dragging himself to his feet.

Lunsford nodded to the guard who raised his pistol and cocked it.

"Now, Captain, you need to just make yourself at home here, as you are likely to be with us for quite some time. I intend to hand you over to whoever the new Roundhead government sends out here. But know this. I'll be willing to show them your grave if you misbehave."

With that, Lunsford turned and walked out of the cell. The guard backed out and the door slammed shut. For a long moment there was silence, then Juba spoke.

No King, No Country

"You in big trouble, Inness. Tell me, what is mutiny?"

Will told Juba his story. Then he lay down and slept.

***

Skirting the main road from town, August Dawes made his way unseen to the waterfront and bounded up the gangplank of the *Fair Wind*. He found that Keogh and Berrycloth were already aware of Will's arrest as were all of the crew. They were gathered now on deck, an angry buzz growing among them. Will Inness might have been a passenger, but to them, he was a shipmate.

Bill Barley suggested they march up to the little gaol and break him out, but Keogh belayed that talk. He'd not approve any open confrontation with local authorities, no matter how justified. A situation like this required patience and, if it came to that, a bit of cunning. And whatever action was to be taken, they would first wait for word from Callie Inness.

So they'd gathered atop the fo'c'sle and waited anxiously for two hours watching the road from the settlement. There was an audible sigh of relief from the score of men at the rails when the slim figure of Callie came marching down from the town. Abraham Keogh waited for her at the top of the gangplank.

"They plan to hold Will until a Roundhead delegation arrives, presumably with a fleet of warships," she informed him. "They'll use him to gain favor with the new government."

Keogh nodded and convened a council of war in his own cabin. Along with August, John Berrycloth and Mathys Beck, he'd invited Jamie Oakley for his knowledge of the settlement. Harry Grey had been seen in the town searching out his mother's cousin, but hadn't returned to the *Fair Wind*. Others eager to lend a hand had to be turned away for lack of space in the cramped quarters.

"Please tell us what you've learned, Mrs. Inness," Keogh began.

"I went to see Sir Thomas Lunsford and was not surprised to learn that it was the Binghams who informed on Will and August."

Oakley spit a wad of tobacco juice into a cup he'd brought with him and frowned.

"Shoulda' dropped that pair over the side off Cornwall," he growled.

Callie smiled at the old waterman, then told the group what she'd told Keogh.

"Lunsford expects Parliament to send a force here to establish their control by the end of the year. He hopes that by holding Will until then he'll curry favor with Cromwell and keep his position."

"Lunsford's a poxy bastard," Oakley observed. "I warned Will about him."

"Poxy or not, he's clever and he just might buy himself preferment from the new regime," Keogh said.

"Will they ship him back to England, Captain?" the girl asked.

Abraham Keogh was a kind-hearted man, but knew this was no time to be gentle. And he reckoned a highland girl could handle the hard truth.

"They'd as likely hang him here, Callie, but we must see that doesn't happen. We'd all of us here be marooned on that damned island in the Bahamas if not for your husband."

"Aye to that!" Oakley said. "I know that gaol. I spent a fortnight there in the dead of winter once. They keep no more than two men there day and night as guards. A half dozen armed men could march up there and have the lad back on board in an hour."

"Those guards will be armed," Keogh pointed out. "What if they resist?"

"That would be their misfortune," the old sailor snarled.

Keogh shook his head.

"I will not countenance killing anyone. We must find another way."

No King, No Country

That brought a silence to the group. No one spoke for a long time, then John Berrycloth slapped his hand down on the Captain's table.

"I've a notion," the first mate announced. He turned to Oakley.

"Go get the cook and have him bring his wine."

For a moment Oakley looked confused by the order, then his eyes grew wide and a gap-toothed smile spread over his weathered face.

"Oh, you're a clever one, sir!" he said and hurried out to fetch the cook.

By now, Keogh had begun to smile.

"It might just work, John!" he said as they waited for the cook to appear.

"Are we to get them drunk?" Callie asked.

Before anyone could answer, the cook came through the door carrying a gallon jug with him. He looked around the room curiously.

"Who amongst ye is costive?" he asked.

"Costive?" August blurted. "What has blocked bowels to do with anything?"

John Berrycloth touched August's arm.

"Lieutenant Dawes, this wine has been seasoned in a cup lined with antimony. It's a purgative for the bowels and the stomach. At sea there are times when food becomes tainted and needs to be…ejected from the stomach. And even if not spoiled, a daily diet of beef can still put a man off his feed and give him cramps. A cup of this wine will make him retch or loosen his bowels—sometimes both."

"I still don't see…," August began, but Callie cut him off before he could finish.

"I will deliver it to the gaol for Will," Callie said.

"For Captain Inness?" Mathys Beck asked, as confused as August. "You would loosen his bowels?"

"He'll never see that wine, Herr Beck."

A look of dawning comprehension came over the German's face.

"Ah, of course! The guards will drink it!"

The German turned to Mr. Berrycloth.

"You *are* a clever man, sir."

"Thank you, Mr. Beck."

The cook set the big bottle down in front of Callie and was turning to the door when it burst open and Harry Grey barged into the room.

"They've arrested Will Inness!" he announced. "We've got to get him out!"

***

Will woke up with a start. Somehow he'd been lifted from the dirt floor and laid on a narrow bench that was the only furnishing in the small cell. His head still pounded, but his stomach had settled and his vision was clear. In the center of the cell, the man Juba was on his knees, bent forward and prostrating himself. He was murmuring something quietly in a language Will had never heard.

He gingerly sat up and watched as Juba rose up, sitting back on his haunches and continuing his recitation. Once more the man bent forward, his palms and forehead flush against the dirt floor of the cell and continued with his ritual. Will looked up at the small window and saw that it was now fully night. He must have slept for hours and felt a bit better for it.

Finally, Juba sat back up, turned and spoke to his right and then to his left in the same strange language, then stood up. Looking up at him now, Will realized that the man was much bigger than he'd recalled when he'd first come to on the cell floor. The African looked to be well over six feet tall and was well muscled. His age was hard to determine in the dim light of the cell, but he did not look to be much older than Will. Seeing his cell mate was awake, Juba smiled at him.

No King, No Country

"You will live, Inness," he said, speaking English once more. "I look at your head. The skin is split, but the bone, not broke."

"Thank you, Juba," Will said, his voice sounding like a croak. Juba dipped a cup in a bucket and handed it to him. The water was tepid, but he gulped it down and asked for another. When he'd finished he stood up unsteadily. The floor seemed to be moving beneath him, but he fought the sensation and gradually it passed. He sat back down.

"What was that you were doing?" he asked, nodding toward the floor where Juba had been kneeling.

"Praying to Allah," Juba said simply.

"You are a Mohammedan?"

"Very much so, Inness. Many Yoruba people follow the Prophet."

"And you pray in this manner to Mohammed?"

Juba laughed.

"Oh, no, no. We do not pray to the Prophet. We pray to Allah, to God only. You are a Christian?"

Will nodded.

"Which kind? There are many kinds of Christians I think."

"Church of England," Will said, the throbbing in his head starting to get worse.

Juba nodded.

"Your prophet is Jesus. Very good man. But why a good Christian Englishman like you in the Jamestown gaol, Inness?"

Will gingerly touched the back of his head and felt where the scalp was split. It needed stitching, but would heal.

"I had ideas the chiefs in England didn't like. I had to run."

"You not run far enough or fast enough, Inness," Juba said flatly.

"It would seem," Will said with a rueful smile. "Why are you here, Juba?"

Juba shrugged.

"My people, the Cherokee, are strong. Other tribes in the southern mountains fear them, though they are not so warlike as the Iroquois."

"Iroquois?"

"Some call them the Five Nations," Juba explained. "Tribes far to the north. Seneca, Mohawk and others. They band together to make war all around the big lakes that are like the ocean. They have the white man's guns. One day, the Cherokee think, maybe the Iroquois come south. They talk to Spanish men further south, but Spanish men won't trade them guns. They send me to the English here in Virginia as I speak their tongue. They offer the English furs for guns."

"For this they locked you up?"

Juba shook his head.

"They lock me up because I'm African man. They take my pelts. They say I lie about the Cherokee! They say I run away from my master, which is true. They see this," he said, pulling up his loose shirt in back to show a horrid patchwork of raised scars, the mark of the whip. "They hold me here until they find who owns me. I am strong. Someone will lie and claim he owns Juba."

The man stopped for a moment, his jaw muscles clenching.

"Nobody owns Juba!"

"Then we must escape," said Will. "I have friends nearby. They will be trying to find a way."

"My friends are far, in the blue mountains where the sun sets," Juba said wistfully.

Will held out his hand.

"You may have friends closer at hand than you know, Juba."

No King, No Country

Jamestown Gaol

The July night air hung hot and clammy over the river as the girl made her way carefully down the gangplank of the *Fair Wind* and started up the road toward the settlement. She had waited impatiently for the night to advance and for the people of the town to retire to their beds before leaving the ship tied up at the pier. Though the dim light of candles and hearths cast a feeble glow from a few windows, most houses were dark now.

It was time.

As Caledonia Inness walked up the muddy lane toward the center of the settlement, the drone of cicadas and the chorus of bullfrogs from the nearby swamp was almost deafening. The heat and the strange noises might have wilted the spirit of a girl from the cool Scottish Highlands, but Callie Inness was on a mission.

Out of sight and a hundred yards behind her, four men crept down the gangplank and followed along in the shadows, watching the girl. She reached the main crossing road in the center of town and marched up to the gaol. One of the two night guards was sitting on the small covered porch smoking a pipe. He straightened up when he saw the girl approaching.

Albert Culpepper knew every female in the town, but had not seen this one and even in the dim light cast from the one window at the front of the gaol he saw she was something special. He got to his feet.

"Well, miss, what have ye there?" he asked pointing to the big bottle.

"I've come to visit a prisoner," she said sweetly, "my husband, William Inness. I thought this wine might ease his confinement."

As she stepped onto the porch and stood more fully in the light, the gaoler leered at her.

"Now aren't you a beauty," he said inspecting her from head to toe. "It's a shame you'll be a widow so young."

Callie feigned distress.

"Oh, I beg you, sir, don't say such things!" she pleaded.

The man shrugged.

"Best face the truth. They say your man will swing for his crime, leaving you all alone."

The gaoler reached over and laid a meaty hand on Callie's shoulder. "Virginia's a hard place, miss. You'll need a good man to look after ye when he's gone."

Callie squirmed away from his touch.

"Please, may I see my husband?" she begged.

The guard frowned, then shrugged.

"Why not," he said and led her through the outer door into a small room where a second guard was sitting in a chair snoring. Culpepper kicked his chair and the man woke with a start.

"What…"

"Up there, Pettigrew! We have a pretty visitor."

The man stood and scratched himself.

"I was just restin' me eyes," he said defensively.

"Well open up the cell so the Missus here can see her man. And I'll take that," he said, relieving Callie of the wine bottle. "Prisoners are not allowed spirits."

Pettigrew picked up a flintlock pistol and trudged over to a heavy oak door secured by a beam that sat in iron brackets affixed to the wall like some medieval castle gate. Culpepper lifted a musket from a rack on the wall and checked the powder in the pan. Cradling the weapon in the crook of his arm, he nodded to his companion who lifted the beam and swung the door out.

"Visitor," Pettigrew announced, then stepped back.

It took Callie a moment for her eyes to adjust to the dim light in the cell. She saw two men rise from a low bench. One came toward her.

"Callie," Will said. "You shouldn't be here."

Ignoring his comment, she flew into his arms and hugged him close. Then she drew back.

"Let me look at you," she ordered, placing her hands on both sides of his face and examining his swollen eye. She turned back toward Pettigrew who was still standing in the cell door and spoke in a voice no longer sweet.

"I need a candle!"

The guard hesitated for a moment, turning toward Culpepper who nodded. Pettigrew fetched the candle from the small desk in the outer room and brought it into the cell, holding it up with one hand to give the girl some light, but keeping his pistol trained on the prisoners.

With better light, Callie could see the other prisoner more clearly. She'd only seen a few African men in her life, one in Tenerife and a few around the Jamestown waterfront, but this man had a look about him, a proud bearing, that the other poor souls had not. He was tall and lean and, dressed in what looked to be deerskin, he cut an imposing figure even in a gaol cell. But the impression was softened considerably by the concerned look on his face as he watched her examine Will's injuries.

Callie tilted Will's head down and felt around his scalp. The hair around the wound was stiff with dried blood, though it looked as though the area had been cleaned up a bit. Callie turned to the guards.

"This wound needs stitches!" she growled.

Pettigrew snorted.

"We ain't leeches," he said, sullenly. "Ye seen yer man, so get along with ye now."

He set down the candle and grasped at her arm, but she jerked it away and pulled Will close.

"Be ready!" she hissed quietly in his ear. Then she turned and stomped out past the guards, slamming the outer door of the gaol behind her.

"That's a pert one," Culpepper said standing now in the cell door and looking at Will. "But I pity the poor devil who gets her after we hang you."

He stepped back and gave a small hand signal to Pettigrew who swung the door closed and dropped the oak bar into place. When Pettigrew turned around, he saw the big man had already taken the cork from the wine bottle.

"We should dispose of this contraband," Culpepper said with a sly grin and took a long swig from the bottle, then passed it to his fellow guard. There was plenty of ale in the colony, but wine was rare and expensive. Neither man would let this go to waste.

Pettigrew turned the bottle up and drank deeply.

***

A bright half-moon cast a ghostly light over the Jamestown settlement as four men and one woman huddled in the shadow of a stable that sat only a block away from the Jamestown gaol. August Dawes, Mathys Beck, Harry Grey and Jamie Oakley sat quietly waiting for some sign that the antimonium wine Callie had left with the guards was having an effect. Both Beck and Harry Grey had firmly insisted on being part of the rescue party, though Callie had tried to dissuade Grey.

"You've family somewhere here in Virginia, Harry. And what of the inn you were to open in Jamestown? You come with us tonight and all that could be done with."

Harry shook his head.

"While Captain Inness was being waylaid, I spent the day poking around Jamestown. I found my mother's cousin readily enough. He was in a grave in the churchyard, having died two years ago of the flux. And Jamestown has an inn—

not a very good one, but better than the place probably deserves. I'd already decided Jamestown was a pest hole before I heard that Will had been taken. I've spoken to Captain Keogh and it's to Maryland for me once we fetch your husband from the gaol. Perhaps the Catholics in St. Mary's Town are in need of an inn or maybe I'll follow Will and August into the wilderness. Your husband's not the only one with a yen to see these mysterious mountains in the west."

Callie could tell the young man's mind was set and said no more. As she looked at the men hidden behind the stables she wondered how this night would end. Keogh had forbidden killing as the price of his cooperation, so none carried firearms or edged weapons. But the Captain had agreed that each could carry a belaying pin, which if properly applied would put a man down without killing him. It had been two hours since Callie left the bottle of treated wine with the guards and the minutes seemed to drag as nothing stirred at the gaol.

"Should it be taking this long?" Callie whispered to Oakley as they crouched in the darkness.

"Depends," Oakley said unhelpfully. "By now some men would be heaving up whatever was in their gut or running for the head. I've seen it take twice that long for others. One way or another, miss, it will hit them before dawn."

Callie sat back, frustrated, but determined to wait it out. They had tried to convince her to return to the ship and wait for them to retrieve Will, but she would have none of it. The men might have belaying pins, but hidden beneath her dress and strapped to her leg was a leather scabbard that held a ruby-handled dagger. Captain Keogh might have forbidden the men from killing anyone, but he'd said nothing to her on the subject. If needs be, she would do what had to be done to get Will free.

It was long past midnight when Harry Grey touched August's shoulder.

"Look!" he whispered.

Harry had been posted at the end of the stable away from the road, but with a clear view of the outhouse that sat twenty yards downhill from the gaol. Callie heard his whispered alarm and crawled down to the corner of the barn to join August, peeking over the young man's shoulder. She recognized the smaller guard who'd been called Pettigrew. He was staggering down the hill tugging at his belt as he came, weaving and stumbling every few steps. Even from fifty yards away, the watchers at the stable could hear him groan.

"Mother of God," he gasped as he flung open the door to the outhouse and stepped in. He'd hardly got the door closed when his fellow gaoler, Culpepper, came racing down the hill. In his haste, the big man tripped and sprawled face down in the dirt. He got to his hands and knees and retched violently in the grass, then dragged himself back upright. He reached the outhouse only to find the door barred. He began to bang on it.

"Out you sod, out!" he roared. The watchers couldn't hear Pettigrew's muffled response, but it clearly was in the negative as Culpepper continued to beat on the door. In desperation, the man stumbled behind the outhouse and dropped his trousers. Squatting in the dark, he never saw August Dawes or the belaying pin that knocked him senseless.

August left Harry Grey by the outhouse door with instructions to deal with Pettigrew once he emerged. The remaining men hurried to catch up with Callie as she ran up the hill to the gaol. She burst through the door with August and Mathys Beck right behind her. The two men lifted the oak bar from the cell door and Callie pulled it open. She held up a candle as Will rose to his feet and shielded his eyes from the light pouring in. He swayed and almost fell backwards, but his cellmate caught him and held him

No King, No Country

upright. August and Mathys took Will's arms and, draping them over their shoulders, led him, stumbling, from the cell.

Callie turned to follow, then stopped and looked at the big black man still standing in the cell.

"Do you speak English?" she asked urgently.

"Yes, miss. I speak it. I am Juba."

"You are welcome to come with us, Juba. We go to a ship on the river, then away from here to the Maryland colony."

Juba hesitated for a moment, then nodded.

"I know not of this place Mary land, but anywhere better than here. I go with you."

***

Captain Keogh stood on the quarterdeck of the *Fair Wind* as the first hint of dawn began to show in the eastern sky. He'd spent the long night anxiously watching the road that ran from the town down to the waterfront. Now in the half-light of predawn he saw them, hurrying down the hill from the town, half carrying Captain Inness. He saw no pursuit behind them, but was sure an alarm would be sounded soon.

He intended to be well underway when it did.

An hour before, he'd posted two men from the morning watch on the pier, ready to cast off the lines. Others were already aloft in the yards ready to unfurl the sails or on deck manning the lines. Bill Barley stood by the sternchaser, the linstock in his hand.

He'd worked the men hard until dark to unload the cargo intended for Jamestown, but there had been no time to take on tobacco or other goods for shipment back to England. Perhaps he could make up this loss if the planters in Maryland had had a good harvest. He consoled himself with the knowledge that he had two hundred pounds of silver from the sale of the *Donker Nacht* that would cover a good deal of lost trade from this hasty departure from Jamestown.

As the weary group reached the pier and made their way up the gangplank to the deck of the *Fair Wind,* he noted that they had taken on an extra passenger. A Negro had followed them down the hill and up the gangplank. Africans were a common sight here in Jamestown, but by his dress and his bearing, this man was no slave.

There's a story there, he thought.

***

The Sergeant of the Guard yawned as he led the five men assigned to morning watch down the road past the Governor's house and toward the gaol. He'd drop off the two replacements for Culpepper and Pettigrew at the gaol, then head out to post the rest of the guard detail at the three outposts that ringed the settlement on the east and north.

It was routine and he'd done it a hundred times.

Then he saw the front door of the goal hanging open, which was odd. As he neared the building he saw Albert Culpepper stumble around the corner holding his head in one hand and holding up his unbuttoned pants with the other.

This was not routine.

***

"Cap'n!" the call came down from the yards.

He'd let his attention wander as the rescue party sorted itself out on deck, but at the lookout's call he jerked his head up toward the settlement and saw trouble coming down the road. Six men, all armed, were hurrying toward the waterfront.

"Cast off the lines," he ordered calmly. His men slipped the heavy ropes that bound the ship to the pilings and scrambled up the gangplank, pulling the ramp in after them as the current began to ease the *Fair Wind* downstream and away from the dock. The movement of the ship did not go unnoticed. An angry shout came from shore.

He ignored it.

"Set the main course," he ordered and the huge mainsail dropped from the yard. "Hard a starboard," he called down to the man on the whipstaff and the bow of the *Fair Wind* swung slowly around, pointing toward mid channel.

No King, No Country

On shore, a man was shaking a fist at him and four more leapt into the dugout canoe tied up at the small dock. They cast off and were paddling furiously to catch the merchantman before it could gain headway. Keogh shook his head.

"Mr. Barley, see those men off, if you please."

Bill Barley blew on the smoldering fuse of the linstock and lowered it to the touchhole of the sternchaser. A roar erupted from the small cannon, loud enough to awaken any who slumbered in Jamestown. The ball splashed ten feet in front of the dugout canoe. The men aboard immediately began to frantically back-paddle as the *Fair Wind* gained headway downstream.

"As you were, Mr. Barley," Keogh ordered. "Time for breakfast I believe."

***

Will winced a little as Callie ran the needle through the edge of the wound, sewing up the six inch gash in his scalp. August sat in the corner of the cabin that had been home to the Binghams on the voyage from England and watched his friend get stitched.

"Oakley says the Indians take a man's scalp as a trophy if they defeat him in battle," he said cheerily. "Perhaps with that scar, they'll leave yours be."

"Let's not find that out," Callie said dryly as she pulled the thread through, drawing the edges of the gash together. She jumped a little when she heard the sternchaser's bark on the deck above her head. Wordlessly, August stood and left the cabin. A few minutes later he returned.

"Four from the settlement gave chase in a canoe. The Captain saw them off with a warning from the sternchaser.

"Keogh will pay for that, I fear," said Will.

Callie nodded.

"Abraham Keogh is an unusual man, a man of principle. He knows there will be a price for what he's done for us."

"What value have we to him?" Will asked.

"You saved his ship," she said as she tied off the last knot in the stitches. "You're the son of a shipper. You should know what that means to a ship's captain. Now lay back and sleep. We need you up and about when we reach Maryland."

***

It was midmorning when the *Fair Wind* reached the broad mouth of the James River and turned north up the Cheseapeak Bay. Having ordered Will to bed, Callie came on deck for some fresh air and Captain Keogh beckoned her to the quarterdeck.

"How fares your man?" he asked as she joined him.

Callie swept an unruly strand of hair out of her eyes as the breeze off the water swept over the rail. She hugged herself and pulled her shawl a little tighter around her shoulders. After the dank heat of Jamestown, the wind on the bay felt refreshing.

"He took a bad blow to the head, but his vision is clear and that's a good sign," she said. "I've sewn up his scalp and the wound looks clean. I credit his African friend for that."

The mention of Juba caused both to stare at the tall black man who stood alone at the larboard rail, watching the shoreline pass by.

"I'm curious about him," Keogh said. "He dresses himself like one of the savages of this land, though different than the Powhatans I've seen."

"Will says he escaped bondage when his ship foundered somewhere along the coast south of here and found refuge among an inland tribe unknown to the English. He speaks our language better than some of my own kinsmen. His people sent him to Jamestown seeking to trade."

"And the colonists took him for a runaway slave," Keogh said, finishing her thought.

"It would seem so," Callie said.

Keogh shook his head.

No King, No Country

"This will be the death of Virginia one day," he said solemnly. "God sent down seven plagues to punish Egypt for holding the Israelites in bondage. Will he not do the same here in Virginia? God does not abide his children in chains. Not the Jews nor the Africans. Not even the Irish!"

Callie wondered about that. The priests said God's ways were a mystery to mortals, but how many generations of Israelites died in Egypt before Moses set them free? And how many would die here? Was there a Moses coming for the Africans of Virginia? Time would tell if Keogh's confidence in God's wrath and the liberation of slaves was justified.

"Captain, what will happen if you come back here to Jamestown in a year? You've made enemies by helping us."

Keogh shrugged at that.

"My father said you could know a man by the enemies he makes."

Callie smiled at that and touched him gently on his sleeve.

"And by his friends."

***

August came off the forenoon watch and saw Juba kneeling on deck facing to the east. Will had told him that the big African was a Mohammedan and that he did this ritual five times each day. August waited until Juba had finished and returned to the rail before approaching him.

"What are you looking for?" he asked as Juba stared at the passing coastline.

Juba took his eyes off the land and looked at August.

"I never come this way before," he said, tapping his forehead. "Maybe I need to come this way again. So I watch and remember."

August shook his head. The only other man he'd ever known to do the like—to fix places in memory like this—was Will Inness.

"Will said you tended to him in the gaol."

Juba nodded slowly.

"He was hurt," he said simply.

"You have my thanks," August said and held out his hand. Juba took it.

"Inness, he is your chief?"

"No, not exactly. We are friends, since we were boys."

Juba considered that for a moment.

"But you follow him."

August grinned.

"I can't argue with that. I've followed him here, half way around the world and reckon I'll keep on."

"Then he is chief," Juba said firmly. He paused for a moment then spoke again. "He say you were fighting men in England."

"We were," August said. "No more."

"I think in this land," he said pointing to the thick forest that grew along the shore, "you will be fighting men again."

***

Will awoke and sat up in the narrow bunk. His hand went instinctively to his head where he felt the raised seam formed by Callie's stitching in his scalp. He swung his legs over the side of the bed and stood up gingerly. Even with the gentle rise and fall of the ship, his head felt clear and his balance solid. He slipped on his shirt and made his way out to the main deck.

The sun was almost directly overhead and the men of the forenoon and afternoon watches were having their midday meal. All paused in their dining to give him a smile and a nod and a few set down their plates to come slap him on the back.

"Go gentle down there," Berrycloth called from the quarterdeck. "I want that man up and about t' lend a hand on the lines!"

Behind the first mate, Callie appeared, a look of mild concern on her face.

"Are you steady, Will?" she called down to him as she reached the ladder.

No King, No Country

"As a rock," Will called back with a grin.

As he waited for his wife, August appeared with a bowl of some sort of fish stew and handed it to him. A day ago any food would have sent his stomach into convulsions, but now the smell of the stew reminded him of how hungry he was. Callie saw him waiting for her as she climbed down the ladder.

"Eat!" she ordered and he was quick to obey. The fish was fresh and the stew delicious. It took an effort of will not to gulp it down, but with Callie watching, he managed to not make a pig of himself.

"So what is the plan now, husband?" Callie asked. "There'll be no boat up the James River."

Will nodded as he finished the last morsel of the stew and set his bowl down.

"There are other rivers," he replied, turning to August.

"Would you fetch my map? And ask Juba if he will come sit with us."

Intent on his careful examination of the land bounding the Cheseapeak Bay to the west, the big African had not noticed Will's emergence from the sterncastle. When August summoned him, he came readily enough and joined them as Will spread the map atop the hatch cover of the hold.

"Here is the river the English call James." he said to Juba, pointing to the bottommost river on the map. "And here is the York, the Rappahannock and, finally, the Potowmac," he continued, moving his finger to trace the shoreline of the great bay northward. Then he pointed inland to the sawtooth line in the west.

"Here is where I wish to settle, Juba."

The African looked at the map and nodded. He pointed to the very bottom of the jagged line.

"Here are my people."

"Do you wish to return to them?" Callie asked gently.

Juba lifted his eyes from the map and looked off to the horizon.

"One day, I will return to my home among the Yoruba," he said slowly. "I have an uncle to kill there, miss. But that day is not yet. I will go back to the Cherokee first and warn them against the English at Jamestown."

Having answered the woman he returned to studying the map.

"What of this area here?" Will asked pointing north of the Cherokee's land."

Juba rubbed his chin.

"None live there now. Some say the land is a place of anisgina…." Juba paused searching for the right English word. "A bad place. A place of…ghosts."

Will and August looked at each other. August spoke up.

"What do *you* think, Juba?"

"I think this is a story to frighten children. I've not ventured far north in the empty land, but what I saw there was a big valley rich in game and ground where corn would grow tall. I saw no ghosts. Still, many grown men believe bad spirits dwell there. There is a path through this great valley that is older than the memory of any Cherokee elder. They call it the Great War Path. It leads north from our mountains all the way to the big lakes in the north that are like the ocean. Tribes use this path to make war and sometimes to trade. But men do not linger along this trail. That is what I know of this land."

Will again caught August's eyes. They had not heard of this valley from Jamie Oakley, whose knowledge of the interior beyond the fall line was, at best, based on rumors. He looked again at the map and saw that the river marked as the Potowmac ran west toward the mountains just as the James had.

"This river, here, Juba," he said pointing to the Potowmac. "Does it lead to the valley you speak of?"

Juba stared at the curving line of the Potowmac on the map.

No King, No Country

"I've not seen this river, but if this is true," he said running a thick finger up the line on Oakley's map, "then, yes."

"Who lives along the river?" he asked.

Juba pointed south of the river.

"Here, Powhatan," he said, then pointed north of the river. "Here are people called Susquehanna. I know little of them. May be folk in Mary's land know more." He paused and pointed to the upper right corner of the map. "Further this way are the big lakes I tell you of and the people of the Five Nations."

Will studied the map for a while longer. From Juba's telling, the empty valley beyond the mountains lay between the fierce Cherokee in the south and the savage Iroquois of the Five Nations to the north. And this river, the Potowmac, would lead them there. Like Juba, he didn't fear ghosts.

Will looked back at Juba and pointed to the dot on the headland that bounded the mouth of the Potowmac on the north.

"We will go here now."

Juba nodded, pointing again to the map.

"We passed this place soon after leaving first river," he said, pointing to the mouth of the York. "I watch for this river," he said staring at the map and pointing at the mouth of the Rappahannock. "It comes soon I think." He continued to trace his finger north to the dot Will had pointed out north of the Potowmac.

"That is Mary's land?" he asked.

"Aye, it's the Maryland colony."

Juba stared at the dot.

"They have slaves there, in Mary's land?"

Jamie Oakley had sauntered over when he'd seen Will and the African studying his map and was looking over Will's shoulder when Juba asked his question.

"Oh, indeed they do," he chimed in, a little too cheerily, "though not so much as back in Virginia."

Juba raised up from studying the map and crossed his arms.

"Then I'll not go to Mary's land," he said firmly.

Will set aside the map.

"Juba, this ship goes to Maryland, then back to England."

"They have slaves in England?"

Will nodded.

"They do."

Juba frowned.

"I'll not go to England," he declared finally and walked back to the rail to stare once more at the Cheseapeak shore. Will followed him and put a hand on the big man's shoulder.

"Juba, if you trust me, come with me to Maryland. We will stay but a few days and when we are ready, we will go to this land beyond the mountains you speak of. We will go up the Potowmac to the big valley and find a home for me. Then you can return to your people."

Juba mulled this over.

"What of slavers in Mary's land?" he asked.

"I will protect you."

"How?" he asked bluntly.

"You will be my servant."

Juba scowled, but Will spoke before the African could.

"They will think you are my slave and you must behave as one. But you and I will know the truth."

"What truth, Inness?"

"That no man owns Juba."

No King, No Country

Mary's Land

The *Fair Wind* dropped anchor just south of the mouth of the Potowmac River as night fell. Captain Keogh did not wish to take his ship into the tributary where St. Mary's City lay in the dark. And while the merchantman's departure from Jamestown had been unscheduled and abrupt, Keogh maintained his tradition of hosting dinner for his passengers in his quarters on their first night under sail. Juba the African declined the invitation and took his meal with the crew.

Despite the unpleasantness of the events in Virginia, this last gathering at the Captain's table for the remaining passengers was a cheerful one. As the spirits flowed, toasts were offered all around. Keogh began it by toasting the capture of the *Donker Nacht,* which had both saved the *Fair Wind* and insured a profitable voyage. Will followed the Captain, lifting a glass to Mathys Beck and his marvelous jaeger rifles that had proved to be of such lethal advantage in their encounter with the privateer.

"Here, here," August said raising his mug of ale and bowing his head toward the German gunsmith.

John Berrycloth raised his cup to both Will and August.

"To you lads who worked like crew, though yer passage was paid. I'll take ye on anytime you've a mind to go to sea!"

August held up thickly calloused hands from his hours hauling on the lines and just shook his head no, to roars of laughter. When quiet returned, Harry Grey got to his feet and looked at Will, raising his cup.

"To Captain Inness, who taught me there is a time to run and a time to fight!"

Will raised his cup back to the young man.

"May your next fight not be aboard a pirate's ship in the middle of a hurricane!"

This brought more laughter from around the table. When the noise died down, Callie rose and faced the head of the table, raising her glass.

"To the resolute Captain Abraham Keogh," she began. "who guided us safely to port and married us along the way." She paused, her cup still held high. "A man who can be judged by the enemies he makes and by his friends!"

This was met with lusty cheering from all at the table and for once, the unflappable Captain Keogh looked flustered. He stood and looked at each person around the table.

"May God watch over you all," he said his eyes welling with tears.

***

At first light, they weighed anchor and rode the incoming tide and a light breeze up the Potowmac and into St. Mary's River, the tributary stream where lay its namesake, St. Mary's City. By midmorning, they were moored off the little settlement's waterfront. The capital of the Province of Maryland was smaller than Jamestown, but better situated, sitting on a slight rise above the river in contrast to the low, swampy peninsula where its sister capital in Virginia lay.

As the passengers gathered on the main deck, a swarm of tenders shoved off from the river bank and descended on the merchantman. John Berrycloth immediately began to sort out this welcoming flotilla and arrange for passengers and cargo to be transported ashore. He and Captain Keogh would follow to see what goods might be available for sale that would fetch a profit back in England.

No King, No Country

A craft suitable to transport the passengers safely to land was selected and its rowers and helmsman waited patiently below the jack ladder as the passengers prepared to take leave of the ship that had been their home for over two months. Farewells with the Captain and first mate having been said the night before, the departing passengers said their goodbyes to the ship's crew they'd come to know so well on the long voyage from England.

Bill Barley threw an arm around Harry Grey's neck and teared up a bit as he recalled the young Cavalier stepping over a dead Knocker Chance to man the sternchaser in their running fight with the privateer. James Oakley, a wad of tobacco stuffed in his cheek, pulled Will aside with a fretful look.

"Yer going away out yonder," the old waterman said, gesturing vaguely off to the west. "Don't let the damned Indians lift yer hair, lad." Oakley's eyes darted around the deck for a moment before alighting on Juba. He leaned in to whisper in Will's ear. "Keep an eye on that one," he said, inclining his head toward Juba who stood patiently waiting to board the tender. "Fella don't know if he's African or Indian, but either way, he ain't like us English."

Will silently gave thanks that Juba wasn't like the English, but said nothing to Oakley who moved off to return to his duties. Men will fear those with looks or ways strange to them. It had always been so. And with fear comes hate. The Irish hated the English, the English hated the French and, if Juba was to be believed, the Cherokee hated the Iroquois who returned that hatred in full measure. Maybe one day, in this new world, that might change, but he doubted it.

When Oakley had gone below, Will joined Juba at the rail as the African watched the tenders jockey for position beside the *Fair Wind*. The big man had stowed his Cherokee garb in a sack at his feet and wore a loose shirt and trousers provided by John Berrycloth, the only man aboard with clothes that would fit. Juba wore no shoes as would befit a slave. He looked up as Will leaned on the rail beside him.

"Sailorman not trust me," he said by way of greeting. Will had to smile at that. Juba missed nothing.

"No, but I do."

That brought a small smile to Juba's face.

"Maybe sailorman smarter than you, Inness. A white man's scalp would be big medicine among my people."

"And a big strong African would fetch a fine price from a planter here in Maryland."

Juba shot him a dark look, but saw the broad grin on Will's face and shook his head.

"I like you, Inness. So I offer a…bargain. I promise to leave your hair be, if you promise not to sell me, once we step off this boat."

Will stuck out his hand.

"Seems fair."

***

Somewhat to Harry Grey's disappointment, St. Mary's City had a perfectly serviceable inn and tavern. The Council Chamber Inn, so named because the building had once hosted the colonial governing council, was run by Willa Martin, a no-nonsense widow who kept the rooms tidy, the food edible and the drinks only a bit watered down. All of the disembarking passengers from the *Fair Wind* found lodging there, with Juba allowed to quarter himself in the hayloft of the stable out back as would befit a slave. At supper their first night ashore the *Fair Wind's* passengers gathered in the inn's small dining room for the evening meal. Over plates of venison stew and pitchers of ale, their talk flowed freely.

"This is tasty!" August proclaimed, holding up a slab of the coarse yellow bread that had been served with the stew. "Good thing too. I've seen no wheat or barley about, but this corn is growing taller than a man's head in every garden in the town."

"I'm pleased you like it, August, as I purchased twenty pounds of the corn meal for your trip upriver," Callie said with a twinkle. "The widow Martin has agreed to show you and Will how it's done, so you won't starve—at least for a while."

"Excellent," August said. "What else is on our menu?"

Callie drew a scrap of paper from the pocket of her dress and scanned the short list she'd made.

"Twenty-five pounds of bacon, a pound of salt and thirty pounds of some sort of beans," she read.

She tucked the list back in her pocket. It was enough, she knew, for no more than a few weeks at best, but there was a limit to how much three men could carry along with their other gear. There were falls on the river where a boat would likely have to be abandoned. Thereafter the men would have to rely on wild game and what they could carry on their backs for sustenance. Will had promised her that they would turn back before starving, but she suspected her husband would push himself to that point and beyond before abandoning his trek.

It gave her some comfort to know that the African, Juba, would be with them. The man knew much of this land, unknown to Europeans. He would know what game there was and much else that would be useful. The thought of the black man sitting alone in the hay barn prompted her to excuse herself. She had Mrs. Martin prepare a large plate of the stew and wrap a slab of cornbread in a cloth for her and she made her way out the back of the inn to the barn.

"Juba?" she called as she stepped into the rough-hewn structure. There was no answer, but she could hear a faint murmur coming from the loft above. She recognized the language that Juba used when he did his daily prayers and waited quietly until the low murmurs stopped and she heard movement above.

"Juba?" she called again, and the big man's head appeared over the edge of the loft.

"Mrs. Inness?" he said, surprised to find her standing at the bottom of the ladder.

"I've brought your supper," she said.

Juba needed no prompting. He climbed nimbly down the ladder and took the plate from Callie.

"You have eaten?" he asked.

"Yes. Please, you eat before it gets cold. May we talk while you have your supper?"

Juba nodded, then sat down on a low bench and dug into his food.

"I am sorry you must stay here," she said looking around the barn. "It's hardly fair."

Juba looked up from his plate.

"I have slept in much, much worse," he said, and Callie's mind went back to the slave ship in Tenerife and the filthy vessel tied up at Jamestown.

For a while she let him eat in peace, but finally spoke again.

"My husband is a brave man," she began "and a stubborn one I think."

Juba looked up from his plate.

"All men stubborn," he said between mouthfuls.

She smiled at that. She'd never heard a man admit it before.

"I want him back alive, Juba."

Juba used a slab of the cornbread to soak up the rich gravy of the stew and smiled at her.

"My woman, she also want me back."

"You have a woman, a wife, among the Cherokee?"

"Oh yes. She much like you."

"Like me?" Callie asked, surprised.

"Yes. She says 'Don't go to meet the English. You not come back!'"

Juba rendered his wife's voice in a comically high sing-song that made Callie laugh. That seemed to please the African.

No King, No Country

"But you went." Callie said after a bit.

Juba shrugged.

"All men stubborn, Mrs. Inness."

Again Callie laughed.

"Well someday perhaps I can meet your woman and we will talk of the stubbornness of husbands."

"She would like that, I think," Juba said. Then his face turned serious. "But she knows, when a man must go, he goes. Do you know that, Mrs. Inness?"

Do I? Callie wondered.

Perhaps she did. She was not a woman to hold her tongue if she had an opinion, but she'd known long before she'd married William that he would be leaving the settlements behind and why. Whatever danger there was out there in this vast wilderness, there could be no peace for them in an English colony with a death warrant hanging over her husband's head. William had to go. And where he went, she would follow.

"Yes, Juba, I know," she said and left the man to finish his supper in peace.

***

When she returned to the inn, the meal was still in progress. As she sat, Will turned to Mathys Beck who'd hardly spoken through dinner. The quiet gunsmith had gone his own way once disembarking at the waterfront and had only joined them at meal time. He sat there now, picking at his food with a somber look on his face.

"You look…troubled, Mathys. How went your day?"

Beck rubbed his chin.

"I fear I've made a grave mistake," he began. "I found an old storehouse near here that I could make serviceable for a workshop, and there is an ample supply of bog iron ore in the region, I'm told, but…" he paused, a stricken look on his face. "There is not a proper iron works! None! In Germany there were ironworks everywhere. Here, they must get good iron from Massachusetts at great cost, or even from England, as they have no works to forge their own. With no reliable source of wrought iron, there will be no rifle barrels!"

Silence fell over the gathering as Mathys Beck described the ruination of his plans.

"You say there is a works in Massachusetts. Will you move there, Herr Beck?" Harry asked.

"Nein!" Beck blurted, reverting to his native German. "Nothing but stiff-necked Puritans there. They would not welcome a man of my faith."

"Then you must build an ironworks here!" Grey said. "What would it take?"

"Everything!" Beck exclaimed throwing his hands up. "A blast furnace and a waterwheel to run the bellows, a forge and a trip hammer to work the pig iron to wrought. It would take a great deal of money, more than I have, but also men. Men who can mine the ore and operate the smelter and the forge. Men who know what they are doing. Where would we find such men or the money to pay for it all?"

When Beck finished his sad recounting of his setbacks, silence fell over the table. Then Harry Grey dug around inside his jacket and drew out the leather bag that held his share of the prize money from the *Donker Nacht*. He dropped it on the table in front of Beck.

"Will this be enough to begin?" he asked, and before Beck could answer, he continued. "And as for where to find men? I say we poach them from the ironworks in Massachusetts."

Beck looked at the sack of silver on the table, then up at the young man across from him.

"But what of your inn?" he asked, his voice grown husky.

Harry shrugged.

"I considered proposing to the widow Martin, who owns this fine place," he said with an amused grin, "but she's twice my age and being courted by some local gentry who owns ten miles of river front for a plantation! So I am in need of another business to invest in."

No King, No Country

Grey extended his hand across the table "Are we partners, Herr Beck?"

Mathys Beck took Harry's hand.

"Partners, Mr. Grey."

***

Little was seen of Harry Grey or Mathys Beck over the next two days as the new partners set about planning their ironworks. Will and August spent their first full day in St. Mary's city inquiring after a boat to take them up the river with hardly more success than Will had had at Jamestown. The dugout canoes that they found were too small to handle three grown men and their supplies and the rowboats all seemed to be gainfully employed in fishing and crabbing around the estuary of the Potowmac and not for sale. Will had returned to the room he and Callie shared with August to help her sort through the supplies they were to take when August burst in, a look of excitement on his face.

"Will, Will," he blurted. "I've something to show you!"

"What is it?" Will asked, curious at his friend's excitement.

August shook his head.

"I won't say. You and Callie come with me…and we should fetch Juba as well!"

The three made their way out the rear entrance of the inn and gathered up Juba as August led them through a cornfield toward the river. At last they reached a small but well-tended dock set a good ways upstream from St. Mary's waterfront. Tied up to a piling on the dock was a canoe.

It was beautiful.

Fourteen feet long with graceful arcs at bow and stern and a hull of some dappled grey and white material stretched over a delicate frame of wooden ribs and thwarts, the thing bore little resemblance to the heavy dugout canoes they had examined earlier in the day. As they admired the graceful lines of the craft, August undid the rope and slid the canoe up onto the bank. Grasping it by the gunwales, he lifted it up and over his head.

"It's made of bark from a birch tree," he proclaimed, his voice muffled as he walked around with his head inside the hull, "and it's light as a feather!"

"Wherever did you find such a wonder?" Callie asked as August lifted it off his shoulders and handed it to Will.

"Indians!" August replied excitedly. "Or at least that's who made the thing. There's a fur trader here who does business with the tribes to the north. He called them the…"

"Susquehanna," Juba said, finishing the sentence. August nodded.

"Three of these Susquehanna arrived in this very canoe as I was taking a stroll along the river after the noon meal. In the center of the boat they had a great heap of beaver pelts to trade for iron goods and colored cloth. It took some dickering with the Indians and the trader, but in the end, the Susquehanna got what to them was a treasure in pots, pans, axes and woolen cloth, the trader got the furs and a bit of my silver and I got us a boat!"

Will lifted the canoe from over August's head, marveling at the lightness of the thing and set it back gently on the river bank. He examined it more closely and saw that the thin skin was sewn together with some sort of fibers and stretched around the wooden skeleton.

"Have you seen such a thing, Juba?" he asked.

"No. Cherokee know of them but not how they are made. They say the warriors of the Five Nations travel far and swiftly in these canoes. Cherokee are lucky all rivers between them and Iroquois run north, not south!"

Will turned to August.

"Well done, Gus! Well done, indeed," he said and slapped his friend on the shoulder. "Jamie Oakley said there are great falls on the river a hundred miles upstream that no boat can navigate. This we can carry around the falls and continue on."

No King, No Country

August started to slide the canoe back into the river, but Will stopped him.

"We've had enough surprises on this trip, Gus. Let's haul this back up to Mrs. Martin's barn for the night. At first light we'll take it down to the river, load it and go."

Juba didn't wait for further instructions. He hoisted the canoe up and over his head in one easy motion and started back toward the inn. Will offered to help, but Juba refused.

"In America, Inness, slaves do the heavy lifting," was all he said.

Potowmac

At first light, squalls swept in off the Cheseapeak spoiling the three men's planned departure upriver. By noon, the sky had cleared, but the tide was beginning to turn, which made for hard upriver travel. But the turning tide was ideal for the departure of the *Fair Wind*, which would sail for the Massachusetts colony on the ebb. Captain Keogh had made up half his lost trade from Jamestown with tobacco from the plantations strung out along the Potowmac and St. Mary's rivers and would call at the growing port of Boston in the Massachusetts Bay colony to take on beaver pelts and lumber.

The former passengers of the merchantman gathered on the small dock on the waterfront to bid a final farewell to the Captain and John Berrycloth. Will took Keogh aside and handed him a sealed note that he had composed the night before.

"This is for my brother Robert, in Liverpool," he said. "If you see him, give him this and tell him I am well."

"It will give me great pleasure to assure him that you are both safe and well married!" Keogh said with an uncharacteristic grin.

"Very well married indeed, Captain," Will said returning the smile.

He shook Keogh's hand and turned to see Callie hugging young Harry Grey. Mathys Beck had learned from Captain Keogh that the ironworks in Massachusetts was largely manned by Scots. They were Catholics and prisoners of war shipped off by Cromwell and the Parliamentarians to become indentured servants in the colony. Harry Grey would take the *Fair Wind* as far as Boston, then would travel on to reach the ironworks on the Saugus River. There he would induce skilled workers to return with him to Maryland by purchasing their freedom and offering them good wages.

"Don't let the Puritans put you in the stocks, Harry!" August said as Callie released him.

"I'll be on my best behavior, Gus, and within a year, we'll be turning out our own iron right here on the St. Mary's river. Then Mathys here can make his marvelous guns."

The young man threw an arm around the dour German who looked uncomfortable at such displays.

"We're going to be rich!" Harry proclaimed.

"We are going to work like dogs and will be poor for a long time," Mathys replied.

"Then we'll be rich!" Harry insisted.

Mathys shrugged.

"Maybe."

After handshakes all around and hugs from Callie for Keogh and John Berrycloth, the three men boarded the pinnace and rowed out to the ship anchored in the channel.

"Shall we ever see them again?" Callie asked wistfully.

Mathys nodded.

"We will I think. The Captain will call here again in a year. I've agreed to supply him ten tons of wrought iron at a good price for shipment to England."

Callie looked out across the water and saw Harry Grey scrambling up the jack ladder to the deck.

Harry was right, she thought *They're going to be rich*!

***

Caledonia Inness and Mathys Beck stood on the banks of the St. Mary's River at dawn as mist hung thick over the slow moving stream. They watched as the last of the equipment and supplies were loaded into the birchbark canoe that lay along the riverbank. The graceful craft tugged at the line securing it to the bank as the river flowed toward the Potowmac, drawn by the retreating tide.

That tide would turn soon and for the next six hours the waters of the Cheseapeak would push back up the Potowmac estuary. Jamie Oakley had sworn that the effects of the changing tide could be felt all the way to the falls a hundred miles upstream. The three men setting out had every intention of using the two flood tides each day to speed their way west.

While a pale moon still hung in the night sky, Will, August and Juba had dragged the canoe down to the river and begun to load their carefully selected supplies in the center of the craft. The big African was dressed once more in the soft leathers he'd worn in the Jamestown gaol. The evening before he'd handed Callie the clothes John Berrycloth had given him. To Juba they were slave clothes and he was done with them.

Along with the food supplies Callie had purchased, they carried three axes, a crosscut saw, wool blankets and the needed tools for cooking. A small barrel of black powder and a hundred lead rounds were carefully secured and lashed to one of the thwarts.

Will and August each brought one of Beck's long rifles and a flintlock pistol. Stowed onboard as well were their two carbines. Beyond their own needs they carried a collection of trade goods selected by Juba should they need to smooth the way with any of the inland tribes.

Will surveyed the canoe and was pleased that, despite its load, the sleek boat seemed hardly weighed down. It would easily handle the added weight of three men. Out in the middle of the channel a fish broke the surface and snatched a dragonfly out of the air, disappearing beneath the swirling water with hardly a splash.

It was time to go.

No King, No Country

He turned to Callie. They'd said their personal goodbyes the night before and there was little more to say.

"Look for us when the snows come."

"I know," she said, "I will."

He pulled her close and kissed her, then turned and stepped carefully into his place in the stern of the canoe. He kneeled and took up his paddle as Juba followed, climbing in just behind the supplies. August was last to take his place in the bow.

Will looked at Mathys Beck and nodded. The German pulled up the stake and tossed it to Will as the current began to pull the canoe away from the bank. Will used his long paddle like a steering oar to turn the canoe's nose toward the middle of the channel as August and Juba dug their paddles deep into the swirling water, propelling the canoe forward like an arrow loosed from a bow.

From the bank, Callie and Beck watched as the graceful craft picked up speed, cutting through the mist that clung to the surface of the river. As the canoe and its three occupants disappeared around a bend in the river, the girl said a silent prayer that it would bring her man back safe to her.

Mathys Beck gently took her by the elbow.

"Come, Callie, we will count the days together."

The German made no mention of the tears streaming down the girl's face as he led her away.

***

Within the first mile, August and Juba found a steady rhythm that shot the canoe forward at speeds they hardly could believe. Surprised flocks of ducks took to the air as this strange creature of the river swept down on them. In the stern, Will gently shifted the angle of his paddle blade and watched as the canoe's nose turned instantly in response.

As boys, he and August had spent hours in small boats on the Weaver and Will had seen every sort of pinnace and rowboat during his years in the shipper's trade, but nothing he'd seen in England could match the speed and maneuverability of this boat made from strips of wood and the bark of a tree. Early on, August had paused in his steady pace and looked over his shoulder at Will and Juba, a look of pure excitement on his face.

"My God!" he called back, "it's like flying!"

It took less than an hour to travel down the tributary that was the St. Mary's river to reach the broad estuary of the Potowmac. The tide was just turning as the canoe left the smaller river and entered the larger. Water from the Cheseapeak was now relentlessly pushing upstream and the canoe danced along on the tidal current. In the wide estuary of the Potowmac, the surface was choppier, but the canoe felt stable as they turned toward the west.

So near to its mouth, the Potowmac was more bay than river and Will could barely see the far shore. He dipped a hand in the water and touched his fingers to his tongue—it was brackish. Before setting out, the three had agreed they would paddle hard upriver until the tide changed, then go to shore to eat and allow Juba time for his prayers. When they set out again they would test the canoe's ability to make headway upriver against the Potowmac's current.

The years he'd spent on the Weaver had taught him that you can take a boat upriver if you kept out of the center channel and stayed close to the inside bank at the river bends. It was hard work, but if they could do that in a rowboat on the Weaver, he knew he could manage it in this canoe on the Potowmac.

As the two men in front dipped their paddles in time with each other, Juba began to sing. The tempo of his song kept time with the strokes of his paddle and the tune had a playful lilt to it, though the language was strange. It was not in the tongue Juba spoke when he prayed. Will wondered if it was Cherokee or from the Yoruba language of his youth.

Whatever the words meant, the tune and the African's booming voice was infectious. After a time, August began to sing along, keeping to the tune and tempo but supplying his own lyrics composed of English doggerel. Having the Englishman join him seemed to please the big African and he sang louder until he stopped in mid verse.

Will looked to the near bank and saw what had made Juba go silent. A long stretch of riverfront had been cleared and row after row of tobacco plants stretched up from the river and out of sight over a rise. Moving up and down the rows were men and women—black men and women—picking the leaves. Sitting astride a horse, a musket resting across his thighs, was the only white man in sight. The man on horseback did not see the canoe as it passed by. He was keeping a watchful eye on his field hands. But one of those field hands saw them. A woman raised up as the canoe passed by on the river below and gave a small wave before bending down once more to pick tobacco. Juba lifted his paddle in a salute, but the woman did not look back up.

There was no more singing that day.

***

For the remainder of their first day on the river they saw not another living soul, though there was much else to draw their attention. A bright blue and orange kingfisher followed them for a long stretch then alighted on a branch to study the water near the bank. Flocks of geese congregated in the eddies and didn't bother to take flight as the canoe approached, simply paddling out of the way. As the sun neared its zenith in the cloudless summer sky, they searched the riverbank for a spot to take out for Juba's midday prayers and saw a herd of deer splash across the mouth of a creek that emptied into the river.

There were a magnificent buck with a fine spread of antlers among a dozen does and yearlings. They were a bit smaller than the red deer Will had occasionally taken in Cheshire, but twice the size of the more common roe deer. As one of the does caught the movement of the canoe, she raised her long tail, its underside covered in a tuft of bright white fur. At this signal of alarm, the herd bolted up a game trail and out of sight.

They took out at the creek and had a hasty meal of cornbread that had been baked in Mrs. Martin's kitchen the night before. When Juba had finished his prayers, they were back on the river. The morning paddle had been an exhilarating ride aided by the tidal surge, but with the turn of the tide in the afternoon, making headway against the Potowmac's powerful current had been hard work. As the sun dipped low in the west, they glided into shore near another creek and hauled the canoe out.

As Will gathered firewood, August struck a spark from a flint into a pile of cattail fluff he'd found in a marshy spot near the mouth of the creek. The tinder flared instantly into a small flame that he carefully nurtured with some dry grass and small twigs. As the two Englishmen dealt with the fire, Juba produced a long string and a fishhook from his small sack.

"Your missus find for me in the town, Inness," Juba said. He had August cut a small piece of fat from their stock of bacon to bait the hook, explaining that as a Mohammedan, he was not allowed to touch pork.

The big man walked back down to the water and dropped the baited hook in. It never reached bottom. With an excited yelp, Juba yanked on the line and hauled in a wriggling catfish. He unhooked the fish and handed it to Will as, without a word, August drew his knife and sliced off another bit of bacon. Will had just begun cleaning the first fish when Juba yanked another from the stream. By the time the fire had died down to glowing coals, a half dozen good-sized catfish and a single perch were cleaned and ready for roasting.

They ate as night fell. Far off an owl boomed and further still its mate called in return. With supper done they doused the fire and Will set himself as first watch. As the others curled up in their blankets he moved off into the woods to

No King, No Country

find a spot well away from his sleeping companions. If any approached the camp in the night, they'd see only two men asleep, not a third awake and armed watching in the dark. It was a thing he'd learned as a young dragoon.

He estimated they'd covered almost forty river miles on their first day, which put them well beyond the limits of the Maryland plantations. A people called the Susquehanna inhabited these lands. Shopkeepers in St. Mary's City had sworn the tribe was peaceable and only interested in trading furs for English goods. But Will would not stake their lives on the opinion of shopkeepers.

They would keep a watch.

***

For two more days they paddled upstream. On both sides of the river the country became more rolling, with high bluffs along the southern shore. This far upriver, the effect of the tides was small and the river's current strong. Their progress slowed and by sundown each day, they were thankful to pull to shore and make camp. Will guessed they'd traveled no more than fifty miles in the two days and on that long stretch of the river they'd seen not a living soul.

But they had seen signs of human presence.

On their third day, when they pulled the canoe ashore near a shallow stream for Juba's prayers, August called them over to a spot where a well-worn game trail crossed the creek. He pointed down and there, amidst the cloven hoof marks of deer, was the fresh print of a moccasin. Judging by its size and freshness it had been made by a man who'd crossed the creek that very morning. Juba agreed it would be best to move further upstream to find a spot for his prayers.

On the fourth day, the high bluffs on the southern bank and the rolling hills to the north gave way to a long stretch of relatively flat country. At midmorning they reached a fork where two channels came together. Will rolled out Oakley's map and noted that the right hand channel was a tributary stream, not the main channel of the Potowmac, and from this tributary they likely had less than a half day of paddling to reach the falls.

With the sun overhead they pushed upriver and soon the land began to rise once more on both sides of the river. On the north bank, a steep ridge rose up and ran parallel to the river while on the southern shore, rocky cliffs loomed five hundred feet above the water. Between the ridge and the cliffs the river had cut a narrow gorge through which it surged and swirled. Will kept the canoe close to the southern bank as the three men fought for every yard of progress. Finally, they saw a break in the cliffs where a narrow ravine came right down to the river's edge. With Juba and August stroking for all they were worth, Will guided the canoe toward the small sandy beach at the foot of this cleft. When they'd dragged the canoe up on the sand, all three fell back, exhausted. The falls were still not in sight, but a distant roar from upriver announced their presence not far ahead.

It was time to portage.

***

A veil of mist hung over the gorge as Will and August hauled the canoe up the ravine and along the cliff top above the falls. Once the two reached the top of the cliffs the going was easier and within a mile they came to a spot overlooking the falls hundreds of feet below. Here the river didn't plunge down the fall line in a single great torrent. The gorge below was a maze of jagged rocks that forced the mighty Potowmac to split into a dozen narrow channels, its green waters whipped into white foam as it dropped through this chaos of stone.

A quarter mile past the top of the falls they found a well-used game trail that ran down through a cleft in the rocks to a flat section of river bank. With the afternoon advancing, there was no time to rest. Will set off immediately to join Juba who'd been left behind to stand guard over the pile of supplies on the sand beach downriver. August stayed behind to watch over their precious canoe.

No King, No Country

Without the burden of the canoe, Will returned swiftly to the sand beach where he and Juba split the gear and supplies between them, each man carrying over a hundred pounds on his back as they followed the trail up and around the falls to join August by the river.

With canoe and supplies now safely above the falls, they paused to take a meal. August began to work on starting a fire as Juba began carefully repacking the supplies in the canoe. Will walked down the river to fill a pot with water. Reaching the bank, he knelt and wearily scooped up his potful of water and was rising when he froze.

Standing on the upstream bank no more than twenty yards from him was an Indian boy. The child was no more than eight or nine years old and he'd stopped in mid-step when he'd seen this tall fair-haired stranger ahead of him. For a long moment no one moved. Will raised his hands to show he had no weapon and smiled at the boy, but it did no good.

The boy turned and fled.

Will did the same, emptying the pot as he ran back up the bank.

***

The last of the gear and supplies were flung into the center of the canoe as the men scrambled to launch it. Where there was a boy, there would be men. How many they couldn't know, but they would be fools to wait and see. August waded into the stream and climbed into the bow as Juba seated himself behind the supplies. Will shoved off and climbed in the stern. All three began to paddle hard upstream.

The Indian boy had been swift in carrying his alarm, for around the first bend they saw a dozen warriors congregating around the lad. Hauled up on the bank were a half dozen fish traps, and three long dugout canoes. Finishing his report, the boy turned and pointed emphatically downriver. The men listening all turned as one to look where the boy was pointing and there was his proof in the middle of the river.

All talk ended as the men scattered to their boats and launched them into the river with a chorus of high pitched whoops and yelps. Will turned the nose of his boat toward the far bank hoping to slip past the slower dugout canoes, but quickly saw there would be no skirting this flotilla paddling out to intercept them.

"Juba, keep us steady!" he called as he lay his paddle down in the bottom of the canoe and fetched his long rifle.

As Juba stroked hard, switching his paddle from side to side to keep the canoe from turning or drifting back down toward the falls, Will poured a touch of powder into his rifle's pan and raised the stock to his shoulder. Fifty yards ahead, the nearest dugout canoe won its race to cut off their escape. Two of the warriors back-paddled, holding their boat in place as one man nocked an arrow and another in the bow brandished a war club. Sighting down the long barrel, Will took a deep breath and held it as the man across the water drew and released his arrow. It buzzed by, six inches wide.

Will squeezed the trigger.

The river valley echoed with the roar of the rifle's discharge and the warrior with the bow lurched backwards, clutching at his right arm where the ball had struck him. He slumped down into the canoe, but his companions refused to flee. Instead, the man in the stern shouted a command and turned their canoe downstream to close with these interlopers in their fishing grounds.

Jamie Oakley had once told him that while the Indians had once feared to face Europeans with guns, they had learned that these long sticks that spit death took a long time to gather themselves between uses. It had become common practice to induce a man to discharge his weapon and then close on him before he could reload. It would seem that this lesson had not been lost on the men in the dugout canoe.

Two of the warriors dug in with their paddles and, aided by the current, the heavy canoe gained speed. As it drew near, the man in the bow, his forehead covered in fierce tattoos, raised his warclub and pointed at August, screaming out a challenge in his own tongue.

In the bow, August frantically searched behind him among the bags of beans and cornmeal for his own rifle, but in their haste to escape the weapon had been buried under their supplies. The enemy canoe was twenty yards away when his hand found the barrel of his carbine. He knew the gun wasn't loaded and there would be no time for that now.

He raised the carbine by its barrel and pointed it at the oncoming warrior.

"Come on then!" he screamed. "Let's see what ye have!"

The warrior, his face a mask of fury hurled back a war cry and swung his club downward in a vicious arc as the two canoes slid by each other. August met the warclub with the barrel of the carbine then thrust the butt of the weapon into the face of the warrior as he passed. Stunned, the man tried to recover, but Juba lashed out with his paddle, its blade catching the man in the throat. He toppled backwards and the dugout canoe listed hard, taking on water.

The second man in the canoe tried to grab the gunwale next to Juba, but the big African brought his paddle down hard above the warrior's wrist snapping his forearm. The man drew it back howling in pain. In the stern of the dugout canoe, the only uninjured man left frantically dug in his paddle to pull away from the lighter craft. With three men wounded, he turned back toward the bank where the boy still stood by the fish traps. But now the current seized the heavy canoe in its grip, pulling it relentlessly toward the falls only a quarter mile downstream.

Men in the other canoes lost all interest in the trespassers as they saw one of their own being swept down river. They broke off their pursuit of the birchbark canoe and paddled hard downstream in a desperate effort to save their fellows. It was in vain. A line of cordage was cast toward the lone man in the stern still paddling mightily, but it fell short and the canoe disappeared over the lip of the falls and was gone.

The three men in the birchbark canoe did not look to see the result. They dug their paddles deep and the canoe pulled away upriver. Will shot a quick glance over his shoulder and saw the boy still standing alone on the river bank. Did the child have a father or brother in the lost canoe? On the voyage to America he'd wondered if the New World would be more peaceable and just than the old. As he watched the boy standing there alone, he had his answer.

***

They paddled on until well past sunset and made camp up a clear stream that came in from the north. August boiled a pot of beans and they ate in silence. Juba took the first watch, but none slept well that night.

At dawn they broke camp and were back on the river despite a morning fog. After the gorge and the falls, the river had settled into a placid pace, its course curving first toward the northeast then making a long loop back to the northwest. The channel here was still wide, but shallower. As they passed above, Will could see huge rocks lying on the bottom. Islands became more common and a good many of the larger boulders on the river bottom rose above the river's surface.

But the canoe had a shallow draft, despite its load, and it handled like a well-trained cavalry horse. By the end of the day, the country on both sides of the river began to rise once more and Juba's mood, which had been somber since the encounter at the falls, lifted. For the first time in over a week he began to sing quietly and his song swelled as the hills gave way to long steep ridges to the east and west.

It was the morning of the third day after the falls that they saw a rocky prominence ahead and there the river split, with one branch running on to the west and one turning sharply south. Juba took but a moment to point his paddle to the south.

No King, No Country

"This river the Cherokee call Shenandoah. It starts far south, almost to Cherokee land. We will go south here."

Will did not argue. To the north were the fierce tribes of the Five Nations and far to the south were Juba's own folks. Between was an empty land where no tribes had settled. Somewhere here in this valley he would find a home for himself and Callie and August. Using his paddle as a steering oar, he turned the canoe's bow to the south and started up the river called Shenandoah.

Shenandoah

The river was as broad as the Potowmac, but shallower, with dark rock ledges visible only a few feet beneath the surface. Hemmed in by high ridges on the east, it bent and twisted like a serpent as the three men powered their canoe south against the river's flow. From time to time, the channel would split to sweep around a rocky island, then come together once more upstream. Dense forests crowded down to the river's edge on both sides and marched up the steep slopes of the eastern ridge. Little could be seen to the west where the land was lower and the wall of trees on the riverbank blocked their view.

But every few miles the trees would give way to a patches of grassland. These large meadows revealed a landscape of gently rolling country covered in tall grasses. Will studied each stretch of the river carefully, both to commit it to memory and to consider whether it might be suitable for a home. As they rounded another bend with the sun sinking behind the trees on the western bank, he saw a bare rock outcropping high up on the eastern ridge.

"There," he said pointing his paddle at the premonitory. "I would have a better look at this valley."

He guided the canoe to a broad sand bar below the overlook where they hauled it out and concealed it beneath the drooping limbs of a small willow. The slope was steep and daylight was short as they climbed up through the trees. The sun was almost down when they reached the rocky crag that jutted out from the flanks of the ridge. Will climbed up on a huge flat slab of rock and looked off to the west. The view made him draw in his breath.

Below them was the twisting strand of the Shenandoah River, glistening in the fading rays of the sun and stretching out of sight to the north and south. Far to the west another range of mountains rose up, higher than the ridge upon which he stood—if he could judge at such a distance. And between him and those mountains was the loveliest valley he'd ever seen.

The valley floor was flat in places and gently rolling in others with stands of ancient trees stretching for miles, interrupted here and there by vast expanses of grassland. Juba explained that the Great War Path connecting the big lakes in the north to the high mountains where the Cherokee dwelt lay in the middle of that broad valley, though never far from the river below them.

"You find a place this side of the river, Inness," he said gravely. "Over there," he said pointing to the land across the river, "too many Indians. No good for English man."

It seemed like good advice to Will. He knew that his new home would not stay hidden forever, but it would be foolish to settle near such a well-traveled path. He knew it was used by the tribes for trade, but it was not called the Great War Path for nothing. He wanted a place that had plentiful timber and a reliable supply of clean water. He would build a strong house on high ground and perhaps a wooden palisade to fortify it. Juba had assured him that most Indian settlements had such defenses.

Somewhere in this vast unpopulated landscape he would find his spot, but for the moment he stood there as August joined him and admired the scene. A sizable meadow lay directly across the river beyond the trees that lined its bank. The grass there was tall and golden brown from the summer heat. As the sun dipped low a large herd of deer had come into the open ground to browse after sheltering during the heat of the day. August took it all in.

"It's beautiful," he said with a hushed voice.

"Yes, very pretty," Juba observed. "Good for meat, good to grow corn and squash, but dangerous place too."

As if to confirm his caution, the deer in the big meadow suddenly bolted, flashing a dozen white tails in their wake as they bounded out of sight. No threat was visible at first, but the men kept watching the meadow and after a time a huge black bear padded out of the trees. It stopped and sat back on its haunches, sniffing the air, then dropped back down and disappeared into the tall grass.

No bears roamed English woods. It was said they'd died out in the dark ages. Will had seen one once. He'd been persuaded by a fellow officer to attend a bear baiting in London. The crowd had found the spectacle of a chained bear being set upon by packs of mastiffs entertaining, even humorous, but the vicious bloodletting had revolted him. He'd never attended another.

"Bear is smart and hard to kill," Juba observed, "but he carry much meat, much fat."

Will nodded. He'd been a skilled hunter and trapper as a boy, but there was much here that was new. The game was different as were many of the plants. He would need to learn fast if he was going to survive in this wild Eden. Juba had not given any notice of when he would depart for his home far to the south, but until that time he would learn as much as he could from the African who had found a way to survive among strangers and in this strange land.

As the sun dropped behind the mountains, they made their way back down to the sand bar and built a good fire. Juba had August bait his hook and snagged a fish of a different sort than his catch on the Potowmac.

"Well bless me," August said as Juba brought the first wriggling fish over to the fire. "It looks like a browny!"

No King, No Country

Will looked up from the fire and saw the fish dangling at the end of the line. It did quite resemble the brown trout they'd caught many times in the River Weaver, though a good deal darker in coloration. Seeing what must be a cousin of the familiar fish he'd grown up with was oddly comforting, a reminder of home. Within a few minutes Juba brought two more trout to be cleaned and what appeared to be another perch. All were set to roast over the coals and were eaten with a simple cornmeal mush heated up in a pot.

As darkness descended on the valley, Juba moved off to stand watch. Will lay on his blanket and stared up at the night sky, speckled with stars. He wondered if Callie would find it as beautiful as he did here in this valley of the Shenandoah. He thought she would.

She was a Highland girl after all.

***

Will had the predawn watch and waited to rouse his companions until the thick mist had started to lift off the river. After a quick meal of fried cornmeal mush, they launched the canoe and continued upstream, passing many streambeds, dry now in late summer. These they ignored. A farmstead would need a reliable water supply year-round. Twice they pulled out where good-sized streams emptied into the river from the high ridge on the east. But each time they found the streambeds ran far up the flanks of the eastern ridge with no level ground for building or planting.

For two more days they continued upstream, finding no promising sites. The morning of the fourth day they slowed their paddling as they approached a sharp bend to watch three buffalo crossing the river ahead of them. A large bull led two cows up on the west bank and shook his great head like a dog, flinging a fine spray of water from the ruff of thick hair covering his head and shoulders. The bull eyed the men on the river and snorted, then turned and led his harem away through the trees as the canoe rounded the bend.

On the far side of the bend was a wide gravel bar with a sizable stream flowing through it and into the Shenandoah. They hauled the canoe across the bar and concealed it behind a pile of driftwood timbers deposited there in some earlier flood. Once again they followed the streambed across a series of broad terraces that bordered the river. When they reached the foot of the great ridge they saw the stream dropping twenty feet down a rock slab from a narrow ravine above. It was a lovely sight, but held little promise as a place to settle. Discouraged, they were about to turn back when Juba pointed to a muddy game trail running down toward the river.

"Buffalo come this way to get to the river," he said.

Will studied the track that had been churned up by the recent passage of the bull and his cows. The path was broad and well used, cutting through a stand of trees toward the riverbank. He turned and looked back up the trail. There he saw it climb up a steep slope in a series of switchbacks, then disappear over a rise.

Juba's eyes had been following the same path.

"Buffalo like flat ground and grass. Buffalo not climb mountains," he said.

Will nodded. If there was naught but steep slopes, thick woods and rock beyond these little falls, there would be nothing there to interest a buffalo. So what lay higher up? He started up the twisting path with August and Juba right behind him. At the top of the rise he saw that this ravine widened out a bit above the falls. It was still narrow and rocky, but looking ahead, he could tell by the light filtering through the trees that the land rose only gently.

They followed the buffalo track as it sometimes veered away from the stream and twice crossed it, always keeping to the most level ground. A mile in, the ravine had widened into a valley a half mile wide. They followed the trail as it wound back down to the stream and emerged from the thick wood into a large meadow. Before them, the stream flowed

No King, No Country

over a low palisade of sticks and mud that had dammed its flow creating a small pond and marsh behind it.

"Beaver!" Juba said and pointed to a brown head watching them from the middle of the pond. The head disappeared followed by a loud clap of the animal's broad tail on the surface. As the ripples spread across the still surface of the pond, Will studied the valley. There were patches of hardwoods and pines on the valley floor that grew eighty feet tall. He'd recognized a stand of black walnut trees along the trail, their limbs heavy with the round green husks covering the nuts inside. Juba pointed to a tree near the pond with large green fruit hanging from its limbs.

"Paw paw," he said. "Good to eat."

Eager to explore, they moved up the valley. Beyond the beaver's pond the stream flowed freely through a patch of aspens and spruce that gave way to another meadow beyond. As they stepped out of the trees and into the open, a covey of quail burst from the tall grass in a flurry of wings. From this clearing they could see that the valley ran on for perhaps another mile, ending as it began in a narrow steep ravine that ran up toward a saddle between two rocky peaks. Will looked at August who was grinning. Both knew they had found what they had come to the mountains for.

"What shall we call it, Gus?" Will asked.

Gus didn't hesitate.

"Eden Valley," he said and so it would be called.

***

The three men sat wearily by the fire waiting for the rabbit to finish roasting on a sharpened stick over the coals. They had spent the afternoon hauling the canoe further into the woods and concealing it there, then packing their supplies up the ravine and into the valley. All were tired, but Will thought it time to address a question that had been weighing on him.

"We have found our place here, Juba," he began. "Will you now return to your woman among the Cherokee?"

Juba didn't answer at once. He stirred the coals with a stick and turned the spitted rabbit that was getting crisp on one side. Then he shook his head.

"My woman is safe with her people, Inness. You and Dawes?" he shrugged. "I think you have much to learn. I will stay until the leaves fall, then I go."

"You do not owe us that," Will said.

Juba nodded.

"I do not," he agreed. "I owe it to your woman. When they come and take you from the Jamestown gaol, it was she who say I come too. She give me back my freedom. So I try to give her back her man. Then, I go."

Will nodded.

"Till the leaves fall then."

***

Callie stacked dirty plates and ran a wet rag over a tabletop in the dining room of the Council Chamber Inn. The noon meal was over and there were dishes to do and kitchen work as well to prepare for the evening customers. It had been a fortnight since she'd watched Will, August and Juba paddle away in the morning mists and she'd resolved that day to not sit idle waiting for their return.

This America was a new land and full of mysteries. While Will and the others explored the land, she'd resolved to learn all she could of its people and their affairs. Maryland might be an English enclave at the edge of the wilderness, but it was not England and had its own peculiar ways. What better place to learn of them than the Inn in St. Mary's City?

Willa Martin had taken her on readily enough. Contrary to local rumor, the widow had no interest at all in the planter who'd been courting her. As a good Catholic, she objected to marrying a slave owner, though she did not hesitate to serve them stew and ale if they had the coin. The inn was a business after all. Her opposition to the slave trade made it difficult to find good help in the little settlement where a great deal of the menial work was done by blacks.

No King, No Country

"White girls are in short supply," she volunteered when Callie first asked about work. "They get married off by fifteen or stole by the Indians. And most would rather be carried off by the savages than to do honest work here at the inn. So you've employment if ye want till yer man comes back."

The widow Martin was a shrewd woman and was not at all surprised when her business picked up markedly with the hiring of the beautiful Caledonia Inness to wait tables. Half the new customers were old married men and the rest were bachelors, some who could barely grow chin whiskers and some old enough to be Callie's father. The girl had made it well known that she was happily wed and Willa Martin noted with satisfaction how deftly she fended off flirtations with firmness and good humor.

Maybe her man won't come back, Willa thought as she watched Callie scoop up the dirty dishes. That she had thought such a wicked thing made the widow blush and cross herself. She knew she'd have to report this to the priest at her next confession.

Callie came through the kitchen to the shed out back where the scraps from the table were fed to three shoats in a pen and the plates were washed in river water. She scraped the leavings for the eager young pigs then set to work on the dishes. As she scrubbed the plates, she thought back on what she'd learned from a new diner that day.

The man had just arrived on a coastal ketch from the Jamestown colony and had been happy to chat with the pretty girl serving up stew and ale. There'd been quite an uproar recently in the capital of Virginia, he told her. Pirates had attacked the gaol and freed a prisoner it seemed. Having rescued their man, the pirate ship had fired a broadside to drive off any pursuit and fled down the river.

The Captain General of the militia had been outraged and the two gaolers who'd let the man escape had been flogged.

Having breathlessly told this tale, the man beckoned Callie close and looked around the inn.

"Some are saying it weren't no pirate at all in the gaol," he said in a hushed voice. "They say he was a Roundhead sent by Cromwell himself to spy on the Royalists in Jamestown!"

"How interesting," Callie said.

Encouraged, the man continued.

"They say this spy'd likely make for the Plymouth colony which sides with Parliament or maybe even Maryland!"

The diner lowered his voice even more and darted his eyes around the inn's dining room.

"Have ye noticed any strangers about, lass?"

Callie shook her head,

"Only you, sir," she said wide-eyed. "And you aren't the Roundhead spy—are you?"

***

For three days the three men explored every part of the hidden valley nestled between high ridges on the north and south and narrow ravines to the east and west. Near its eastern end a small knoll rose up beside the stream. Some long ago fire had burnt the old growth there and the little rise was covered with saplings and blackberry brambles. From the top of the knoll it was a short walk down to the stream and once the saplings were cleared, the site would afford good views up and down the valley. Will and August agreed that it was here they would build their cabin.

When they weren't exploring the valley and its surroundings they set to work preparing their homesite. They'd brought three long-handled axes and two spades with them and began clearing the saplings from the little knoll by the stream. It took them two weeks of sweaty labor in the August heat to clear and level the top of the hill.

One day as they worked, Juba held up his axe and shook his head.

No King, No Country

"Do you know what the Cherokee use to fell trees?" he asked. "Fire and stone axes! The whites have steel and my people have stone," he said sorrowfully. "It cannot end well for us."

Will wanted to tell him he was wrong, but knew that would be a lie and said nothing. Thankfully, Juba was not one to dwell on melancholy things for long and soon began to sing one of his Yoruba chants, tearing into the saplings with a vengeance using the white man's steel axe.

They used some of the saplings to build a rough lean-to to keep out the weather, others they set aside to use as roofing for the cabin. Among the young trees, Will found a small elm that yielded two good staves for longbows that he put aside to cure.

They saved a few clusters of blackberries to provide some fruit and found big patches of blueberries up the sides of the valley. They weren't the first to discover this berry patch as bear scat was there as well. Juba said the bears fattened up on the berries as they neared time for their long winter sleep.

The African had been true to his word and took every opportunity to teach the two Englishmen the knowledge he'd acquired from five years with the Cherokee. Early on he showed them how to take a patch of deerskin and fashion moccasins, cutting the skin to fit the foot and stitching up the sides with sinew.

They'd worn holes through the soles of the cavalry boots they'd escaped England in and were eager to try the new footwear. The soft leather underfoot felt odd, but as there were no bootmakers within a hundred miles they'd need to get used to the new footwear. Within a week, both wondered why they had stumbled around in their heavy boots for so long.

In the evenings, Juba taught them the language of the Cherokee and each morning quizzed them on the words they'd learned the night before.

"Some tribes speak a tongue much like Cherokee," he told them. "Others not. Powhatan language I do not understand. Iroquois tongue has many words same as Cherokee. An old chief once say that long time back, Iroquois and Cherokee are one people. Maybe so, but now, they blood enemies."

No love like that between brothers, Will thought. *Nor hate either.* In civilized England brother had been pitted against brother for six long years.

Early on, the three hiked to the eastern end of the valley and climbed the steep ravine there to a saddle between two rocky summits to the north and south. From the top of the saddle they could see all the way to the foothills that stretched out of sight to the east.

They slipped down the eastern side of the saddle and killed a good sized buck that still had velvet on its antlers. Juba had advised them to leave the valley to hunt so nearby game wouldn't become scarce. Come winter, having meat nearby could be crucial. They skinned and cut up the deer, packing it back to the valley, where Juba showed them how to smoke the meat.

Near the end of the month, they discovered a small limestone cave under a rock overhang not far from the home site. The entrance was narrow but the space opened up a few feet in. They fashioned torches and cautiously stepped into the darkness from the bright August sunlight. Inside, the cave's interior felt wonderfully cool and the ceiling rose to twelve feet. Somewhere, further back, they heard the sound of running water, but this outer chamber was dry.

Their torches revealed that they were not the first men to discover this cave. In the center of the chamber were the unmistakable remains of a fire. The charred wood was cold, but there was no way to tell if the fire had died a month ago or years ago. It was a good place for a man to shelter or to hide, and for the farmstead Will planned, it would serve as a cool dry place to store root plants and other perishables.

No King, No Country

As they turned to go, Juba stopped abruptly and raised his torch. There, above the entrance to the cave a figure had been carefully scratched into the soft limestone. It was the unmistakable image of a deer of some sort. The drawing had been skillfully crafted and the animal appeared to be in mid-flight. A close looked revealed the shaft of an arrow in its rump.

"Awiequa," Juba said in a hushed voice. The African made a little sign with his hand then scrambled up and out of the cave. Will and August stayed behind, studying the drawing.

"Looks like a red deer stag," August said and the huge antlers on the drawing fit that description. As young men, the two had once hunted in the high country of Derbyshire and had seen just such a beast on a far ridge, but had never gotten close enough to attempt a shot. After a time, they followed Juba out into the sunshine to find the man sitting well away from the cave mouth.

"Juba, do you think the man who made the fire drew the picture on the wall?" Will asked.

Juba shook his head gravely.

"There are pictures like this in the land of the Cherokee. They are very ancient. The Cherokee call the picture-makers 'The Old Ones,' and fear their spirits dwell in places where they leave these marks."

Will didn't press the man further. Juba might not believe in ghosts, but he clearly did not wish to cross paths with the spirits of The Old Ones.

***

In the London Guildhall, Oliver Cromwell paced back and forth in his small office, stopping finally to gaze out the one window. The situation in Ireland had gone from bad to worse over the summer. The rebellious Irish Confederates had allied themselves with the remnants of the English Royalists and had gained control over the entire island, save for Dublin.

He'd shipped Edward Whalley's regiment there a month ago, both to shore up Dublin's defenses and to get the Colonel and his men out of London. Whalley was a cousin and a brave soldier, but his men were rabble-rousers and Whalley was hesitant to deal with them with a firm hand. To his dismay, the discipline of the army had become a political issue of paramount importance and Colonel Whalley's weakness in that regard made him a liability.

In another fortnight he would leave to take command of the army in Ireland and could ill afford to leave politically unreliable men here in London. As he looked out over the rooftops of the capital he felt both relieved and anxious to leave the city.

London.

In his eyes, the city was the new Babylon, a place overrun by tradesmen and lawyers, where any excess was tolerated and all discipline scorned. It was a city where honest country men feared to tread, a place where a scurrilous rumor could spread like wildfire from Whitehall to the Tower in half a day and summons an angry mob in a moment. Just that morning such a rumor had reached his ears and it troubled him.

It had been three months since the execution of the army mutineers—long enough for London to have moved on to other concerns, but now there was talk that one of the mutineers had escaped the gallows and that this missing Captain Inness was behind a secret faction within the army that was growing in strength. Led by Inness, the rumor went, the conspirators were plotting to free the Leveller leaders from the Tower and seize control of Parliament and the army.

It was all nonsense of course. This Captain Inness was no doubt hiding somewhere in the west country, afraid to show his face, or more likely run off to America. But rumors such as these were dangerous. It encouraged the damned Londoners and emboldened malcontents in the army. The

No King, No Country

mood of the London mobs didn't worry him overmuch, but he could ill afford more trouble in the ranks of the army just now.

He'd hoped that the mercy he'd shown by sparing some of the mutineers would quiet the unrest that had plagued the army these past months. Now this notion that some fugitive captain was keeping alive the men's grievances and plotting against him and Parliament would keep things stirred up. Were it not for these rumors, he'd have been content to let the memory of the outspoken Captain Inness simply fade away, but now....

Inness had to be found and hanged, wherever he might be hiding.

There was a rap on his door.

"Come!"

Major Binford entered the office and saluted.

"You sent for me, sir?"

"Yes, Major, I have an assignment for you."

"Yes, sir," Binford replied eagerly. He'd been relegated to supervising the patrols collecting drunken soldiers from the back alleys of London since his failure to apprehend Captain Inness and Lieutenant Dawes in May and it had galled him.

"A ship will depart from Gloucester in ten days, bound for the Americas. I am sending an emissary to visit each of our colonies to gauge their loyalty to the new government. A full fleet and sufficient regiments will be dispatched after the Irish campaign is finished to further establish our control there."

"Very good, sir," Binford offered.

Cromwell frowned. He didn't like toadies, but Binford had a certain talent that he needed.

"You will be my emissary, Major, and in addition to judging the loyalty of colonial officials, you will discover if our slippery Captain Inness and his friend Dawes have shown up there. If they have, you will find them and bring them home. A company of foot will accompany you. Understood?"

"Perfectly, sir."

"And, Major, I want them alive. So I can hang them on Tower Hill for all to see."

That brought a small smile to Binford's lips.

"Very good, sir. Put an end to the rumors," he said.

Cromwell felt a twinge of annoyance that Binford had known of these rumors, perhaps even before he did. Still, it showed that his Provost Marshal had not lost his instincts for sniffing out trouble.

"Dismissed," he said, and Binford saluted and left.

No King, No Country

Trouble in Eden

Will and Juba muscled the pine log up to shoulder height and set it down into the notches that had been carefully shaped by August with his hand axe. The log settled firmly into place and the two men stepped back to examine their handiwork. The cabin walls were now shoulder high on all four sides, the product of a week of heavy labor.

Setting the foundations had taken a fortnight of hauling stone up from the streambed and the tall pines needed for the cabin walls had to be felled from a stand a quarter mile away. Each day they arose at first light, sending one of their number to hunt or gather nuts and berries as the cornmeal and bacon were gone. The others felled, trimmed and hauled the timber to the cabin site to be measured, cut and set in place.

August had designed the cabin based on log houses he'd seen in Jamestown and St. Mary's City and it was unlike any house in England or, according to Juba, any dwelling of the Cherokee. A wattle and daub house would have been much easier to construct, but a house on the frontier had to serve as a fortress if it came to that and thick logs would offer far better protection from bullets and arrows than a structure of woven limbs and mud.

Once the walls were as tall as Juba, saplings they'd cleared from the knoll would serve as sturdy roof timbers. Juba showed them how to cover the saplings with moss that could be peeled up from the forest floor. Moss would shed water and be hard to catch fire. Clay from the fringe of the beaver pond supplied the daub to seal the gaps in the logs and to keep out the cold and rain. Flat stones from the stream formed the fireplace and chimney. The African also suggested they surround the little knoll with a palisade of logs in the Indian fashion, but that would have to wait until the cabin was complete.

Will wiped the sweat from his eyes and admired the growing structure. It looked sturdy and oddly beautiful to him. He lifted his eyes to the high ridges that surrounded this sheltered valley and felt certain that Callie would approve of their new home. She was a Highland girl after all and one could scarcely imagine a more beautiful mountain valley than this. He was picturing her standing in the door of their new cabin, when August tapped him on the shoulder.

He didn't speak, just inclined his head toward the stand of aspens down by the creek. The dense patch of trees still sported the bright green leaves of summer, but here and there a few had turned from green to gold. It was now mid-September by their best estimate and the leaves would last no more than six more weeks. When the aspens were bare, Juba would leave.

Soon after, it would be time to return to St. Mary's City. Will had promised Callie he would come before the snows and he intended to keep that promise. If all were well in the settlement, they would winter there then set out in the spring for this valley. For now, there was much work left to do.

Will shouldered his axe and headed back to the pines.

***

Early October brought an end to the heat of summer with crisp cool days followed by chill nights. High on the ridgelines autumn announced its arrival with patches of yellow, rust and red that crept further down the flanks of the ridge with each passing day. By mid-month, the first frost had arrived and the aspen, birch and maples were ablaze with color on the valley floor.

They'd finished the cabin, and though it was snug and warm when a small fire was set in the fireplace, on clear nights they often chose to sleep outside under the stars. It was on one such night that Will sought to know more of Juba's past, before he'd come to live with the Cherokee.

"Why did your Uncle sell you to slavers?" he asked.

"My father was of the obeye, the ruling class of the Yoruba people. He and his brother, my uncle, were advisors to the great Alaafin, Ajagbo, who is like your king in England. They were rivals for the Alaafin's ear and grew to hate one another over the years. I'd seen twelve summers when my father suddenly fell ill of some wasting sickness. My mother thought it to be witchcraft or poison, as my father was a strong, healthy man. One day as he lingered near death, my uncle summoned me to his compound. He well knew that should my father die, I, as his first born son, would take his position. Nor could he doubt that the hatred my father felt for him had already been handed down to me and burned in my heart. I was clubbed and awoke bound with a rope about my neck and led off to the coast where I was sold."

"Your father?"

"I know not if he died or if he lives. That no longer matters. I will kill my Uncle before I breathe my last."

***

With autumn advancing and leaves beginning to fall, the men redoubled their efforts to prepare for the winter and for leaving the valley. One of the meadows was cleared of burnt out tree trunks and stones to ready it for the plow come spring. August, who'd become deft with his hand axe, fashioned saplings and woven reeds into chairs and sleeping platforms for the cabin. Will, judging his elm staves sufficiently cured, set about paring the first down into a bow shaft, drawing his knife carefully along the grain.

As the shavings gathered in little mounds at his feet, the shape of the bow emerged, flat in the belly and rounded at the front. It was a shade over six feet long when he'd nocked the ends. Its like would have been instantly recognized by any archer on the field of Agincourt or Crecy.

For the second bow he would carve tips from the antlers of the deer, but he was anxious to put the first into service, both to save precious lead and gunpowder and to test himself. It had been over six years since he regularly hunted with a longbow and to be proficient with the weapon took time and practice. So as August built furniture, Will practiced. Juba had shown him how to find arrow shafts among the shoots at the base of an ancient hazel tree and how to fashion serviceable arrow heads by knapping jasper and flint.

As they worked, wild geese passed high overhead winging south ahead of the cold. Their calls stirred something melancholy in Juba who sang little now. Will could tell the African was soon to take his leave and on a day when it seemed that summer had returned, he and Juba set off down the western ravine to look for game beyond the river in the big valley of the Shenandoah. They'd discovered that the spot where they'd seen the buffalo cross the river was shallow enough for a man to cross without swimming, though the water in places was chest deep.

Will carried his longbow and Juba carried one of the carbines that Will had taught him how to shoot. They'd hunted the big valley across the river twice before with great success and a final deer would give them all the meat they would need until they left the valley.

The trail down to the river passed near to where the canoe was carefully hidden. As they neared the spot they could see that its hiding place had not been disturbed and they did not approach it. They would not risk having others find their tracks and discover their prize. At the river's edge they tightened the leather ties on their moccasins and waded into the current holding their weapons over their heads. The water was cold, but in this late warm spell it was tolerable.

Climbing out on the far bank they took the same path the buffalo had made to the west. It passed through a fringe of woods that ran along the water, then crossed a big meadow where deer liked to graze. As the two men reached the edge of the trees, they stopped and stood very still. Standing alone in the tall grass was a bull elk.

"Awiequa," Juba whispered—and the beast, for all the world, looked like the drawing they'd seen in the little cave. Will slipped an arrow from his quiver and nocked it. It was a long shot, well over a hundred paces, but it was a big target. Juba looked at him skeptically. He'd seen Inness fashion his long bow and practice with it in the valley. The Englishman was a good shot and got better with practice, but he'd not aimed at any target this far off. A shot from this distance would likely do nothing but spook the animal and a great deal of meat would be gone on the hoof. But Inness had proven to be a man who would do what he'd set out to do, so Juba said nothing.

Will elevated the bow, then drew the arrow back until the fletching touched his ear. He held, then loosed. The arrow leapt across the meadow. Juba thought he'd undershot, but he had not seen the full power of a longbow and the shaft flew true, burying itself above the shoulder of the elk. The animal reared, then sprang down a trail, fleeing for the cover of the trees there. Will and Juba ran to pick up his trail. It was not difficult. The bull was losing much blood as it fled and was slowing. Will caught a glimpse of its haunches as it stumbled and fell in a little clearing. He unsheathed his knife and hurried forward. Then he froze.

Standing in the clearing were more than a dozen Indians, who looked as shocked to see him as he them. Between them, the dying elk thrashed for a moment then laid down its great head and died. When the elk lay still, Will slipped his knife back into the sheath and set down his bow, raising open hands to show he held no weapon. This was no war party as there were more women and children than men. Will only counted five warriors and two of these were hardly more than boys. The oldest man, a tall handsome warrior with a proud bearing, had his own knife drawn, but made an elaborate display of returning it to his belt. Will looked over his shoulder at Juba who was eyeing the group suspiciously.

"They have trouble, Inness. Not our affair. Give them a haunch of meat and we go."

Will could see with his own eyes that Juba had the right of it. This little band was weary and gaunt as though they had traveled far with little rest or food. The two boy warriors were hauling a litter behind them which they gently set down. A woman, old beyond telling, raised her grey head and eyed the elk and the men standing across the clearing.

"Oginalii," she croaked and slumped back on her litter.

Will looked at Juba.

"It is word for friend in the Cherokee tongue," Juba said.

A young woman knelt beside the litter and stared defiantly at Will and Juba as though doubting that these strange looking men could be friends. She pulled a knife from somewhere in the folds of her buckskin shift and brandished it at them. The tall warrior spoke sharply to her and she glared at him, but tucked the knife away.

"Ask them what their trouble is."

Juba frowned.

"Not our affair," he said again, more firmly now.

"Ask them."

Juba shook his head, but stepped forward and addressed the oldest man who was clearly the leader of the band. From his study of the Cherokee tongue, Will understood many words the two spoke but had trouble stringing them together into anything meaningful until Juba turned to him and explained in English.

"His name is Dancing Crow. They are Hurons, come from far to the north, near the big lakes. They speak the

No King, No Country

Iroquois tongue but are not of the Five Nations. They say there is a great war in the north over fur. The Five Nations have turned on all their neighbors and the northern streams run red with blood."

Will looked at the sad little band. The woman on the litter looked near death and all looked half starved. The leader had a half-healed scar on his left arm from his shoulder to his elbow. The man stood very straight, but in his eyes, Will could see desperation. Whatever the nature of the war in the north, these people had certainly lost.

"Where do you go?" Will asked the warrior called Dancing Crow in the Cherokee tongue.

Dancing Crow pointed off to the south then spoke at some length. Will could only catch part of his meaning, but that part was worrisome.

"They are pursued?" he asked Juba.

Juba nodded.

"He says Seneca war party seek for them. He says when Seneca drive them from their village, they seek shelter with tribes south of the lakes, but all feared the Seneca and turned their face from them. Twice the Seneca catch them and twice Dancing Crow's people get away, but each time they lose men. These five are all that's left. They do not know where to go, so they just keep going. They ask me if Cherokee take them."

"Will they?"

Juba shrugged.

"The girls and the children, mayhaps," he said. "The men…maybe no."

"Why do warriors seek you so far from your home?" Will asked the Huron. Dancing Crow spoke slowly, understanding now that Will was new to the tongue.

"When Seneca overrun our village, I kill many warriors," he said and spit on the ground in contempt. "One I killed I see before. He was son to a Seneca chieftain. His brother, a warrior they call Crooked Knife, has sworn to take my scalp in revenge."

"Will they follow this far south?"

"It is far from their lodges, but yes, they may follow."

"How close?"

Dancing Crow thought for a time before answering.

"Two days, maybe more, maybe less.

Will nodded and turned to Juba.

"Could you speak for them with your elders of the Cherokee, Juba? They need help."

Juba shook his head.

"I can speak, but other voices have more weight at council. I could not promise that the men would be spared. But that matters not," he said, inclining his head toward the group. "It is many, many days travel to the villages of the Cherokee. If the Seneca are on their backtrail, these Hurons will never reach there."

Will knew that Juba spoke the plain truth. He'd seen the condition of these people and knew they were on their last legs. He looked at them now, one by one. The smallest children were strapped to the backs of their mothers. Older girls held the hands of those old enough to walk. Their faces were dirty and their cheeks hollow. He'd seen much the same on the roads of England as towns were plundered and people fled from Royalist and Parliamentarians alike during the civil war. As part of an army on the march, there was little he could do for the English refugees he'd seen, but he was no longer in the army and this was not England.

"I will take them to our valley," he said to Juba.

"It is a foolish thing to make enemies of the Seneca, Inness," Juba said urgently.

"Juba, you will go back to your people soon and we will have no friends in this empty land. We could use some."

"Better no friends and no enemies!" the African said firmly. "Seneca will follow these new friends of yours right to your cabin door and your woman will weep that you do not come back to her."

"If the Seneca come, they will find my scalp hard to lift." Juba sighed.

"You are a strange man, Inness," he said and drawing his knife, knelt in the clearing and began to gut the elk.

***

They followed the old buffalo track from the meadow to the river, hoping their tracks might be lost amidst the welter of hoof prints. Will and Juba helped Dancing Crow and one of his young warriors carry the litter across the ford. The rocks on the bottom were slippery, but the men were steady and the old woman arrived dry on the far bank of the Shenandoah.

Weeks of being hunted had made the Huron women and children watchful and silent. But there was some whispering among the women when they emerged from the dark confines of the ravine into the sunlit valley beyond. As they passed the pond, the resident beaver used his broad tail to slap his alarm and dove out of sight, much to the delight of the younger children who pointed and nudged each other but did not speak. Will wondered when these young ones might become children once more.

The Hurons made their camp in the aspen grove that lay between the pond and the cabin. The women immediately set about starting a fire and further butchering the elk, which had been hastily cut into pieces in the clearing and packed across the river. Those not working on the elk carcass began cutting off straight limbs from the aspens to fashion rough shelters. Dancing Crow sent one of his young warriors to watch at the river ford to give warning if the Seneca should follow. With the women at work and a watch set, the Huron leader followed Will and Juba further up the valley to the cabin.

August had been sitting on a stump sharpening his hand axe on a whetstone, but stood when he saw his two friends approaching with a stranger. Will hailed him.

"August, we have guests in the valley. This is Dancing Crow. He is a Huron from far to the north. He and his people will be staying here for a time. They speak a tongue close to Cherokee, though many words are different."

August studied the newcomer. He was a striking looking man—tall and muscular, his head shaved bald save for a cockscomb of black hair in the center. He wore beautifully worked soft deerskin leggings, but like the man himself, they looked hard used.

He looked back at Will.

"You said 'his people'?"

"There's over a dozen more down amongst the aspens," Will said. "Mostly women and children."

August nodded. He'd been studying the Huron but couldn't help noticing that Juba was unhappy. He beckoned for Will to come close and turned away from the Huron, lowering his voice.

"Juba looks worried, Will. Is there trouble?"

"Could be bad trouble, Gus. There's war in the north between the tribes. Men from the Seneca nation hunt these Hurons and they might not be far behind. Juba says we should turn them out, but I could not be party to that."

Will turned and looked August in the eyes.

"You are your own man, Gus, and half this valley is yours. If you say nay, I'll send them back across the river and point them south. But if I do, I go with them until I see them safe—or the Seneca catch us."

August sighed, then turned and sank the blade of his hand axe deep into the stump he'd abandoned.

"Let's go have a look at this wretched lot," he said and started down the hill toward the aspen grove.

***

No King, No Country

The smell of roasting elk greeted them as they neared the aspen grove. August hung back a little at the sight of this band of Hurons in the valley. The only natives of this land he'd encountered had tried to kill him at the great falls on the Potowmac, but this scene could not have been more peaceable. The older women had wasted no time in setting spits over the fire and were picking off small pieces of elk meat to feed the children. The rest were waiting eagerly for the meat to be done. One of the young warriors squatted near the fire, feeding the flames with dead wood.

Down at the pond two of the older girls knelt near the cattails, scrubbing the dirt from their faces. That done they rose and walked back up toward the stand of aspens. Will recognized the taller of the two as the one who'd stood beside the woman in the litter and brandished her knife at them. She was called Two Rivers and as the girls came up the path from the pond, she moved with a grace that belied their weeks on the run. When they neared the encampment she laughed out loud at something amusing the other had said.

The sound of a girl's laughter in this valley where only the rough voices of men had been heard for months seemed out of place, yet charming. Dancing Crow left the three men and walked up to the fire. One of the young mothers scooped up a boy sitting by the fire and tumbled him into Dancing Crow's arms. The little boy wrapped his arms around the warrior's neck as the Huron plucked another piece of meat off a spit and gave it to the child.

August shook his head and turned to Will.

"They stay," he said.

***

Will, August, Juba and Dancing Crow sat down at the end of the day to speak of the Senecas and the threat they posed. From the big valley of the Shenandoah, their valley was well hidden and they had taken care to cover their tracks as much as possible, but a determined Seneca war party would not be easily deceived. They had to prepare to fight.

"They will see where the elk was butchered," Dancing Crow said. "They may keep searching to the south, but if they find no tracks there, they will return. Then they will find this place."

Will turned to August.

"What would the dragoons do, Gus?"

August rubbed his chin.

"Well, we have these now," he said, touching a hand to the stock of his long rifle. "We can sit on the high ground above the ford and kill any man before he gets to midstream. That should discourage them, but if that should fail, we must hold the ravine above the falls. There's good ground there to defend. If they come in strength and get into the valley, it will go hard for us."

Juba agreed.

"We must watch the ford, night and day. When they come we must meet them there or in the ravine where their numbers will not count for as much."

Dancing Crow agreed that his four young Huron warriors would be the watchers at the ford and that the two Englishmen and the strange Cherokee, Juba, would camp near the ravine. There they could come quickly if the watchers at the ford raised the alarm. This they would do until the Seneca came or the danger had passed.

Dancing Crow sent the first of his watchers back through the ravine to watch the ford and ordered the older girls and women without children to make shelters for the three men near the ravine. Will, August and Juba returned to the cabin to fetch bedrolls, weapons and other necessaries and made their way down to their new campsite.

A half dozen of the women had cut and shaped limbs to frame an overhead shelter between four saplings and were covering the frame with spruce bows to keep out the rain.

No King, No Country

August set down his bedroll, hand axe and fry pan to watch the women and shook his head in amazement at their energy.

"We'd have had the cabin up in a week with this lot," he said.

As they stood there, the youngest of the girls stared at them. She could not have been more than seven or eight years old, and seemed fascinated by these strangers, two white and one black, who had offered them refuge. August saw her gawking and rummaged in his coat pocket, pulling out a cloth where he'd wrapped the last of the fat blackberries taken from the bush by the cabin. He unfolded the cloth and beckoned to the girl who came shyly forward. He held out the ripe berries and the girl plucked two from the pile, popped them in her mouth and chewed thoughtfully. When she'd finished, she looked up at August and suddenly stuck her tongue out. It was stained black by the fruit. August made a face at her display and, laughing, she ran back to join the other women working on the shelter.

Will noticed that Two Rivers had been watching this encounter as she worked. She spoke to the younger girl when she rejoined the women. The girl pointed at August and waved at him, still laughing. The older girl smiled, then turned back to her labors. But as the afternoon wore on, Will saw her glancing more than once at August. His friend seemed not to notice her at all.

***

The sun was setting as Crooked Knife studied the bloody remains of the elk that lay across the trail. He was surprised that the Hurons had managed to kill the thing. Surely an elk would have smelled the stench of a dozen Hurons long before they were near enough to strike with lance or arrow. From the prints, the animal had come from the meadow he could see just ahead in the fading light. Had it blundered into them here on the trail? It made no sense.

He squatted and put a hand to the grass where the elk had bled out. It was still damp. The Huron were no more than half a day ahead of them now! His heart leapt with savage joy, but he was cautious. This band of Hurons had proven hard to catch and harder to kill. Twice they'd closed on them and twice the Hurons had set clever ambushes for his warriors. He'd left his lodges in the north with twenty-two men, all eager to take the scalp of the Huron, Dancing Crow. Now he had but seventeen left.

It galled him, for there would be lamentations in the villages of the Seneca at these losses and he would be blamed for the deaths if he returned without the scalp of Dancing Crow hanging from his war lance.

Crooked Knife knew where they were bound. Crossing the big river called Potowmac by the Susquehannas meant one thing only. They would follow the Great War Path south and seek protection from the one tribe in these mountains powerful enough to defy the Five Nations—the Cherokee. As the light failed, he made a small hand sign and set off toward the meadow, following the well-worn path south that had been a wilderness highway since ancient times. He must catch these stinking Hurons before they reached the high peaks and the lands of the Cherokee.

***

For four days the Hurons watched the ford and waited, but no Seneca showed his face. In the ravine, Will and August tramped over the ground and selected concealed positions with good fields of fire. In the valley, the women braided cattail leaves into strong cordage and set snares and trip ropes along the most likely paths up the ravine.

Each day at morning and evening, the women would come to the Englishmen's camp with food. After a few days, Will could not help but notice that the tall girl who went by the name of Two Rivers seemed to linger whenever his friend August was about. When he'd first seen her in the clearing across the river she'd been boldly defiant, but now she was bold in a way hardly different than any English village girl showing interest in a boy.

No King, No Country

But all this passed entirely by August, who was polite enough, but otherwise ignored the girl. It had ever been so with his friend. Will resolved to let nature take its course for a time, but at some point, if August was too blind to notice the girl's obvious interest, he would take his oldest friend by the collar and spell it out for him. Till then, there were more pressing things to worry about.

For the last of the leaves were off the aspens.

***

Will found Juba sharpening the long-handled axe by their new camp and sat down beside him.

"It is time to go back to your woman, Juba."

The African continued to run the whetstone over the axe blade for a time before replying. Then he set the axe aside.

"Trouble is coming here," he said gravely. "These Seneca, they won't rest until they have scalps to take to their lodges."

"This is our trouble, not yours," Will said.

"I promise your woman."

"And you have kept your promise. See?" Will tugged playfully at his hair that had grown long since his flight from England.

Juba snorted.

"It will look pretty in the lodge of a Seneca warrior."

Will stood.

"It is time you went to your woman," he said, "and you should not return to your people empty-handed." He handed Juba the carbine he'd taught the African to shoot, a bag of powder and bag of shot.

Juba took it and set it beside the axe. He did not look up at Will.

"I will come back in the spring to see if you are here," he said, and said no more.

On such things as the fall of leaves do men set their courses and decide their fate. At dawn, Juba rose and gathered his belongings. He solemnly shook hands with

August and Will and took a long last look around the hidden valley.

"It is a good place," he said.

Then he turned and set off down the ravine. Will and August watched him until he was lost to sight among the bare trees.

No King, No Country

Bloodhound

The *Sparrow* tied up at Jamestown's dock on the 15th of October after a stormy six week passage from Gloucester. Major Simon Binford was the first passenger to disembark followed by a squad of Parliamentarian infantry. The Major had to restrain himself from going down on his knees and kissing the solid ground. The *Sparrow* had taken the northern route to the Americas despite the lateness of the season and Binford hadn't fared well in the crossing. Unused to the solid footing beneath him, he found himself swaying as though in one of the North Atlantic tempests they'd sailed through. With a groan, he rushed to empty his gut into the James River as his military escort stood stolidly in ranks on the dock.

The purging helped and the swaying gradually subsided as he led the squad from the dock to the waterfront and hailed a man.

"I am here to see the Governor," he declared. "Kindly direct me to his palace."

The man looked at Binford oddly and spit a wad of tobacco juice dangerously close to the toe of his shiny boot.

"If it's Sir Billy yer lookin' for," the man said pointing to a tall, patrician-looking gentleman ambling down the hill toward them, "here he comes now."

Binford marched up the hill and intercepted the Governor before the man reached the quay.

"Sir, I am Major Simon Binford, dispatched by Parliament to take stock of things in the Commonwealth's colonies in America."

Governor William Berkley eyed the razor thin Binford mildly.

"Well, that sounds like a very big job, Major. What may I do to assist you?"

Binford had been rehearsing for this encounter since the lookout had first sighted land off the coast of New Amsterdam. He cleared his throat and began.

"You, sir, will cease providing sanctuary for traitors. The King is dead. Parliament rules. There will be a fleet here come spring and at that time, a full accounting of your stewardship will be expected."

As Berkley listened patiently to this speech, he slipped a small locket from his vest pocket, took a pinch of snuff from it and inhaled the brown powder. The result was a lusty sneeze to punctuate Binford's address.

"Well, yes, of course, a fleet, an accounting, and all that," Berkley said with a dismissive wave of his hand. " Now if you will excuse me, Major..."

"Binford."

"Yes, Binford. I have a barn full of tobacco to sell to your Captain."

With that, the Governor of the Virginia Colony resumed his amble toward the waterfront. Binford chased after him and tugged on his sleeve.

"Of immediate concern," he began, "is an arrest warrant I have here for a Captain William Inness and a Lieutenant August Dawes. Are they here?"

Berkley scratched his head.

"Inness? Why there was an Inness arrested three months ago and held right up there in the gaol. Got away, though. Some said rescued by pirates."

Binford was both elated and appalled. He'd never thought Inness was hiding somewhere in the west country of

No King, No Country

England! He'd been certain the deserter had fled to America, but his satisfaction at being proven right was dampened by the news that Inness had been in custody right here in Jamestown, but now was gone!

"Escaped you say?"

"Aye, that's what I said. If you want more on the subject, speak to Lunsford. He handles enforcement of the King's... eh, Parliament's laws here in Virginia. Second house past the church," he concluded, pointing vaguely toward the center of town.

Berkley did not wait for further inquiries from the bothersome major, but hurried his steps down to the dock. Other planters were already starting to gather there and he did not want to miss this opportunity for a sale.

***

"It was an unfortunate incident and one entirely beyond my control," Lunsford explained to Major Binford as he led the man into his parlor. "I had Inness arrested as soon as my wife informed me that he was wanted by Parliament and General Cromwell. I'd every intention of turning him over to a representative of the new government, but alas..." As they entered the parlor, he paused to introduce the two people already seated there.

"I believe you may have met my wife, Lady Anne, and her brother, Sir James Bingham?"

Binford eyed the two and scowled.

"Aye, I remember them well," he snarled. "I searched their damned ship in Liverpool!"

James Bingham rose hastily.

"Major, we were unaware that the criminals you sought were concealed among the crew! Had we known, we would have turned them over instantly. As it was, we reported their presence to the authorities here as soon as we disembarked."

Then Anne Lunsford spoke up.

"I believe you will find, sir, that more folk in Virginia are inclined to welcome the new government than you might expect."

"That's good to hear, miss, as a fleet with a regiment of infantry will be here in the spring," he said, more for Lunsford's benefit than the Binghams. He turned back to Lunsford.

"In the meantime, Sir Thomas, I must know more of Captain Inness."

"This story of pirates is poppycock," Lunsford said with a dismissive wave of a hand. "I have it on good authority that crew from the merchantman *Fair Wind* broke him out of the gaol, then fled down the river. They poisoned two of my men and nearly killed four more with a cannon shot when they tried to stop them. The ship was bound next for Maryland. I would seek for your Captain Inness there. And once you have him, you should arrest that Irish ship captain, Keogh, as well."

Binford nodded and was turning to leave when Lady Anne spoke up again.

"It might aid you to know that Inness is married now," she informed him. "You may recall her. She was the red-haired servant girl with our party when you came aboard at Liverpool."

Binford remembered.

***

Had the *Sparrow* made port in St. Mary's City on any day save Sunday, Callie, who'd made many friends among the men who worked the waterfront, would have been forewarned of the Provost Marshal's arrival. But it was a Sunday morning and Mass had just begun when the ship dropped anchor in St. Mary's River. She and Mrs. Martin had no warning as they exited the chapel that Major Binford and a squad of soldiers would be waiting for her outside.

At the sight of the soldiers, Callie instinctively drew back toward the open doors of the church. But the entrance was jammed with other congregants and she had nowhere to turn as Binford lunged forward and seized her by the arm. Callie tried to jerk away, but the Major kept his grip and pulled her aside. It was then she recognized the man who'd come aboard the *Fair Wind* in Liverpool to search for Will and August.

"Mrs. Inness, is it now?" he asked gruffly, though it was no question.

"I've committed no crime," she snapped.

"Oh, but I think you have. You've aided the escape of a wanted man and that is most definitely a crime!"

He turned to his squad of soldiers.

"Take her to the gaol, wherever that is in this hog wallow of a town and keep watch. The fools in Jamestown let her husband escape and that is not to happen here. I'll be along in a bit."

Two soldiers stepped forward to flank Callie and marched her away from the chapel toward the center of town. Binford turned to Willa Martin who stood there glaring at him.

"You are a friend to Mrs. Inness?" he asked.

"Aye, and no friend to the likes of you!"

"I'm not here to make friends. But you could help yours if you told me where to find her husband."

"He run off and left the poor girl," she snarled. "I don't know where he run to and neither does she."

Binford did not know whether to believe this crone's claim or not. After all, these Papists always stuck together. Perhaps Inness did desert his wife, just as he had the army, but he'd find the truth of it soon enough, either from the girl or someone else. St. Mary's City was a small place. Sooner or later, someone would talk.

Binford stalked off down toward the waterfront to see that his baggage was offloaded properly. It seemed likely that he would be in this nest of Catholics for some time and he would need to requisition adequate lodging. A group of men had gathered in front of the chapel watching Callie being led away by the red-coated soldiers. All but one of the men were recent arrivals, brought to Maryland by Harry Grey from the ironworks in Massachusetts. At their center was Mathys Beck their new employer and a devout Catholic himself. Beck had recognized Simon Binford from their brief encounter in Liverpool months ago, but was shocked that the major had turned up in St. Mary's City and outraged that he had ordered Callie placed under arrest. This Provost Marshal was like many men he'd dealt with over the years—a small man with too much authority.

Mathys Beck had had his fill of such men.

He hurried up the street toward the small office he shared with Harry Grey.

***

Harry Grey had returned from the Massachusetts Colony two weeks before with nine experienced iron workers, all former Scots prisoners of war, whose indentures he'd purchased with half their prize money from the *Donker Nacht*. Now he paced anxiously back and forth in the office he shared with Beck.

"We must go to the governor," he urged. "He must be informed of this outrage!"

Beck shook his head.

"While you were recruiting men in Massachusetts, I have been studying affairs here in the Maryland colony. Lord Baltimore has sought to gain the new government's favor for himself and leniency for Catholics. He has appointed William Stone as the new governor. Stone is a Protestant with connections to Cromwell and the leaders of your Parliament. He's allowed Catholic worship to continue, but will do nothing to challenge the authority of this Major Binford to carry out a warrant from Cromwell. We must find another way to help her, Harry."

"Then we break her out, as we did for Will at Jamestown!" he snarled, pounding a fist on the office's lone desk.

No King, No Country

Again Beck squashed his idea.

"Jamestown had two fools for guards. Here there is a squad of Parliamentarian infantry posted to keep watch over her."

"What then?" Grey demanded in exasperation.

Beck shook his head again.

"I don't know, Harry. I don't know."

Seneca Dawn

Still Fox stared at the ford over the Shenandoah as he had for six nights and tried to stay awake. It was an hour yet until dawn when his older brother would replace him on the watch and his eyes were heavy with sleep. The days they'd camped and rested in the hidden valley had restored much of his strength, but there was a lingering weariness that had been hard to overcome. He rose from the log he'd been perched on and crossed to the stream. He bent down to splash water on his face. He never heard the soft tread of moccasins behind him.

***

Crooked Knife knelt beside the dead boy and drove his knife blade into the dirt to cleanse it of blood. They'd wasted three days following a welter of moccasin prints south along the Great War Path hoping to catch the fleeing Hurons. Instead, they'd come upon a trading party of Shawnee returning from the north. Realizing the tracks they'd followed were not those of their enemies, they'd turned and hurried back north, until they once more reached the place where the elk had been killed. There he ordered his men to search more carefully and they picked up the trail they'd missed amidst the buffalo sign. It led down to the river and ended there.

Crooked Knife made certain none of his warriors showed themselves on the river bank. If the Hurons had crossed here, then someone would be watching on the far bank. From the shelter of the trees, he studied the high ground opposite. A stream came down through a ravine and emptied just upstream from the crossing. Perhaps the Hurons had taken to the high country following that stream.

He led his men back south, following the twisting course of the river until he found a spot where the water ran more swiftly. Carefully he edged into the stream and found it shallow as he expected. They'd crossed and rested until the moon rose high overhead, then they'd started back north. If a Huron was watching the ford at the buffalo track, they would be looking the wrong way.

The Seneca's heart had leapt when he'd seen the boy sitting on the log in the moonlight gazing down at the river. With great care, he'd worked his way uphill and across the stream, testing each footstep before putting his weight down. No twig snapped beneath his moccasins as he crept close. Then he froze as the boy suddenly rose and went to the stream, passing no more than ten feet from the Seneca before kneeling.

It had been easy.

He slipped his knife back in his belt and cupped his hands around his mouth, issuing a soft ululating call that mimicked the screech owl. Seventeen Seneca warriors rose from hiding and followed Crooked Knife up the ravine.

**

The young Huron stopped dead in his tracks when he heard the screech owl's call. It was one he had heard many times, but this was wrong. The owls called at dusk and in the early evening, but not in the wee hours before dawn. That the call had come from far below, down near the river where his younger brother stood watch troubled him. He hurried now, being careful to avoid the trip ropes the women had strung along the path. Halfway down the ravine he caught a brief flash of movement on the trail below. He eased himself down and watched. And there they were!

He counted more than a dozen warriors, picking their way up the trail towards him and knew then that his brother was dead. But now was no time for lamentations. He slid backwards until he was well out of sight, then he rose and ran back up the path like death was on his heels—for in truth, it was.

***

Will sat up and laid a hand on the long rifle that lay beside him. He'd been roused from sleep by the sound of running feet coming up the trail in the ravine. On the far side of the shelter he saw that August had heard as well. He didn't have to tell his friend that trouble was coming their way. The two men piled out of their shelter and were waiting when the Huron boy came charging out of the woods.

"Seneca!" was all that he said, but that was enough.

Breathing hard, the young warrior told them a dozen enemy warriors were climbing up the ravine on the river side. Will didn't ask how the enemy had gotten so close without the alarm being raised. There would be time later to speak of that—if they survived the day. He sent the young warrior to rouse Dancing Crow at his camp in the aspens.

Above the high ridges to the east, the sky was beginning to lighten, though it was still as dark as midnight on the valley floor. Will and August took up their long rifles and slipped their twelve apostles over their shoulders and across their chests. Will grabbed his longbow and quiver and August picked up his carbine. Together they headed down the trail.

They'd walked this ground both in daylight and dark and deftly avoided the snares and trip ropes concealed along the trail. When they reached a place they'd scouted as a fallback should they not be able to hold the Seneca at the river or further down the ravine, he motioned to his left and August slipped away in the darkness toward a jumble of boulders he knew lay in that direction. Off to the right of the trail, Will slipped into a natural redoubt formed where three trees had fallen in a tangle from some long ago windstorm. He leaned his long rifle against a trunk and strung his longbow.

Then he waited.

***

The moon was low in the sky, but still cast some illumination through the bare limbs of the trees in the ravine. Will watched as a warrior came around a bend in the trail fifty yards downhill. The man dropped into a squat to study the ground ahead. Seeing nothing, he rose and started forward. Will counted until a dozen men had followed the first, then drew his longbow and loosed. The arrow buzzed past the first warrior's ear and struck the second in the throat. The rest vanished before the dead man hit the ground.

Will nocked a second arrow and waited. Nothing moved down the trail as he strained his eyes to penetrate the darkness. A faint sound came from behind him and he whirled. It was Dancing Crow and his three remaining warriors. All were armed with bows or war clubs and Dancing Crow carried his lance. Wordlessly they moved off to either side of the trail and vanished into the gloom. In the ravine, all was silent.

As a dragoon, he'd seen his share of night action and had learned that patience was a virtue when you couldn't see your enemy and he couldn't see you. A concealed man sitting still was almost impossible to see in the dark, but a man who must move risked giving himself away and it was the Seneca who had to move.

Will knew they must wonder if the bowman above them was a lone rear guard sent to delay them or something more formidable. Either way, he expected they would fan out and try to flank the trail. His guess was confirmed when the silence was broken by an anguished cry off to his left, followed by the blast of a carbine. It all happened in a matter of seconds, followed by a return of silence.

The strangled cry he'd heard had not sounded like August, but that might just be wishful thinking. He knew from experience that his old friend was a hard man to kill, but the first dim predawn light gave him some relief when he looked across the ravine and made out August's familiar shape, crouched behind a jumble of boulders, a dead Seneca lying beside him.

He knew the advancing light would change the balance of this fight. Beyond the few spruce and low hollies, the bushes and trees were bare. With such sparse cover, the Seneca would find it hard to move without revealing themselves. By the same token, they would find it easier to see and to count the defenders. He looked up the sides of the ravine. If he was commanding a company of dragoons, he'd send men along the high ground on both sides to get in behind defenders below.

It was time to move.

He caught August's eye and gave the him the old dragoon signal to withdraw. Not far off he saw Dancing Crow look his way and he pointed back up the trail toward the valley. They'd hoped to stop the Seneca as they crossed the ford or in the narrow western ravine, but that had failed. It was time to change the plan.

Will watched as August slid down the side of the ravine. When he reached bottom he stood and an arrow buried itself in a tree trunk a foot from his head. He did not look to see from whence he came, he just broke into a run over the rough ground, weaving and changing direction as he made for the main trail. Another arrow missed, shattering against a slab of granite as he passed. Will climbed out of his concealed spot and sprinted for the main trail. Dancing Crow and his warriors had already melted away back toward the valley.

August reached the trail and was moving fast as Will fell in behind his friend, the two running for the valley as the report of two more muskets sounded behind them. Will heard an angry buzz as a ball passed by his ear and more arrows fell around them as they ran, but none struck home.

Behind them, fierce war hoops echoed through the ravine as the Senecas took up the chase.

***

Dancing Crow waited patiently beyond the bend in the trail with his three young warriors. They crouched behind a huge cluster of rhododendron, hidden by their mass of evergreen leaves. They watched Will and August come pounding up the trail and let them pass. The Englishmen were aware of the traps that the Huron women had laid at this bend and avoided them. The Seneca were not so lucky.

Below, Crooked Knife ordered his men to fan out as the ravine widened to make certain that none of the Hurons slipped through their net. But two of his bolder warriors, seeing their enemies break and run, could not resist the chance to take the first scalps. They bounded up the main trail in hot pursuit.

The first man did not see the tough cattail cord strung across the path at the bend in the trail and fell headlong on his face. Seeing him go sprawling, the trailing man pulled up short. He had a steel tomahawk in one hand and brought it down in one swift motion, cutting through the trip rope. As he rose up, Dancing Crow burst from the rhododendron just off the trail. The Seneca lurched backwards, raising his tomahawk, but it was of little use as Dancing Crow drove his lance deep into the man's belly.

The Seneca on the ground was scrambling to his feet when a young Huron leapt from the cover of the bushes and brought his war club around in a vicious stroke, shattering the Seneca's ribs. As the man doubled over in pain, the Huron finished him with a crushing blow to the back of his head.

"Aiyeee!" he cried and reached for his knife. It would be his first scalp. As he grasped his enemy's top nock a musket sounded from down the hill and a ball took the Huron between the shoulder blades, toppling him over atop the dead

Seneca. Dancing Crow retrieved his lance and with his two remaining warriors ran up the trail toward the valley.

***

At their council of war, they had agreed that, should the Seneca penetrate into the valley, they would retire to the cabin, where they would have the protection of its log walls and good fields of fire. As Will and August ran past the beaver pond, they saw that the Huron camp was empty, the women and children gone to take refuge in the Elk Cave.

They reached the cabin only a little ahead of Dancing Crow and his two warriors. When they burst through the door, they were surprised to find Two Rivers there, a knife in her hand and fire in her eyes.

"Why are you not with the women and children?" August demanded. His words weren't perfect, but she understood his question well enough.

"Seneca come to kill all. First men, then us. I'll not wait in hole in the ground to die!"

Before August could reply, the Huron warriors came charging through the door and an arrow buried itself in the logs at the front of the cabin. Will and August slammed and barred the door as Dancing Crow shouted at Two Rivers. The girl shouted back and the words between them came too swiftly for Will and August to follow. The Huron leader did not like having his orders defied, but there was nothing to be done now as the Seneca gathered a hundred paces in front of the cabin.

Knowing that such a day as this might come, they'd cut windows in each wall, large enough to let in a little light and to provide good fire ports, but too small for a man or bear to climb through. Will and August took up positions at the front wall while Dancing Crow and his warriors kept watch on the sides and back. Two Rivers stood in the corner and sulked.

In the tall grass down the hill, the Seneca warriors stood boldly in the open and Will counted fourteen in all. There could be others still out of sight, but if it came to close fighting, fourteen would be more than enough for the Seneca to prevail. Inside the cabin were five fighting men plus Two Rivers, who Will thought might very well take at least one Seneca with her in a fight. As he watched the Seneca down the hill, he realized why they were standing so calmly this close to the cabin. They thought they were well beyond the range of a musket—and they were.

But they were not beyond the range of Mathys Beck's long rifles. August had already poked the long barrel of his rifle through one of the front windows and Will did the same. Will uttered a quiet command and both men squeezed their triggers at the same time. The Seneca did not react instantly to the sound of gunfire from the cabin, but when two of their number lurched back, one struck in the forehead and the other in the chest, all dropped to the ground as one.

***

Crooked Knife peered through the high grass at the cabin and for the first time felt a worm of doubt. He'd seen such structures before. They were built by the whites, but no whites had ever found their way this far from the coast. Yet here in this remote valley near the Great War Path was the cabin of white men. If such men were aiding the Hurons, that would explain the musket fire that had surprised him in the ravine. Against the Hurons they'd faced nothing but arrows, lances and war clubs. Somehow the Hurons had acquired firearms or allies with guns—and such guns!

Could a musket ball fly true at that distance? The Seneca had been trading furs for muskets for years, but he'd never seen a musket that was accurate much beyond a lance throw. He might have counted losing two warriors at this distance as sheer chance, but there had been two shots and two hits. That was not chance!

He signaled to his men and, shielded by the tall grass, they moved well to the rear, leaving their dead behind. Rising once more to his feet, Crooked Knife glared at the little cabin on the rise. If there were white men there he would ensure that they died very slowly and in agony before he took their scalps. Then he would see what guns they had.

***

For hours the men in the cabin watched the approaches, but the Seneca did not show themselves.

"They will come in the dark," Dancing Crow said at last. "Then your guns that kill far off will not help us."

Will nodded. He'd come to the same conclusion as they'd watched and waited through the long afternoon. The Seneca would wait till full dark then use the tall grass to draw near to the cabin walls. He wasn't sure if they'd take their axes to the door or scale the walls to the roof and hack their way inside, but either way, fighting in such close quarters would negate the advantage they held with the long rifles.

"We must meet them in the dark," he said, "but they must not expect we are there. Some must stay here and draw them to the cabin."

As the sun dipped toward the ridgeline at the western end of the valley they made their plans and waited.

***

The night was overcast and that suited Will. The better to slip out of the cabin undetected. They'd dug around the base of one of the foundation stones beneath the rear wall and managed to pry it loose. The hole was tight, but big enough for a man to force his way through. Once the last of the twilight was gone, Will squeezed through the opening. August passed him his long rifle, bow and quiver through the makeshift tunnel. With his weapons in hand, he crawled on his belly into the tall grass behind the cabin.

Dancing Crow and one of his warriors followed. August had agreed to stay in the cabin with the last Huron warrior and Two Rivers, who had stopped sulking and now looked eager for a fight. Outside, the two Hurons and one Englishman fanned out, crawling through the grass to places

No King, No Country

they'd picked out while it was still daylight. Then they waited.

***

Crooked Knife was pleased that the night sky was filled with clouds that hid the moon and stars, the better to conceal his warriors as they crept near to the white man's log house. They'd spent the afternoon preparing for battle. Muskets were cleaned, weapons sharpened and as evening drew near, each man sat alone with his medicine pouch, communing with the spirits who would protect him in the fight to come.

Crooked Knife held his own communion with the spirits and renewed his blood oath to take the scalp of the man who'd struck down his brother. He'd ordered a ram to be cut and picked four warriors to smash in the door of the cabin. While men were breaking in the door, others would be hoisted up to the roof and cut their way through the timbers to fall on the Hurons and whites inside. It would be a great slaughter. Later, when the snows lay deep around the lodges of the Seneca, men would sing of this night!

***

Will had studied the ground in front of the cabin carefully during the long afternoon. There was a cluster of blackberry bushes they'd left standing only twenty paces from the front of the cabin. Its fruit and leaves were gone, but it still provided good cover and was a likely place from which the Seneca could launch an attack. Will had crawled well clear of the rear of the cabin and now made his way around the little knoll to a spot twenty paces from the bush. Somewhere on the opposite side of the knoll, Dancing Crow and one of his young warriors would be lying in wait.

Will rolled on his back and took up his longbow, nocking an arrow and rolled back to his stomach, his long rifle beside him. The night was dark and quiet, the summer sounds of insects and frogs gone with the first frost. He strained to hear any sound that would reveal his enemy's approach. For a time a chill wind picked up, stirring the long grass and whistling through the naked limbs of the trees. But then it died. It was then that Will heard it.

It was the rustle of something moving through the grass close by, but he could see nothing. Then, from the other side of the hill he heard a strangled cry. Someone had died over there and he hoped it wasn't Dancing Crow. The death cry seemed to stir the Seneca into action. They came in a rush, rising out of the grass like ghosts and charging toward the cabin. From the front window of the cabin a shot rang out dropping a Seneca before the rest closed on the cabin.

Two of the charging warriors fired their muskets at the narrow window sending wood chips flying into the cabin, one ripping a gash in August's chin. A third shoved his musket barrel through the window on the side wall and pulled the trigger. The blast lit up the room inside but the ball buried itself harmlessly in the opposite wall. The Huron warrior standing at the window grabbed the barrel before it could be withdrawn and the two men struggled over the weapon until another Seneca helped to yank it back outside.

Four men had waited behind the blackberry bush for the first rush to reach the cabin, then they rose up, the ram between them, and sprinted for the front door. An arrow leapt out of the darkness and took one of the four in the side. He fell but the other three reached the front of the cabin and swung the ram forward. It struck the door with a crash, ripping loose the leather hinges, though not breaking through the bar that secured it from the inside.

Will stood and aimed his long rifle at a Seneca manning the ram, but the warrior tripped and went to one knee, the shot passing harmlessly over his head. The three Seneca by the cabin door turned at the sound of Will's rifle and saw him standing alone. They dropped the ram and charged down the hill toward him. With no time to reload, Will slipped the ruby-handled dagger from the sheath at his side and waited to meet them.

No King, No Country

***

At the cabin, four Seneca had managed to gain the roof and began to hack through the timbers there. August had reloaded his long rifle and waited as debris began to rain down from above. He handed the carbine to Two Rivers who took it readily and backed into a corner waiting for the roof to give way. The young Huron warrior, his eyes wide, stood staring at the roof, his war club at the ready.

As the Seneca tore away the moss and saplings overhead, August caught a glimpse of the night sky. Then, two warriors broke through and dropped into the center of the small room. One landed so close to August that he couldn't bring the long barrel of his rifle to bear. He swung the butt of the weapon in a vicious uppercut, catching the Seneca in the groin and dropping him writhing to the floor. Across the room the second Seneca ducked as the Huron swung his war club in the cramped space, then lunged forward, driving his knife into the young warrior's chest.

As the Seneca bent over his victim to take his scalp, August lifted the long rifle and shot from the hip, striking the Seneca in the back of the head just as two more warriors dropped into the room. The first slashed at August, his knife not sinking deep, but slicing through the Englishman's shirt and leaving a bloody gash down his left arm. He drew back for another blow, but August grasped his wrist and the two tumbled to the floor in a death struggle.

The second warrior saw Two Rivers in the corner and came at her with his axe. She leveled the carbine, closed her eyes and pulled the trigger. The blast flung the Seneca warrior across the room and into the cabin wall.

Stunned, she dropped the carbine and staggered back into the corner. Too late she saw that the warrior that August had dropped with a blow to the groin had recovered enough to get to his feet. He screamed a war cry and lunged at the girl. She dodged the axe blade which buried itself in the wall, but when she stabbed at him with her knife, he grasped her wrist and twisted until the blade fell to the floor. Pinning her down, he reached for the knife and closed his hand on the grip.

As he raised the blade, the cabin erupted as a flintlock pistol fired from across the room. The ball struck the warrior in the neck and flung him off the girl. Dazed, she sat up and saw August sitting across the cabin, a dead Seneca draped across his legs and the smoking pistol in his hand.

They were the only living souls left in the cabin.

***

Outside on the grassy hill, the three warriors separated as they moved down toward the white man, each hoping to be the one to take his scalp.

"Aiyee!" the cry came from behind Will and he whirled to meet the threat. To his relief, it was Dancing Crow, a knife in one hand and bloody war club in the other. But the Huron leader had come alone. The young warrior who'd crawled from the cabin with him was nowhere to be seen.

The Huron took up a position next to Will and the three Senecas slowed their approach. This white man they didn't know, but Dancing Crow was a man with a reputation. He'd taken many Seneca scalps and that demanded caution. The three began by circling the pair, feinting attacks, but not closing.

The arrival of Crooked Knife with another Seneca warrior signaled an end to this standoff. He uttered a terse command and the five warriors surrounded the two men standing alone by the blackberry bushes. Crooked Knife drew his knife and tomahawk and glared at Dancing Crow in triumph.

"My brother's spirit will rejoice at your death!" he taunted.

"Your brother will ask 'Where is your hair?' when you meet him in the spirit world tonight!" the Huron spat back. "Tell him Dancing Crow has it!"

"Kill the white man," Crooked Knife snarled to his men. "The Huron dog is mine!"

No King, No Country

Will and Dancing Crow turned back-to-back as the five Senecas closed in, certain of victory. One warrior, eager for glory, swept in at Will. He was young and strong and feinted with his knife low, but it was a move Will had seen more than once in a sailor's brawl and he did not take the feint. As the warrior raised his tomahawk, he stepped in close and drove his long dagger into the man's throat. The Seneca staggered backwards, clutching at his neck trying to stem the flow of blood, but quickly sank to his knees and toppled over. Enraged, the other Seneca pressed in from all sides.

Then, out of the darkness, a carbine spat fire. One of the Seneca's spun around, struck in the arm by the ball. The others seemed frozen in shock as a tall man, black as the night, waded into them with a long-handled axe, a Yoruba war cry on his lips.

Juba wielded the axe as though he was felling saplings and another man went down under his deadly blade. The remaining Senecas recoiled from this unexpected attack. All began to back away from this frightening specter. The man wounded in the arm by the carbine ball, in his haste to retreat, tripped on an old stump. Dancing Crow leapt forward, crushing his skull with his war club. Crooked Knife, with but one warrior left, broke and ran, his lone follower fleeing behind him. Dancing Crow raced off into the darkness after them, but Will simply staggered over to Juba and threw an arm around his friend's shoulder.

The attack was over.

***

Up the hill, August and Two Rivers stumbled out of the wrecked cabin door and Will ran to meet them.

"They're gone?" August asked.

"Aye, Gus, what's left of them. How bad is your wound?"

He made a sour face.

"Hurts like hell, but she says it is a scratch that will heal quick."

The Huron girl clung to August's side as the weary Englishman leaned against the front wall of the cabin. He saw Juba following Will up the hill and hailed him.

"I wondered who was making that God awful war cry out here," he said with a grin. Then he turned serious.

"Thank you, Juba," he said, at a loss for any other words to say.

"I was going south and see the Seneca come back north on Great War Path. I think this time they find you, so I follow." The African paused for a moment, then pointed at Will.

"I promise his woman."

***

Somewhere beyond the ford on the Shenandoah, Dancing Crow lost the track of Crooked Knife and his lone Seneca warrior. In disgust, he turned back toward the hidden valley where he would mourn the loss of his warriors and see to the Huron women and children.

A mile north, Crooked Knife paused to rest. He heard no sound of pursuit behind them. Beside him, his last warrior was bent over, taking deep breaths after their desperate flight from the carnage in the valley. Crooked Knife stepped quietly in behind him and slit his throat.

When he returned to the lodges of the Seneca alone there would be an outcry. Where are our sons, our brothers, they would ask. There must be no one to challenge the story he would tell—a story of white men invading the empty lands, of secret alliances between Hurons and the whites, of a brave stand in the Shenandoah where only he managed to escape with his life. Many would believe, but some would not. He knew, as he started back north along the Great War Path that he must return here to avenge these losses or become a little man among his own people.

That he couldn't abide.

No King, No Country

Return to Eden

Callie sat up in her tiny cell and pulled her shawl tight around her shoulders. A chill wind was blowing through the barred window high on the wall, reminding her that winter was not far off. She rose from the narrow sleeping cot and looked up at the small patch of sullen grey sky visible through the bars. For a moment, a tiny sparrow, buffeted by the blustery wind, seemed suspended against the grey sky. It beat its wings furiously but made little progress. Then the wind dropped abruptly and the bird was gone.

She guessed it had a nest in the rafters of the stable next door to the gaol and hoped it was well-feathered and cozy. The wind picked up again, making her shiver. She wondered if snow had come yet to the western mountains and hoped it had not. Will had promised to return with the snows and, above all, she hoped he would break that promise. For there was a platoon of Roundhead infantry waiting patiently in St. Mary's City for his return.

She heard the familiar sound of a key in the lock of her cell door and turned to see Willa Martin standing with a tray in her hands. Each morning the widow brought Callie a decent meal from the inn, the food at the gaol being only fit for a pig's trough.

"Mornin'" she said with a smile.

"Morning, Willa," Callie replied, taking the tray and sitting back on her narrow cot. "Looks like the weather's changing."

"Aye, lass, the geese have all come down from the north and the last of the leaves are gone. Winter soon."

As the guard closed the door, the talk of weather ended.

"Your friends, Mr. Grey and Mr. Beck, have posted men down at the waterfront and on the west road to watch for your man, Callie. They'll give him warning of what's waitin' for him here."

Callie nodded.

"Where did they find men they could trust? We're all new here in the colony."

"Oh, Mr. Grey found a passel of able young lads up in Massachusetts. Brought 'em down to run the new foundry, but that's being built upriver and won't be ready till spring. So Mr. Beck has them watching the river and the roads for your Captain Inness."

The news was a relief for Callie. Both Mathys Beck and Harry Grey had been to see her twice in the fortnight she'd been locked up and she knew that both men would pull whatever strings they could to help. But such strings were few as no one in the little Maryland colony would dare to cross the representative of Oliver Cromwell and the new Parliamentarian government. At least Will and August wouldn't blunder unawares into the trap Binford had set.

How she would ever get free to join him, she didn't know, but she'd been captive aboard a privateer's sloop in a hurricane and Will had saved her then. Surely he'd find a way to get her out of this gaol.

***

Simon Binford picked his way down the main street of St. Mary's City avoiding as best he could the dung piles left by oxen and the rain-filled holes in the roadway. Each day at random times, he inspected the five-man guard detail he'd posted at the town gaol to keep watch over the Inness girl. He was determined that there would be no gaol breaks here as there'd been at Jamestown!

No King, No Country

After a week, Simon Binford knew that the girl was not going to tell him anything. Perhaps she truly didn't know where her husband was, but that didn't matter. In a small town, someone *always* talked and St. Mary's City had not disappointed him in that regard. No one seemed to know where the two fugitives had got off to, but it was common knowledge in the settlement that Captain Inness and Lieutenant Dawes had gone off into the wilderness and would return to the Maryland colony with the first snows. That was all the information Binford required, for with Caledonia Inness safely tucked away in the town gaol, all he need do was wait and watch. And the weather was turning colder by the day.

The waiting had not been pleasant. For a fortnight, he'd endured this primitive backwater where the streets were hardly more than cow paths, ankle-deep in thick, clinging mud after the slightest bit of rain and where accommodations were spartan at best. There was only one inn in the place, owned by the belligerent widow Martin. The room the old shrew had assigned him was no bigger than the tiny berth aboard the *Sparrow* where he'd suffered on the long voyage over from England. And each morning, when he arose, he seemed to have a new constellation of red bites on various parts of his body.

But Simon Binford was a man of iron discipline and neither mud nor bed bugs would deter him from his duty. He consoled himself with the vision of marching Inness and Dawes into the Guildhall and presenting them personally to General Cromwell. That would put an end to days rounding up drunks in the London alleys!

When he arrived at the squat structure that served as a storehouse and gaol for the colony, the Watch Corporal saluted him smartly and the men appeared to be well turned-out and vigilant. Satisfied, he didn't bother to look in on Callie Inness. Her only value to him now was as a lure to draw her husband in. When she did, he'd clap Inness and his friend Dawes in chains and order the *Sparrow* to set sail for England on the next tide.

***

Juba left at first light, taking his carbine and ample powder and shot with him.

Will shook his hand solemnly as he took his leave.

"You've been a true friend, Juba. Should you ever be in need, send for me."

Juba nodded.

"I think you are the only white man worth sending for, Inness," he said with a wry smile.

When he'd gone, Dancing Crow approached Will and August.

"This is a good valley," he said. "We wish to stay if Inness will share the land."

Will looked at August who'd been spending much time with Two Rivers in the days after the Seneca attack.

"It's a big valley, Will, and we could use some neighbors," he said with a sheepish grin.

And so it was agreed. The Huron's would make a more permanent camp down among the aspens and would stay in the valley over the winter. It would be a hard time with no corn stored away, but game was plentiful in the mountains and fish swarmed in the river. They could also trap for pelts, but Will warned Dancing Crow to leave the beaver family in peace.

The next day, Will and August retrieved the canoe from its hiding place, loaded it with enough food for a week and launched it into the Shenandoah River.

***

Alexander Macintyre huddled in the lee of the cooper's shed down by the St. Mary's River. The shed blocked the wind, but not the cold. He had a wool coat, but it was threadbare and barely kept out the chill. It was two hours until his release at dawn, but he didn't mind. What was a little cold to a free man?

He'd been laid low at Sterling in forty-eight along with many another Highlander. He'd woken up in a filthy pen with two hundred other captives. They'd been marched west to Glasgow and given little food or water. Many had perished. Then it had been prison for a time until at last the decision was made to bind them over as indentured servants in the colonies. He and forty of his fellows had been put on a ship and delivered up to the Puritans in Massachusetts to labor in their new ironworks on the Saugus River. The work was hard, but he'd learned fast and when Mr. Grey arrived in Saugus with a proposition, he'd not hesitated.

It had been a good decision. Ironworking was hard, but honest work and he'd learned the trade well. His new masters, Mr. Beck and Mr. Grey, were good men, even if one was a German and one an English Protestant. As promised, they'd torn up the indenture papers and offered them a decent wage. Maryland wasn't the Highlands, but what was left for him there now? He'd resolved to build a new life for himself here in this new world.

He stamped his feet to keep feeling in them as he kept a watch on the river. There were a half-dozen rowboats and small sailing ketches anchored in the channel or tied up at the one dock that jutted into the river. All were dwarfed by the big, three-masted merchantman anchored at midstream. The *Sparrow* had been there since the day he'd arrived from Massachusetts and if his new boss Mathys Beck would give him enough gunpowder, he'd gladly row out to where she swung at anchor and blow a hole in her hull. For the *Sparrow* was home to a company of Parliamentarian infantry and he had scores to settle with the Roundheads.

He cupped his hands and blew on them, his breath a cloud of white vapor. He'd know to bring gloves the next time he had the night watch. As he looked around he could see that the waterfront was silent and deserted, no honest man having any business there at this hour. He turned back to the river and blinked. Coming toward him was a boat of some sort, its white hull glowing in the reflected moonlight. Two paddles rose and dipped as the craft glided effortlessly across the dark water. Macintyre stepped out of the shadow of the cooper's shed and raised an arm in greeting and the paddlers froze. He beckoned to them and they once more dipped their paddles and slid up to the riverbank. Two men leapt out and pulled the canoe out of the water.

"Captain Inness?" he asked tentatively.

"I'm Inness," one of the men replied. "Who are you?"

"I am in the employ of Mr. Beck and Mr. Grey. I'm to bring you to them in secret as there are men here from England to arrest you. Alexander Macintyre's the name."

"Thank you for the warning, Mr. Macintyre," Will said, "but should you not take me to my wife first? She lodges at the Council Chamber Inn."

There was an awkward silence from Macintyre, but then he spoke up.

"Mrs. Inness is in the gaol, Captain."

***

After the men hid the canoe upstream, Alexander Macintyre led Will and August though back alleys to the building that housed the offices and sleeping quarters of Beck & Grey Ironworks. They roused Mathys Beck and Harry Grey who lit a candle and set it on the desk he shared with Beck.

"It's Binford," Harry said. "He arrived a fortnight ago with a company of infantry and the warrant for your arrest."

"When he couldn't lay hands on you, the bastard arrested Callie on the steps of the church!" Beck said bitterly. "He's held her ever since, waiting for you to return."

"Mathys spoke with the Governor," Harry added. "We have some influence here as we are investing in an ironworks that will greatly profit the colony, but the man will not challenge a warrant signed by Cromwell himself!"

No King, No Country

"Callie....How does she fare? Is she well?" Will asked.

"Aye," said Mathys. "Mrs. Martin feeds her and we visit when we are allowed. She's a brave woman and not cowed by this Binford, but frets that you will fall into his hands. That's why I set my lads to watch for you."

"So what is to be done?"

The two men looked at Will with pained expressions.

"Binford posts a squad of your Roundhead infantry to guard her day and night," Harry said. "We see no easy way to get her free."

"Then we'll have to find a hard way," Will said grimly.

He pulled up a chair next to the desk.

"Tell me about this gaol."

***

Things were quiet on this overcast November day in St. Mary's City, but as evening fell, nine drunken Scotsmen stumbled down the street from the Council Chamber Inn toward the center of town. They sang a rowdy song of the Highlands and seemed in good spirits until one said something to another who took exception. Then quicker than summer lightning, fists began to fly and the street in front of the gaol became a melee.

The red-coated guard posted in front of the gaol ignored the uproar at first, content to let the locals beat each other's brains out, but the Scots could not seem to contain the violence to the middle of the street and it soon began to drift toward the gaol. When a burly Scot stumbled backwards and bowled over a private, the Watch Sergeant had enough. He ordered his men to port arms and they began shoving the unruly men back into the street.

This seemed to make the Scot's forget their grievances against each other and focus on the Englishmen trying to herd them away from the gaol. Words were exchanged and the ensuing brawl had participants on both sides sliding around in the mud. Up and down the street people peered out of windows to see what the horrible din was.

***

In her cell, Callie heard the commotion out front and wondered what it could possibly be. As the noise grew, she heard a new sound much closer at hand, a rasping sound of metal on metal. She looked up to see the blade of a steel saw passing back and forth along the bottom of one of the iron bars that blocked the window above her head. She stood on tiptoe to see what was happening. Framed in the window was a bearded face. The sawing stopped for a moment.

"Callie," Will whispered.

Callie dragged her sleeping cot beneath the window and reached up. Will reached through the bars and touched her hand. That was all. Then he returned to his labor.

***

It had been Mathys Beck's idea. He'd gone into the storeroom next to his office and retuned with a canvas bag full of tools. From the bag he produced a long thin sawblade with a wooden handle.

"This will cut a gun barrel to length," Beck said. "It should make short work of the cheap iron that bars the windows of her cell."

All that was needed was a diversion to draw the attention of the guards and mask the sound of the saw. Harry turned to Macintyre, who'd been sitting quietly in the corner.

"Callie Inness was once Callie MacDonell, he said. Would you and the other Scots lads risk possible arrest to help free her?"

Macintyre got to his feet.

"A MacDonell of Glengarry?" he asked.

"Aye," Will answered. "The same."

"Did the lass have a father and brother die at Philiphaugh?"

Will nodded.

"I fought for a time with Montrose and knew of them," Macintyre said. "What is it you'd have our lads do, Mr. Grey?"

"Start a fight," Harry said.

"Startin' a fight comes natural to a Scot," Macintyre said with a laugh. "Are we allowed to win this one?"

***

The saw performed as Beck said. In a little over a minute he'd cut through the first bar and went to work on the second as the sound of the fight in front of the gaol waxed and waned. As the saw cut through the second bar, Will seized it near the bottom and pulled. It bent almost as easily at it had cut and within a minute he'd forced the two bars up and out of the way. He stuck his head in the window of the cell and reached down to grasp Callie's wrists.

"Up you go, Mrs. Inness," he said as he hoisted her up until she could haul herself through the opening. When her feet touched ground, she flung her arms around Will and whispered in his ear.

"I knew you'd come!"

He laughed at that and kissed her hard on the lips. Then he pulled her arms free and spun her around. Harry, Mathys and August stood there beaming at her. She hugged each in turn then stepped back.

"True friends all," she said, a catch in her voice.

"We'll be here if the wilderness doesn't suit you," Mathys Beck said, his voice husky.

"I'll inform Mrs. Martin that you're safe away," Harry said with a smile. "She'll miss you, and so shall I."

On the opposite side of the gaol the noise of the fight was starting to wane.

"Go, go!" Beck said, shooing them off down the dark alley with his hands—and they went.

Will took Callie's hand and with August leading they ran through the back alleys of St. Mary's City to reach their canoe. Inside were supplies placed there courtesy of Beck & Grey Ironworks and the widow Martin. Cornmeal to help see them through the winter, seed corn and squash for the spring planting and Callie's clothes from the Council

Chamber Inn had been carefully packed in the center of the canoe.

August climbed in the bow as Will helped Callie settle herself just behind the stack of supplies. There was a chill wind rippling the surface of the river and Will fished a wool cloak from Callie's pile of clothes, wrapping it around her shoulders. He pushed off from the bank, hopped nimbly into the stern and turned the nose of the canoe south, toward the wide Potowmac. As the two men dipped their paddles into the dark water, Callie looked into the night sky, held out her hand and laughed.

It was snowing.

No King, No Country

Historical Notes

My first historical fiction series, The Saga of Roland Inness, was set in England, France and the Holy Land in the last decade of the 12th century. I got drawn into that era by reading about the Third Crusade, which in turn led me back to England as the long reign of Henry II was coming to an end. It was a fascinating period with larger than life characters—Richard the Lionheart, Saladin, Eleanor of Aquitaine, Prince John and William Marshal to name but a few. It was a wonderful backdrop for a story about a boy coming of age with a longbow in his hand. But as boys do, Roland Inness grew to be a man and I got a yen to explore another place and time closer to home.

The age of the crusades was coming to a close as Europeans discovered that there was a new land to the west inhabited by people wholly unknown to the Old World. This New World seemed to offer a canvas even larger than medieval England, so I pressed the fast forward button to the year 1650 to begin my new story.

By the mid-17th Century, the English, and others, had carved out footholds on the edge of a vast continent, the beginning of a relentless drive to conquer and settle the land. Governments far away in the Old World tried to control this drive, but it was primarily individuals and small groups who pushed the frontier ever westward. My story touches on the plans and policies of governments, but focuses on the hope and dreams of individuals.

The history of the settlement of the Americas by European nations has received renewed attention in the past twenty years, with new scholarly works exploring the native cultures that existed prior to the arrival of Europeans (*1491,* by Charles C. Mann) and the experiences of early English settlers in the new colony of Virginia (*The Barbarous Years*, by Bernard Bailyn; *Marooned*, by Joseph Kelly and *Roanoke*, by Lee Miller) among others.

Everywhere one looks in these new histories of the era, one finds a messy, human story. Greed, heroism, ambition, endurance and betrayal were manifest in the Europeans who established the first settlements at the very fringe of the new land. The same could be said of the native peoples who already occupied these lands. In the end, the more advanced culture (in terms of technology, weaponry, etc.) simply undermined and overwhelmed the less advanced native cultures. But it didn't happen quickly, or easily, or bloodlessly.

Historical Figures:

The following are actual historical figures that appear in the story:

Charles I, King of England: Charles came to the throne of England, Scotland and Ireland as the second of the Stuart dynasty in 1625 and ruled until his execution by beheading in January, 1649. Charles believed firmly in the divine right of kings and that his authority was absolute since it was ordained by God.

He would dissolve Parliament in 1629 and rule alone for twelve years. This was a period of considerable religious upheaval. Henry VIII had made England a Protestant country, but there were schisms within the new Protestant faith. Catholics, meanwhile, were systematically oppressed during this period. It did not help the King's standing that his queen was Henrietta Maria of France, a Catholic. During this period, unrest grew and ultimately so affected the King's ability to collect revenue that Charles was forced to call Parliament back.

No King, No Country

Determined to restore its traditional role and curb royal abuses, Parliament passed a number of reforms, none of which were supported by the King. By 1642, the King raised his standard in Nottingham and the English Civil War began. Defeated in that war by the Parliament's New Model Army, the King was executed in January, 1649. Thereafter, England became a Commonwealth for ten years until the restoration of the monarchy under Charles' son Charles II.

Oliver Cromwell: Cromwell was from Cambridgeshire and socially of the minor gentry. He rose to prominence early in the English Civil War when he raised a regiment of cavalry for the Parliamentarian side and, despite a lack of military experience, proved to have a natural knack for leading men and for battle tactics. It was his regiment of horse, nicknamed the "Ironsides" who broke the Royalist cavalry at Marston Moor in 1644 and again at the Battle of Naseby in 1645. With the reform of the army mid-way through the war, Cromwell was made Deputy Commander under Sir Thomas Fairfax.

Cromwell's political life was based on his control of the army. His rise to power is a far bigger and more complex story than can be covered here, but it ultimately led to his ruling England, Scotland and Ireland as Lord Protector with near absolute power for nearly ten years until his death in 1658.

John Lilburne: Also known as "Freeborn John", Lilburne was an English political figure before, during and after the English Civil Wars. His political movement which came to be known as the Levellers was based on his theory of "freeborn rights," rights with which every human being is born, as opposed to rights bestowed by government or human law. He joined the Parliamentarian army at the start of the Civil War and fought with distinction at Edgehill and Marston Moor, rising to the rank of Lt. Colonel. He was friends with Oliver Cromwell, but his growing influence within the ranks caused a falling out. Lilburne agitated for suffrage for all adult men, not just those who owned property, and for freedom of religion. He was imprisoned in 1645 for denouncing members of Parliament for living in luxury while his troops went unpaid and arrested again in 1647 and held in the Tower. He was tried in 1649 for treason but found not guilty. In 1656 he was imprisoned in Dover Castle. He died while out on parole in 1657. Lilburne's works have been cited in opinions by the United States Supreme Court.

Colonel Edward Whalley: A distant cousin of Oliver Cromwell, Whalley rose to command the Ironside regiment of horse in the Parliamentarian army. He distinguished himself at the battles of Marston Moor and Naseby. It was a company in his regiment that fomented the Bishopsgate Mutiny in 1650 over orders to fight in Ireland. Later, Edward Whalley was one of the signatories to the death warrant for King Charles I.

Sir Thomas Lunsford: Lunsford was a somewhat infamous figure in his day. In his youth he was said to have a violent temper. As an adult he fell into a feud with his neighbor and was imprisoned for poaching deer on the neighbor's land. He subsequently attempted to murder the neighbor outside of church, but missed with two musket balls. For this he was imprisoned in Newgate Prison. He escaped Newgate and fled to France.

He would return to England to fight for King Charles I in the Civil War. With the defeat of the Royalists, Lunsford fled to Holland and then to Virginia where he was made Captain General of the Virginia Militia. In this post he furthered his reputation as a man inclined to sadistic violence.

Clan MacDonell of Glengarry: This clan joined the Marquess of Montrose in fighting for the royalist cause until defeated at the battle of Philiphaugh in late 1645. They remained one of the few clans to keep their Catholic faith after the English Civil war and rose with the Jacobites to fight for Bonny Prince Charlie. After the Battle of Culloden the MacDonells of Glengarry were mostly driven in to exile as part of the Highland Clearances of the early 19th century. Many settled in Glengarry County, Ontario, and parts of Nova Scotia.

Native American tribes of the East Coast: The coast of North America was far from an uninhabited wilderness when the first English colonists began to arrive. A patchwork of tribes and tribal alliances held sway over large swathes of land, though there were regions inland such as the Shenandoah valley that were largely vacant. In Virginia, the English encountered the powerful network of Algonquin tribes known collectively as the Powhatan Confederacy.

South in the Carolinas were the Eno and Tuscarora and farther south, the Catawbas. To the southwest along a broad stretch of the southern Appalachians, the powerful Cherokees were dominant. To the north were the Susquehanna and the fierce tribes of the Five Nations (Seneca, Mohawk, Oneida, Cayuga, and Onondaga) also known as the Iroquois League.

These tribes fought bloody wars among themselves, a fact that the Europeans exploited. For the tribes, the newcomers brought astonishing and valuable technologies such as iron and gunpowder. They also brought European diseases for which the natives had no immunity. Various plagues carried by the early Spanish explorers in what is now the southern United States is thought to have killed up to 90% of the native population of the lower Mississippi Valley. Smallpox and other European diseases also ravaged the tribes of the eastern seaboard leaving them vulnerable. Still, the tiny outposts of settlers near the coast could have been wiped out easily in the beginning, but the tribes found their trade goods too valuable to resist.

When the Dutch began providing the Iroquois with firearms in exchange for furs, other tribes had to do the same, which made them even more dependent on the new European settlements.

Places:

Jamestown: After the failure of the Roanoke colony in the 1580s, a more ambitious effort was made to plant a British colony in North America. The first settlement on the James River was established in 1607 and barely survived famine, Indian attacks, and feckless leadership in its early years. Between 1608 and 1610, eighty percent of the colonists died. The arrival of more settlers and the emergence of tobacco as a reliable cash crop slowly began to stabilize the situation. In 1619, the first African slaves were sold at Jamestown and the slave trade grew steadily along with tobacco acreage.

By 1650, settlements had spread up the James River to the fall line near Richmond and the Powhatan Indians had largely been forced out of the coastal plain. The colony did harbor strong Royalist sympathies in 1650 and many royalist refugees from the English Civil War. Fun fact: The nickname of the University of Virginia sports teams is "Cavaliers."

St. Mary's City: St. Mary's City was founded in 1634 as the capital of the new colony of Maryland. The colony was intended to be a refuge for persecuted English Catholics, though all religious faiths were tolerated.

Hammersmith Ironworks: The first ironworks in English America was the Falling Creek ironworks established on a tributary of the James River in 1619. It was short-lived as the workers were massacred by the Powhatan Indians and the works destroyed in 1622. A more successful attempt at production of iron in the colonies was made in the

No King, No Country

Massachusetts Colony where a large ironworks was constructed on the Saugus River in 1646.

The Hammersmith Ironworks was as modern as any in Europe and while most highly skilled positions were originally filled by Englishmen, a great deal of the labor was performed by Scottish prisoners of war who were shipped to the colony as indentured servants. Many of these men eventually completed their servitude and fanned out to create forges throughout the colonies.

The Great War Path: This was the network of trails used by Native Americans for both trade and warfare that ran through the Great Appalachian Valley. This system of footpaths branched off in several places onto alternate routes and over time shifted westward in some regions. It extended from what is now upper New York, through the Shenandoah Valley and deep into Alabama.

Things:

Antimonial wine: Wine doctored with antimony was used by the Romans to induce vomiting at feasts. In the Middle Ages it was routinely used as a purgative for the stomach and bowels. It was still in wide use in Europe through the 18th century. Of course antimony in sufficient doses is a poison. Some researchers believe Mozart died of antimony poisoning while using it as a purgative.

Haul Away Joe Shanty: This was a tradition sea shanty originating in the 18th Century.

Useful Terms

Political/Military Terms:

Apostles: Small wooden flasks that hold pre-measured charges of gunpowder. A dozen (hence the term "apostle") are typically attached to a sash slung across a musketeer's chest.

Buff coat: A thick leather jacket of buff color able to absorb some sword slashes. Worn by mounted troops of both sides, but primarily by Parliamentarian cavalry.

Cavalier: Royalist cavalry, often men of aristocratic birth who favored flamboyant dress.

Carbine: Shoulder-fired weapon with a shorter barrel than a musket originally developed for dragoons who rode to battle but fought on foot. Easy for a man on horseback to handle but not very accurate.

Dragoons: Mounted force that rode to the battlefield but generally fought on foot like infantry. Often used for reconnaissance.

Flintlock: A musket or rifle that used a piece of flint to strike a spark on the frizzen, which ignites the powder in the pan and fires the round. An improvement over the matchlock.

Frizzen: Metal piece positioned above the powder pan of a musket. When the trigger is engaged, the flint strikes the frizzen sending a spark into the pan, igniting the charge in the barrel and firing the weapon. The failure of the powder to ignite the main charge in the barrel is the origin of the phrase "just a flash in the pan."

Jaeger Rifle: Early long gun with rifled (spiral-grooved) barrel. Rifling imparts spin to the ball giving it greatly increased accuracy. German gunsmiths brought the Jaeger rifle to the early colonies where it evolved into the later Kentucky long rifle of Daniel Boone and Davy Crockett fame.

Levellers: A derisive name given to a faction within the New Model Army calling for more fundamental changes in the political system. They advocated for freedom of religion and votes for all adult men, not just landowners. These ideas had significant support in the cities, but Parliament and the leaders of the Army felt these changes were far too radical and suppressed the Levellers.

Matchlock: A musket that used a slow-burning length of fuse to ignite the gunpowder in the pan to fire the round.

New Model Army: The army of Parliament. Local militias were reconstituted as a standing national army by Oliver Cromwell to prosecute the civil war against King Charles I.

Regiment of Foot: Infantry units armed with pikes or muskets.

Regiment of Horse: Cavalry units.

Roundhead: Derisive term attached to Parliamentarian soldiers who often were Puritans favoring short haircuts as opposed to the long curled wigs of the Cavaliers.

Nautical Terms:

Aft: Toward the stern of the ship.

Bow-chaser: Cannon mounted near the bow to fire forward.

Braces: Lines attaching to the end of the yards to adjust the angle of the sails.

Close-hauled: Sailing a craft as close as possible into the wind to generate maximum speed.

Forecastle or Fo'c'sle: Raised structure forward of the main deck of a sailing vessel.

Foremast: The forwardmost mast on a ship.

Forward: Toward the bow of the ship.

In irons: Sailing too close to the wind causing the sails to "back" (having the wind strike the front rather than back of the sail) forcing the boat to go dead in the water or move astern.

Jack ladder: A flexible hanging ladder. It consists of vertical ropes or chains supporting horizontal, historically round and wooden, rungs.

Larboard: The side of a ship that is on the left when one is facing forward. Later commonly called "port."

Line: A rope. Individual names are given to specific lines, like halyards or braces or stays depending on their usage.

Mainmast: The tallest mast on a ship. If three-masted, the center mast.

Merchantman: A ship devoted to commerce. Not a warship, but often lightly armed with cannon.

Mizzenmast: The rearmost mast on a ship.

Nine-pounder: Small cannon, often used as a bow-chaser or stern-chaser.

Pinnace: A small boat used by large ships to ferry cargo and people to and from shore.

Quarterdeck: Raised deck aft of the main deck and above the sterncastle.

Rat lines: The horizontal lines attached to the shrouds allowing sailors to climb up to the yards.

Rigging: The system of masts and lines on sailing vessels.

No King, No Country

Ship's Bells: Ship's bells mark each half hour passed in a watch. There are 8 bells at the start and end of a watch and one bell at the first half hour mark of the watch, two bells at the end of the first hour, etc.

Ship Watches:
- 1st Watch: 8:00 PM to 12:00 AM
- Middle Watch: 12:00 AM to 4:00 AM
- Morning Watch: 4:00 AM to 8:00 AM
- Forenoon Watch: 8:00 AM to 12:00 PM
- Afternoon Watch: 12:00 PM to 4:00 PM
- 1st Dog Watch: 4:00 PM to 6:00 PM
- 2nd Dog Watch: 6:00 PM to 8:00 PM

Shrouds: The main lines that run from the chains to the mast to stabilize and secure it.

Sloop: A sailboat with a single mast typically meaning one headsail in front of the mast, and one triangular mainsail aft of (behind) the mast. Often used by privateers and pirates for its speed and maneuverability.

Sounding: Using a line and a lead weight to measure the depth of water. Depths were called to the Captain in fathoms (fathom=6 feet).

Square-Rigger: A type of sail and rigging arrangement in which the primary driving sails are carried on horizontal spars that are perpendicular, or "square", to the keel of the vessel and to the masts.

Starboard: the side of a ship that is on the right when one is facing forward.

Sterncastle: Raised structure aft of the main deck.

Stopper: Rope attached to the anchor.

Topgallant: The topmost sail—above the topsail.

Tops: Platforms above the lower course of sails on a mast.

Topsail: The sail above the mainsail.

Tween Deck: Deck on a sailing vessel between the main deck and the hold. Often used for crew quarters and storage.

Twelve-pounder: Medium cannon.

Stern-chaser: Cannon mounted near the stern to fire aft.

Whipstaff: Steering device used on square-rigged sailing ships before the invention of the ship's wheel—basically a long lever attached to a tiller and controlled from the steerage room in the stern.

Yards: The horizontal spar from which a square sail is suspended, e.g. the main yard suspends the mainsail.

General Terms:

Dons: English slang for the Spanish ruling class.

Ironmonger: a person or store selling hardware such as tools and household implements.

Books by Wayne Grant

The Saga of Roland Inness:

Longbow
Warbow
The Broken Realm
The Ransomed Crown
A Prince of Wales
Declan O'Duinne
A Question of Honour

The Inness Legacy

No King, No Country
The Long Rifles

Have a craving for more adventure? Check out the tale of Will Inness' ancestor in The Saga of Roland Inness. A boy, a bow and an evil Earl—what more could you want?

https://www.amazon.com/dp/B00OHZGQQG

About The Author

I grew up in a tiny cotton town in rural Louisiana where hunting, fishing and farming are a way of life. Between chopping cotton, dove hunting and Little League ball I developed a love of great adventure stories like *Call It Courage* and *Kidnapped*.

Like most southern boys, I saw the military as an honourable career, so it was natural for me to attend and graduate from West Point. I just missed Vietnam, but served in Germany and Korea. I found that life as a Captain in an army broken by Vietnam was not what I wanted and returned to Louisiana and civilian life. I later served for four years as a senior official in the Pentagon and had the honor of playing a small part in the rebuilding of a great U.S. Army.

Through it all, I kept my love for great adventure stories. When I had two sons, I began making up stories for them about a boy and his longbow. Those stories grew to become my first novel, *Longbow*. From there I spun the story of Roland Inness over six more books.

Having completed the story I set out to tell in *The Saga of Roland Inness*, I turned to a new story that had been floating around in my head for years, a story of the early settlement of America, which begins with *No King, No Country*.

To learn more about me and my books, visit my website at www.waynegrantbooks.com or the Longbow Facebook page at www.facebook.com/Longbowbooks

The picture was taken in the Shenandoah Valley of Virginia in August, 2020.

Printed in Great Britain
by Amazon